**Tor Paranormal Romance Books by
C. T. Adams and Cathy Clamp**

THE SAZI

Hunter's Moon
Moon's Web
Captive Moon
Howling Moon
Moon's Fury
Timeless Moon

THE THRALL

Touch of Evil
Touch of Madness
Touch of Darkness

TOUCH OF DARKNESS

C. T. ADAMS &
CATHY CLAMP

A TOM DOHERTY ASSOCIATES BOOK
NEW YORK

This is a work of fiction. All the characters, organizations, and events portrayed in this novel are either products of the authors' imagination or are used fictitiously.

TOUCH OF DARKNESS

A Tor Book
Published by Tom Doherty Associates, LLC
175 Fifth Avenue
New York, NY 10010

www.tor-forge.com

Tor® is a registered trademark of Tom Doherty Associates, LLC

ISBN-13: 978-0-7653-5962-9
ISBN-10: 0-7653-5962-6

First Edition: August 2008

Printed in the United States of America

0 9 8 7 6 5 4 3 2 1

DEDICATION AND ACKNOWLEDGMENTS

As always, this book is dedicated first and foremost to Cathy's husband, Don, and to Cie's son, James, and then to all the family and friends who have helped along the way. Special thanks go to Merrilee Heifetz and her able assistant, Claire Reilly-Shapiro, of Writers House; and to Anna Genoese, Heather Osborn, Jozelle Dyer, and the rest of the wonderful staff at Tor. Finally, we want to thank you, the readers, for coming along to play in our worlds. It would mean nothing without you.

Note from the Authors

The airport described in Las Vegas doesn't exist as envisioned here. It's located approximately where McCarran currently sits, but liberties have been taken with the design. Also, Mesquite Hills, Texas, is a nonentity, as are Beaver Falls and Murphysboro. We tried not to mangle Colorado criminal legal procedure too badly, but it's an alternate reality, so Kate's world isn't quite like ours. The new St. Elizabeth's has been moved to an actual medical complex, but I believe the real-life Veterans Affairs hospital is set to go in and will have opened and been in use by the time this book hits the shelves.

All our characters are imagined people with the exception of one friend who specifically requested that their name or description be put in the first book of this series and who has been mentioned in the following two. Otherwise any similarity between fictional and real people is purely coincidental. (And if you think we were that effective in bringing a character to life, we're flattered.)

We hope you will enjoy this, the concluding book in the Thrall/Kate Reilly series. In truth, while we write for love and for a living, we mostly write for you, the reader.

TOUCH OF
DARKNESS

1

Tiny needlepoints of pain dragged me up through layers of sleep. Increasingly insistent, the repeated puncturing resisted my best attempts to drop back into the warm and inviting dreams of my soon-to-occur wedding. I vaguely remembered rolling over beneath the heaps of down comforters. The resulting yowl of a startled and indignant cat pried open my eyes.

The room was pitch black—that enveloping depth of darkness you only get after a power outage. We forget how surrounded by light we are normally, even at night . . . from the soft glow of the clock to the little dots and rectangles of hibernating electronics.

But I'd been prepared for this after watching the weather report at bedtime. I reached to the nightstand, nudging aside the soft bulk of my cat, who refused to stop digging claws into my arm. A click later, and the yellowish glow from a battery lantern pushed away the black. As my brain started to function a little better, I heard the wind howling outside. It's not completely unheard of to get early-season blizzards in Colorado, and this one was going to be a doozy. Even in the dim light I could see icy patterns on the window ledges high above the bed, and driving snow that moved sideways across the glass. I groaned in response and curled deeper under the covers.

Again Blank jumped on my chest with a weight that pushed the air from my lungs hard and fast, like airplane turbulence. He was named *Blank* because of his unfinished appearance. A bare canvas that only required a splash of color to be real. But his whiteness had dulled to a dirty gray in the light, even while his pale, nearly clear eyes reflected it. They became headlights that made me squint. As I lifted his body off me, I thought he was purring, but then I realized it wasn't a purr that rumbled his chest.

It was a growl.

He combined the warning with claws digging deep into my wrists and I was suddenly fully awake. Adrenaline pounded my pulse as I listened for danger. I hadn't had any trouble for awhile now—no women with knives, men with guns, or even Thrall vampires trying to slice open my veins. So it was probably time for them to appear again. Damn it. Just when life was going pretty good.

A little snow wouldn't bother the Thrall. They're not vampires of legend that slow down like reptiles in the cold—making them little threat before they've fed. No, they're ordinary humans, turned superhuman by sentient psychic parasites, but fully capable of shopping for winter clothes at the mall in broad daylight.

Even in flannel pajamas, the chill that hit me when I threw off the covers was enough to make me shiver. Apparently, the power had been out for longer than I'd thought. My feet found the slippers on the wooden floor by touch. Good thing, since I couldn't see that well yet. I picked up the handle of the lantern and walked to the dresser to turn on the second lantern. This one was bigger, an eight D-cell monster that, with a flick of the switch, filled the bedroom with comforting incandescent light.

Sometimes, just having a light turn on is enough to scare away an intruder, but I didn't hear any footsteps or panicked voices downstairs. No scents of unfamiliar cologne or sweat found my nose. A quick glance at the wind-up clock on the bookshelf showed it was 2:00 A.M. That's when I heard the sound . . . a rumbling, cracking sort of noise and sensation that I couldn't place. The cat hissed and leapt down from the bed to stand next to me. The guttural thrum reminded me of the approach of a distant trash truck. The sound faded away after a moment, leaving only the wind and snow beating against the windows. There are a lot of windows in my loft, formerly a factory in the lower downtown of Denver, called LoDo by the locals. I renovated the place so that the old, thick industrial glass would rise above the floor on the west side for two full stories. Rain and snow hitting the wall of glass tend to set up a rhythmic vibration that becomes white noise after years of hearing it.

Blank stayed with me, crouched low next to my feet as I descended the staircase to the main level, carrying my little circle of light. He was looking all around, taking in everything, as though he couldn't place the sound either, but didn't like it. When I reached the bottom of the stairs, while I was still surrounded by walls that gave some measure of defense, I opened up my senses. Being psychic has advantages at times, and this was one of them. I can touch minds that are nearby, can communicate telepathically with family and loved ones in danger. But mostly, as much as I hate it, I can sense where the Thrall are. They've tried repeatedly to turn me into one of their own. They've come so damned close to succeeding several times now that if one was in my apartment, I'd know.

But they weren't here, or even there. Though the whole Denver hive should be up and about at this time of night, I was met with a smooth, flat wall of . . . nothing. Either my ability to touch the hive was being blocked by the queens, or they were holed up, sleeping out the storm like sane people. Since a lot of the Thrall hosts tend to be abnormally athletic people, hence slightly *insane* in my opinion, they're probably out in this mess. My fiancé, Tom Bishop, would say I was the pot calling the kettle black, since I'm a former professional athlete. It's part of why the Thrall has been trying to capture or kill me for years. But even I'm not nuts enough to be outside in a Colorado blizzard. I played volleyball . . . *beach* volleyball. Warm sun, soft sand.

So, I was betting it was option number one, which was a bad thing. They only block me when they don't want me to know what they're up to. It's an effort for them, because I'm pretty strong, so they don't do it for long.

But you know what they say—you're only paranoid if you're *wrong*. If you're right, they call you *proactive*, and in my many encounters with the Thrall, I've been exceedingly proactive.

The wind stopped for a few moments, the calm before the next blast of snow. In that brief silence, I heard the sound I'd been missing. A steady trickle of water that was like a dripping faucet, but more hollow. It seemed to come from ahead of me, but there was nothing along the wall of windows that had pipes, except the dripper lines in each of my potted plants for when I go on trips. I suppose the sudden cold could have split the plastic hoses. It made me sigh, because it would be a mess to clean up if it was in more than one place. The tension in my muscles was replaced with a weary resignation.

I have a *lot* of plants.

My brother Joe called me Jungle Kate for the sheer volume of greenery . . . well, he did back when he was speaking to me, anyway. The last time he spoke to me was at his wedding months ago. It was just a tense *thank-you* in response to my congratulations, and only after being prodded in the ribs by his new bride. Then he'd turned his back and walked away. He even returned the gift Tom and I had given them, unopened. That had brought on the first of many tears. But we're both stubborn, and I refuse to apologize for being psychic . . . for being a target of the Thrall. I hate that the vampires keep attacking my family because they're trying to kill or capture me. But I don't know what to do except keep trying to destroy them, and keep protecting those I love to the best of my ability.

The power chose that moment to flicker on. Both Joe and the Thrall were instantly purged from my brain by the horror that made me gasp and Blank hiss and dive for cover, almost simultaneously.

2

My wall of windows was a waterfall—literally. Spiderweb cracks had appeared across the panes in a pattern that reminded me of a baseball line drive to a windshield. The inside was still warmer than outside, so the snow was melting as it hit the glass and was seeping through the cracks to drip on the floor. My gaze was pulled upward because no way should those windows be cracking. I'd been forced to heave a woman who was trying to kill me through the glass a year earlier and her body had only managed to break out a single pane. It had taken months for the glazier to find a sheet of quarter inch, blue-tinted glass big enough to replace it. I'd had him check the integrity of the whole wall when he'd finally returned, and the panes were as solid as the bricks surrounding them.

But not anymore, and I could see why. Apparently, a *lot* more snow had fallen than they'd forecast, because the ceiling was bowed down nearly a foot where it met the windows. Either several tons of the white stuff, or a military transport plane, had crash-landed on my roof.

A rapidly growing puddle was crossing the hardwood floor and seeping down into the pit area toward my sofa and entertainment center. But they were the least of my worries as the rumbling sounded again, this time accompanied by the very particular sort of squeaking that metal makes when it's being stretched beyond its limits. I instinctively ducked and Blank darted back under the coffee table when sizzling and popping came from above. One of the industrial-sized ceiling fans that keep the loft warm or cool stuttered and began to smoke. The ceiling dipped further. There was no time to do anything but run for my life.

I dove for the floor and grabbed the cat, who responded by clinging to my chest with all four feet, claws extended. The cat carrier was already by the door because he was going to be staying downstairs with my tenant, Connie Duran, while I flew with Tom to Las Vegas for our wedding. My flight was supposed to be later today, and Tom planned to follow tomorrow at the end of his shift at the firehouse.

Those plans might be changing.

Another ominous series of creaks and groans hurried my feet, and I suddenly didn't care that I was wearing pink and yellow pajamas with fuzzy bunny slippers. I did care that it was snowing outside and I might freeze to death, though. Thankfully, Tom had left a pair of boots next to the couch, and my coat was with the jump bag I keep in case of emergencies in the downstairs closet. It has spare clothes, toothbrush, and weapons. I grabbed it quickly, pulling the strap onto my shoulder.

Blank went into the carrier without any fuss for a change and I snapped the metal gate closed just before slinging on my coat and tucking slipper-clad feet into the boots. I'd guessed right that they'd be darned close to a perfect fit that way.

The door to my apartment is one of the old fire doors from the original factory. It takes a pretty tough person to open it under normal circumstances. My shoulders are my strongest feature, so I can open it, as can Tom. Of course, he's a werewolf, so that helps. But I hadn't ever tried to open the door with weight on the door frame. I could already see the heavy steel beginning to flex down, and I wasn't sure what would happen if I yanked it open. Would the whole header collapse down on my head before I could get out? Would it start a chain reaction that would take out the windows and bring down the roof?

The only other option was the old freight elevator that would deliver me right into the basement where there's a small parking garage for the people who live here. Right now, the only car in the place should be Connie's—if she's not out on a call. She's a bail bondsman (or is that bail bondswoman?), so she keeps odd hours.

My own truck was stolen a year ago, and I had to use the replacement money to pay bills instead of getting a new set of wheels, so that spot is vacant. As a werewolf, Tom isn't allowed to have a driver's license, much less own a car. Damned prejudice anyway.

But I had no way of knowing if the elevator frame had been damaged. Would I get inside it just to have it get stuck halfway down, where I wouldn't be able to get out? No, better to take my chances with the door. Tom had used the CAD program at work to make an escape plan for the building so that I could post it on the walls for future tenants . . . and it didn't include either elevator.

So, it would be me against my building. Well, I'd forced it to my will once when I renovated it from a mouse-infested dump—and I could do it again. After patting the top of the cat carrier for luck, I steadied my stance and grabbed the knob with both hands. As I'd expected, it didn't give on the first tug. Not only did it not give, but the rumbling increased tenfold and the spider cracks sped up. *Well, shit.*

The second tug nearly pulled my arms from their sockets but I did get a hint of fresh air from the hallway that encouraged me. Blank mewled piteously from the back corner of the carrier as I bolted away from him to the kitchen, where I keep the crowbar. Normal people don't keep crowbars in their kitchen, but normal people aren't the building manager and maintenance department rolled into one. And, I hate trudging to the basement every time I find some old rusted thing that needs a helping hand. It happens more than I like to think about. It's in the bottom drawer, right next to the WD-40 . . . another handy item for the task at hand.

I set the black nylon jump bag onto the kitchen floor. It would only be in the way while I worked.

A fine trembling was beginning in the floor, which was starting to panic me. People make mistakes when they're panicked, so I tried not to listen to the noises of the building that was threatening to collapse onto my head. My mind focused down to, *insert crowbar in doorway, throw weight against wall. Ignore big hole in drywall and move crowbar down a notch. Hose down hinges with lubricant. Repeat.*

Inch by inch, the steel door fought against the steel frame weighted down with bricks and snow. I was winning but it wasn't fast enough. A crash sounded behind me and I looked back to see that the bedroom where I'd been sleeping was now buried in what was probably a ton of steel supports, asphalt roofing, and sizzling electric wires. A rush of cold wind and snow hit me in the face and the air stank of smoldering wood and hot metal.

Dear God. Is this what Tom feels like every time he goes in a burning building? My heart was pounding a mile a minute and my terrified cat was yowling while clawing and biting at the metal gate to the carrier to escape. The crowbar was down to the floor and the doorway was still only open about three inches—not quite enough to get a good grip with my hands where I could brace myself. Blank got picked up and moved to the left and then I used every bit of my leg strength to kick those steel-toed boots into the crowbar. It hit the baseboard with a thunk and the door popped open so hard and fast that I would have gotten knocked out if I hadn't lost my footing and wound up on my butt. *Woo! Here's to clumsiness!*

More of the ceiling crashed to the floor, taking out Tom's relatively new flat-screen television and the rocking chair that was one of the few things left from my mother. The kitchen, too, disappeared under a pile of rubble. But the header over the door held. A pile of snow the size of a child's snowman fell through the new opening and hit my back just as drywall dust coated me. I started coughing, both from the sudden blast of cold air and the swirling dust.

Pinging, cracking, and more screeching filled the air and a brick bounced off the wall about head height. I struggled to my feet and grabbed the carrier. The bag was toast, so I left it. I ran down the hallway toward the staircase. It's an old metal tread emergency stair and the fire inspector promised me it would outlast the building. I prayed he was right as I headed down to the second floor. Tom's old apartment is on that floor, but most of his stuff has been in my place since we got engaged. I didn't need to knock on the other tenant's door either. Rob Jameson and Dusty Quinn are members of Tom's pack but they're already in Las Vegas with—saints be praised!—my luggage and wedding gown. Dusty had half-jokingly suggested I allow her to take my luggage since I didn't have a very good track record of making it to the church on time. I originally objected, but something *had* come up time after time in the past ten months since Tom proposed. So, I dutifully packed my bags and sent them off with her, while Tom shook his head indulgently.

I'll bet this particular situation hadn't occurred to either of them.

I reached the main floor and bolted down the hallway. "*Connie!* Wake up! We have to get out of here," I yelled as I banged on the door with my fist. There was no time to check the garage to see if her car was there. Thankfully, I heard movement inside and a light flick on under the doorway.

She opened the door, rubbing eyes still bleary with sleep. Her hair was in curlers and a scarf. I didn't think *anyone* still did that. I always figured she had a perm. "What's wrong, Kate?" She yawned wide and then her eyes focused on me, widening as her jaw dropped a second time. "Oh, my God! Katie, you're *bleeding*. What's wrong? What's happening?" Connie was suddenly alert and reaching for her shoes. "No, never mind. If you say we get out—we get out. Talk later. Action now."

Was I bleeding? Probably. I tend to have that happen and not realize it in the heat of the moment. I didn't feel woozy, though, and all my limbs were working, so whatever damage there was could wait. Still, I checked what I could see of myself, but I didn't notice any blood. "The roof caved in from the snow. My apartment's gone. If the walls go—"

I didn't have to finish the thought. She did it for me. "The floors won't hold all that brick. No shit we need to get out of here." She was busily grabbing logical things, like her purse, cell phone charger, and flashlight. Wish I would have thought of that before they got buried. "Is there time to get my car?"

"Don't know. This floor is pretty rock solid, but—" The lights went out again. Whether from the storm or the rest of the roof cutting the lines, I didn't know. Connie switched on her big Maglite flashlight, one of the four-cell models, and turned it my way.

She let out a frustrated growl. "Doesn't matter much now. We won't be able to get the gate to the drive open. Or is there a manual chain to open it?"

I nodded. "Yeah, but it's not an easy open. It'll take a ladder, and time, to switch the gate over to manual, and I don't know that we have either one right now. But the ladder's in the basement if you think it's worth giving it a try."

Connie shook her head. "No, we're not going down a floor if we don't need to. We'll hope for the best. C'mon, let's get moving. We can use my cell to call 9-1-1 when we get outside."

The rumbling started again overhead and I could see fear etch across Connie's face in the dim reflection from the flashlight beam. I was beginning to feel vibrations underfoot and when I placed the flat of my palm against the wall, it was moving . . . swaying from side to side slightly. This was an interior wall, so if *it* was moving— "Crap! The whole thing's coming down."

There was no more talk. Connie opened the closet door and pulled out a green vinyl gym bag. It strained her arm muscles, so heaven only knew what was inside. She caught me looking and smiled . . . although it had grim overtones. "Overnight bag. I always keep one packed so I can look decent at odd hours. Clothes, toiletries, toothbrush. That sort of thing."

A crash to my left turned both our heads. Something had collapsed inside the stairwell. Billowing smoke and dust poured out and chased us down the hallway as we bolted for the front door. As we crossed the stunning mosaic tile entry floor, I caught the eye of the woman who'd been lovingly immortalized in bits of glass by an unknown someone when the building was built. I'd spent weeks carefully uncovering the tiles and replacing the few bits that had been damaged by the cheap linoleum someone had put over it before I bought the place.

By the time we opened the door and exited the building, she'd been covered over by dust—lost again to view.

It was dark outside . . . no street lamps or headlights lit the snow that billowed and floated down between the skyscrapers. It was drifting across the sidewalk, but even the drifts were only up to my knees.

Odd—

"Yes, that's right . . . the whole roof's gone. I can see where part of it's come down." I couldn't help but hear as Connie recited the address and flicked the phone closed. My eyes moved upward as Connie turned her beam toward the top of my building. Rough edges had replaced the smooth, straight brick lines of the old factory. Two of the panes of glass started to fall inward, pushed down by the wind coming off the mountains—they fell like a slow motion building implosion. I winced at the resulting crash as the panes shattered.

"We should get across the street, in case the wind shifts." My voice sounded flat and emotionless to my ears. I changed the cat carrier to my other hand and flexed my fingers to get the feeling back. Blank's no lightweight and the wind was making my skin raw. He let out a little *mmrrr* and moved to the other side of the carrier in response to the wind shift. Yeah, he's got fur and he lived outdoors for a time, but it was still freaking cold outside.

Connie and I trudged across the unplowed street and found a place that was mostly sheltered against the opposite building. I put Blank in the most protected corner I could find and knelt down beside the cage to scritch his chin through the wire. After a long moment of both of us just staring at the collapsing building, Connie spoke. "So, what happened? Did you hear something, or did the whole thing just come down on top of you?"

LIGHTS, SIRENS, AND people filled the empty streets as the fire department arrived. One of the cops who'd responded to Connie's call had caught sight of tendrils of smoke mixing with the snow and had called in an alarm.

The pumper truck didn't have any problem negotiating the snowy street, but the police cruiser had slid around quite a bit when it first arrived. I'd never really thought much about the men and women who have to brave weather like this just to do their jobs until I'd met Tom. Now every time I hear about a rescue during a flood, or earthquake . . . or snowstorm, I offer a little prayer, asking for protection of those who choose to serve.

As the firefighters stepped out of the cab of the big truck and began to move around purposefully, I saw one helmet-clad man approach the chief and speak to him. The chief nodded and the man began to look around frantically. I raised my arm and he sprinted my way. He *sprinted*.

As bad as the day had been so far, I couldn't help but smile as Tom threw his arms around me and held me close. "God, Katie . . . when I heard the address of the call—" He turned my head from side to side with thick warm gloves that heated my frozen ears and cradled the back of my head. When he let go his glove tips were smeared with red. What with the cold, I didn't even feel it and it didn't look like there was much blood. In a flash of movement, I was suddenly pressed against his chest in a nearly suffocating hug. "I love you so much."

My voice was a little muffled by his fire-resistant jacket. I was a little surprised he was still in uniform, instead of in wolf form. Werewolves have a hard time holding their human form when they get an adrenaline rush. It's one of the reasons for the no-license thing. "I love you too, Tom. It's okay. Everybody's out and we're fine." I pulled away slightly, even though he didn't want to let me. His eyes were turning from golden wolf eyes back to their normal chocolate brown. "Go. Do your job. You don't need any more trouble from the guys."

The little chesty snarl and frown told me he didn't care what his peers thought of him. But he knew I was right. He's been taking a lot of shit from the guys he works with after he deserted his post to save Joe from a madwoman who was, coincidently, also going to blow up one of the local hospitals. The fact that Tom managed to help take her down, save a mother and child, *and* tell them where to find the bomb that was going to blow up the ICU ward were the only things that saved his job.

By the time they'd raised the cherry picker to look inside the building and pour down water to contain the small fire—the chief was smart enough not to send anyone inside—the snow had stopped and the news vans had arrived. *Them* I didn't say a prayer for, since I could do without any more coverage after the year I'd been having. I'd been brutalized by the press for my battle with the Thrall. They'd turned me into a media monster, without even asking for my side of the story. The only reason I hadn't been run out of Denver with sticky feathers was the Barbara Walters interview that put me in a good national light. But as for the local press . . . phooey. Let 'em slip off the road.

I was thankfully spared having to talk with any reporters, which now included news choppers that scanned the area with searchlights, because I was spending my time with the cops and fire department. They were asking logical questions about what happened and I was doing my best to answer them. At one point, I felt a hand on my shoulder. It squeezed lightly, the touch of a friend or comrade, but by the time I turned my eyes, the person was gone. Or, at least, whoever had done the squeezing wasn't someone I recognized. Still, for that brief moment, it had been comforting, because the enormity of the situation had finally dawned on me.

Tom found me at the end of two long hours, as they were rolling up to speed toward the next problem. "Okay, so I'll see you in Vegas tomorrow night. Right?"

My jaw probably dropped. "Tom! The *building* just fell down. You can't possibly think that I can—"

He held up his hand, as though expecting my protest. "No. We're *doing* this, Katie. You've talked to my grandparents. You know how much they want to meet you; want to be witnesses to our wedding. The building is *condemned*. The cops are putting up the tape now. You can't stay here. I can't stay here. The police will guard the building to prevent looting until we can get a fence company out here to secure it. We already have plane tickets and reservations in

Vegas for the next three days. It would be stupid for us not to use the hotel room. And—" He held my shoulders firmly in those strong, glove-covered hands. "I *will* marry you. Even if I have to drag you to the altar. The day after tomorrow you're going to be Mrs. Kate Bishop."

Despite the snow, in the shadow of my destroyed building, his words still made me smile. How could they not?

3

"ate, are you all right in there?" Peg's voice came to me through the door to the hotel suite. I hit the mute button on the television, silencing the familiar voice on the weather station, and wandered over to let her in.

"Is there anything more pathetic in the world than a would-be bride sulking alone in what was supposed to be her honeymoon suite?" I snuffled pitifully as I pulled open the door.

She put on a sad pout for my benefit and tucked her arm around mine. "It's not Tom's fault, sweetie. A freak hundred-year blizzard in Denver on the heels of a regular snowstorm—closed airport. You can't say he didn't *try*." She walked a few steps into the room with me and then just stopped, staring around, while I continued on.

I'd done the same thing when I'd arrived. It was worth a stare or two. The suite was gorgeous. Tom had made the arrangements and had gone all-out. When you first walked into the suite you came into a seating area. Everything was done in shades of champagne and jewel tones, with dark wood furniture pieces polished to a warm glow. There was a white marble fireplace, and white marble tile squares on the section of floor in front of the fireplace that flowed seamlessly into the white marble of the ensuite spa. The bedroom had a king-sized four-poster bed and matching dressers and an armoire that hid a plasma television. Sliding doors led to a balcony that overlooked the lights of the strip.

When I'd first come in I'd found a table set up in the conversation area with champagne on ice, plus fondues with white, milk, and dark chocolate to have chocolate-covered strawberries. The perfect romantic moment for the arriving happy couple.

Sigh.

Everything was plush and elegant, not in the least bit tacky. We might be in Vegas, but this was high-end Vegas.

Tom's not wealthy. But he's conservative enough with his money that it goes a long way. At least he's *usually* conservative. I couldn't imagine how much he'd paid for all this and he wouldn't tell me. But after waiting so long—what with the marriage classes at the church, and one thing and another—he'd wanted everything perfect. It would have been, too, if he wasn't riding a bench at Denver International

Airport. He couldn't even get back along Peña Boulevard to a hotel. They closed it after his cab arrived.

"I know, I know." I sounded as sullen as I felt. Damn it anyway. Tom and I have been through so much to get together. Why couldn't *this* at least go right? But no. No such luck.

Peg gave me a *look* and announced, "You need a drink."

"The champagne was complimentary with the room. Part of the wedding package."

"Fine. Champagne it is." She strolled across the carpet to the ice bucket. It only took her a moment to get the bottle open. She's had a lot more experience at that sort of thing than Tom or I have. Either of us would've bungled it, but she managed to open and pour without any mess, fuss, or giggles.

I took the crystal champagne flute from her hand and took a long drink. I'm not a big champagne fan, but this actually tasted good. Surprise.

"It's a big storm, but you've both safe and sound. You've waited this long; a couple more days won't kill you." She sipped her drink as gracefully as she did everything else. Peg is my best friend and I love her, but she's also close enough to perfect that it sometimes gets on my nerves. Petite, blonde, she is the epitome of well-groomed WASPdom. I'm so not. I, Kate Reilly, stand six foot one in my bare feet, have red-gold hair that is completely uncontrollable unless pulled into submission, and confess to a penchant for black leather. Striking. I can give myself striking. But I'm not pretty, or beautiful, and I can never seem to manage the kind of pulled-together look that Peg achieves so easily.

We met and became friends in the course of business. She's a flight attendant. I have my own business as a bonded air courier. She's worked a number of different routes over the years, but she particularly likes the DC/Tel Aviv run that I use most often.

"I had to call Tom's grandparents and cancel at the chapel. His grandmother was heartbroken. They're old, and not in good enough health to drive themselves to Denver for the church wedding, and he won't fly. The marriage here was really, *really* important to them." Important enough for Tom to come back, despite a lot of problems from his past that he hadn't wanted to talk about. But Peg didn't need to know that.

"Besides, in four days I'm supposed to be in Tel Aviv doing a diamond run."

Her snort spoke volumes. "Didn't give yourself much time for a honeymoon, did you?" She strolled over to the couch and sat down, turned, and reclined with her back against the armrest and her stocking feet crossed on the cushions.

I shrugged and took another sip. "Tom had to be back anyway. He has a shift."

"He couldn't get time off?"

I sighed and took another fortifying drink. I knew I was drinking it too fast. I'd end up with gas for sure, and possibly drunk. But right now I didn't really care. "He probably could've, but we're still walking on eggshells."

"I thought he was cleared of charges—"

I crossed over to the chair opposite her and collapsed into it. I didn't like thinking about the night that Samantha Greeley captured and tortured my brother Joe. Nine months and I was still having nightmares and dealing with the fallout. Joe was having a worse time, though. He had scarring, both physical and mental. His legs were in braces, and he had PTSD—posttraumatic stress disorder.

"The night Tom came with me to save Joe, he left his crew. They don't completely trust him anymore. I think they're still worried that he might 'run off' if he has to choose between his duty as a firefighter and me or the wolf pack. It didn't help that he asked the chief to search for me the second they arrived last night. Yeah, he lived there too, *but*. . . . Nobody *said* anything, but I watched how they treated him differently than last time I saw them together."

"So they haven't forgiven him. Great." She shook her head. "God, Reilly, the life you lead. Do you have some sort of mega-great-grandfather in your past who ticked off a leprechaun or something? Some Reilly family curse that dooms you to bad luck?"

I snorted, but some days I wonder the same thing. My life can, and frequently does, suck. Once upon a time things had been relatively normal. But that had been a *long* time ago. Long enough that while I could wax nostalgic, I didn't really *remember*.

"So, what's this I hear about your baby brother? Did Bryan really check himself into one of the vampire halfway houses?"

I stared at her with anger probably plain on my face. I know that I nearly choked on the sip of champagne I'd just taken. "Yeah, you heard right, damn it. I can't believe how stupid my brothers are being. Joe and Bryan both know the truth about the Thrall—better than most. They're vampires, Peg. Blood-sucking parasites that kill the host they infest within a matter of two to ten years."

"Or sooner," she agreed. "I mean, with you being Not Prey and all, I figured Bryan would steer clear of them. What's to say that he won't be a target to get to you once they've got him locked up?"

"That's what I mean. They should know better. God knows I have the scars to prove they're violent. But now that's supposed to be *ancient history*. Wonderful Larry, who tortured poor Dylan and turned Monica into a nutjob who I was supposed to battle for the *honor* of having a slimy parasite attach to my brainstem to make me a queen. I mean . . . *ewww*." I raised a hand in a stopping motion. "And let's not even *discuss* Monica's little plan to take over the world. I'm sorry, but I just can't forget how many times they've tried to kill me, with no provocation, I might add—and accept their new warm and fuzzy, *can't we all just get along* campaign. Bryan might buy into it, because he's only got my word on some stuff, but Joe? He knows better. Hell, he's criticized them himself. Yeah, they might be using their psychic abilities to bring back coma victims and Eden zombies, even helping them readjust to normal life in their shiny "New Dawn" halfway houses around the country, but what's the cost? Huh? Where's their food coming from? Who's donating blood to them? How can you call zombies willing donors? Hmmn?" I put the delicate champagne flute down on the table after my little rant, before my clenching fist snapped the stem in two. "Good guys—yeah, right."

Of course, what I didn't need to bring up . . . especially to my best friend, is that if the vampires are the good guys, then people like me get cast as the villains. *Just* what I need.

My anger turned to pain so I picked up the flute again to self-medicate. "I heard about Bryan checking himself into New Dawn in Texas from a reporter— a *reporter,* for pity's sake—who was trying to get a reaction shot."

"Oh, my God!" She looked just as horrified as I'd felt that day. "Katie, that's terrible. I'm so sorry."

"It sure worked. The picture of me on the front page of one of the tabloids was priceless. I looked hurt and horrified, just like the jerk planned." I didn't bother to mention the next few minutes. Peg probably figured out that as soon as I'd gotten somewhere a little more private I'd tried to contact my baby brother psychically. No luck. That was unusual, and would take a lot more concerted effort than he was usually willing to expend. I'd tried dialing his cell number the minute I'd climbed into a cab. It had been disconnected. My next call had been to Joe.

"And Joe knew about it? He didn't bother to tell you about Bryan's decision?" I heard the sadness in her voice as she tried to decide who to feel sorriest for. She'd loved Joe once, before he met his new wife, Mary.

"He was my next call. And let me tell you—*that* didn't go well. He gave me a lecture about how, if I was just a little less self-centered, I'd *know* what was going on in the family. But no, never mind, I was too busy what with my new-found celebrity and all."

She looked suitably angry and sympathetic. I had to admit it was making me feel better to talk about it. I love Tom desperately, and he usually takes my side in things like this. But he's so damned practical. He keeps thinking of *solutions*, when sometimes I just want to rant and have the person make the right noises.

"Joe meant the words to *hurt*, Peg. A part of him knows that I didn't deliberately seek fame, and anyone can see I don't enjoy it. But it has started to consume my life, and it makes it hard to do all the family things I used to do. I wind up planning everything I do to avoid the glare and preserve what's left of my privacy."

She couldn't decide how to respond to that, so we both just sipped champagne and thought our own thoughts for a bit, while watching the mute moving pictures on the television. After a moment, she started channel flipping, the sound still off, while I mulled.

I keep hoping that the whole situation will die down. I mean, actors and actresses are "hot" one minute and then never heard from again until *Entertainment Tonight* does a special on "Whatever Happened to—." But so far, it hasn't worked that way for me. The good news is I don't have trouble at bus stops and riding the light rail. I guess people figure it isn't "me," that "real" celebrities don't ride the bus. I wouldn't, either, if I had managed to get myself a new vehicle, but I don't want to spend the money until the situation with the car rental company is settled. The negotiations are nearly over, I just don't know the final result. I may wind up having to buy the blasted thing. It wasn't a bad vehicle, but it's not the one I'd have chosen.

She sighed after a time and tucked another pillow under her head before refilling her glass from the fast-emptying bottle. "Still, things aren't all bad, Kate. You and Tom found each other. You own a building in lower downtown Denver. I'm sure it's still fixable. You can fix anything. And while Bryan might not be making the choices you would, he's in his own mind enough to actually *make* choices. That's something."

She was right, and I nodded, my eyes misting over just a bit at the realization that I might be mad with him, but I *could* be mad with him. Less than two years ago he'd been an Eden zombie—completely helpless, trapped in his own mind without will or personality. No, things were not all bad. I glanced up and mouthed a silent prayer of gratitude.

"Don't get me wrong, Reilly." She took a long pull of champagne and pointed at me. Her words were getting a little slurred, but who was I to talk?

"I'm not blind. You've definitely got your share of faults, but neglecting your family is not one of them. If Joe says it is he needs to get his head examined, his ass kicked, or both." Her expression grew fierce and then amused, her perfect brows arching prettily. "If I asked nice, do you think your fiancé the werewolf could take care of the ass-kicking part?"

I grinned. I couldn't help it. Peg always seems to say just the right thing to cheer me up.

My cell phone rang. I reached over to grab it from the nightstand and checked the number. Speaking of my favorite werewolf, Tom was on the line.

Peg grinned at my expression. Sad to say, she could tell who was calling just from the look on my face. I'm in love. It shows. A lot. I should probably be embarrassed, but generally I'm too happy to let it bug me.

"Go ahead and talk to Tom. I'll dip another strawberry. Tell him he's missing quite a feast."

She didn't have to tell me twice. "Thanks." I hit the button and took the call.

"Hi."

"Hey, gorgeous. I miss you." I know it's silly, but just the sound of his voice on the line warmed me to my toes, making me feel better about Bryan, postponing the wedding . . . everything. I've heard that kind of reaction wears off with time, but we're at two years—the first danger point for most relationships—and there's no sign of fading yet. He still thinks I'm wonderful. I know better, but I'm certainly not going to argue.

"Oh, my *God*. Look, Kate. They've got your building on the weather station." Peg pointed with her glass at the television screen.

My gaze followed her pointing finger to look at the television. What I saw nearly made me drop the telephone. My building made the national news. Standing outside next to the building . . . even having been inside during the collapse, hadn't really given me any scope. But the chopper gave me the whole view. The cameraman panned across the scene to show the chunks of brick, glass, and twisted metal that had rained down into my apartment, and later onto the sidewalk.

The scene cut to street level on the bundled-up newscaster from the local news talking to Connie. Yeah, she'd played it up to the max. She'd waited to talk to the press until she was sitting on an ambulance gurney with Blank's cat carrier beside her while an EMT worked on a tiny scratch on her face.

Peg grabbed the remote before I could and hit the button to turn off the mute:

". . . at the residence of local celebrity Mary Kathleen 'Kate' Reilly. I am speaking to Connie Duran, a tenant in the building. Tell me, Ms. Duran, do you know if anyone else was home at the time of the collapse?"

"Just me and Kate Reilly, the owner. My two neighbors are in Las Vegas this week." She patted the cat carrier as though it were her own. *"Thank God for this cat! Kate was sleeping, and he just hopped*

on the bed and wouldn't *leave her alone. He was acting so weird it got her to wandering around her apartment. That's when the whole building started to creak and water started pouring down the walls of the stairwell. We ran for our lives, and only just made it out. If it weren't for this cat, I'd be* dead."

Well, water wasn't exactly *pouring* down the walls, and she was never in the stairwell with me. But hey . . . at least she kept the press off my back.

Wait! I saw a flash of myself for the briefest moment as the camera was panning. It was when I felt the hand on my shoulder and turned to find nobody there. But there had been someone there. Peg noticed too. "I didn't know you knew Lewis Carlton. I thought he retired from the NBA and moved to Detroit. Does he live down in LoDo now?"

My mouth went dry, because I should absolutely have noticed Carlton at the accident scene that night. Carlton is ex-NBA all right—a former power forward and all-around bad boy. He wears the ring, the bling, and the ride for a man who left at the top of his career. But at seven foot two inches he's also the most lethal Thrall queen I know. Head of the newest nest, in Pueblo, he'd saved my life once when an enemy tried to kill me. But, and I ticked off the questions on mental fingers: Why would he appear at the collapse of my building? Why was he in Denver at all, not to mention squeezing my shoulder? Where would he get enough oomph to blind me to his presence . . . and for what reason?

A new image appeared on the screen. Peg grabbed the couch as her knees started to buckle. "Oh my God, Kate. I didn't realize—"

"Kate . . . *Katie* . . . talk to me." Tom's voice was growing panicked, but I couldn't seem to speak. The image, one shot today, froze as though the satellite signal stalled. It was . . . gone. It was finally coming home to me as I stared. Both walls had collapsed inward, down to the main floor. It was a pile of rubble. My mind wouldn't focus enough to form coherent thoughts: my building . . . my *home* . . . everything I owned—

"Breathe, Katie, breathe." Peg grabbed the phone from my limp fingers and raised it to her lips.

"Tom, it's Peg. We were watching the weather channel and they showed Kate's building again. I think everything just hit her."

I could hear him swearing, hear her filling him in on what was being shown on the news. I didn't even try to contribute. All I could do was stare, transfixed, at the scene frozen on the television screen.

The signal blipped and lines flashed before it returned to the program. Peg knelt down on the floor in front of me as a commercial break came on. Very gently, she pressed the phone into my hand, and moved my hand to my ear, as if she didn't trust me to do it myself. She might well have been right. There was a lot to process at the moment.

"It's going to be all right, Katie." I heard Tom's voice as if from a distance. The connection was fine. I wasn't. He knew it, or guessed, because he was speaking very carefully, gently. Even long distance, over the telephone, he could tell I was in bad shape. "I wasn't going to tell you about the walls until later. Dave at the station called me here at the airport to let me know that none of our guys were inside at the time. I'm sorry you had to find out like this. But it could have been so much worse."

Right. I should be grateful. It could've been worse. Things can be replaced. People can't. But oh *God*, my *house,* our furniture, my pictures . . . *everything.* It wasn't too bad in my mind when the walls were standing. A roof can be fixed. But a whole *building*—

The room phone was ringing, and Peg rose to her feet. She ducked into the bedroom and snagged the extension. I could hear her talking in the background as I listened to Tom telling me how he loved me, and we'd get through this, just like we'd gotten through everything else . . . together.

I desperately wished he was here. I actually ached to feel his arms around me, smell the scent of his skin as I buried my head against his neck. I'm strong. I'm tough. I've spent most of my life taking care of business and taking care of myself. It's only been these past few months with Tom that I've been able to let myself be vulnerable again, let myself trust someone else to take part of the load.

"Say something, Katie." His voice had gone soft and worried.

"I love you." My voice sounded odd, thick, and choked with tears.

"I love you too." He sighed. "God, I wish I was there, or you were here. That we were together." There was a frustrated growl to his voice. I hoped he was somewhere private, or that he stayed calm enough not to change.

The thought of what might happen if he changed forms in the middle of DIA brought me out of my shock. "Me too." My voice was still shaky, but better. I tried for a weak joke. "We'll have to time our disasters a little better next time."

"Right. I'll take a note."

"Do that." My voice didn't break, and I *hoped* he couldn't hear the tightness that came from trying to hold back yet another set of tears. I don't cry often, or well, but today just seemed to be the day for it.

"Are you going to be okay?"

A harsh snort that wasn't quite a laugh escaped me. "Do I have a choice?"

He gave a rueful laugh. "That's my girl, always the realist."

"Katie," Peg interrupted, she held out the phone to me, her expression serious. "I hate to say it, but you'd better take this."

Now what? "Who is it?" I knew Peg wouldn't bother me unless it was important, but I really *really* didn't want to talk to anyone but Tom right now. I'd just had a serious shock. I wanted time to myself to . . . well, *wallow* I suppose.

"Some girl named Ruby Willow. She says it's an emergency and sounds pretty panicked."

Oh, shit. Ruby was one of the two surrogates for Tom's werewolf pack. Werewolf females are sterile, so the pack encourages the males to find human females to breed with, marry, and have babies that the pack helps raise. The Denver pack currently had two surrogates, Dusty and Ruby. Both were pregnant, and both were staying in a hotel down the block with Rob. But while Dusty and Rob were a happy couple, Ruby's boyfriend Jake had been killed in a battle with the Thrall, leaving his teenaged future bride pregnant and relatively alone. The pack took care of her well, which was good . . . because I knew her family had disowned her. But she'd loved Jake desperately, and she'd been having a very hard time dealing with the loss.

"Tom, Ruby's on the other line and says it's an emergency. I'll call you right back."

"Shit. Yeah, do that."

I closed the cell, cutting off the call without saying goodbye. I knew he'd understand—approve even. Ruby had been living on the streets when she'd met Jake. She was tough and had been through enough that if she said it was an emergency, it was. She wouldn't, pardon the expression, cry wolf.

I grabbed the phone from Peg's hand.

"Kate here."

"Oh thank God!" Her voice was breathless with relief. In the background I could hear fierce growling and barking accompanied by swearing, sirens, and a woman's moans.

"What in the hell is going on?"

"Dusty's in labor. We're at the emergency room at a hospital here in Vegas, but the ob-gyn on duty in the emergency room is a Thrall host. You know they're enemies and with her defenseless and all . . . well, Rob sort of went nuts and changed form and now he's blocking the whole hallway, snapping and barking. He won't let anyone near her, and they're going to call the police. Kate, I don't know what to do!"

Shit! "Have them call in another doctor to treat her."

"They have, but I don't think he's gonna get here in time. Her contractions are only two minutes apart! I've been trying to time them, but I didn't attend all the partner classes like Rob did."

I took a deep breath and tried to think rationally. This was insane. Why in the hell was she calling me? What was *I* supposed to do about this? I mean, I'm probably the only other person in Vegas who knows the Denver werewolf pack, and I'm Not Prey, but neither fact was likely to be useful in the current situation—

Unless . . . inspiration hit. It might not work, but it was sure worth a try.

"Put the vampire on the phone and make sure Rob can hear me talk."

"Got it."

There was a pause, during which the barking stopped. I still heard low, menacing growls, but there wasn't much I could do about it.

"Dr. Drewrey here."

He talked with just the slightest bit of a lisp, a dead giveaway that he'd only recently gotten his fangs. Unless, of course, he'd lisped before. But I doubted it.

"My name is Kate Reilly. Do you know who I am?"

"I've heard of you." His voice was cold, bitter. I wasn't exactly surprised. To some of the lesser vamps I'm something of a "bogeyman." After all, the only way you can get to be Not Prey is to survive an attack. To do that involves killing the vamp attacking you. I've survived more than one, and wiped out two entire *nests* in the process, including most of the human herds the nests had fed on. Far as I know, I've killed more vampires than anyone else on the planet. Which is why the vampires hate me so much. But I'm Not Prey. While they detest me and want me dead, by their own rules they have to treat me with the respect they would treat a queen vampire and they can't lie to me. It's a handy thing that might just get me out of the current mess.

"I'm Not Prey. You can't lie to me."

"I'm a little busy here." His sarcasm made the lisp more pronounced. Okay, I had to think quick now and try to imagine any possible problem with delivering a baby.

"Just reminding you of the rules, *doctor*. Because I want you, right here and now, to *honestly* promise me that you will treat Dusty Quinn to the best of your medical ability, as if you were a human doctor and she was just another patient. I want to hear you say that you won't harm her or the baby in any way because she's a surrogate for the werewolves . . . that you won't withhold treatment or deny drugs, or *give* drugs or treatment that are wrong for her or the baby, or make mistakes or omissions for any other reason." I paused and then, before he could speak, added, "And . . . that you and the queen collective won't let anyone else in the hive attack her or the baby or harm them while they are patients in the hospital." I had to take a deep breath after all that. But it should cover most of the issues.

The trick to dealing with the Thrall is to use a lot of compound sentences. You have to cover all sorts of weird, improbable, or impossible situations and pray hard that they don't find a loophole. Because they will if they can. There are tens of thousands of minds in the collective for them to draw on. And I knew at least a few of them were attorneys who were skilled at contract negotiation. One of them is P. Douglas Richards, Esq., the queen of the Denver hive.

I heard him take in a slow, hissing breath. He wasn't happy with the request. But doctors take oaths to "do no harm." I would have expected a simple agreement, or at least a grudging affirmative. Instead, there was a long silence as he and the hive considered every nuance of what I had said. *That* made me believe Rob had been right. Something was definitely fishy. I automatically opened my psychic senses to their full extent, trying to catch a hint of what was going on within the hive. Unfortunately, the queens had anticipated that, and my mind was met with dead silence.

Terrific. Just terrific.

I could hear Dusty panting and whimpering in the background. Judging from the sounds she was making, the baby would be arriving soon. Since I'd gotten involved with Tom and his pack members had moved into my apartment complex I'd learned a lot about surrogates and werewolf pregnancies. Werewolf deliveries are almost always complicated and difficult. Dusty needed medical attention *now*. If not Drewrey, then at least one of the ER docs.

I decided to try a telepathic link to Rob, but didn't have any luck. He's been working with Tom to retain more of his human mind when he changes form, but he still has a long way to go. Stressed as he was, I wasn't really surprised that human Rob wasn't "home." Disappointed, but not surprised.

Finally, the doctor spoke. The words came out haltingly, as if each individual syllable was being pulled out by force. "I personally, and the queens, on behalf of the collective give you our word that the girl and her . . . *spawn* will receive the best medical attention available at this hospital and that no one connected with our people will do anything to harm her or the infant while they are at this hospital."

The growling stopped and Ruby grabbed the telephone. "Oh, thank-you, Kate! Whatever you did worked. Rob's backed off and is letting the ER doctors work on her. Thank-you, thank-you."

Hallelujah! It wasn't perfect, but it was enough for the moment. Dusty and the baby were safe. But I couldn't help but notice the promise had only been *while they are at this hospital*. Which made me wonder just *exactly* what we'd be facing when they left. I'd warn Mary. We'd work out some sort of protection when the time came. In the meantime, Dusty and the baby were as safe as I could manage.

But oh yeah, right, I almost forgot. The vampires are supposed to be the "good guys" now.

4

There are reasons I don't generally drink much. First, I don't want to lose my edge. My life is too dangerous, too violent to take that kind of risk. I was dealing with the second reason this morning. A hangover made my eyeballs feel like they'd been packed in sand, my head ache enough that my thought processes didn't quite seem up to speed. I hadn't thought I'd had *that* much champagne. But the thing about alcohol is that it affects your judgment— including about how much alcohol you can handle.

If I hadn't made plans I'd have stayed in bed and slept it off. But I was due to meet Tom's grandparents at 9:00 at the nearby family-style restaurant for breakfast.

Maybe it wasn't the hangover that was giving me dry mouth and making my stomach queasy.

Calm, Reilly. Calm. Yeah, right. Like that was going to happen. I climbed out of the tub and grabbed one of the oversized, fluffy towels. It was actually *soft.* One of the biggest differences I've encountered between mid-range hotels and the really high-end ones is the linens. I've owned couches smaller than the bath sheet I was using, and the high thread count bed sheets had been seriously amazing. I might, just might, have to break down and get myself some when I was replacing everything. It seemed ridiculously decadent to spend that much money on linens, but it was sorely tempting.

I padded naked to the bedroom area and stared down at the clothes I'd chosen for the day. I'd picked plain blue jeans and a peach-colored polo style shirt. Nothing fancy. From what I'd been able to drag out of Tom his grandparents were "simple folks." His mother's parents, they were fully human. They hadn't really approved of her choice to be a surrogate, but they'd loved her, and their grandchildren, desperately. It had nearly destroyed them to lose everyone but Tom to the fire.

While pulling on my clothes I remembered the conversation Tom and I had when he'd asked if I'd be willing to have the Vegas wedding. He'd been so sad, so *earnest.*

"Why didn't they come with you to Denver? I mean, you're all the family they have left. Why stay?"

His eyes had grown shadowed. His body language changed ever so slightly. I'd had a flash of insight that had nothing to do with psychic talent, and everything to do with knowing the man I loved. They'd said no. He'd wanted them, asked them. They'd refused.

"Vegas is their home. But more than that, my mom's grave is there. They won't leave. Ever."

I'm not a big one for visiting graves. To me, the body is just the shell. The soul, the essence that made the body a person, has moved on to something better. But there are people to whom it matters a lot. Apparently Tom's grandparents were among them.

"But we could fly them out for the wedding at least."

"Gramps won't fly, and neither of them passed their last driver's test."

I could tell it meant the world to him. I could also tell he was nervous about it. He swore up and down that it wasn't fear of my meeting his family, but he wouldn't say what the problem was. Which made me nervous.

I pulled on tube socks and a pair of running shoes and went to check my reflection in the full-length mirror.

The clothes fit well, looked good in fact. My face, however, needed some work. I was pale, and not in a good way, my eyes seriously bloodshot. Thank God for eye drops. If I was lucky they'd actually live up to their commercials. Because I wanted to make a good impression.

My stomach lurched. I wished Tom was here. It wasn't fair for me to have to do this without him. But it was snowing again in Denver. The news said it would be at least one more day, maybe two or three, before they'd be reopening the airport. Mr. and Mrs. Thomas had made it very clear (in the most amazingly polite way) that they would be hurt and insulted if I canceled our breakfast just because Tom couldn't join us.

I'd caved.

A quick glance at the clock told me I'd better get moving. I didn't want to be late. Late would be bad. Oh hell, why couldn't Tom *be here*? This just *sucked*. I hurried into the bathroom and grabbed makeup from the case. Blush I could manage; a little eyeshadow. I didn't trust myself with eyeliner. My hands were shaking too much to draw a straight line. I'd probably just end up poking myself in the eye—which would totally negate the positive effects of the eye drops.

I put my hair in a simple braid that hung in a thick rope down the middle of my back. Wearing it loose is more flattering, but is a pain to deal with. It blows around, getting in the way. Almost the only times I wear it down is when Tom specifically asks me to.

I took deep breaths, counting slowly to calm my nerves. I was being ridiculous. This was Tom's *family*. It made no sense for me to be afraid of them.

But what if they don't like me? What if they believe everything the press has been saying? What if—

I gave myself an actual, physical shake. That kind of thinking would just make things worse. I love Tom. Tom loves me. They love Tom. He loves them. I could get through this. Really.

I kept telling myself that all the way through the short cab ride to the restaurant, up the sidewalk, and through the double wooden doors. I was still reciting it like a mantra as my eyes adjusted to the dim lights and loud bustle of the restaurant.

"Miss Reilly."

I turned at the sound of my name spoken in a gentle wheeze. A man stood bent, his weight supported by an aluminum walker hung with a bright blue nylon bag that held a green metal oxygen tank whose clear plastic tubes snaked up to his nose.

His skin had that thin, blotchy crepe texture of the very old, stretched taught over sinews and knotted blue veins. What little hair was left on his head was in four small patches: one above each ear, the rest in a pair of remarkably bushy eyebrows. Still, the eyes behind the coke-bottle glasses were clear, the look assessing. He'd dressed in a charcoal gray suit with subtle pinstriping. It was almost the exact double of the suit Tom wears to most formal functions, right down to the crisply starched white shirt and striped tie.

"Mr. Thomas?"

He nodded. "We've taken that large table in the corner." He gestured in the general direction with his head as he shuffled the walker into position. "I hope you don't mind. Edie brought pictures."

I looked past the bustling waitress to the table he was indicating and had to grin. It was one of the big corner booths meant to seat a small army. Its lone occupant was a tiny, wiry woman whose bright brown eyes sparkled behind glasses not one whit less thick than those her husband wore. Her eyes, and a mop of frizzy gray curls, were all that was visible over a towering stack of photo albums.

Ed Thomas caught the grin and returned it, with interest. "She was so nervous—afraid we wouldn't have anything to talk to you about. I told her not to worry. But this was her solution. I just hope we don't spill anything on them at breakfast. It'd break her heart."

"I've been nervous too," I admitted. "The two of you mean so much to Tom . . ." I let the sentence drag off unfinished.

"Do you love him?" Ed stopped so abruptly I nearly ran into him. He stood in the middle of the aisle, turning to face me. His eyes flashed behind the thick magnifying lenses.

"Oh God, yes."

"That's all I need to know." Small laugh lines appeared at the corners of his eyes, and his mouth twitched slightly. "Edie, however, may take a little more convincing." He shook his head. "She worries."

"I understand." I meant it. Nobody can worry you like family. I might not have a child, or grandchild, but I had my brothers. I know they're adults, fully capable of living their lives without supervision. But with Mom and Dad gone, they're all I have left—at least the only ones I'm willing to acknowledge.

He gave me a long, assessing look. "Maybe you do at that." He admitted it grudgingly, muttering the words under his breath as he turned to make his way forward. When we reached the booth he gave his wife a bright smile and gestured toward me with his left hand. "Look who I ran into on the way back from the restroom."

"Hello, Mrs. Thomas."

"Mary Kathleen?"

I nodded my assent as I waited for Ed to lower himself carefully onto the bench seat. It was a slow, tedious process. I would've offered to help, but I wasn't sure how. Besides, I was pretty sure he'd be insulted. He struck me as being the proud, stubborn type who wanted to do things for himself. Not, of course, that I've had *any* experience with people like that.

"You can call me Kate, Mrs. Thomas. I'm only Mary Kathleen when people are mad at me."

She smiled. "Then you must call me Edie. I can't tell you how much Ed and I have been looking forward to meeting you!" She patted the bench next to her. "Sit down, sit down. Tell us how you met our Tommy and how he's doing in Denver. He always *says* he's fine . . . but then, he *would* now, wouldn't he."

She knew him well. "We met when he was looking for a place to live. I own an apartment building in lower downtown Denver, and he came to see it. We started out as neighbors and moved on from there."

"Ah yes," Mr. Thomas chimed in. "I remember him telling me that you renovated the place yourself. Sent us pictures so that we'd know it was a nice place." Edie was nodding her agreement, patting one of the photo albums with her hand for emphasis.

"That had to have been a lot of work," he continued.

"It was," I admitted. "But I enjoy that sort of thing."

"It must've just broken your heart to see it collapse like that. It's a miracle no one was hurt." Edie shook her head. "They said on the news they're investigating—that it may have been sabotage. Such a terrible thing."

I was saved from having to respond by the arrival of the waitress. Just as well. My throat had tightened up painfully enough that it would've been hard to speak without crying. I didn't want to cry, not in public, not in front of Tom's family. Oh, they'd probably understand. But I still didn't want to. And oh, Lord, the authorities were *investigating*. The mere thought made me shudder. I've been *investigated* a time or three in the past couple of years. It's never pleasant. Innocent until proven guilty might rule in a court of law, but it absolutely *didn't* in the court of public opinion, or in the minds of the police.

We placed our orders. My choice was coffee, black, and one of the special breakfast offers that was heavy on protein. Ed and Edie ordered from the senior menu. Siobahn, our waitress, was cheerful, brisk, and efficiently managed to clear enough space for our coffee and future plates without toppling the albums before disappearing in the direction of the kitchens. Once she was out of hearing range, Edie leaned toward me across the table.

"Do you think it was the vampires or the pack?"

I choked on my coffee. I managed not to do a spit take, but only barely. My eyes watered. My nose burned in that way that only happens when fluid backs up.

When I could finally speak I managed a hoarse, "I can't imagine the wolves would do such a thing."

"Really?" She didn't bother to hide her disbelief. "Then your pack in Denver must be *very* different from the one here in Vegas. There isn't much the alpha here *hasn't* done at one time or another."

Edie's voice was cold, hard, and brittle enough to make me shiver. It didn't take a psychic to see that she meant every word.

Ed spoke softly. "When our daughter and her husband died we were appointed guardians under the will. The pack took us to court. When that didn't work, the pack leader tried exerting . . . pressure to force us to give Tommy up." His eyes met mine, and for just an instant I saw the man he'd been before age stole his vitality—a man of courage and toughness who would do whatever it took to protect his family. You wouldn't discourage such a man; wouldn't succeed by threats either. The only way past would be to put him in an early grave. That he was here to tell the tale meant that either the pack hadn't been willing to go that far; or he'd beaten them. Something in his expression, and hers, told me it was the latter.

"Mary Connolly is the pack leader in Denver. She's tough, but she's honest, and fair."

"So Tommy said." Ed gave a sad smile. "I was almost afraid to believe him."

"It's not like that here in Vegas." Edie shook her head. "Hasn't been since Elaine Johnston took over the pack all those years ago." Her lips compressed into a thin line of disapproval.

"And now she's heading up the Conclave." Ed spoke over the rim of his coffee cup. "Makes her a very powerful enemy to have."

"Why do you think she's my enemy?"

"You're human," Edie said simply.

I blinked rapidly, at a complete loss for words.

"It's a little more complicated than that," Ed chided.

"Not much." Elaine's jaw thrust forward aggressively. Two bright spots of color had marked each of her pale cheeks.

"She's all right with humans she can control," Ed pointed out gently. "She just won't tolerate *anyone*, human or wolf, who gets in her way." He turned to me, giving me the full weight of his gaze. "And if she can't control you, you're in her way."

I've met humans with that kind of single-minded, ruthless determination. They can be damned dangerous. A wolf would effectively double that. *Shit.*

"Tommy says you can take care of yourself. God knows the press makes you out to be some kind of a superwoman . . . but you'll need to be careful of Elaine."

"I will."

The food arrived. I managed to eat without making a mess of myself, or the stacked books on the table. By the time the plates were cleared away and we were on our after-brunch coffee the tense mood of earlier was gone and Edie'd settled in, ready to show me her pictures.

I loved it. When Mom and Da were alive they'd taken lots of family photos. Mom's favorites were taken with the old Polaroid *her* mother had given her. It was the kind where the soon-to-be picture shot out of the front of the machine and you'd shake it in the air while it developed before sticking it on the backing. Somewhere, unless my aunt pitched them, there were dozens of little square images of three red-headed children. I know Mom would have adored digital photography.

Edie was much the same way. There were shots of her as a young woman with Ed, followed by literally hundreds of photos of their little girl, Tom's mom, from birth through childhood, her senior prom, and her wedding to Tom's father.

Their daughter Audra had been a pretty child, and a beautiful woman, with long honey-colored hair and the same long-lashed, chocolate brown eyes I so loved on Tom. There was a strong physical resemblance between the two of them, no doubt about that. Still, the pictures with his father left no doubt whose son he was.

We moved to the next book. These were the shots I'd looked forward to the most. Tom as a child, alone and with his sister.

I recognized some of them, pictures that Tom had made copies of, that had graced the photo wall in our apartment. I felt a very real stab of pain at the realization that they were gone, along with everything else. *Damn it.* Tears stung my eyes, but I blinked them back as I ran a finger over the edge of plastic cover protecting a cherished school photo.

An age-withered hand settled over mine. "It's all right, dear. I understand. We can make you copies of any picture you like."

"Would you?" I met her eyes. "I know how much those pictures meant to Tom, and they're all ruined."

"Of course! You're family after all."

After breakfast I'd shared a cab ride with Ed and Edie to their house. It was a nice white two-story with green trim and a wide front porch in a quiet neighborhood far off the beaten track. Despite their age, and the obvious effort it took, the lawn was as perfectly groomed as any golf course. Pots of bright red geraniums decorated the porch railing on either side of what had originally been a steep set of concrete stairs. As far as I could tell, the only accommodation they'd made to age and infirmity was the gently sloping ramp that had taken its place.

They were tiring by the time they'd finished showing me around, taking particular care to tell me that the upstairs guest bedroom was "saved" for Tom and me any time we cared to use it. (With a broad hint that they expected it to be often.) Last, but not least, I was shown into the game room. It was a large room, dominated by a beautifully polished billiard table. But when Edie flicked the switch for the overhead lights my eyes were drawn to the far wall. There, in glass-fronted cases, was a formidable display of glittering trophies—*shooting* trophies. Some of them were four-foot tall monstrosities that had to have come from national titles. Beside them another case hung on the wall next to a gun safe. The case displayed a wide array of edged weapons, daggers and knives of various shapes and sizes. Despite loving care, many of them showed hints of use.

Grandmama, what big teeth you have.
The better to defend you with, my dear.

5

I was going to meet Tom at the airport. After three days the storm had finally cleared enough for air traffic to get into and out of DIA. We'd have a few hours together, then I was off to Tel Aviv.

If I hadn't had my breakfast with the Thomases the other morning I would have been confused and shocked by the pack's attitude. As it was, I put up with it by avoiding them as much as I could. It wasn't as easy a task as it sounds, either.

The local wolves didn't trust the vampires' promise to me, so they had guards all over the hospital protecting Dusty. More wolves were bodyguarding Ruby. Even in human form there was no mistaking them for harmless. The Acca, head of the local pack, seemed to have an almost unlimited supply of burly, surly men and even more aggressive females, none of whom seemed to like me.

I'd expected tension. After all, it was no secret that the wolves were against my relationship with Tom. They wanted him to marry a sweet little surrogate who could breed werewolf babies. I'm sterile. It's a by-product of having been bitten by a queen. Apparently you can still have babies without any problem after a "normal" vampire bite. But there is some sort of toxin in the queen's saliva that makes a human woman sterile. I don't know the details. The doctors are still studying it. But I know the results . . . intimately. I proposed the possibility of him being a sperm donor, but the werewolves have a real prejudice against that sort of thing.

I'd expected resentment and tension. But there was more to it than that. I felt their anger and it felt *personal*. I tried to fish it out with my psychic senses, but the same magic that lets Tom help me block the vampires kept me from being able to. Tom had promised to explain everything, in person. I was looking forward to hearing it.

Since I didn't need, want, or rate bodyguards I only ran into them when I was around Ruby or came to the hospital at least once a day to visit and check on Dusty and the baby.

I like Rob and Dusty and the baby, Robert Thomas, captured my heart from the moment they set him in my arms. Chubby and cute, he has a head of shaggy blond hair and the bluest eyes I've ever seen. He hasn't changed yet, which has Rob a little worried.

Dusty just laughs and tells him to give the boy time, but I know he won't be happy until he *knows* for sure that the little one really will be a werewolf. But despite my affection for them, I could only hang out at the hospital so long before I got restless.

Also, while I would never admit it to anyone else, I got jealous as hell. Because it will never be me. I'll never get to have or hold a baby of my own. Won't get to name it after my best friends, do the whole new parent thing. It makes my heart ache, and that kind of sadness has no place in the nursery—especially when the mom's a psychic.

So I had time on my hands. I tried gambling, but discovered it isn't really my thing. The noise gets on my nerves and I'm not comfortable risking money I've worked so hard to earn. I didn't really want to go to the shows without Tom. So, I wound up spending most of the days back at the hotel with Ruby. She's a nice enough girl, but her incessant chatter was hard to take.

But that was almost over. My heart sped up at the thought. I glanced down, checking my appearance. I hadn't dressed up . . . exactly. I was wearing black jeans and sneakers, but the top was one of Tom's favorites, a pale peach tee with a low scooped neck that fit just tight enough to show off my figure. The short sleeves bugged me a little. I'm used to wearing clothes that conceal my knife sheaths. But I was going into an airport. Homeland Security would frown on the armament, even if I do have a concealed carry permit. After all, I was here on a social errand, not carrying valuables. I'd left my hair down, too, with only the front sections pulled back by a pair of gold combs. Usually I keep it braided, but Tom likes it loose. Today I needed to see his smile, so loose it was.

I was shocked at how much I'd missed him. It's not like we don't spend time apart. My job takes me all over the world for days at a time. His has shifts where he'd be gone for two and three days. Too, I've spent most of my life being pretty much of a loner. I don't have a lot of friends and am not all that comfortable with most people. But Tom had wormed his way into the very core of my life. I'd come to count on him when things went wrong. And right now things were definitely not right.

Part of the problem was the Las Vegas pack. I'm not good with people, but compared with the local wolves I was a regular social butterfly. I couldn't fault their security measures, but their hospitality left a great deal to be desired.

The thought made me glance over at the woman in the passenger seat. Annie the werewolf was second in line in the Vegas pack. She was probably in her mid-forties, short, stocky, and plain as an unpainted fence post. I'd only seen her smile once, very briefly, in response to a particularly sarcastic remark I'd made to Doc vampire. The rest of the time she'd been dead serious, alert, and in full bodyguard mode. I wondered if she'd be glad to hand Ruby off to the Denver wolves. Probably. She hadn't said so. Then again, she hadn't said much of anything.

She and Ruby had caught a ride with me because Mary and a couple of the other wolves from Denver were due to fly in as well. They'd caught a flight with a different airline. Normally, they'd be getting here an hour and a half before Tom, but their flight had been delayed. Now there was only a half hour between the two. Kind of silly to take two cars under the circumstances. Although, truthfully, I'd wanted to. But Ruby had begged; almost groveled. She didn't want to be alone with just the Vegas wolf for company. I'd caved, but I was already regretting it.

I pulled the van into the short-term parking garage and began circling, looking for a spot. The closest ones were blocked off with concrete barriers—the result of security measures put in place after 9/11. It created a wide, open area that just begged to be used and never would. I sighed as we rounded the corner and headed up the ramp to the next floor.

The silence was getting thick and tense without even music from the radio to cut it. I did my best to ignore it and pulled to a stop. An elderly gentleman in a huge old Caddy was pulling out of his parking slot. It should be just big enough to fit the van. I glanced at my watch. We were definitely cutting it close. When I'd called earlier the flight had been listed as running on time.

I threw the gearshift into park and unbuckled my seat belt. I climbed out of the van and slammed the door closed with more force than was strictly necessary.

God, how I wanted out of this airport, this *city*. With Tom, on our honeymoon, Vegas would've been wonderful. Instead, it had been a disaster.

I should've waited for Annie and Ruby. But I was just too damned tired of both of them to spend another second listening to a bullshit argument that didn't really *mean* anything. I moved away from them, down the incline with long strides, my tennis shoes nearly silent on the smooth concrete.

"Katie, wait!" I heard the slap of Ruby's flip-flops as she ran toward me. Pregnant as she was, she had all the grace of a lame hippo. If she fell, I'd feel responsible.

I made myself stop, but I didn't turn around.

"I'm sorry." She set her hand on my arm. I tensed, but didn't shrug off the contact. "I don't mean to be so much trouble."

Okay, at this point I was supposed to lie and say it was no trouble at all. Unfortunately, I couldn't do it. In fact, as I turned to look at her I had to bite my tongue not to say something regrettable. After all, the girl couldn't help being a teenager, *and* she was dealing with baby hormones, *and* she'd lost the baby's father under rotten circumstances that were connected enough to me to make me feel really, *really* guilty. So I bit the offending bit of flesh until I could practically taste blood and looked around for a change of subject.

Annie hadn't caught up with us. I turned to find her standing near one of the long open "windows," talking earnestly on her cell phone. She looked even surlier than usual. I pointed toward the terminal, and she waved us on with a gesture.

That was odd. Definitely odd. Still, she didn't have to tell me twice. "Come on, let's go. She can catch up."

"Are you sure?"

I gave Ruby a *look* that held all of the frustration I'd been feeling. "Fine. Wait if you want. I'm going."

She decided to come. We hurried to the stairs and made our way down. I didn't hear Annie behind us, but honestly, I didn't care. I didn't expect any trouble, and if there was any I'd deal with it.

We exited the parking garage and crossed the lanes of traffic without incident. When we made it through the front doors I hurried to the first bank of monitors and looked up the flight. It had arrived early, which meant they should be here any minute.

I heard Ruby gasp, and turned to look where she was pointing.

As I watched, the crowds parted like water. I didn't blame them. Even from here I could feel the energy pouring off the four werewolves. Mary was in front, pulling a wheeled bag. She wore black jeans and boots under a black leather bomber jacket. It would have been intimidating enough without the hostile body language. As it was, her entire body was rigid, her face set in stony lines. My sister-in-law is not big, but she's compact, strong, and tough as old boot leather. I've seen her angry plenty of times—usually at me. But I'd never seen her like this. I couldn't imagine how she was keeping her beast in check.

The two women behind her were obviously sisters. They weren't twins, but they'd probably only been a year or so apart. Both were tall, blonde, buxom, and had features that, while not beautiful, should have been pretty. But the taller one was flushed with anger. When she caught a glimpse of me her eyes narrowed, and I felt a psychic blast of hatred so pure and undiluted it took my breath away. I didn't know who she was. I certainly hadn't done anything to her. But her hatred was a living, breathing thing.

Her sister grabbed hold of her arm, whispering something urgently, but she shook off the grasp. Dropping her bag she shoved past Mary, coming straight over to where Ruby and I were waiting.

"Oh shit." Ruby was almost whimpering. She ducked behind me. I couldn't honestly blame her. That blonde was trouble, no doubt about it.

I held my ground, letting Ruby cower behind me. She was a kid. She was pregnant, and I don't like bullies.

The blonde stopped barely an inch in front of me, deliberately invading my personal space, trying to intimidate me. It was the wrong approach. It didn't scare me, it just pissed me off.

"What in the hell are you doing here? And where is your bodyguard?" The words were for Ruby, but the glare and the anger were all for me. "You're supposed to be at the hospital with Rob and Dusty. We arranged with the local pack for them to protect you. The Acca was supposed to send someone to pick us up."

"Annie's right behind us. She was taking an important call." I kept the words calm, without so much as a hint of hostility.

"Then Ruby should be with her." She growled over my shoulder. *"She,"* the blonde pointed a manicured finger at my chest, *"isn't pack.* She *isn't a wolf."* Hatred had twisted her face into an ugly, menacing snarl. "As a surrogate your *duty* is to keep yourself and the baby safe—under our protection."

The other wolves had arrived, and I saw a security officer speaking into his walkie-talkie as he hurried our way. Homeland Security plays a big part in airport security. If trouble started here it could get very ugly very fast.

"We should probably take this outside." I kept my voice low and addressed Mary. She was the Acca for the Denver pack. That meant she was the one in charge. I'd let her deal with the crazy lady.

"This is pack business, and none of yours," the second blonde snarled.

"Oh for God's sake, Betty, she's just being reasonable." Each word Mary uttered was crisp, as if controlling the words would help her control the wolf inside her. Hell, maybe it did. I wouldn't know. She turned to the woman in front of me, her expression

grim. When she spoke it was with the tone a drill sergeant would use to a new recruit. "Janine, back *down*
before you get us all arrested."

"You're not Acca any more, Connolly," the woman
in front of me turned to glare at my sister-in-law as
she spoke. "*I* am. You can't tell me what to do."

I felt my jaw drop, and I shut it with a snap. *That*
was news. Mary *wasn't* their leader anymore? What
in the hell had happened?

"Fine," Mary sounded more than a little bitter.
"You wanted the job and now it's yours." She gave a
vicious little smile. "But I don't know how well
you'll be able to rule from a Homeland Security
kennel."

"They wouldn't dare," gasped the woman called
Betty.

The hell they wouldn't. And she was an idiot if
she couldn't see that. "Every security officer in this
place is armed with a tranq gun and trained in how
to use it." I spoke with confidence. I'd learned all
about it talking with my friend Leroy, a security officer at DIA. "They'd have you all down and out before you even knew what hit you."

I watched the information sink in, watched as
Janine swallowed all that rage, forced herself to control both her temper and the beast that was so very
close to coming out. She clenched and unclenched
her fists again and again through long seconds of
tense silence during which I never once moved or
took my eyes off of her. When she'd finally mas-

tered herself, she said "Fine, we'll go outside. But this isn't over."

I gestured toward the doors, letting her take the lead. As she stormed past one of the five armed security guards who had stationed themselves around us he gave me a curt nod of acknowledgment. I don't generally carry cargo out of Vegas, so I hadn't been to the airport since they rebuilt it. I didn't know him personally, but he'd figured out that mine was the voice of reason getting us out of his hair. Me, the voice of reason. Who'd have thought?

"Be careful, Katie. Janine—" Mary leaned in close, the words a mere breath of sound. She didn't say more, because Janine whirled and growled when she saw our image reflected in the glass doors.

Our happy little group tripped out of the terminal and across the busy drop-off lanes to the relative privacy of the concrete parking garage. Honestly, I didn't want a fight with the werewolf. There was too much chance I'd lose. But I also wasn't about to back down. As far as I was concerned I'd done nothing wrong. I'd been *nice*. I'd been *helpful*.

Janine didn't slow until we reached the open space in the shadowed lower level of the parking garage. Only then, when there were limited witnesses and as much privacy as we could reasonably expect, did she whirl around and open her mouth.

"Let me be really clear on this, Reilly. I'm not married to your brother. I didn't go to high school with you. I couldn't care less that you're a 'big bad vampire killer.' I think you're a liability to us and Tom has no business dating you let alone thinking about marriage. It's nothing personal, but your relationship with him is over as of now."

"Bullshit." My answer wasn't politic, but it was succinct. "Tom and I dealt with this months ago. Tom will leave the pack if he has to, but we're not breaking up."

"It's not just the pack." Betty's voice had a sly satisfaction that made me want to slap the smug look from her face. "Mom's in charge of the International Conclave. She's scheduled a meeting and it's on the agenda."

"So?"

The collected group caught their breath as though I'd just announced that the sky was green and werewolves didn't exist.

I turned to the one Acca I knew for help. Mary's expression was troubled, but she kept her mouth shut. No, the person who interrupted the tense silence amid all that cold concrete was the last one I would've expected: Ruby.

"You *bitch*." The tiny blonde with her hugely distended belly stepped from behind me and faced Janine full on. She looked ridiculous, her bleached white hair teased into spikes, maternity top stretched taut across her abdomen, and her silly looking flip-flops with their pink feathered flowers. But she was angry enough that it didn't matter. There are people in this world who won't stand up for themselves, but will fight to the death defending others. Apparently Ruby was one of them.

"You fucking *bitch*. You're not doing this 'for the good of the pack.' You want him, and if you can't have him back, you'll make damned sure nobody else can have him either."

Um . . . *excuse me?* I was suddenly missing big chunks of this conversation that everybody else seemed to know. Ruby was shouting loud enough that her voice was echoing off of the concrete walls. Out of the corner of my eye I could see people who had been taking this route to the terminal moving nervously away from the scene. In the distance, Annie was hurrying toward us. One man pulled out his cell phone. I hoped he wasn't dialing 9-1-1, but I wouldn't be surprised if he did. Hell, it's what I'd have done in his place.

Janine's face purpled and twisted into a mask of pure rage, her breathing harsh.

Ruby should have been frightened—the look on Janine's face wasn't sane, and werewolves are dangerous as hell at the best of times. But she continued inexorably on. "Tom won't be coming back to you. Ever. He doesn't love you. He loves Kate."

Oh, crap. That had never occurred to me, but it should have. Now I suddenly understood the hostility. Tom had mentioned he once had a werewolf girlfriend in another pack, and that it had ended badly. But he'd never mentioned names.

There was one of those odd, frozen moments that seem to happen sometimes in high-adrenaline situations. I felt what Janine was going to do, or I'd never have been fast enough to stop it. Those last words went that one step too far. Something inside Janine snapped. Her fist swung out in a blur of speed, and at the same time her power surged and her body began to shift and change.

Mary was opening her mouth to shout a warning, and then the magic hit her and she began to shift. She lunged toward Janine while her body was still changing shape.

Instinct and training took over. I pivoted, bringing the bulk of my body between Janine and Ruby, raising my left arm in a standard block.

The pain was instant and intense. I actually heard the bones in my arm scrape against her teeth, felt the rip of razor claws tearing through the skin and muscle. Blood rained in a long arc following the path of my arm as the power of her blow forced movement.

I staggered, letting out a cry of both rage and pain. I kicked out and caught her in the jaw, rolling her backward for a brief moment. Ruby was screaming, long and loud, her voice echoing hollowly. In the distance I could hear the crackle of radio static, the sound of running feet. Help was coming. I only hoped that they got here in time. Because both Janine and her sister were fully wolf now. Pony sized, their fur was silver gray—the thick neck ruff fading into white belly fur. Whenever Mary closed with one sister, the other tried to get me. I had no weapons, and my death was in those flashing golden eyes.

I was starting to get woozy from loss of blood and I didn't dare extend any limbs toward them that they could get teeth into. So, I concentrated on feinting to stay out of their way, and getting in a judo throw when I could. Mostly, I was worried about Ruby because she couldn't move fast, so I tried to stay between them and her.

Annie and the cavalry arrived after what felt like hours, but was probably only a few minutes. The uniformed airport security officers all held tranq guns to dart the wolves. I would've argued, but I couldn't. Not really. The fighting between the wolves was too intense to separate friend from foe. Each movement was a blur, almost too fast for the eye to follow. The wolves held nothing back, fighting not to wound, but to kill. Blood was everywhere, staining the concrete floor and supports. It's a good thing lycanthropy isn't contagious.

Shots rang out in rapid succession. The noise was deafening. I watched the darts strike home, burying themselves deep in the wolves' thick fur.

It wasn't like the nature programs on television, where the drugs slowly take effect, and the animal staggers around a few minutes before settling down to sleep. No, whatever was in those darts was potent stuff. Each wolf yelped in pain as the dart hit home. In a matter of seconds eyes glazed and they fell, barely breathing, to the floor. A moment or two after that eyes closed on the sisters.

My eyes sought and found Mary. She was hurt. Hell, they all were hurt. Wicked damage from teeth and claws that had torn through the thick fur protecting their skin. Blood matted her thick black fur, but it wasn't spurting like arterial blood, or flowing steady as if they'd caught a vein. I wanted to go to her, but I couldn't. A bearded redhead the size of a professional linebacker was holding me back. My ears rang. I could hear, but not clearly.

"We need an ambulance, and a wagon for the animals." A whipcord thin black man with close-cropped hair called. He was squatting next to the wolf I thought was Janine. Of course, it could've been the sister. I wasn't sure. I only knew it wasn't Mary.

"Where are you planning on taking them?" I heard myself say the words, but I was having a hard time focusing. I've been hurt before, badly hurt. But I'd never felt quite like this. I was light-headed and more than a little bit nauseous. Shock. It had to be. Thing was, I couldn't afford shock. Not with a friend on the ground with hostile officers who really weren't paying a whole lot of attention to what either Ruby or I had to say.

I shook my head, trying to clear it. "One of the wolves was protecting us. Please." I looked directly at the redhead, speaking with every ounce of persuasion I could muster.

His expression darkened. "Did you hear that, Rog?"

A frustrated snort and then he looked from wolf to wolf. "Yeah, I heard. Can you tell us which one?"

I nodded toward Mary and our eyes met just before her lids closed. "The black female."

He sighed. I could tell he wasn't happy, but I wasn't sure why. "Fine. We'll take the black female to holding and have the on-duty vet monitor her until the drugs wear off."

There was something in his voice, a hint of something I didn't like. "How long will that be?"

"Two hours for the tranquilizer. Four for the paralytic."

"Paralytic?" I thought I knew what he meant, but I was hoping that either I was wrong or he was joking. No such luck.

A young blond man came up. "Inhibits muscle movement. Makes them totally helpless. Piece of cake to transport them."

He sounded almost obscenely happy about it. Personally I found the thought horrifying. So Janine wasn't asleep but paralyzed? Shit. To be completely alert and utterly incapable of movement. I shuddered at the possibilities. There's a lot of people who hate and fear werewolves and don't consider them humans, or people at all. And the vampires, God, what would happen if the vampires found out about the drug?

I couldn't expose Mary to that. Hell, much as I disliked Janine, I couldn't even wish that on her. *Shit.*

"I want to go with them."

The redhead shook his head no as he slid an inflatable pressure bandage around my arm and hit the button to activate it. It hurt, a lot. I felt the air rush out of my lungs and it was all I could do not to pull the arm away from him. Not that it would've done any good. He'd been expecting it and had a good, solid grip.

"Not a chance, Ms. Reilly. Not with that arm you don't. You need to get a shitload of stitches. Plus, that bone might be broken. Won't know until after an X-ray."

"How do you know who I am?"

He snorted in derision. "I do read the papers. Please! Your face is on half the magazines they stock in this place." He sighed. "How are the wolves connected to you?"

I nodded toward Mary. "The black female is my sister-in-law."

A look of disgust flickered over the face of the younger man. He stifled it, but not quickly enough for me not to notice. I felt my face flush, not with embarrassment but with good, old-fashioned anger. It was enough to burn off a few of the cobwebs in my head.

I could hear an ambulance siren in the distance. We needed to make a decision now.

"Send them to the hospital with me."

"No."

I tilted my head to meet the redhead's eyes. There was no hint of compromise there. None. I had to do something. The problem was, there wasn't much I *could* do. Security Agent Evans (I just now noticed the neat brass nameplate on the breast pocket of his gray uniform shirt) held all the cards.

"I can't leave them like this. They're completely helpless." I hadn't meant to glance at the blond, but I couldn't help myself. Evans's eyes narrowed, his lips tightening into a hostile line as he followed my glance.

"You and the surrogate go to the hospital. I'll stay here and stand guard." I jumped at the sound of Annie's voice. I was just that unused to hearing her speak.

"Miss," Evans turned to face her, his expression stern. "Under the circumstances, I can't—"

"No." She interrupted him, her voice firm. "Kate's right. Somebody needs to be here to make sure no one hurts them while they're helpless." She gave him a nasty, saccharine smile. "After all, we wouldn't want the press to start poking their noses into what *really* goes on in those holding cells, now would we?"

I didn't like the sound of that one bit. What *had* been going on in the holding cells? My eyes narrowed and I glared at the guards. I'd protested on instinct, not based on any knowledge. But Annie's words had definitely hit a nerve.

I wouldn't have thought Evans's expression could sour more, but he managed it. All the other agents were looking to him to make the decision. It would be his head on the block if something went wrong and he knew it. If he refused us and something happened to the wolves, he'd be in a world of trouble with the law, his superiors, me, and the wolves.

If he didn't refuse, and something went wrong, he'd be in just as much trouble. I almost felt sorry for him.

Annie turned to me, her eyes dark with meaning. "We have an attorney on retainer. I'll have the Acca send him here to deal with whatever charges are brought once they've reviewed the security tapes." She gave me a grim look that finally held some hint of respect before turning to the surrogate. "Ruby, stay with Kate until they take her to surgery. She'll protect you until we can get somebody to the hospital."

"Thank-you," I sighed. "Somebody needs to meet Tom's plane, let him know what happened."

She nodded brusquely. "We have a couple people inside the airport. That's the only reason I let you go in ahead of me. I'll let them know what happened. Consider it an apology for the arm. If our people had been where they were supposed to be, Janine would never have gotten close to you." She sounded disgusted and angry. I'd have given odds that some of the Vegas wolves would be getting a serious dressing-down when the crisis was over.

My nod of acknowledgment was met with a look of weary gratitude.

I got in the ambulance without further fuss. In truth, it felt good to lay down. It must've shown, too, because Ruby sat in uncharacteristic silence next to the gurney in the back of the ambulance for the entire ride.

The ambulance took me to the same hospital where Dusty had given birth. She was recovering nicely—probably would be given her walking papers today. Too bad. We could've shared a room.

I spent very little time in the emergency room before being wheeled into X-ray. Just enough time to sign forms and give them my insurance information. From X-ray I was taken straight into surgery. Yeah, the wound was that bad. It made me nervous as hell, being put under anesthesia in a strange hospital, without either Tom or Joe to keep an eye on things. But there really wasn't any choice. So I had to hope that the surgeons, doctors, and nurses assigned to me were not only skilled, but that they weren't under the influence of the vampires—something that wouldn't have been nearly as much of an issue if I hadn't had to negotiate for Dusty's safety just a couple days before. I didn't think the Thrall would be as reasonable about me as for her.

The last thing I saw before they wheeled me down the hall and the anesthetic took me under was Ruby, standing in the middle of the wide white hall. She was hugging herself with skinny little arms, with tears and mascara streaming down her face.

HEY, NIFTY! I came out from the anesthesia. Hearing came back first. A calm female voice asked me the answer to a simple math problem. I got it right, and managed to open my eyes. They didn't focus all that well at first. But eventually I saw that I was in a mid-sized room with dim lighting and all sorts of machines being monitored by a pair of nurses in colorful scrubs. The elder was middle-aged and gray haired, with an efficient if slightly macho manner. She slid a blood pressure cuff on my good arm, inflated it, and slid a cold stethoscope against my skin to listen.

"One-twenty over eighty-five," she announced. The second nurse wrote it down with a smile. Good numbers on the blood pressure and the ability to answer properly meant that I'd probably come out of the anesthesia in good shape. In fact, it earned me a smile and a trip down the hall to a semiprivate room.

I slept. I'm not sure how long—but long enough that I woke to find Mary sitting up in the bed next to mine. She looked distinctly worse for wear in a gaudy souvenir tee-shirt and the kind of cheap shorts you can pick up on sale at your corner drugstore. The shorts made her legs look stocky. The kiwi green of the shirt looked awful with her coloring and emphasized the dark circles under her eyes. Her hair was even unkempt, unusual in a woman whom I knew to be almost obsessively tidy by nature.

The curtain between the beds was open and the door closed, so we were able to talk without worrying about being interrupted or overheard.

"Tom?"

She nodded toward the door. "He's been sitting by your bedside fretting ever since you arrived, but his grandparents wanted a few minutes with him. He's talking to them in the hall. Figures you'd open your eyes while he's out." She shook her head. The gesture made her dark bangs fall into her eyes, and she brushed them back with an irritated gesture.

"Actually, I'm glad we've got a minute. We need to talk."

She sounded grim. I reached for the controls to the bed and pushed the button. Whatever we were going to talk about, I'd feel better—less helpless—if I wasn't looking up at her from flat on my back. When I was sitting upright I let go of the controls and turned to look her in the eye. It was as I was turning that I noticed the cast, an old-fashioned plaster job that was dyed black. What the hell happened in surgery? But that wasn't a question for Mary, so I asked the one that she *could* answer.

"What's up?"

"How much do you remember of what Janine and Betty said in the parking garage?"

"All of it."

"Good. I'm not Acca any more. Some of the wolves thought I had too much going on in my personal life, that I needed a break. Some just flat disagreed with how I ran things. Any way you slice it, Janine is the new elected Acca."

I didn't answer. I didn't know what to say. The pack had been Mary's whole life for a very long time. Now she has Joe. But losing the pack had to have been a real blow.

Mary's golden-brown eyes met my gaze and held it. "Ruby wasn't wrong. Janine dated Tom for a while before he met you. She got serious. He didn't. He broke it off. She never got over it. Somehow she tracked him down and came to Denver after him." She leaned forward intently. "The thing is, the shit the vampires are pulling plays right into it. We had enough problems before, when the average man on the street thought they were a myth. Now that they're real and *helpful* the wolves are the ones who are the *monsters*."

I understood that. Hell, I'd been experiencing the same thing as a Not Prey.

"Most of the wolves think that we need our own good press. Tom's handsome. He's a fireman and a hero. He rushes into burning buildings and saves lives."

"The wolves want to use him."

"You bet your ass."

"And they think I'm in the way."

She sighed and shook her head. The look she gave me was almost pitying. "You *are* in the way, Reilly. The way they see it, every good thing he's done is offset by something negative about you."

I flinched, even as she shrugged.

"I don't agree. But I'm just one wolf, and I'm not even Acca anymore. Worse, they think I'm prejudiced in your favor because of Joe."

"They've obviously never met Joe." I couldn't keep the bitterness from my voice. I love my older brother desperately, but there are times when I don't *like* him. We get along for a while, then I do, or say, or don't do *something* and we're back to square one with him pissed and pissy and me not even knowing exactly what I've done wrong. "I just wish I knew what I did to turn him against me again. Something happened at the wedding, and I just don't know what."

Mary sighed and stared at the wall for a moment, thinking. I let her, because I was thinking too. It's all I'd been doing since Joe sent back the wedding gift. But I was still coming up with nothing.

"Okay," she said after a moment. "I'll give you enough hints to figure it out for yourself. But as far as Joe is concerned, we never had this talk. I'll deny it to your face to the point of beating it in if you tell him."

Well, that was certainly direct. I raised my brows and realized I could. The drugs must be wearing off a little. I took the opportunity to try sitting up. I managed it, but the process wasn't pretty. Mary didn't offer to help, and I didn't expect her to.

"You know Joe's been in therapy since the . . . *accident*." I nodded, but she didn't even notice. "We call it that, because he still can't handle words like *kidnapped* or *tortured*. In a way, it *was* accidental. He was in the wrong place, born into the wrong family."

That stopped me cold and I couldn't keep the shocked anger from my face or scent. She stared me in the eye, a meeting of equals. We always had been—the two toughest girls in Catholic school, rival captains when we played the same sports. Of course, at the time, I hadn't known she was a werewolf. But we'd still always been fiercely loyal to one another. I counted Mary as one of my few friends. Had that changed?

"Yeah, it's all about you, Reilly. How can it not be? Joe competed with you always, from the day your parents died. But it wasn't until you got the Not Prey title that his life changed . . . and not for the better. You brought Bryan back. Terrific. Joe was massively grateful for that. But then you did the same damned thing to Bryan his *friends* did all those years ago when he overdosed. You dumped him— left him on the side of the real world road to handle shit all on his own." I opened my mouth to protest that I've always made myself available, but she anticipated the comment. "Yeah, yeah, I know. Nobody called. But, see, your own life sucks so bad that nobody *dares* ask you for help. Your tiny little bit of sunshine is Tom, and you're so damned happy with him that nobody wants to be the one to ruin it by intruding."

She swung her legs off the bed and turned to face me with arms crossed over the hideously green shirt. "It's like the time Joe leased the Hummer and you got pissed. He didn't ask about how much you were paying Father Mike in expenses for Bryan's care, and you didn't volunteer the info. So, you mortgaged yourself to the point of foreclosure and got pissed off, and he nearly lost his cookies when he found out how bad off you were. No communication. You think that's somehow miraculously changed just because Bryan's cured?" She snorted, and it sounded like a bark. "Try again. But that's not the worst part. When Joe finally got rehabilitated enough to go back to work, he expected a hero's welcome. But what he got was *pity*. Candy stripers helping him walk down the hallway. Special ramp additions for his braces that are in the way of every doctor in the ER. And sure, shit happens. But his therapist figured out that every single nightmare, his reaction to his braces, his job, his friends . . . it all comes back to *you*."

I sat there, open-mouthed but speechless, because I couldn't figure out what to say for the life of me.

She took a deep breath. "The day of the wedding, there was a trauma victim that came in at St. Elizabeth's. It was Joe's specialty and I won't even pretend that I can understand, or even pronounce, what the issue was. But they didn't call him." She looked at me with fierce eyes, turning golden with repressed adrenaline. "Not because it was his wedding day. Not because they didn't know where he was. But because of how they think of him now. He's not a brilliant doctor to the upper management anymore, not a specialist with skills that are worth accommodating. He's a *victim* in the eyes of his peers there, and he can't handle it." Another deep breath, during which she could only stare down at her chewed nails. "A man died that day in the ER, and Joe could have saved him. I'll let you work out all the things that have been eating at him since a day that should have been the happiest of his life."

The part of me that had been fed a diet of Catholic guilt since birth wanted to vomit. The part that had grown up knew it wasn't his fault . . . or *mine*. But that didn't change the fact that a man died when he might not have had to. For whatever reason. And it was definitely something Joe was going to have to come to terms with. The senseless death of innocents was something I'd been forced to deal with a long time ago—about the same time I first encountered the Thrall.

Mary shook her head and wiped a quick palm across her eyes. "But enough of that. Like I said, we never discussed it. Anyway, Janine's mother is not only the Acca here in Las Vegas, but she's also the head of the Conclave. I know Tom hasn't told you anything about the Conclave, because I ordered him not to. Until you actually were on the far side of the altar, it didn't matter to your life. But I'm not the Acca anymore, so feel free to ask him. I know you won't give up Tom, and he'd rather die than lose you. But I have to warn you. Things are going to get really ugly."

I opened my mouth to say something, anything, but she waved me to silence. Tilting her head at some sound I couldn't hear, she abruptly changed the subject. "Thank-you, by the way."

"For what?"

"For everything." Mary began ticking off items on her fingers. "For dealing with the hospital about Dusty, for protecting Ruby, for making sure somebody was there to guard me while I was unconscious." Her expression darkened. "It shouldn't have been necessary. Janine—"

"Janine is nuts, and dangerous." Tom said the words as he stepped through the door carrying cups of coffee.

My breath caught in my chest at the sight of him. I blinked a couple of times, trying to bring my mind back to the conversation at hand. Tom noticed, and gave me a dimpled grin that made my heartbeat speed up just a little. He crossed the few steps from the door to the bed, handed Mary both cups of coffee, then leaned down to kiss me hello.

It was a great kiss: it started warm and gentle, building slowly. His left hand cupped my cheek . . . his touch delicate as his tongue slid gently into my mouth. His right hand pressed against the bed for balance as I leaned into the kiss, savoring the warm strength of him. Lust is wonderful, and God knows I always lust after him, but it was the steady unshakable love that had built between us that I treasured most. We'd been through a lot together. We'd probably be going through more. But I didn't doubt that whatever trouble came up we'd face it together. I wasn't alone. Not any more.

Mary gave a very deliberate cough. We broke the kiss. I blushed. Tom laughed. It was a joyous sound, and I caught a wisp of thought from him that let me know just how much he enjoyed the effect he had on me—which made me blush even harder.

"I can't believe Janine tried to attack a surrogate. She needs to be put down." Tom turned to Mary, deliberately changing the subject. He took one of the cups from her hand, using the bulk of his body to block her view of my face. He was giving me a chance to recover from my embarrassment. As far as I could tell he was never embarrassed, at least not about anything to do with me. Maybe it was upbringing. I'd been raised with all of the sexual taboos *firmly* in place. Things that made me writhe in mortification didn't bother him in the least. In fact, he thinks it's *cute*. I hate *cute*. But it tells you something about how smitten I am that I can't even hold that against him.

I watched him bring the cup to his lips, and couldn't keep the wistful expression from my face. Tom gave an amused shake of his head and handed me the cup. Now *that* is love. I took a long pull of the steaming liquid, letting the heat and taste soak into my poor, abused body.

"You have to do something." He spoke to Mary.

Mary shrugged. "What am I supposed to do? We're not in our home territory, and even if we were, I'm not in charge any more. But if what happened at the airport gets out beyond the Vegas pack, there's going to be even more bad press. Knowing Janine, she'll try to lay it right at Kate's door."

"But it wasn't Kate's fault," Tom protested.

Mary waved her hand to silence him. "I know. I *know*. But that won't keep them from blaming her, now will it?"

6

"If you were alone, we'd *insist* on keeping you overnight." The doctor was grumbling. His choice of words told me that he wanted me to stay anyway, but wouldn't force the issue.

"My fiancé is a fireman," I replied. "He's also had EMT training. I'm sure I'll be fine."

The doctor didn't like it. I could see it in his eyes. They clouded, and his mouth tightened into a grim line. He looked from one to the other of us, trying to find the weak link.

"I'll make sure she rests, and will bring her in if there's any sign of any problem," Tom promised. There was a coolness to his voice that was unusual. I dropped my shields enough to know that, sure enough, the doctor tingled of Thrall. Not as bad as if he'd been fed from recently. In fact, it could just be from associating with the doctor who'd been in the ER when Dusty came in. Whatever the reasons, Tom was going to get me out of here one way or another. I was glad. I *so* didn't want to spend the night at the hospital. I didn't want any trouble with the vampires. I just wasn't up to it. Besides, I might not feel great, but I'd feel just as good (or bad) sleeping in the hotel bed with Tom as I would in a hospital next to the garrulous old lady who'd moved into the second bed. The minute they'd wheeled her in she turned the television on to *Jerry Springer* at top volume, and started in on a litany of complaints.

Seeing that we were completely united, he said, "I'll have the nurse bring the form indicating you're signing out against my recommendation." He gave up with ill grace, turning on his heel and starting to walk away without another word, his back as straight as if someone had shoved a poker up his butt.

"By the way, doctor . . . can I ask a question?"

He turned his head, but left his body ready to leave on a moment's notice. "Yes?"

I raised my arm with the heavy plaster cast. "Why do I have plaster on my arm? What sort of surgery did you have to do?"

Tom must also have been wondering because he nodded and raised his brows. It actually pulled a small smile from the doctor. "Nothing more than stitches. But your brother suggested the cast. He mentioned your past history of being . . . *hard* on healing wounds. We use acrylic now, but it's not as sturdy. Had to order out special for plaster. The black was the wolf lady's suggestion. Said it matched your wardrobe."

"My *brother* suggested?" I couldn't imagine Bryan setting it up. "When did Joe come by?"

The doctor took one step closer to the door and turned the handle. "He didn't. I called him. Met him at a conference in California last year and got to talking about you. He had to leave suddenly, but we've kept in touch. And after all, we want to be certain you don't have reason to come back here. I'll go get those releases ready." He left without another word, the smile wiped from his face.

Ah yes, he'd need to cover his ass in case something went wrong. Fair enough. I didn't think anything was going to go wrong. I trusted that instinct. Ever since I healed Rob up in the mountains, and even more so since I healed Bryan and the Simms girl, I've had kind of a feel for the extent of injuries. I knew my arm would be fine eventually. Oh, I'd end up with some more choice scars, and probably another bout of physical therapy, but in the end it would be fine.

"He's probably right, Kate. You probably *should* stay overnight. If he didn't smell of vampires—" Tom said it softly, so that our neighbor wouldn't hear. God knows she was trying. She was straining so hard I was afraid she'd fall off the bed. I didn't know if she recognized me and wanted juicy tidbits to give her acquaintances, or if she was just the nosy type. I didn't care, either. I just wanted out.

I gestured to the stand between the two beds. The phone was there, along with the thick Vegas telephone book. "Can you go downstairs and get me something to wear? They took my clothes for evidence. I'll call us a cab."

"All right." Tom leaned down to give me a quick kiss. "But I don't like leaving you alone."

"What do you mean alone!" The old girl snapped from the next bed. "I'm here, aren't I? I'm tougher than I look too. You just do what you're told!"

Tom fought not to laugh. "Yes ma'am." He kissed me again. "I'll be right back."

As he passed through the door she shook her head and passed judgment. "Handsome, but not terribly bright. You could do better, dearie. Still, can't say as I blame you. He is quite the looker."

I might have defended his intellect, but the cab company picked up the line. I asked them to be at the front entrance in forty-five minutes and gave them the name Bishop. They said they'd wait if need be, but I'd be charged for it.

As it turned out, I'd given us more than enough time to get me checked out and downstairs. I'd expected to have forms to fill out, and to spend at least a few minutes talking with Mary and with Tom's grandparents. Turned out, Mary had already gone off to meet with the locals. Tom's grandparents stayed only briefly, just long enough to make sure I was going to be okay and to extract a promise from Tom that we'd call them in the morning.

The sun was setting as the two of us settled onto

one of the small concrete benches that lined the hospital entrance. I had my bag with prescriptions and paperwork resting on the seat next to me. Even with the drugs, the arm hurt abominably.

There hadn't been anything to wear in the hospital gift shop, so Tom had walked down to the corner drugstore. He'd come back with lime green drawstring shorts and a cheap souvenir tee-shirt with hot pink flamingos wearing sunglasses in front of a neon sign that said "VEGAS ROCKS."

I slid across the seat, giving him room to sit beside me. When he was settled beside me I asked the question that had been hovering between us.

"So, what's the situation in Denver?"

"Do you want the bad news, the worse news, or the really horrible news first?" He was quoting me from an incident some time ago, trying to keep the tone light by reminding me of a night from our past. It might have worked, but his eyes gave him away. They were serious, even worried. Still, I played along, giving him the response he expected.

"Gee, honey, you make them all sound so wonderful. You choose."

I was rewarded with a sincere, if tired, smile.

"The good news is, Harry Zorn transferred out of the department."

"Okay." I didn't know why that was good news, but I'd take his word for it.

Tom's smile grew broader. "He's the one who was keeping everybody worked up about what I did. He just *kept* agitating. I think he was trying to get me fired. When he saw I got accepted to smokejumping school he had a fit and quit."

"You got accepted!" I forced myself to smile brightly and act excited. He'd always wanted this, after all. I can *do* the supportive girlfriend thing. But oh, shit, he got accepted.

"Yeah!" His eyes were sparkling now, and he was practically bouncing up and down on the seat with excitement. "It's so great!"

That was debatable. But I *so* wasn't going to say it. Oh no. Nunh unh. Nope, nope, nope. Time to change the subject before I gave away my real feelings.

"But you said *bad* news," I prompted him and was immediately sorry. All that bubbling joy just drained away.

"Mary's not Acca any more. She's been replaced by Janine."

"I know." I raised my left arm. "And you're right, it's the worst. Janine's nuts."

"Did you know that she's my ex-girlfriend? That she came out to Denver from Vegas looking for me?" He was angry, even bitter about it. But at the same time I could see he was worried how I'd react. He needn't have worried. After all, who was I to throw stones? I've got my own share of not-so-glorious ex-relationships.

"It came up." He flinched. I hadn't meant my tone to be that harsh, but thinking of Janine made me angry all over again. I was surprised Mary hadn't told him about the argument that had started the violence at the airport. Then again, she might have figured it was something best left between the two of us. "Janine's gotten her mother to call an emergency Conclave and put our relationship, or the end of it, on the agenda. Care to 'splain to me about Conclaves? Mary said to tell you that since she's not Acca anymore, any orders she gave you are out of force."

I was glad the cab was late. It was giving us time to talk. But someone had taken a seat on the next bench over. I could only hope he wasn't eavesdropping.

Tom stared at me for a long moment. I could feel the tension build as he tried to come up with the right words. His face moved from anger to fear and then to something I didn't recognize but had *wolf* written all over it.

"I've been wanting to tell you—" He paused and looked at me with worried eyes. I shrugged, not so much angry as tired. It was yet another thing he didn't feel confident enough to tell me. Yeah, I know the wolves are a matriarchal society, but sometimes I find it frustrating just how *obedient* the males are to the Acca, who is always a female. He even took a beating from Mary that would have killed a lesser man, just because he refused to break up with me.

Of course, that got me to thinking about Carlton again, because it was he who had rescued Tom from the side of an icy mountain road to bring him home after Mary worked him over. Again with the *why*? Thralls are evil. Thralls don't do nice things without reason—and certainly not for a *werewolf*.

Yet, Carlton seemed to be able to flout the rules of the collective as easily as the ones on the court.

Tom's voice interrupted my musing. "The Conclave is like the United Nations. Each of the dyad family units and pack hunting units answers to the Acca. The Accas, in turn, answer to the Conclave. Representatives are chosen from the Accas to sit on the Conclave council. The Conclave decides *everything*. They are the ultimate law." He turned to me and took my hand. It was then I noticed his palms were sweating. "Kate, I didn't know we were on the agenda. God! This changes *everything*. It's one thing to leave the Denver pack if they object to us. But the Conclave could have us driven out of not only the Denver pack, but blacklisted so that no pack would take us. I don't know that I'm strong enough to become a rogue."

That sounded like a title that had real meaning, and if it scared him that much, I needed to know what we were facing. I squeezed his hand and turned his face with my damaged arm so I could see his eyes flickering yellow as he neared changing. We needed to keep him calm. I don't know what would happen if he changed in the back of a taxi in Las Vegas. "What's a rogue, Tom? This is important. Hold it together here."

He locked his jaw so suddenly that I heard the muscle pop and I steeled myself for the worst, my body pushing back into the leather car seat. "If I'm declared rogue, every pack in the world will be under orders to drive us from their territory on sight.

There's not much land that isn't considered part of *some* pack's territory. From what I've heard, rogue wolves seem *accident prone*—to the point where they have a really short life expectancy. To my knowledge, there aren't *any* rogue wolves alive at this precise moment."

"*What?*"

He closed his eyes in evident pain. Reaching across the seat, I took his hand in mine and gave it a squeeze. It seemed to strengthen him, because he continued. "I love you, Kate. I do. But I can't subject you to that sort of life. We need to figure out some way to get off the agenda, or get a champion, or something. This is big. I don't know if you realize just *how* big. I need some time to think about this. Sadly, though, that wasn't the bad news I was going to give you and now that the moment's ruined, I might as well. Your insurance company is denying the building claim. They say it was sabotage, and think the claim is fraud."

Time froze. It was hard to even think straight. Yes, Edie had mentioned the possibility of sabotage, but I hadn't really *believed* it. Silly me. Now everything I owned had been destroyed or damaged, Tom might be heading for slaughter, and there was a good chance that I might not have a home for years. To say nothing of the inevitable lawsuits, running for our lives, and bad press. Assuming word leaked out—which, eventually, it would. I've had run-ins with the police before, and the courts, and the wolves. I'd been cleared, but now my name was on the official

radar at a national level. I was becoming *infamous*.
And, like it or not, there are always going to be
those folks who think "where there's smoke there's
fire," that because I've been suspected of wrongdo-
ing, I *must* be guilty.

It was rapidly reaching the point where I might
have to change careers, change my name, or get a
new face. First off, legal problems would put my
bond and concealed carry permits at risk *again*. But
worse, notoriety is the last thing clients want in an
air courier. They want their valuables to pass in safe
and pleasant anonymity from place to place with
thieves not knowing who to target. I have a very
distinctive appearance. It wouldn't take a particularly bright thief to put two and two together if they
saw me at an airport with a briefcase cuffed to my
wrist. While Gerry Friedman and some of the other
clients who had become friends over the years we'd
worked together would hate having to hire someone
else, they'd still do it. I couldn't even blame them.
After all, business is business.

And if I was running for my life from rabid wolf
packs, I couldn't do much to keep money coming
in if Tom couldn't find steady work in his trade.

Which is why it was no real surprise to me when
Tom broke the last bit of bad news. After everything
so far, it nearly made me laugh. Gerry had called my
cell phone while I was unconscious. The Tel Aviv
run was being "postponed" indefinitely.

"I'm sorry, baby." Tom spoke softly so that
passersby wouldn't hear.

I felt like crap, physically, mentally, and emotionally. Everyone has a breaking point and I was getting damned close to mine. So much of my life was completely out of control right now. I didn't dare meet Tom's eyes, or I'd lose it. So I stared out at the glow of the lights of the strip in the distance, my throat too tight to answer him.

It was at that point the cab finally arrived. As he pulled to the curb Tom and I rose to our feet and crossed the sidewalk.

"It's not all bad news." Tom gave my shoulder a gentle squeeze, enough contact to show support, but not enough to push me over the edge. "Joe came to see me at the station. He told me to let you know that we can stay with him and Mary until we get a new place and that he and Mary are taking us out to Guiseppe's for dinner so he can apologize for being such an ass."

I saw the drop of my jaw reflected in the car window. Closing my mouth, I turned to look Tom in the eye. I had to be sure he wasn't joking. After what Mary just told me, I couldn't believe that it was that simple.

"Yeah," Tom grinned. "I know. Kinda threw me for a loop too. But it's the truth. He was off work because of the suspension—" Tom opened the car door for me, I peered inside and confirmed with the driver that this really was our cab before climbing in and sliding across the smooth vinyl seat.

"Suspension?" Crap. Mary hadn't mentioned that, but it made sense if the brass didn't trust his judgment anymore.

Tom winced. "The press got to him." He pulled the door closed. "They started asking about you, and what he thought about you having killed vampires now that we know how helpful they can be to mankind."

Uh oh. They'd played him like a concerto, pushed all the right buttons: his family and his work. The parasites may be working on good press right now, but the fact is, you get infested, you've got a remaining life expectancy of five to ten years—if that. And Joe, like me, is more than a little suspicious about this newfound helpfulness in the bloodsuckers.

"You can guess how it played out."

The cabbie pulled out into traffic. For a long moment the only sound was the crackle of voices on his radio as the dispatcher routed the various drivers to their destinations.

I could imagine how Joe would react. Badly. I shook my head, not trusting myself to speak without it becoming a string of swear words.

"They showed the tape of it on the news—every station. I made a copy for you. He defends you, and blasts them. My favorite part was when he said "McDonald's doesn't *save* cows, and the vamps aren't *helping* us. We're food and shelter. Period.""

Oh God, I could just hear him saying it. And wouldn't that just give the hospital administrators fits. After all, they were working hand in hand with the vampires to bring coma victims and Eden zombies back to consciousness.

Tom shook his head. Just that simple movement told me that he felt sorry for Joe, thought he was a fool, and at the same time admired him. I wasn't surprised. Joe engenders mixed emotions in just about everybody, me included. He sighed. "They wanted him to issue a public apology. When he refused, they put him on suspension."

"For how long?"

"Indefinitely."

Ouch! I'd met the hospital administrator. A bigger ass you've never seen. He'd expect my brother to back down at the threat of losing his job. He'd be wrong. Joe doesn't react any better to threats than I do. Look in the dictionary under hard-headed, you'll find a picture of our family crest.

"But there's a second spot of good news. Figured I'd save it till last. Our wedding present from Mike arrived."

Something in the way he said it, so soft and serious, made me worry a little. *Father* Michael O'Rourke had been my first real love, right up until he chose the priesthood over me. We've remained the closest of friends since. Until I found Tom, Mike had always been the one I went to: when I fought with Joe, when Bryan became an Eden zombie, when my former fiancé became part of the Thrall and tried to trap me into doing the same. Last year the same lunatic who'd captured Joe had tortured Mike for information. I'd been in hiding. She wanted to know where I was. She'd been sure he'd know—and intended to use the information to kill me. With everything she'd done to him, he hadn't broken. She'd wound up getting the information off of his answering machine.

Mike lived, but he was horribly scarred, and paralyzed from the waist down. The amazing thing is, he doesn't blame me for any of it. Apparently, unlike Joe.

But not unlike me. I miss Mike. I feel guilty and sad every time his name comes up. I feel even more guilty that I'm *relieved* he's gone to Rome to work at the Vatican. Because, guilt aside, there was a tension building between him and Tom that I didn't like.

I knew we needed to talk about it, but I wasn't sure I wanted to do it with the cabbie right there. As if in answer to an unspoken prayer I heard the driver's cell phone ring. As I watched he hit the button to his hands-free headset and was chattering away.

"He sent us tickets to Italy for next month. He's arranged hotels, sightseeing, everything. He's giving us a honeymoon."

Wow. Okay then. That was unexpected. And *not* cheap. I knew that the church did right by Mike, particularly now that he was on their International Youth Council, but *that,* that was impressive to the point of being scary. I wasn't sure what to say. Hell, I wasn't sure what to *think*.

Tom's smile grew wistful. "I feel kind of guilty, really."

I felt my eyes widen. "Why would *you* feel guilty, for heaven's sake?" I mean . . . *me,* sure.

He shifted uncomfortably in his seat, and wouldn't meet my eyes. "I've always been more than a little jealous of Mike. And I'm pretty sure he was jealous of me too. But then he goes and does something like this, and—"

I reached up to cup his cheek in my good hand. "You do not have any reason to be jealous of Mike."

Tom sighed. When he met my gaze his eyes were oh so serious. "You loved him, Kate. He was your first true love. If he hadn't joined the priesthood the two of you would be celebrating your anniversaries and raising kids together right now. Hell, a few months ago he was ready to die rather than give you up to the monsters."

The car was slowing to pull into the hotel driveway and the cabbie had ended his personal call. This was a big subject, and there wasn't enough time or privacy right now to do it justice, but I had to try. I caught Tom's gaze, and kept it, putting every ounce of intensity I could in my expression and in the words I was about to say. "Mike was my first love, and he is a terrific guy. When I was younger I couldn't imagine finding anyone better for me, loving anyone more. But he chose the church. His calling is more important to him than I was; than anything, really. If he had to choose again, he'd make the same decision." I steeled myself, this next was the hard part. Saying it out loud, admitting my true feelings, would make me completely vulnerable in ways I hadn't dared *since* Michael. Not with Dylan certainly, and not with anyone else. "But the truth is, if I had to choose again I wouldn't choose Mike. I'd choose you. I love *you*. Completely. I don't want anyone else. I can't imagine being with anyone else. You mean everything to me. I just wish there was some way I could prove that to you."

"You mean that." He whispered the words, his voice tight with emotion.

"Hell, yes I mean it!"

"Well, I can't even imagine my life without you—and I don't want to. Just the thought of losing you. . . ." He shook his head to clear it of the unwelcome thought. "I won't give you up, Katie. Whatever happens, I'm in it for the long haul."

I leaned in, laying a gentle kiss on his lips before whispering. "I love you, Tom Bishop."

"I love you, Mary Kathleen Reilly. And if you weren't injured I'd drag you up to the suite and demonstrate how much in all sorts of new and creative ways."

"It's only my arm." I smiled when I said it. Yes, the arm hurt, but the pain pills had taken the edge off, and I wanted to do whatever I could to ease the hurt I'd seen in Tom's eyes. "If we're careful—"

Tom paid the cabbie and grabbed his bags. We moved with almost indecent haste through the lobby, past the colorful rows of slot machines and the equally colorful characters playing them. The ringing bells and clink of change were loud enough to give me a headache. I saw Tom wince, and realized how painful all the noise must be to his sensitive wolf ears. It was a relief when the elevator doors whooshed shut behind us, and the only sound was muted Muzak. I was digging in my pocket for the key before the elevator got off the first floor. If anything, Tom was even more impatient than I was. What could possibly go wrong?

Just having the thought was tempting fate. I should've known better. But no. Leave it to my luck.

Wrong, in this case, took the form of a very large middle-aged werewolf standing outside the door to the hotel room. In human form she was only an inch shorter than I was, but she was probably a solid fifty pounds heavier and all of it was muscle. She wore a navy tank top with matching shorts that had white piping and little slits up the side that only emphasized just how buff her legs were. The black curls she'd pulled back into a ponytail were liberally streaked with silver. The gray hairs looked good on her, going well with faint wrinkles that were just starting to line her features. I recognized her from the description Annie gave. Her name was Elaine Johnston . . . the Acca for Las Vegas, the elected head of the Conclave—and oh, and let's not forget, Janine and Betty's adoptive mother.

"Good afternoon, Ms. Reilly, Tom." Her voice was a pleasant alto. The words were delivered seriously, but without menace.

"Acca." Tom addressed her by her title, giving a respectful nod of his head.

"We need to talk."

I felt a surge of irrational anger. Not at her necessarily, although frustration was making me annoyed. More than that, though, I was really beginning to hate that phrase. Every time I heard it lately I was getting seriously bad news. I didn't want more bad news. I had enough on my plate at the moment. I sure as hell didn't want to "talk" with the head of the freaking Conclave. But, there you go.

I shifted the plastic bag the hospital had given me onto my left arm, but the moment the strings wrapped around the cast, I realized it was a stupid thing to do. A wave of pain hit my brain that the painkillers couldn't handle. Tom looked panicked for a moment and then touched my bare skin. I felt a soothing wave of warmth flow through my arm . . . felt the pain dissolve in the magic of his wolf. He can do that, and has for me before. I luxuriated for a brief second in feeling no pain, but then I shook my head. I let him know with a glance that this was no time to show any weakness because I was *only* human.

He frowned the tiniest bit but did as I asked. He pulled away his power and then the pain was back, sharp and immediate. I took a deep breath to swallow it back in and then slid the card key into the slot on the door and pulled it out slowly. The light turned green, the lock switching open with an audible click.

It was Tom who turned the knob and opened the door, holding it so that Elaine and I could precede him.

She stopped a step or two inside the room, taking a long look around. I saw her back stiffen. Watching the expressions chasing across her face, I decided that Elaine wouldn't be much of a poker player. She was too obvious. And while there wasn't any physical resemblance between her and her foster daughters the body language similarities were striking.

"A honeymoon suite." She took a seat without invitation, lowering herself onto one of the chairs next to the table where the food had been the first night.

"We were coming here to get married," Tom observed. "You knew that."

"Yes." Just one word, but there was a thread of anger that set off my psychic alarm bells. "You called ahead and got permission from my seneschal, just like you're supposed to."

I hadn't known about that. Then again, I don't know much about the wolves and their culture. I'd always thought that was a part of Tom's life that really didn't involve me so I hadn't taken time to do any research or learn the customs. My mistake.

"But you didn't call *me,* now did you?"

A tense silence stretched between the two of them. She stared at him, daring him to defy her. He didn't, but he didn't back down either. I might not know werewolf culture, but I know dominance games when I see them. I moved, deliberately drawing her attention, breaking the standoff. "You said we needed to talk. What about?"

She glared at me, her eyes gleaming eerily

golden, with almost no whites showing at all. "Are you planning on pressing assault charges against my daughters?"

I thought about it. What Janine had done was violent, wrong, and *stupid*. I didn't doubt that there were going to be all kinds of criminal charges filed that I had no control over whatsoever. Did it really matter if I, personally, pushed for the district attorney to pursue assault? Probably not. I couldn't imagine it making that much difference.

I was taking too long to answer. Her expression darkened, and I could feel the power of her magic begin filling the room.

"She attacked a surrogate." This time it was Tom's turn to provide the distraction. When he spoke he didn't even bother to hide his disgust.

Elaine turned her head to him very slowly. There was something oddly inhuman about the motion, but she managed to keep her beast in check.

"What Janine did is inexcusable." Elaine's voice had dropped almost an octave and had taken on a growling undertone. "And she *will* be punished. But assault charges, and a trial, particularly with *you* involved, would bring the kind of publicity we least need right now. Our attorney thinks he can manage the rest of it discreetly if you and the surrogate don't push the assault issue." She stared at me with those odd, unsettling eyes for a long moment before continuing. "The girl will follow your lead. So I ask again. Are you planning to press the assault charges against my daughters? You don't want me as your enemy, Ms. Reilly."

I smiled tightly. "No. I don't. I'm just not sure how wise it is for me to turn my back and leave an enemy loose behind me."

"You consider Janine your enemy?" she snarled.

I held up the black cast and stared into those oh-so-golden eyes. "She made it clear she considers me hers."

She nodded once, slowly, acknowledging the distinction. Her gaze shifted, following Tom's movement as he made his way to the full size, padded bar and grabbed an overpriced bottled water. "Would you like something to drink, Acca?" he offered.

"Please."

She watched him as he busied himself pouring her drink into one of the glasses that had been provided with the room. I didn't sense any sexual tension, or threat. It seemed almost as if she were measuring him against some inner standard. Only after she took the glass from his hand did she turn her attention back to where I'd taken a seat in a burgundy and forest green upholstered wing chair that would have looked at home in Napoleon's palace.

"Janine is facing a number of serious charges. It will take some time for it to go through the legal system. We'll put that time to good use—get her enrolled in anger control classes, therapy, anything and everything to impress the prosecutor, judge, and jury that she's not a menace to society. I can't promise you one hundred percent safety. But I can, and do, assure you that I'll be keeping her under *very* close *personal* supervision while we work through this mess. She won't be getting off scot-free from us either. She deserves harsh punishment for what she did, and she'll damned well get it. I didn't realize how often she'd been using my position as a club against others. That will stop."

Elaine meant what she was saying. The problem was, there was only so much she'd be able to do. Her political position and clout with the werewolves would help, but ultimately it would be up to Janine. Was she sane enough to act in her own best interest? Maybe. But I wouldn't have wanted to bet on it. While I would love to believe that either therapy would help or she'd get put in jail for a good long time, I didn't. Not really. Therapy generally seems to work best if you *want* it to and are willing to put in the effort. Janine didn't think she needed help to get over Tom. She wanted *me* out of the way.

But pressing charges wouldn't help the situation. It would piss Janine off more. Too, my name would make it practically certain the press would be all over it. The werewolves didn't need that kind of bad publicity.

"I won't press charges."

I watched the muscles of her back and shoulders unclench as she let out a slow, careful breath. "Thank-you."

"You're welcome."

She gave me a wry smile that softened her features,

made her look more human. "Connolly was right about you."

I raised an eyebrow at that. I realized I'd started to cross my arms over my chest, but the cast wouldn't cooperate—leaving one hand resting on the opposite shoulder. It probably looked as odd as it felt, so I dropped my hands back to my lap.

"I talked to her before I came over here, while you were still in surgery."

"Dare I ask what she said?" I sounded almost as wary as I felt. There's not much about me, good or bad, that Mary doesn't know. I like her. I respect her. Thinking about it, I realized that her good opinion mattered a lot to me.

The smile turned into a grin. "She said that you were one tough cookie and stubborn as hell, *but* ultimately you'd do the right thing. She also told me not to even bother trying to use bribery, intimidation, or influence peddling; that it would just piss you off. That if I wanted something I should just ask."

It had been good advice. I don't like bullies. It really doesn't matter whether they use power, money, or physical threat. It's still bullying, and it gets my back up but good. Stupid really, and God knows how much trouble it causes me, but true. It also told me, albeit indirectly, that Mary had expected her to threaten me.

"She knows me well."

"Yes, she does." Elaine looked at me with serious eyes. "I was going to order Tom not to marry you. Not because of Janine, but for the good of the wolves.

Our situation really is getting fairly desperate. We need all the good press we can get, and to avoid as much conflict with the vampires as we can." She sighed, and for just a minute she looked old. I watched her pull herself together in front of my eyes, rebuilding the persona she presented to her people. "I *was* going to order him. Not now. Instead I'm asking you both. Please. Wait. Not forever, just for a while. Let us get a handle on things."

She looked from me to Tom and back. I looked away from those oh-so-serious eyes, seeking, and finding Tom. I knew what he wanted without telepathy. He wanted me, as his wife and his lover, but he didn't want to endanger his people, or complicate an already tense situation. I gave a slight nod, letting him know that I understood, but I let him answer.

His voice wasn't resigned, or angry. It was adjusted to let her know that we were making a reasonable concession . . . not giving in. "We'll wait . . . for now."

She didn't even try to hide her relief. It showed in her face, and in the sudden relaxation of muscles she'd held tense.

"Thank-you." Elaine rose, extending her hand to me. I shook it, and felt a shiver of electric power pass between us. Her eyes widened just a fraction, and she let go of my hand abruptly. "You're a dangerous woman, Kate Reilly. I don't think I realized until now just how dangerous."

She left the room before either of us could respond. Just as well. I didn't have a clue what to say.

7

I cleaned up in the shower and we went to bed early. Despite the setting, neither Tom nor I was up for sex. Too much had happened, most of it bad. Instead, we slept.

I woke in the morning spooned against him, his arm wrapped around my waist. When I stirred, he made a small protesting noise, pulling me closer against him so that I could feel his body hard and ready against my buttocks.

Are you up? I sent a tendril of thought his way. He responded by brushing my hair aside with gentle fingers and laying a kiss on the spot where my neck met my shoulder.

"Oh, yeah." He moved his hand down my abdomen in a gentle, sure movement, his fingers caressing the tender skin, sliding down until he could brush them against the most intimate parts of my body. I writhed against him, and felt him grow even harder.

"You must have had good dreams. You're wet." His whisper tickled my ear as his finger moved inside of me, making me shudder with pleasure.

I didn't remember dreaming, but I was definitely wet, and ready; so incredibly ready. I'd missed everything about him. But I'd really missed this. Tom hadn't been my first lover, but no one had ever moved me the way he could. Just looking at him could make my body ache with the need to touch and be touched.

He nibbled my shoulder as his finger sought the sweet spot and began stroking it over and over, until I couldn't help but writhe and moan.

"I missed you." He released me so that I could roll over onto my back. It was difficult to move the cast around easily. The pain killer had worn off and I winced. This time, when he sent soothing magic my way, I happily gave in and felt the pain dim and then float away, until all that was left was pleasure.

I looked up into his eyes and the expression on his face took my breath away. There was just so much emotion, such intensity. Then he smiled, and it was like the sun coming out from behind the clouds. He leaned down and kissed me, warm and hungry, his mouth opening mine so that our tongues danced and played.

He slid his right hand from my waist to hip and lower in a slow caress that ended with his hand beneath my knee. With gentle strength, he lifted and spread my legs. My body arched so that the tip of him rubbed against my opening, drawing a low moan from his lips against mine.

I lowered my hand to find him, hard and ready, the blood pulsing beneath my hand as I stroked his silken flesh with my thumb. His body shuddered, and he pulled away from the kiss. His eyes were a little unfocused, his breathing faster than normal. I used my hand to guide him, and he slid inside me, fast and hard enough to make me cry out, but not in pain. It felt so good, so incredibly good, to have him moving inside me. I bent my knees, bringing them up so that my calves could wrap around his waist. It changed the angle just enough, so that each thrust rubbed against that perfect spot. I felt the orgasm building slowly at first, then faster, my breath coming in pants as my body strained and reached for the release it craved. My hands cupped Tom's ass, and I could feel the muscles moving as his body pounded into mine in an ever increasing rhythm.

I felt Tom's body tense and shudder as the orgasm hit him, and it was all that I needed. My body spasmed around his, my nails digging furrows into his flesh and a long, loud scream of pleasure left my lips.

We collapsed as one, our frantic heartbeats slowing, relearning how to breathe.

I let Tom take his shower first. I couldn't move. I doubted I'd be able to for a while. It had just been that good.

When I could finally bring myself to stir, I used

Tom's laptop to print out our e-tickets while Tom was in the shower. We'd go back to Denver, deal with the police and the insurance investigators, and see if the building inspector had determined the place was safe enough for us to recover what we could from the apartment. I was dreading the whole thing. I'd worked so hard for so long. It just about broke my heart every time I thought about everything I'd done sitting in ruins, so I was trying hard *not* to think about it.

The phone rang, breaking into my reverie. I leaned across the bed to grab the nearest extension. "Hello?"

"Kate, it's Mary. Can you and Tom meet us downstairs in a few minutes for breakfast?"

"Both of us?"

"Please."

"He's in the shower right now, but we can come down as soon as he's dressed."

"Thank-you."

She hung up without explaining why she wanted to meet. Not good. On the other hand, she hadn't sounded particularly upset. It was at that moment I realized that we hadn't talked to her since we'd met with Elaine. Shit. We probably needed to tell her what had gone on. We probably *should* have told her last night. Tom hadn't mentioned it, and I honestly hadn't thought about it. I'm too used to acting on my own to handle the wolf power structure very well.

Well, if she got pissed, she got pissed. We'd just have to deal with it.

"Who was that?" Tom stepped out of the bathroom wearing only a hotel towel tied loosely at the waist. He was using another towel to rub his dark curls dry. He looked positively scrumptious, but I was still a little sore and plenty satisfied from our earlier exertions. Still, I couldn't help but drool a little. It should be criminal for anyone to look that good.

"Mary wants us to meet her downstairs for breakfast."

"Do we have time? When does our flight leave?"

"Not for three hours. We should be okay if we don't dawdle."

"Right. No dawdling." He gave me an impish grin that flashed those irresistible dimples. "Good thing we took care of business earlier."

I blushed, just like he'd planned. Seeking revenge, I grabbed one of the throw pillows from the top of the bed and lobbed it at him, but he was too quick. Laughing, he ducked through the bathroom door. The pillow bounced harmlessly off to lie pitifully on the floor.

I stood, and picked it up, and went into the bathroom. If I was really, *really* quick I had time for a shower. Since I didn't really want to meet Mary for breakfast smelling of sex, I hurried. As I scrubbed myself virtuously clean I could hear Tom in the other room talking to his grandparents on the phone as he got down to the business of packing. It was a smart thing to do. If we had everything ready to go there'd be less chance of us getting caught in a panicked rush to the airport and leaving something behind.

I quickly toweled myself dry, and pulled on the outfit I'd chosen. It wasn't the most comfortable thing to wear, but I'd chosen it more to impress Tom than for any other reason.

I stepped into the doorway, and came to a complete stop.

He looked good. Spectacularly good. Somewhere he'd found a tailored dress shirt in a color that was somewhere between brown and copper. He'd folded back the cuffs twice, which showed off his muscular forearms. The color of the shirt looked amazing against his skin, and brought out the gold and copper flecks in his eyes. His hair was still damp and looked almost as black as the pair of brand-new black jeans that fit like a glove over his well-toned backside. He'd opted for a simple pair of black running shoes rather than his usual boots—the better to get through the inevitable shoe search.

"You're staring," He teased.

"Can't help it," I admitted. "You look amazing. I love the shirt."

"I thought you would." He gave me a pleased, possessive smile. "You're looking pretty spiffy yourself."

I was glad he'd noticed. I'd packed for a honeymoon, so I had brought some of my most flattering clothes. This morning I'd picked a scooped neck tee in a soft shade of daffodil yellow with tiny flowers embroidered in a daisy pattern on it. The neckline was low enough to show off actual cleavage—a feat obtained through the use of a very effective, if relatively uncomfortable, push-up bra that (while he wouldn't see it until later) exactly matched the lacy panties that were currently hiding under my most flattering pair of jeans. They've been washed enough that the color has faded to an almost powder blue, and the denim is soft to the touch.

Despite a fair amount of pain, I'd worked yellow and white ribbons into the braid hanging down my back and was even (gasp) wearing makeup and jewelry. It was all very soft, very feminine. The only sour note was the black cast, but hey, you can't have everything. I'd have been a little disappointed if he hadn't said anything. Silly of me. But I only go to the effort of dressing up for him. Before he came into my life my clothing was all about function and accessories were guns and knives. When I'm working I still make sure to wear clothes that allow for a concealed carry. I am, after all, guarding other people's valuables. But for Tom I go girlie. It takes a little effort, but he rewards me in the most *creative* ways.

"Thanks."

He came close. Putting his arms on my waist, he pulled me in to his body. I rested my head against his chest, listening to the steady rhythm of his heartbeat. He buried his nose in my hair, breathing in the scent of my shampoo.

I'd never really paid too much attention to scents until I started dating Tom. But werewolves have an incredibly acute sense of smell. It's as important to them as their eyesight. Once I learned that, I started paying more attention, and I found *myself* noticing things as well. Like the fact that he'd used his usual soap instead of the stuff provided by the hotel. Or that the maid had been using carpet freshener in the hallway. Little things, but it added up to a whole new appreciation for so much I'd simply overlooked.

"Thank-you." His breath moved against my scalp as he whispered the words.

"For what?" I tilted my head to look up at him. He sounded so very serious.

"For everything." He smiled, but it carried a hint of sadness. "I don't know too many women who wouldn't have thrown a fit about having the pack force them to call of their wedding plans."

"Not call off." I corrected. "*Postpone*. You are *not* off the hook." I poked my perfectly manicured nail into the middle of his chest. I was going for playful, trying to cheer him out of the odd mood he suddenly seemed to have fallen prey to. Besides, I'm just a little bit superstitious. I didn't want to even invite the possibility of the wedding being called off for good. "And I'll be expecting a really spectacular wedding band for my patience."

"Already taken care of." He gave me a quick, sweet kiss. "I sent a picture of the engagement ring to Gerry Friedman and had him design our wedding bands. They're gorgeous."

"Ooh, let me see." I started to pull back and turned toward the luggage. I hadn't *seen* any jewelry boxes, but they had to be in there somewhere.

"Can't. They're in the hotel safe."

"Rats!"

Tom laughed. Pulling me close again, he gave me a quick hug. "I love you, Katie. Oh, and just in case you were wondering, the folks think you're great. But I'm supposed to tell you to be more careful next time."

I gave a wry chuckle. "I'll do my best." I tilted my head up to kiss him. A quick meeting of the lips, but just that simple touch made me shudder in reaction.

"We need to go to breakfast."

"Right. Breakfast."

We took the luggage downstairs with us. I waited at the door to the restaurant as Tom went to retrieve the rings from the safe. The two of us walked together into a dimly lit restaurant area filled with the wonderful aromas of a breakfast buffet and freshly brewed coffee.

Mary was sitting at a table for four in the corner next to the windows looking out over the outdoor pool. The harsh light wasn't kind to her. She was looking more worn and tired than I'd ever seen her. Dark circles shadowed her eyes, and her clothes seemed to hang loosely on her rugged frame. Whether it was a reaction to the drugs she'd been given yesterday, or something else, I didn't know, but it surprised me. She'd seemed well enough at the hospital. But if something was wrong, she didn't seem inclined to confide it. Instead she led Tom and me through the buffet line, then settled down at the table.

While we ate she was all business, telling Tom

that Dusty, Rob, and little Robert Thomas would be on the same flight with us, ordering him and asking me to "keep a close eye on them. I want them back home and safe."

"I'm surprised they're letting them fly. I mean the baby's only a few days old."

"The doctors cleared it. I even checked with Joe. He said it wasn't *optimal*, but if Dusty and Robbie are both okay, it shouldn't cause any problems. And I want them back in Denver. Sooner rather than later."

"What are you and Ruby going to do?"

"We'll drive back in Dusty's car. She's too far along, the airlines don't want her to fly, and frankly, I want to spend some time alone with her. There are things we need to discuss."

Poor Ruby. That didn't sound promising at all to me.

"Have you got your weapons with you?" Mary asked.

"No. *Why?*"

She seemed poised to say something, but changed her mind at the last minute. "Nothing. I'm sure it's nothing. Just keep an eye on them for me."

"Mary—" Tom started to say something but she shook her head.

"Tom, if I knew for sure something was wrong, I wouldn't send them. I just have this feeling. It's probably nothing." She gave me an inquiring look, as if to see if I'd *seen* anything. Unfortunately, my psychic gifts really aren't that controlled. Most of my precognition has come either in dreams, or when I've done my meditation. I hadn't done my meditation exercises for almost a week now, and I didn't remember any dreams—good or bad.

I gave a small shrug, and her shoulders sagged even more.

"We'll be careful," Tom promised.

"Thanks." She smiled, her expression lightening fractionally. "When you get to Denver, tell Joe I miss him, and I'll be back in a couple of days, not to trash the house."

"I'll do that."

She rose. Pulling a large bill from her wallet, she dropped it onto the table to cover the tab. Her parting words were to me, and they made the heavy breakfast sit uneasily on my stomach.

"I wish you were armed."

8

Some babies are just fine in airports and on planes. They eat, they sleep, the other passengers barely even know they're on board. Robbie was not one of those babies. He started screaming the minute we walked through the glass doors of the terminal. The screams changed to a penetrating, headache-inducing whine shortly after we boarded the plane.

There was no assigned seating on the flight, so the four of us stuck together and took the back two rows. That put a wall at my back, and me on the aisle between Dusty, Robbie, and the world. Tom and Rob sat directly in front of us. It wasn't perfect, but it was as good as we were going to get.

Dusty tried feeding, burping, changing, rocking, cooing at him, anything and everything she could

think of without much success. He was making so
much noise when the plane took off that I honestly
couldn't hear either the engines or the stewardess's
emergency lecture. Of course, since I knew the lecture
by heart, it wasn't a problem.

Finally, in desperation, Dusty passed the baby
over to me.

Robbie nuzzled his little head against my neck,
pulled fistfuls of hair out of my braid, and quieted. I
held him close, singing one of the old Irish lullabies
my mom had used on my brothers and me as children. He was so tiny, and yet that little body practically vibrated with strength. I held him, singing
softly, with tears in my eyes and wished fiercely for
something I'd never have. Meeting Tom's eyes over
the back of the seat in front of me, there was no
hiding how I felt. He unfastened his seat belt and
reached over the seat. I'd expected him to caress the
baby, and he did, but not until after he'd cupped
my cheek in his hand.

"I love you anyway."

The words helped. I felt the tightness in my chest
ease just a little. I might never have a baby of my
own, but I had Tom, and I had friends and family,
most of whom, now I thought about it, would probably be *more* than happy to have an on-call babysit-
ter. Smiling, I took a deep whiff of that soft "clean
baby" smell. The smile turned to a wince as the little
one gave a good solid yank, taking several of my
hairs out at the roots.

I didn't yelp. Yelping would've woken him and

brought down the justifiable fury of all my fellow passengers. But *OW!* I mean *jeez.* That *hurt.*

I spent the rest of the flight sitting as still as I could so as not to wake the little guy. Dusty and Rob took advantage of the break to sleep the sleep of the utterly exhausted. Tom spent his time browsing through the airline catalog, describing various cool things that we could spend a small (or not so small) fortune on to refurnish our house. Before I knew it, the stewardess was moving through the cabin, gathering up the trash and empty drinking cups, and the announcement came on with the light, telling us to fasten our seat belts, move our seats into the full upright position, and make sure our tray tables were up and locked.

Laying a gentle kiss on the baby's head, I turned to look out the window. There, in the western distance, lay the mountains, their tops shrouded in clouds. Below, the sprawl of a white-covered Denver and the suburbs. We were home.

The descent was smooth. I passed Robbie back to his mother's waiting arms so she could tuck him snugly into one of those baby carriers with the plastic handles that Rob had stowed in an overhead bin. Since I'd checked all my luggage, I was given responsibility for the diaper bag. The thing was thick, bulky, and surprisingly heavy. It made me wonder what the devil she'd packed for the little guy. I mean, disposable diapers and bottles couldn't possibly weigh that much, could they?

What with all the baby kerfuffle, we were the last

ones to disembark, with only the flight crew to walk behind us through the tunnel from the plane to Concourse C.

By the time we reached the staging area for the train to the terminal I was tired. My arm hurt. I hadn't taken anything for pain because I wanted to stay alert. Mary's warning had made me nervous. I'm supposed to be the psychic one. I hadn't felt anything wrong, hadn't had any visions, no psychic stuff at all for days. I stopped abruptly enough that Tom ran into me. *I hadn't had any psychic stuff for days.* That had never happened before. Not even before I was attacked by the Thrall for the first time. All my life I've just *known* things—little stuff mostly: who was calling on the phone or at the door. Ordinary enough for the most part. After Larry attacked me, and even more after Monica laid the eggs in my arm and the hatchling tried to infest me, it's been constant. Until the past few days.

Oh, shit.

"Katie, what's wrong?" Tom asked. "You've gone white as a sheet."

I ignored the question, fighting to control the panic clawing at my innards. "Dusty," I tried to make the question casual, and failed miserably. "Have you had any psychic premonitions or anything in the past couple of days?"

She set the baby carrier to rest on the floor for a second, tilted her head to the side, and thought about it. "No."

"Is that usual?"

She looked startled, and was getting more than a little nervous. Was my fear contagious? Probably. I know Tom sensed it. Both he and Rob were looking carefully around, watching the people surrounding us with cautious eyes.

"No."

The announcement for the arriving train came over the speaker, the pleasant feminine voice telling us to stay behind the warning line for our own safety and letting us know that this particular stop would put us on a train to Concourse B, Concourse A, and the main terminal.

I deliberately took a few steps away from Tom and let the shields I keep around my mind drop, willing myself to sense what was out there—expecting to hear the buzz of the Thrall collective. A few feet away, Dusty was doing the same thing.

There was nothing. Utter silence. A solid blank wall of will that was terrifying in its perfection.

My mouth went dry, my heartbeat sped up dramatically. Ironic, most of the time I wished the psychic abilities "gone," particularly with regard to the Thrall. Now that they were, I was terrified. Because the only times I'd ever felt them shield me out was when they had plans, *bad* plans, generally involving me.

"I can't feel anything."

I barely heard her whisper over the sound of the train, and the milling of people moving toward the doors.

It was at that precise moment, when my shields

were down, my mind completely vulnerable, that the Thrall struck.

Pain, white hot, and blindingly intense. It drove me, screaming, to my hands and knees on the cold concrete floor. My vision blurred with tears, so that I could barely focus. Still, I saw Dusty collapse, falling unconscious to the floor as four of the people surrounding us pulled weapons from their bags. Tom and Rob changed form in a wash of magic, only to be felled by darts like the one that had taken Mary in the airport at Las Vegas.

A man appeared as if from thin air. He wore an expensively cut, pin-striped navy business suit and leather shoes polished to a high gloss. He stepped forward, calmly taking the baby carrier by the handle. I blinked stupidly and tried to scream, but no sound would come out. I tried to force my body to move, and couldn't. It was all I could do to look up. I stared, stunned and helpless, as Dylan Shea boarded the train with Rob and Dusty's baby.

It couldn't be Dylan. Dylan was dead and buried. But while the hair had been cropped close to his head, and his nose was broken and scarred, it *looked* like Dylan. But that made no *sense*.

The announcement came on. The doors whooshed closed on the crowd of passengers staring blankly, their minds completely enthralled by vampire powers.

I fell forward, and my outflung arm touched Tom's. Just that small contact was enough for me to pull from his magic, mute the pain enough to think.

Keeping that hand on his, I used my other hand to rummage in my pocket for my cell phone. With desperate haste I dialed 9-1-1 and told the operator we had an abduction of a newborn at DIA, that we needed to shut the place down, followed by a request for medical assistance for Dusty and the boys. At the same time I used my contact with Tom to pull strength from the pack—just as I'd done in my fight against Samantha Greeley. It wasn't easy. But I fought my way to my feet. Leaving Tom and the others to the care of strangers who'd stumbled upon us on the way to the train, I staggered toward the stairs. Determination was fueled by panic and rage—the powerful emotions of an entire pack in fear for the child they'd all hoped and prayed for. The emotions had power, power they poured into my mind and body so that I was able to brush the last of the vampire's attack from my mind and *run* after the train and save the baby.

I ran, ran as if the hounds of hell were at my heels, dodging travelers and their unwieldy luggage, ignoring the calls of security guards. I'm not a lycanthrope. I can't change form. I don't have their supernatural speed and agility. But I work out, hard, and I run several miles nearly every day. I gave it everything I had, letting the wolves' panic fuel my own adrenaline to augment my natural abilities.

I didn't know how fast the train traveled. It didn't matter. My knee was grinding, objecting to the strain as I twisted and dodged my way through Concourse B. Passengers stared, open-mouthed with shock as I moved past them in a blur. I was at the top of the escalator leading down to the train when I heard the announcement and the doors whooshing closed. *Shit!* I'd come so close. I was gaining on it. I had to push harder: *had* to. Just a little more.

I felt a stitch starting to form in my side as I dodged around a pair of women staring at one of the glass-encased art displays. Ignoring the pain, I pushed on.

I had reached the escalator and stairs down to the train level between Concourses A and B. I was close, I could *feel* it. A man's voice behind and to my left called for me to halt. I ignored him, lunging forward for the stairs.

A shot rang out. I felt a stab of pain, and the sensation of falling forward into empty air as my legs missed the stairs and collapsed from under me. Then . . . nothing.

9

I couldn't move. Couldn't even lift my eyelids. It made me panic, but even the rush of adrenaline provided by my terror couldn't overcome whatever they'd shot me with. I felt my pulse speed, but the muscles simply wouldn't respond. I struggled against the effects of the drug until I was exhausted. But it wasn't useless. Because when I stopped struggling, and was too weary to maintain my shields, they fell. My mind slid free from my body, my psychic senses seeking outward.

Is she dead? A single voice separated itself from the hive. I don't know how, but I knew it was Carlton. Lewis Carlton was a former NBA all-star and current Thrall queen. He was huge, he was tough, and he was *not* someone you wanted to mess with. Despite all that, I liked him.

Not yet. Why does it matter to you?

This, too, was a single voice addressing an *individual*. That was . . . different. It almost felt as if the entire collective had changed. Before, when my mind had brushed theirs, every decision, every *thought* had taken a moment or two, as it passed through the entire group of queens, and their collective reactions were sorted into a single well-thought-out plan almost as quickly as an individual mind could think. There was a sense of separate *will* there, too, and white-hot rage that was far more personal than anything I'd ever felt from the hive. In fact, the impressions I was getting from them were much more what I'd felt from the late, unlamented Monica Mica—the Thrall queen who'd held enough of a personal grudge to risk everything to infest me.

My mind instinctively pulled away from the collective at that thought. Monica was dead, but she'd been stark, raving mad. If another like her had taken over the collective mind—It didn't bear thinking about. Worse, I couldn't risk letting her/it/them know that I knew.

Carlton's voice came through again. *If she doesn't die, there'll be hell to pay. She protects her people, just like we protect ours.*

Are you afraid of her? The interior voice was scornful.

Not afraid. But I do respect her. She's killed Larry, Monica, the abomination, and Samantha Greeley—everybody she's come up against. By underestimating

*her, you risk us all. There are plenty of other babies,
from other packs.*

*But this baby was perfect. Exactly what we need
for my plans to work. It was worth the risk. I can
handle Kate.*

I felt a chill that would've made me shudder had
my body been able to respond. The voice sounded
so smug, so very confident.

PAIN! Instant, white-hot, powerful, centered in
my chest. It brought me back to my body in a rush,
and my eyes popped open. I tried to scream, but
couldn't quite manage. Not that it mattered. The
baby in Dusty's arms was screaming enough for
both of us and then some. I could hear him, could
see the tented roof of the airport towering above the
faces of the EMTs. Apparently I'd missed things.
Lots of things. Dusty had the baby. That was good.
But she was pale and wide-eyed, her entire body
shaking with a fine trembling as she clung to the tot
like a lifeline.

I tried to form words, but it was too hard. No air.
It was as if a giant hand was squeezing my chest. I
couldn't seem to breathe against the pressure of it.
Darkness ate at my vision. The last thing I heard
was the heart machine as it emitted a long, steady
warning bleat and the EMT's shout.

"We're losing her. Clear!"

*I was in the back of a battered truck that stank
of diesel fuel, sweat, and fear. Half a dozen people
were crammed into the small space behind the boxes
of produce that had been stacked to the ceiling to*

simulate a full load. One of my fellow passengers, a white-haired man, old, but tough and sinewy, was talking in Spanish to a boy of about fourteen. I didn't know what he was saying. What little Spanish I'd taken in school didn't cover situations like this.

I shifted uncomfortably. The ride was miserable, made more so from the fact that I needed to piss. Not that I'd get the chance any time soon. I shifted positions, trying to get more comfortable without disturbing the woman next to me. She was dozing fitfully. I wished I could. I was too miserable, too afraid to let myself relax that much.

Quit bitching and be grateful. It could be worse. You got out. You're alive. Once you get back across the border you can get the information to Mike, let Katie and Joe know you're all right, get back to your life. One step at a time.

Bryan? Is that you?

I felt the realization that I was there, in his thoughts, hit my brother like a blow.

Katie! Oh, God. Is it you? Look, you have to tell Mike. He was right. I have the proof. I got away but they're after me.

Who's after you? What proof?

I struggled to hold onto the connection, but it was fraying fast. Vision went first, then sound. Instead of the closed confines of the panel truck, I was in an elevator, on a gurney with IVs strapped to my arm. I could hear the EMT breathing a sigh of relief. "She's back." I wanted to scream, this time with frustration. But though I could still taste stale air and sweat on my tongue, there was no going back. The connection was broken, and I was too tired, too weak, to reforge it.

To MOST PEOPLE, one emergency room looks pretty much like the next. Sadly, I've seen enough of them to be able to tell the difference. They'd taken me to Denver General rather than one of the other hospitals. I was a little surprised. Usually you go to the closest, unless you need a trauma center. Then they'll probably go for DG. Since this wasn't a gunshot wound, stabbing, or major car wreck, I would've expected to be taken to the new place they built out here by the airport.

Not that it mattered. It just surprised me; gave me something to think about besides fantasies of throttling my brother Bryan, Michael, Dylan . . . let's see, was there anybody else?

As if in answer to my question, Joe appeared.

Ah yes, Joseph. If my elder brother hadn't looked like something the cat dragged in I probably would've lit into him. Because I was pretty sure, really almost positive, that he'd manipulated me into that last fight we had so that he wouldn't have to explain to me what the hell Bryan was doing. Worse, it had worked.

Unfortunately, I'm just not good at kicking someone when they're down. And he was. I could tell by the way his shoulders slumped, and the fact that he'd actually come out in public wearing paint-splattered sweat pants and a torn gray tee-shirt. The fabric of the trousers bulged oddly in places because of the braces he had to wear to walk. Samantha Greeley had taken him, tortured him to get to me. Mary, Tom, and I had managed to rescue him and kill her, but he'd never be the same. The scars on his abdomen were hideous, and he'd never walk normally and without pain again. But even at that he counted himself lucky. He wasn't dead, and he hadn't been paralyzed like Mike was. Someday he might even be able to sleep without nightmares.

Unlike me.

Today his hair was unkempt, his jaw sported stubble, and there were circles as dark as bruises beneath his eyes.

Still, you can take the doc from the ER, but you won't get the ER out of the doc. The first thing he did when he stepped through those curtains was grab the clipboard with my information and review the treatment notes. Apparently they were doing everything right, because he gave a little grunt of approval and slipped the clipboard back into the little plastic file holder they had mounted on the wall next to the bed.

"Can you move yet?"

I could, but it still wasn't easy. Whatever they'd given me had been potent stuff. I managed a nod, and to shift a little in bed so that I could see him more clearly.

"You were lucky." He bent down and started adjusting the pillows behind my back to make me more comfortable. "One of the EMTs recognized you, knew you were human and wouldn't be able to process the drugs like a lycanthrope. They gave you something to counteract the worst of the effects almost immediately. Otherwise, you'd be dead." He shook his head, and a surprisingly gentle smile crossed his face. He reached down, and planted a light kiss on my forehead. "But you did it again. You saved the day. The baby's back with his mother. Tom and Rob will be fine in a few hours. Dusty is watching over them. Whatever the vamps were trying, you stopped 'em cold."

I wanted to say I didn't; I hadn't; that they had gotten what he wanted. Whatever that was. Instead, what came out of my mouth was some sort of a croak with all vowel sounds. Apparently the small muscles involved in speech weren't up and running yet.

He reached over to hook one of the metal stools the doctors use with his left hand and pulled it close to the bed before pulling the blue fabric curtain closed. "Katie, there's something I need to tell you." He swallowed hard enough for me to watch his Adam's apple bob. "You're gonna be pissed about it. All I can say is I'm sorry. I'm really, really sorry." His voice cracked on the last words. Right then and there I forgave him. He was just hurting so bad. Besides, Joe never apologizes. His pride won't allow for it. Bending this much deserved a reward. And I love him. So sue me.

I fought for enough muscle control to move my hand toward him. It was more of a twitch than an actual movement, but he got the idea, and took my hand. The expression on his face was one of almost wonder. "You don't even know what I did."

"Bryan." I tried to say the word. It came out more like "IA" but he understood that too. Maybe I'm not the only psychic in the family.

Joe took a deep breath, squeezing my hand tight, as if borrowing strength and courage from the contact. Looking furtively around to make sure nobody would overhear us over the bustle of emergency room traffic and the moaning of the woman a few cubicles down. He started talking in a furtive whisper, the words almost tumbling over themselves in his haste to get it said.

"There's something wrong with the humans the vamps have brought back. Not all of them. The first ones seem just fine. But starting about six months ago something changed. They're not themselves, not like Bryan is. And it's especially true of the ones from powerful families. That Middle Eastern prince was one of the first to really notice. And because Michael is the head of the church's zombie program, he talked to Mike about it."

Joe's eyes met mine, and I could see the guilt he was feeling reflected in his gaze. "Bryan's the only zombie who wasn't brought back by the vamps. The only one we could be sure wasn't contaminated."

That wasn't quite true. I'd rescued a girl at the same time I'd saved my brother. Not that it mattered. From what I'd seen of the inside of her mind she wouldn't risk a broken fingernail to save someone else, let alone her life. No, it made perfect sense that

Mike had asked Bryan to look into it. And with everything Mike has done for Bryan and our family over the years there is no way he would refuse.

"He's been sending e-mails or calling to check in every other day. Just to let us know he's okay."

Another deep breath, and his hand spasmed around mine so hard it hurt. "But we haven't heard anything for three days now. Nothing. Mike's inside informant says Bryan's not there—that he's just disappeared. The records say he checked himself out, but he didn't. I'm scared, Katie. Really scared."

I tried to form the words to reassure him, but my mouth just wouldn't work. Only incomprehensible sounds came out. I tried using my psychic talent, but for whatever reason, I couldn't get through to him. It was so incredibly frustrating. I pushed as hard as I could, and only succeeded in setting off all of the monitoring machines so that the nurses came running in. They shooed him away, and he let them. By the time they'd calmed down, and the machines were back to their normal beeping, he was gone.

10

*E*ven with the drugs they gave me to counteract the tranq and paralytic it took hours longer for me to get back to normal than it did the wolves. In the meantime the press had a field day. Somehow or another they managed to get hold of the 9-1-1 recording and video surveillance tapes from the airport that showed the abduction and my panic-driven dash through the concourse. I was a hero.

Of course it didn't keep the police from politely requesting my answers to questions about the abduction: over, and over, and over. The main sticking point was that the abductor looked like Dylan Shea. You'll note I didn't say it *was* Dylan. Not to the cops. Nope, nope, nope. Dylan Shea was dead and buried. You don't accuse a dead man of kidnapping. But I could say he looked like Dylan. Even that was enough to net me plenty of extra attention, and to have them check with the docs to see if the drugs could cause hallucinations. As it turned out, they could. Which meant every word out of my mouth was suspect. Of course, that didn't keep them from questioning me. In fact, by the time they were finished with me I felt as though I'd been through the wringer. I knew they were only doing their job, but I wished they'd get done with it already. I wanted to see Tom. I *needed* to see him. Yes, it was silly. Intellectually I knew he was all right, that the drugs had worn off and he was outside the room somewhere waiting for me. But intellectuality be damned. I wanted to be held. I wanted to smell his aftershave, and the scent of his skin, feel his arms around me as he told me everything was going to be all right. Wussie of me, but I didn't, *don't* care. Besides, we needed to make some decisions. It was already late afternoon and God alone knew what had happened to my luggage.

That was an unwelcome thought. Because if those clothes were gone I was so screwed. Everything at the house had been exposed to the weather for days. If my bags were gone I was left with only what was left of the clothes I'd been wearing this morning. Considering I was currently in a hospital gown I couldn't even be sure they'd survived. And oh, *damn*. The wedding rings were in Tom's bag. If they were gone I was going to be really, truly upset.

"Ms. Reilly." The ER doctor stepped through the curtains as the cops were stepping out. He'd been working on me for a while, but this was the first time I'd felt well enough to really look at him. He probably stood six foot two, thin, and balding. What hair he had was that sandy shade between blond and brown, as were his brows. The lashes that framed his hazel eyes were practically invisible behind a set of thick rimless glasses. Every inch of exposed skin was covered in freckles. He had my clipboard in his left hand and a pen in his right. "I think you're ready to be released. I don't see any need to keep you overnight, so long as you have someone staying with you—as you *obviously* do."

I found myself blushing. From his tone of voice I could tell that Tom had been making his presence known. Normally he's very laid back. But don't push him. And he is very, *very* protective of me. And of course Joe was here, and he's just *so* subtle.

The doctor smiled, but it didn't warm his features. It was a reflex only, bedside manner, not something he really felt. "I want you to take it easy for the next couple of days. Get plenty of rest. You're going to want to set an appointment to follow up with your regular physician, make sure there are no lingering effects. There don't appear to be, but it's better to be safe than sorry."

I agreed wholeheartedly. For one thing, I still felt like crap: physically, mentally, and emotionally. The sad part was, I was probably going to be pushing myself anyway. I needed to find out the status of the claim on the building collapse, find a place to stay, deal with the mess with Bryan, avoid the press, figure out what the hell the vampires were up to. It made me exhausted just thinking about it.

"*Rest,* Ms. Reilly. I know you were a professional athlete. Your physical condition is *still* impressive—especially considering you didn't even rip out your stitches under the cast. But the human body can only go so far before it collapses and suffers permanent damage. You're coming perilously near that point."

"Yes, doctor." I said the words, but I didn't really mean them.

"Fine. Don't listen to me." He actually snarled. It startled me, let me know that he was dead serious. Scary.

"I am listening. I just don't know if I can do what you're telling me to. It's not like I've gone out looking for these things. I'm not *that* stupid."

He gave me a long, significant look that started with meeting my eyes, then moved, slowly, to the cast on my arm, to my shoulder, then to the scars that decorated my knees. Not one word was said, but he'd made his point.

I shuddered, and gave him the best answer I could. "I promise that I will do my absolute best to take it easy over the next few days. Barring disaster—" He interrupted me.

"I don't care if there is a disaster. Sit it out. Let someone else handle it." He looked at me over the top of his glasses. It wasn't a friendly look. "If you don't, you'll wind up back here. And when you do,

I'll see to it that you're admitted, with no visitors, and you *will* rest, like it or not. Even if it has to be in the psych ward."

He was exaggerating. He had to be. He couldn't do that. But the threat did drive home the point nicely. He viciously tore the patient orders off of the sheet and shoved them at me. "Go."

"Thank-you, doctor."

With a sound that was a cross between a growl and a snort he ducked out between the curtains and was gone.

I rose carefully: very carefully. As soon as I stood I saw my clothes, folded neatly in a stack on the counter, between the box of plastic gloves and the tongue depressors. It was all there, and hallelujah, not even damaged.

Dressing was a challenge. My coordination still wasn't up to par and the fingers weren't working very well with the cast restricting my forearm muscles. It's surprising to most people how much a person needs those muscles. Fortunately, and sadly, I was pretty accustomed to doing things with vital muscles not working right.

Still, this time it was as though my body couldn't quite remember how it was supposed to work. When I tried to stand on one foot to step into my trousers I fell over into the wall. In the end, I wound up having to sit down and put both legs in before standing to pull them up. Even that was tricky. The bra and top weren't much easier. But the worst, tying the shoes—that was a real challenge. It was ridiculous. I was just glad nobody was around to watch. By the time I was done I was exhausted and grumpy.

"Can I come in?" Tom's voice came clearly through the thin cotton "walls."

Just four words and my irritation disappeared. Magic. "Absolutely."

He stepped in, wearing loose-fitting black jeans and a black tee-shirt that was just a little too tight to be comfortable, but showing off every rippling muscle. I wasn't sure where the clothes had come from, but they looked good on him.

He answered my question with a shrug, without my having to voice it out loud. "Dusty made some calls. One of the pack members came out with clothes for Rob and me and formula and diapers for the baby." He crossed the room as he spoke, took me in his arms for a long hug, then pushed me back to take a good look at me.

"You look like hell."

"Gee, thanks." I put as much sarcasm into the words as I could. Humor as a defense mechanism. There's nothing like it. And usually, for Tom and me, it works. We can face almost anything if we can laugh. When he didn't even smile, I knew we were in trouble.

He shook his head, his expression so very serious. "Kate, don't. Don't joke about this." He moved his right hand up to cup my cheek, his thumb gently stroking a sore spot that was probably a bruise. I hadn't seen a mirror yet, so I couldn't be sure.

"What do you want me to say?"

"I don't know." He dropped his hand and started to turn away, but stopped when I reached out to touch his arm. "I couldn't protect you, couldn't protect Dusty or the baby. Mary warned us to be careful, but they took him without any trouble at all. They could've killed him—could've killed us all."

I raised my arms, resting then on his chest. Bending my elbows, I stepped in close, until the full length of our bodies was only a fraction of an inch from touching.

"Tom, you can't blame yourself. There's nothing anyone could have done. They were ready for us. It was an ambush." I wasn't convincing him. I could feel it in the tightness of the muscles under my hands, the way he stood so close, and yet may as well have been a million miles away. "And you did help."

"How? Name one thing I did." His voice was so bitter it hurt me to hear it; his hands balled in fists at his sides.

"When I touched you, it blocked their psychic attack. *You* gave me a link to the pack. *You* gave me the strength to make the 9-1-1 call and run. Dusty was still out cold. I would've been, too, if not for you."

"Don't lie to me, Katie." There was a dangerous thread of anger in his voice.

I looked up, deliberately meeting the anger in those chocolate-brown eyes. I put everything I had into that look, willing him to believe me. "I'm not lying. I swear. You can smell it when I do. Bring in

Brooks if you want. I'll tell him the same thing."
Detective John Brooks was the only other "Not
Prey" living here in Denver. The rules set down by
the vampires put "Not Prey" as being equivalent to a
Thrall queen or werewolf Acca. We weren't allowed
to lie to each other. If we did, we'd lose our status,
and that status offered some (not a lot, but some) protection from the predation of the vampires. I couldn't
lie to Brooks, and I wouldn't lie to Tom.

He stared at me for a long, silent moment. Finally,
he unclenched his fists and slowly moved to take me
into his arms. His head fell forward, so that our fore-
heads touched. In a whisper that was barely more than
a brush of air I heard him say "I was so fucking *helpless.* That's never happened to me before . . . not even
in a fire."

It broke my heart to hear the pain in his voice. I'd
have done anything to take it from him. But I
couldn't. He *had* been helpless. So had I. I'd just recovered from it sooner. I think I hated the vampires
more at that moment than I had at any time since
they'd kidnapped Bryan almost two years ago.

When he spoke, his voice was breaking with emotions too strong for him to control. "The worst part is,
I keep thinking. What did they do to him? Why did
they take him? *Why did they give him back?* Because,
Katie, they could've kept him if they wanted. They
had that whole crowd of people getting on the train
enthralled. They had you and Dusty down, Rob and
me out. There's no way the vanilla humans could've
stopped them, cops or no. So why give him back?

Why take him at all if they weren't going to keep him? It doesn't make any sense."

I didn't know what to say. There really wasn't anything to say. He was right. It didn't make sense. I know the parasites intimately from years of forced psychic contact with them. Everything they do has cold logic behind it. They make plans and execute them with ruthless efficiency. The hive mindset makes them more than willing to sacrifice the individual for the good of the whole.

The kidnapping made no sense—particularly coming in the middle of their very successful positive PR campaign.

"You two 'bout ready? They're needing the room." Joe shoved the curtain aside and stepped through into a well of tense silence. I don't know if he'd heard us. We'd been fairly quiet, especially compared with the chaos that was going on in other parts of the ER, but you never knew.

"As we'll ever be." Tom answered for both of us. He shifted positions so that he was standing next to me with his arm around my waist. A smart move on his part as I was still unsteady on my feet.

"Then let's go."

It took a little sneaking around, but we made it out of the hospital and to the vehicle without incident. The fact that it had become unusual says something sad about my life. Still, I was glad. Just walking that far had exhausted me. I sank gratefully into the heated leather seats of Joe's SUV. Normally, I'd have considered heated seats frivolous, but I was dressed for Vegas, not snowbound Denver, so it felt awful good. After the shivers subsided, I watched the sun set out the side window. It was gorgeous . . . the clouds tinted crimson, orange, and purple behind the ridge of the western mountains. I've been all over the globe, but Denver's home, and I really don't think there's anywhere more beautiful.

As soon as the car doors were shut, and we had as much privacy as we were going to, I turned to Joe. I had to let him know what I'd seen about Bryan. He might still be in danger, but he was alive, and Joe needed to know that. Assuming, of course, he believed me. He's always been a little skeptical about the psychic stuff. It's ridiculous considering there's empirical proof—in the form of Bryan's recovery, the Thrall's hive communication, and God knows how many case studies. But it's not quantifiable, and it's not *controllable* so he has a very, very hard time dealing with it. Joe is, after all, *all* about control.

But either the new wife was teaching an old dog new tricks, or I'd underestimated him, because I saw his breath catch in what was almost a sob of relief. "He's alive. You're sure?"

"He was alive a few hours ago, and relatively safe. They were after him, but he seemed more worried about getting word to Mike about what he'd found than about his safety." Of course, that could've changed, but I didn't say it. I didn't need to. Joe's seen firsthand what the vampires do to people they're pissed at, and has the scars to prove it. I shuddered, deliberately pushing away a wave of useless guilt.

Every time I look at Joe I wonder what if and wallow in guilt. Stupid, but I can't help it.

"Can you find him again?" Joe's question cut through my reverie like a scalpel.

I thought about it for a second before I answered. "If I get some rest, yeah. Right now I'm useless. I can't even think clearly in the here and now." I felt bad saying it, but I knew it was true. Instead of the background buzz of the Thrall hive that I've learned to live with over the years, there was silence. Maybe it was them blocking me out again. I didn't know. It could be that, or just as easily, exhaustion. Because when I closed my eyes I couldn't feel Tom's presence, and he was right here in the SUV with me. It sucked, because I wanted to know Bryan was all right as much as Joe did, but trying now would just wear me out more, and make it take even longer before I was capable. It made me wonder if the ER doc had been right.

I sighed, and turned my attention out the window. We were driving down Speer, but we were headed toward Cherry Creek instead of downtown. That wasn't right. I hadn't even had a chance to stop by my old place, take a look at the damage, see if it was salvageable.

"We should go by the building."

"No," Tom and Joe both chorused.

"Really. No," Tom repeated.

"I need to see it in the daylight."

"Not today, Katie." Joe spoke gently but didn't take his eyes off the road. "It got worse after the second blizzard—way worse, and you've had enough for today. You need to rest, and not just so you can find Bryan. It'll still be there tomorrow, when you feel better. Tom, Mary, and I got a lot of your stuff out the other day when the guy from City allowed it. You haven't lost everything."

I sighed and dropped my head. "It's that bad?"

Tom reached over the seat to squeeze my shoulder. When I lifted my eyes to meet his, I saw sympathy. It *was* that bad. Shit. I'd known, but I'd hoped . . . I felt my throat tighten, and tears threatened. I was *not* going to cry. I wasn't.

I cried. I've been doing a lot of that lately. I don't like it. For one thing, I don't do it well. I know other women who have silent tears stream delicately down their perfect cheeks. Not me. I get blotchy, reddish purple and wrinkled, gasp for air like a fish out of water, and generally get as unattractive as it is possible for a human being to look. Thankfully, Tom didn't care, and I knew Joe didn't either. They let me cry it out. One of them, I don't know which, handed me a box of tissues—those little ones that take two or three to make up a real one. I blew my nose noisily, took a few ragged breaths, and forced myself back under control.

I felt better. I don't like crying, but this had been cathartic. It had been a rough week.

We were nearly to the gated community in Cherry Creek that my brother currently calls home. It's nice. *Very* nice, and not cheap. Personally, I'd hate it. It's covenant controlled. And I do mean *controlled*.

There are rules about everything. They dictate what colors you can paint your house and trim, how many vehicles you can park on the street, even the kind and color of flowers you can have in your four by four patch of "lawn." But it gives the neighborhood an almost militaristic tidiness that would appeal to both Joe and Mary's sense of order. Joe pulled the SUV up the concrete drive leading to a pretty brick and shingle colonial-style with attached garage that was one of the three style options offered. A popular choice; its appearance was echoed all up and down the street.

I tried not to shudder. Conformity is *so* not me. Tom either for that matter. We shared one of those *looks* that couples sometimes get, where you know exactly what the other is thinking. A kind of non-verbal shorthand. If we could salvage the lofts we would. If not, we'd be looking for another place in the next few days, but it wouldn't be here.

Joe struggled up the steps to the front door. Neither of us helped him, because he would feel insulted, so we hung back, taking baby steps for each of his. After a few seconds of fumbling with his key ring, he unlocked the dead bolt and let us inside.

Mary had done a nice job decorating the living room. Bright sunlight shone through the sheer curtains over a wide picture window onto a spotless white wall-to-wall carpet. The furnishings were tasteful, high-end colonial with gold and white striped upholstery on the couch and matching loveseat and polished cherry and brass end and coffee tables. A polished cherry armoire hid the big-screen television and the wide selection of movies my brother had amassed over the years. The only piece that didn't "fit" was a huge old La-Z-Boy recliner that faced the armoire. It was Joe's baby. He'd had it for years and wouldn't have parted with it without a fight.

"Sit," he ordered. "Rest. I'll fix us something to eat."

It sounded like a wonderful idea and I figured Joe was a lot more familiar with his own kitchen than me, and Mary had probably set it up for him to manage things alone. I collapsed into the recliner, tilting it back to a position that was perfect comfort. A quick pull of the lever and the footrest sprung out. I closed my eyes, thinking I'd just rest for a minute or two.

Tom woke me an hour later. Joe had heated up some high-end frozen lasagna for dinner. I fell asleep in the middle of it, almost literally. One minute I was awake, listening to Joe talk about his job prospects. The next Tom was carrying me upstairs to the guest bedroom. He made big, tall muscular me feel like a child in his arms. Let's hear it for werewolf strength and stamina, 'cause baby I wouldn't have been able to make it up those stairs on my own. It wasn't fair that he had to, admittedly. He'd been drugged too. But I let him. I vaguely remember him giving me a gentle good-night kiss, and then I was out.

I woke alone at 7:00 the next morning. I was completely disoriented for a few seconds, the way you sometimes are when you sleep too hard or in a strange bed. I blinked a few times, bringing the pretty sunlit bedroom with its white walls and floral print drapes into better focus. I was at Joe and Mary's. Right. Okay. That meant the bathroom was down the hall and to the left. Good to know. And the coffee and cinnamon rolls I smelled (bless you, whoever thought of them) would be in the kitchen downstairs.

I didn't remember Tom undressing me, but he must have. I was naked under the crisp cotton sheets, and there were some truly spectacular bruises decorating a good portion of my body—almost as if I'd fallen down a flight of stairs or something.

I threw off the covers, snagged Tom's tee-shirt from the floor, and pulled it on. It wasn't much, but it covered enough that I'd be decent if I ran into anybody in the hallway. Not that I was likely to. From the sound of the voices I was hearing everybody was downstairs in the kitchen helping themselves to breakfast.

The upstairs bathroom in Mary and Joe's house isn't large. Painted sunshine yellow, it is just big enough for a shower, toilet, and sink with a minuscule cabinet. The curtains have white and yellow daisies printed on a gold background. A bright yellow throw rug lies on the white tile floor. Everything looked, and smelled, amazingly fresh. It almost seemed a shame to use the facilities, but I did. *And* started a shower to boot.

Not to put too fine a point on it, I stank. I'd been terrified most of the day yesterday, and the nasty scent of stale sweat rank with fear clung to my body. If I hadn't passed out from exhaustion, I would've showered before bed. As it was, I was amazed Tom had been able to sleep next to me. It had to be true love for him to put up with the stench rather than sleep on the couch.

I pulled the ties and ribbons from my hair and tossed them into the trash. They might have been salvageable, but I didn't really care. I was just glad my hair had been braided. I couldn't even imagine the tangled mess it would have been after yesterday if it hadn't been. Tom thinks it's prettier loose, but sometimes sensible has to win out over pretty. I winced as I finger-combed the braids out. There was a lump the size of a chicken egg on the back of my head. I supposed I should be grateful for my thick Irish skull. I'd fallen down a tall flight of stairs. It could easily have resulted in a concussion. But in that, at least, I'd gotten lucky.

I slid the glass shower door open and worked myself around so that I could keep the cast dry while showering. At least it was only on my forearm. Last time I was in a cast, it covered my whole shoulder and I wound up having to buy a stack of dry cleaner bags to cover half my body, which I then had to sponge down. I set the water as hot as I could stand it, and put shower massage on high and just stood there for the longest time, letting the heat and pulsing water work on the knotted muscles in my shoulders and neck. When they were as loose as they were likely to get without a massage, I lathered up with soap one-handed and used the shampoo sitting on the built-in shelf.

I had to scrub carefully. In addition to the knot on my skull I had a wide assortment of bruises. They ranged in color from a sickly green to that deep, purplish black that means serious business. Looking at them seemed to make them hurt more, and scrubbing them was murder. But I did it anyway, and when I was done I was *clean*, and felt all the better for it.

I turned off the water, slid open the door, and stepped onto the bath mat. Grabbing one of the pretty yellow towels, I wrapped it around my dripping hair. I used the other one to start drying myself off and discovered a message traced into the fog on the bathroom mirror. While it wasn't at all good that I hadn't heard someone walk in the room, the pitty-pat of my heart wasn't fear. Tom had drawn a heart with our initials in it. Right below that, an arrow, pointing directly down at a huge mug of steaming coffee.

Awww—

If he'd been here I'd have kissed him. If I hadn't already agreed to marry him, I might've proposed. As it is, I swear sometimes that man knows me better than I know myself. Coffee first, then clothes and toiletries. A plastic bag in the sink held a toothbrush, my favorite brand of toothpaste, deodorant, and a comb and brush set. A brand-new pair of black jeans and a matching tank top sat folded neatly atop the toilet lid along with a black lace bra and matching panties with the tags still attached. Since it was too early for most of the stores to be open I guessed he'd gone shopping last night after I passed out. It was an incredibly thoughtful thing for him to do; and he'd even gotten the sizes right.

I inhaled the coffee in between getting dressed and combing out my hair. Then I brushed my teeth, dressed, and was ready to face the day.

Other than the bruises, I looked okay. Grim, a little pale, but then I always look pale when I wear black. I usually compensate for it by putting on more makeup, but he'd either run out of money, or forgotten about cosmetics. I didn't mind. It would've taken a professional with considerable skill to cover the marks that showed on my face and arms. I left my hair loose for the moment, giving it a chance to dry. It hung down the middle of my back in loose curls that were a darker red because of the water. The tank emphasized my shoulders. They don't need the help. They're plenty broad enough without it. But it was also cut to emphasize my bust, and the bra Tom had picked out helped with that too. I had cleavage. Oh, not a lot, but enough to actually warrant notice.

I carried my nearly empty coffee mug carefully downstairs. The white plush carpet was beautiful, but it had to be hell to keep clean. Give me hardwood floors and a dust mop any day. Still, it sure was pretty. The entire house was made up of clean lines and bright colors with lots of sunlight. I could see how it suited both their tastes, and it made me happy that Joe and Mary had found each other. They were good together.

I stepped through the swinging doors into a kitchen done in gleaming white and navy blue. Everything was spotless and sparkling and I felt a twinge of envy. I love a clean house. I hate house-work. I can't imagine having the time to keep things this nice, but I didn't think Mary was springing for a housekeeper either.

Joe was talking on an old-fashioned navy blue wall phone as I came in.

"Right. I'll call Greyhound and give them my credit card number for your ticket. In the meantime, *be careful.* You may not have completely given them the slip." Joe was finishing up his phone con-versation as I walked across the room. He turned to face me, his expression just a little bit guilty.

"So," I gave him a smile sweet enough to warrant a trip to the dentist. "Where's Bryan?"

Tom choked on his coffee, trying not to laugh, but I ignored him, keeping my gaze locked with that of my older brother.

"What makes you think that was Bryan?"

Tom still couldn't talk, but he was shaking his head no. Good guy that he is, he was trying to warn my brother not to step into something smelly up to his eyeballs. He probably assumed I'd used my psy-chic powers to find out who was on the phone. I didn't need to. Joe had just sounded that relieved, and that *guilty*.

I set my coffee mug on the counter, and reached for the half-empty pot on the burner without uttering a word. If I said anything, argued at all, Joe would use it as an excuse to storm off and leave me behind. By saying nothing, he had nothing to fight against. It's not a tactic I use often. I'm too hard-headed. But Mother used it on Da to good effect when we were growing up and Joe is *so* like our father.

I stayed pleasantly silent, leaning against the counter and alternately sipping my freshly poured coffee and nibbling on the cinnamon roll I'd snagged from a blue and white floral serving tray on the white tile counter. It took a couple minutes, but in the end, he caved.

"*Fine*, it was Bryan," Joe admitted sourly. "He called collect. He doesn't have a dime to his name and is stranded in this tiny town just over the Texas border, a place called Mesquite Hills. I offered to come get him, but instead he asked me to just pay for his bus ticket and a little spending money." He sighed. "You were right, by the way. He had to make a run for it from New Dawn, and sneak back over the border with a bunch of illegals. But he's fine, and he has *some* information for Mike. And before you ask, he wouldn't tell me what."

"I see." I kept my voice bland and pleasant, the sweetest of smiles on my face.

Joe gave me a suspicious look. I could tell he expected me to argue, or say something withering about the whole "spy" fiasco. A part of me did want to. Another, wiser part told me to keep my mouth closed. It was all water under the bridge at this point anyway. I hate that Mike asked Bryan to do it—hate that Bryan felt compelled to agree. Most of all, I hate how the three of them deliberately deceived me. But unless I wanted a full-out battle, there was no point in starting the discussion. So I didn't. If God gives brownie points for discretion I figure that earned me a bunch of them.

"I need to call Greyhound."

"Feel free." I gestured toward the phone with a wave of my hand. He didn't move. He just kept staring at me, as if he was waiting for the other boot to drop. Eventually I completely lost patience with it.

"Oh for the love of God, Joe, just *get over it*. I don't know what you're expecting, but I'm fine. I think it was a stupid thing to do—but you already knew that. Let's just clean up the mess and move on." I grabbed my cup and went to take the chair next to Tom, who was chuckling softly.

The suspicious look vanished, replaced by a sheepish smile. "I'm sorry. I'm just not used to you being this reasonable."

Tom stopped chuckling abruptly. "Watch it, buddy," he said, pointing a single finger at my brother across the room. In a voice that was only half-teasing he advised, "You'd best stop right there, before you put your foot in it up to the hip."

Joe's smile broadened to a grin. "No doubt." And without another word he turned his back on me to rummage in the kitchen drawers for the telephone book.

While he was chatting with Greyhound I shifted positions and started a conversation with Tom. "So, what are your plans for the day?" I asked. He'd dressed as though he was planning on doing something physical. He was wearing one of his oldest and most battered pairs of jeans and a blue plaid flannel shirt that had faded almost to gray, with the sleeves rolled up to just past the elbows.

"I figured I'd stick around, help you go through the stuff in the garage; maybe go with you to check out the ruins and deal with the insurance company."

I opened my mouth to tell him it wasn't necessary. He anticipated it, and answered me before I could say a thing.

"I know you don't *need* me to. But I want to. Besides," his expression soured just a little, his eyes darkening with suppressed anger, "Call it a hunch, but I'm pretty sure the insurance investigator is going to be a *lot* more polite if I'm there with you."

He was probably right. I can handle myself. But there are still people out there who don't take women as seriously in a business situation as men. It's not fair, but life, in general, isn't. I'd only dealt with the investigator in one brief telephone call before the scene with Janine in Las Vegas. He'd been marginally rude and condescending as hell. Tom had met him in person. If he believed I needed company, I probably did. Even if it was only to keep me calm enough not to do something "unfortunate."

Tom continued, "Joe has an 8:30 interview. Mary called, she doesn't expect to be back until some time this evening. We'll have the day to our-selves."

Joe had an interview. Well, that explained the ex-pensive navy suit and tie. I gave him a second look. He looked good. The white dress shirt had enough starch in it that it might well have stood up without him. All traces of stubble were gone, and his hair was freshly cut and styled.

I heard my brother finish his conversation and hang up the phone, so I turned to him to get the details.

"Where's the interview?" I asked him.

"Denver General."

I grinned at him. I couldn't help it. DG is a trauma center, the big leagues for an ER doctor like my brother. It would be a great job for him—and a slap in the face to the jerks at St. Elizabeth's who'd suspended him.

"What're you smiling about?"

"The interview. DG—that's *so* cool."

He rolled his eyes. I guess I was supposed to be too old to say *cool*. Whatever. I was still proud of him, and happy that he was looking for a job where he wouldn't have to deal with the likes of Edgar Simms. Dr. Simms was the kind of administrator who gave "politics" a bad name. He was a world-class, certified, Grade A ass who had close ties to the vampires. I'd brought his daughter back from being an Eden zombie at the same time I'd cured Bryan, and while I knew he was grateful, it didn't keep him from being solidly against everything he thought I stood for. It had made things very *tense* for my brother. "I'd better go. I want to make a good impression by getting there early." He sounded a little nervous, but other than his face being a little flushed, he seemed to have his act together.

"Good luck." I walked over and, careful not to get icing on the suit, gave him a hug and a peck on the cheek. "Not that you'll need it. You'll be fine."

"Thanks." He gave me a crooked smile. Grabbing his keys from the counter he started out the door. His parting comment was "Take it easy today. It's going to take a while for the drugs to work their way completely out of your system."

"Right. Will do."

He gave a half-hearted growl. On his way out the door he turned to Tom and said, "Don't let her overdo."

"I'll do my best, but you know how she is."

"Hey!" I resented that. It might be true, but I still resented it. Besides, I did intend to be careful. For one thing, I still didn't feel "right," and honestly, the doctor had actually managed to scare me. But there were simply so many things that needed to be accomplished, and some of them needed doing in a short time frame.

"Are you going to tell me I'm wrong?" Tom asked.

I didn't dignify *that* with a response. Instead I grabbed the telephone book my brother had left out on the counter and started looking up some of the numbers I'd need.

I started with a couple of phone calls. First, to the airport, to see if they knew yet what had become of our luggage. Next, I called the insurance office. No one was there yet, so I left a voice-mail letting them know I was back in town and giving them my cell phone number. That accomplished, Tom and I took the cordless phone and went out to brave the mess in the garage.

The minute I opened the door I was hit by the smell of mildew and a wave of depression.

This was it. Everything that was left of my home. Stacked in molding boxes with the logos of various brands of liquor, boldly emblazoned with magic marker words such as "books," "pans," and "linens."

"Are you okay?" Tom stood behind me, his hand outstretched, as if he wasn't sure whether or not he should try to touch me.

Hell no, I wasn't okay. Straight ahead of me, nearly buried under three layers of boxes, was my mother's hope chest. It had a long, splintering gash like a wound cutting through the polished cedar surrounded by innumerable smaller scratches. To the left, leaning lopsidedly against the wall, was the family coat of arms I'd paid a small fortune for. It was *dented,* scratched, and the hand-calligraphed write-up that went with it was in a smashed frame and had significant water damage.

"We dropped most of the clothes off at the cleaners. They said they thought they'd be able to salvage all of it except the leathers."

Something in his voice, an odd inflection, made

me turn around. There was something he wasn't telling me.

I met his eyes, my mind brushing gently against his, asking permission to join his thoughts, but he had his shields clamped down tight. I couldn't get in unless I tried to force it, and I didn't want to do that.

"What aren't you saying?"

His hand dropped to his side, and he sighed. He looked around the garage, not meeting my eyes. "The leathers weren't ruined in the collapse, Katie. They were shredded to ribbons. It was like someone had taken a utility knife to them." He gave me a long, steady look, assessing how I was taking the news. "There wasn't much scent: too much water. But I checked the weapons safe. Your guns, your knives, all your weapons are gone. So is the neck brace and all your meditation stuff."

I didn't speak. I didn't know what to say. I just stood there, blinking stupidly at him for a long moment.

"I didn't tell Joe. I wasn't sure how he'd react. I did call Brooks about whether I should file a police report about the weapons being gone."

"What did he say?" My voice was a little breathy from shock. I felt shaky all over. Enough so that I had to stick my hand out and balance myself against the wall.

"He asked me if I was sure, that maybe you'd taken them with you."

"I didn't."

"I didn't think so." He stepped forward and put his

hands on my shoulders. I could feel the strength of those hands, could almost feel him willing that strength into me. God help me, I needed it. I'd told myself I was ready, I'd understood intellectually what it meant to have lost the building, my home and belongings. I'd even known the authorities were pretty sure the building had been deliberately sabotaged. But intellectual knowledge and actually seeing the damage up close were two very different things.

"He told me to have you call him, let him know what was missing. He'll talk with the right people to get the process rolling. He said he owes you that much."

"There's an inventory in my safe deposit box at the bank."

"Good. We'll go there, then stop by the cleaners. After that, we're hitting the leather shop at the mall." He started to lead me back out the door we'd came in through. I didn't fight him. In fact, a part of me was downright grateful.

"What about this?" I waved wearily at the mess.

"It's not going anywhere." He sounded resigned. "And I don't like you going around unarmed when the Thrall are up to something."

"The Thrall are always up to something."

"Exactly."

11

It had been a busy day. The cab pulled into my brother's driveway at 9:15 P.M., just as he was coming out the front door. He was wearing a heavy turtle-necked sweater and jeans, without a jacket or gloves. The night was warm enough for him to get away with it. One of the nice things about Denver is that even a major blizzard is normally followed by warmer weather to melt it away. There was still snow stacked up along the curbs and piled high on the grass, but it was dissolving fast.

Watching him, I realized just how hard it was for him to walk, even with the leg braces hidden beneath his trouser legs. He moved stiffly, and had to hold tight onto the railing just to stop himself from falling down the two small steps from the front door to the sidewalk. I hurt just watching him.

I climbed out from the back seat and walked up to meet him at the door of his car. It left Tom and the cab driver to take care of our packages and luggage, but I didn't think they'd mind. Besides, I could tell something bad had happened.

"What's up?"

"Bryan called. Something went wrong. He's stranded in a little town downstate by the name of Beaver Falls. Ever heard of it?"

"Nope."

"Me either." He shook his head. "Thank God for MapQuest. Apparently, it's in the mountains west of Pueblo—one of those new pop-up towns. Anyway, I'm headed down to pick him up."

"How far is it?"

"About four hours, assuming I don't get lost."

I fought down a snort of laughter. Unless somebody else does the navigating Joe *always* gets lost, even with directions, maps, and an on-board computer. I know why, and I even understand it. Joe questions *everything*. Nothing can be taken at face value. He can't just take the computer's word for it— or anyone else's either. So he questions, and doubts, and ends up *not* following the instructions and, consequently, lost. At least he doesn't adhere to the old saw about not asking directions. If he did, he'd probably still be wandering around somewhere in Kansas from when he left to go to medical school.

"Nice jacket, by the way."

"Thanks." I smiled at him and turned from side to side to model it for him. It had taken Tom and me most of the evening to find this. The leather store at the mall had biker-style jackets, but the leather had been cheap, and too lightweight to offer any protection at all. The goth shop had some really cool trench coats, but, again, too lightweight. We'd ended up taking a cab to an actual biker shop on 38th Avenue. Once there I'd had the challenge of finding a coat big enough to fit my shoulders. I'd wound up with a men's extra-large, which had the added bonus of having sleeves large enough to slide over the cast if I left the zipper undone.

I'd had to special order the matching boots. My feet are long, but narrow. Nothing in stock anywhere ever fits. It's a nuisance, but I could live with it. Especially when I stepped up to the cashier's counter and saw a perfectly lovely selection of knives.

"I'm glad you replaced it. Did you get any weapons while you were out?"

In answer I moved my arm a little so he could see the hilt of the knife I'd slid into my cast. "I just have to be careful not to cut the gauze."

He nodded, approvingly. "Nice."

"Tom thought you hadn't noticed about the weapons."

Joe shook his head. "I noticed. I'll make you a new neck brace this weekend. I don't like you doing without."

"Neither do I."

Joe had worked with a friend years ago to invent an acrylic shield to protect the neck and chest from vampire bites. He'd given it to me when I'd gone into Queen Larry's lair to save Dylan. That neck brace had saved my life that night, and on more than one occasion since. I didn't like that it was gone. I don't wear it often, but not having it available made me feel naked, vulnerable.

"This time I'm going to line it with something. Then maybe it won't itch so bad."

I didn't know how he knew about the itching. I'd never dared complain to him. It would've been too ungrateful. Still, now that he'd mentioned it, I certainly wasn't planning on arguing. "That would be *lovely*."

We turned at the sound of a car door slamming. The cabbie was taking off. Tom was gathering up the packages to take them inside. I knew I ought to help, but I was afraid if I did Joe would drive off and leave without us. I didn't want him doing that.

Tom walked up to us, juggling parcels like a pro. "So, where are we going?" The smile he gave my brother was calm, confident, pleasant, and still managed to convey a complete and total lack of compromise. God, how I wish I could master that look. It would save me *so* much trouble and unnecessary arguments.

Joe's expression grew pained. He looked from me to Tom, and back again. He started to open his mouth to argue, changed his mind, and closed it, all in a matter of seconds.

"You're not supposed to drive that far with your leg anyway," I pointed out helpfully.

"That's rich. *You* lecturing *me* on following doctor's orders."

He had a point. A very *sharp* point. And I was absolutely determined to ignore it. I turned to Tom. "We're going to pick up Bryan. He's stuck in some podunk town in southern Colorado."

Tom gave Joe a puzzled look. "I thought he was taking the bus?"

"He was. The vampires tracked him down. He went across the street from the bus stop to grab a bite to eat, and saw them drive up. He got away by hiding in the back of somebody's pickup truck underneath the tool box and wound up in Beaver Falls. He told me he was heading up to the church to see if he could get the information sent off to Mike. I was going to meet him there."

"Does he know how they found him?" I asked.

"No."

"They may have just checked all of the public transportation hubs. It's what the cops do," I suggested.

"In that case he should be safe." Tom tried to sound hopeful.

Famous last words.

12

It was a little after midnight and we were nearly there. I'd driven the first two hours, but Joe had insisted on taking over when I'd pulled over to get gas and give everybody a bathroom break. Tom was in the back seat. I was riding shotgun for this leg of the trip. I had the window partway down to get rid of the stale greasy smell of french fries left over from the food we'd picked up at the stop.

I was scared, and trying not to show it. Almost a half hour before I'd felt a burst of panic, but before I could trace it, find out if it was Bryan, and determine the cause, it just disappeared. Now all I could see in my head was a smooth, solid white wall.

My stomach tightened into a knot of fear as we passed a green-and-white sign announcing that we were four miles from Beaver Falls. Something was wrong. I knew it. I just couldn't pinpoint *what.*

Tom sensed what I was feeling, or maybe smelled the change, because he reached over the seat to give my arm a reassuring squeeze as Joe hit the brakes to take a curve.

There, just ahead, I could see the hint of light pollution above the trees. Not much, but enough to be noticeable. I watched the speedometer dip below the triple digits for the first time in a while. When we cleared the next corner I got the first glimpse of the outskirts of the town. On the left, a brightly lit convenience store and gas station that boasted of being open 24/7. On the right, at the bottom of a hill, an old church cemetery with an elaborate wrought-iron fence surrounding one large mausoleum and several other, more modest monuments to the honored dead.

The SUV slewed sideways as Joe slammed on the brakes. He'd almost missed the narrow gravel drive that wound past the cemetery up to the small stone edifice that was St. Michael of the Archangels Catholic Church.

I had to brace myself, one hand against the dashboard, the other on the door as the vehicle bucked and lurched on the rutted track. Up ahead I could clearly see the church, a well-lit gravel parking lot, and what looked like a tool shed for the construction site of a new building or addition in what had once been an empty field between the church and the mesquite woods edging the burial grounds.

They'd used earthmoving equipment to create a

plateau of sorts to build on, but it was in the early stages. The rip in the topsoil was like an open wound, the ground rocky and uneven. The area was marked with surveying stakes, their pink plastic banners hanging limp in the still night air.

I did not see Bryan, anywhere. There was no movement, no sign of a light coming on. My stomach tightened into a hard knot. Something was wrong. We'd made a lot of noise pulling in. He would have heard us coming.

Joe hit the horn as he pulled the vehicle to a stop in front of the steps leading up to the arched doorway. The church wasn't large, maybe twenty-five feet across, probably a hundred feet or so deep. It was two stories tall at the pitched roof, with the steeple rising a few feet above that. The main structure had been built of tan and caramel colored stones, fitted together with minimal mortar by expert craftsmen from generations past. The wooden steeple gleamed with a fresh coat of brilliant white paint that matched the trim around the stained glass windows spaced along the length of the building.

I threw open the car door and climbed out. Tom was right behind me, in wolf form. I wasn't sure when he'd changed, but I wasn't sorry. Tension rode the still air, and I could taste metallic fear on my tongue even over the gravel dust that was settling from our passage.

Joe turned off the engine. When he slammed the door shut I whirled around and jumped a good foot, letting out one of those ridiculous, high-pitched half-screams that slip out sometimes when you're startled.

"Can you track his scent?" Joe's voice was flat, cold. He stood in the harsh artificial light, holding his medical bag, his face set in grim lines.

Tom let out a swift bark, and put his nose to the ground. Almost too quick to follow he began running across the uneven ground, through the construction site.

I followed close behind, with Joe laboring to keep up. The braces on his legs were making it hard for him to maintain his balance. I could hear him swearing under his breath. I stopped, turning to offer encouragement.

Three things happened at once. Joe stumbled, I saw a blur of movement from behind the construction shed, and the lights went out.

It wasn't totally dark. The moon was too close to full for that. But it took a second or two for my eyes to adjust. I drew the knife from where I'd concealed it in my cast and began moving back toward Joe as quickly as I dared.

A shadowed figure moved with blurring speed to slam into my brother, who fought to keep his footing. As I ran toward the action, I heard the thud of bodies impacting each other, Joe's oath, and a nasty crunching sound.

"Joe?" I didn't even try to keep the fear from my voice.

"I'm fine. She's not."

He stood, and stumbled, falling hard on his ass

next to the body of a fallen Thrall. Even in the uncertain light I could see that the neck had been torn out of the heavy turtleneck he'd been wearing, and moonlight gleamed off of what looked suspiciously like heavy acrylic. His leg was at an odd angle, the brace bent until it had torn through his trousers, metal shining bright in the silver moonlight.

I opened my mouth to say something, but was interrupted by frantic barking that ended in a yelp.

Tom!

"Go! I'm calling 9-1-1, then I'll catch up."

I had to go, but I couldn't leave him unarmed, not when he had no chance to run. So I tossed the knife blade into the ground beside him as he flipped out his cell phone. Then I turned and ran before he could say anything to object, ran in the direction of the vicious snarls that were coming from deep inside the cemetery.

I stopped just short of the woods because I felt something moving in the flickering shadows between the stunted trees.

I lowered myself into a crouch, searching for something, anything, to use as a weapon. Because someone was in there. Now that I was on alert the faint hint of cheap cologne came to me over the scents native to the woods.

The site was remarkably clean: no tools left lying around, no scrap lumber. The best I could do was squat down and pull one of the surveying stakes from the ground.

As weapons went it wasn't great, but it wasn't bad

either. The wood was unfinished and splintery, but it was long, and the end had been sharpened to a nice point—perfect for driving into the ground, or into a vampire. I could've done without the cute little plastic flag, but beggars can't be choosers.

I was just starting to rise when I saw a blur of movement from the corner of my eye. I heard Joe shout.

There was no time to look. No time for anything. I dived sideways, rolling out of the way. The cast hit the ground with a thud and sharp pain made me suck in my breath. But it held. I'd have to remember to thank Joe for that.

I tried to get to my feet, but a hand like iron grabbed my left shoulder, rolling me onto my back. I moved with it, using my body to hide the stake in my right hand. In one smooth movement I slammed the cast into the vampire's jaw and then drove the stake at an upward angle through the thin fabric of his black tee-shirt. It tore through the skin beneath his ribcage at an angle designed to take out his heart.

Between the broken fangs and the chest wound he screeched, an eerie high-pitched death wail, his mouth open wide, revealing ragged stumps where his fangs used to be. Spittle sprayed my face from an inch away. Hot blood poured over my hand and down my arm. I shoved him off of me, pulling the stake free. Blood sprayed from the wound in gouts with his every heartbeat. He was dying.

I didn't stay to watch. I had to find Tom; had to save Bryan. The wall of will that had trapped me inside my own mind by blocking my psychic gift was crumbling. I knew, *knew* that I had to get to them *now* or all would be lost.

I ran through the trees, bloody stake gripped in my hand. Low branches slapped at my face and arms, the uneven ground making it hard to gain any speed at all. Only when I burst through the trees and made it onto the gravel cemetery road was I able to run full out. My knee was grinding in protest. It didn't matter. Nothing mattered but getting to the new grave site just beyond the large crypt by the entrance.

I passed a large, brindle-furred form lying dead on the ground, its throat ripped out. It wasn't Tom. Tom was a few feet away, his huge form half-buried as his paws scrabbled frantically into the fresh soil, sending clods of dirt flying in an arc.

I dropped the stake, fell to my knees, and began digging frantically with one hand, the other rendered useless again by the recent battle. I could feel the cracked bone moving under the cast and wetness seeping down the arm. Probably ripped the stitches. Damn it. Well, they'd just be bigger scars. I could still feel them healing, so I wasn't going to have the cast cut off and the stitches redone. Not when the chunk of plaster had been so useful thus far.

But none of that mattered as we uncovered the still, still form of my younger brother. He wasn't buried deep. Only a foot or so down. Just enough to conceal him, to smother him. They'd drained him damn near dry, and when he was too weak to do anything, they'd buried him alive. I gave a howl of anguished rage at the knowledge as I pulled his upper body from the enveloping ground. Desperately, I sought for a pulse. It wasn't there. But his body was still warm to the touch. And my mind could feel . . . something. Some tiny thread of him remained. He wasn't completely beyond reach.

I cleared his mouth and airway, breathing air deep into his lungs. Nothing. I screamed for Joe at the top of my lungs. Tom was in wolf form and the adrenaline in his system wouldn't allow him to change back until he was calm, which wasn't going to happen anytime soon. He couldn't help with CPR. But he could lead the EMTs to me. I didn't see him run off, but I felt it. I was too busy pushing the heels of my hand into my brother's chest in the prescribed rhythm, ignoring the screaming pains that shot up my left arm with every thrust; too busy pulling air into my lungs to expand his while I tried to breathe for both of us.

As I pounded on Bryan's chest and prayed, I heard sirens from the direction of the church. Then shouts and running footsteps. Help was coming.

I opened my mind and the last of the barrier was gone. There was no need for it now. We'd found what they were hiding. I felt the presence of the hive in my mind, and knew they were waiting with smug satisfaction to hear what I would say.

"I will kill you for this."

A laugh filled my mind—a single laugh that was male and confident, just before the reply. "You can try."

13

Three days passed in a very ugly blur. Bryan had been transported to the county hospital in Murphysboro in critical, but stable, condition. Murphysboro was the seat of a newly created upscale mountain county, and thus home of the spanking new county jail. I'd been taken into custody the night of the attack and was being held without bond, awaiting prosecution for the death of the man—whom prosecutors wouldn't readily admit was a vampire.

The jail was clean. I was the only female prisoner, which meant that I got the entire four-bed area to myself, showered alone, and slept on an ordinary twin bed, staring at cinder block walls painted with pale yellow high-gloss paint. The food was passable. The guards polite. It was boring, but all things considered, it could've been one hell of a lot worse.

Fortunately, the town had a hotel, and a Wal-Mart where Joe could pick up clothing for everybody and put it on his credit card.

My hearing was scheduled for first thing Monday morning. The day dawned clear and cold. The guard came to get me bright and early so that I could get first crack at the showers. My attorney had arranged for me to wear street clothing to the hearing. Joe had chosen an inexpensive brown suit that, while it was technically my size, didn't really fit. It was too big in the bust, too tight across the shoulders, and the shoes didn't fit so that my feet started aching the minute I'd forced my way into them. I did, however, look considerably better than the men I'd caught a glimpse of climbing into the other transport. Those poor souls were stuck wearing "jailhouse chic": orange cotton, one-size-fits-all jumpsuits that really don't fit anybody.

Sheriff Beall himself escorted me, along with the largest of his deputies. In addition to my street clothes I got to wear shackles on my ankles and handcuffs that were only partially obscured by the long sleeves of the jacket. The shackles made a jingling noise as we passed through the hall leading out of the jail to the spot right outside the door where the sheriff's cruiser was parked and waiting.

I got to ride in the back, of course. It wasn't comfy, but it wasn't meant to be. There was no back seat, just a simple bench molded out of a piece of hard plastic. I could see through the "cage" bars into the front seat, hear the radio dispatcher explaining that we would have to wait until they got somebody over to the courthouse to direct traffic.

We waited. It seemed to take hours, but in reality it was probably only a matter of minutes. I was nervous enough that time seemed to be passing oddly—crawling endlessly at some points, then lurching forward abruptly.

When we got the all clear the sheriff started the car and pulled out. The jail was only three blocks from the courthouse, so I could see the crowd almost immediately.

Representatives of the press were there. Not a lot of them, but enough to take up a bunch of the parking slots and snarl up traffic around the courthouse. I, of course, was thrilled to death by *that* development. After all, I needed another dollop of infamy. You betcha. And having the most humiliating experience of my life broadcast over the Internet and on national television was a dream come true.

Sheriff Beall was driving slow and steady, keeping the vehicle moving through the press like a hot knife through butter, getting me safely to the courthouse. He wasn't a tall man, maybe five foot eight or so, five foot ten with the cowboy hat. He was built compact and wiry. He had a face that was gracefully moving toward the tail end of middle age. There were wrinkles in the leathered skin, and deep laugh lines around his brown eyes, but he seemed comfortable with them. His face was dominated by a drooping iron-gray moustache. It suited him, went well with his rough-cut features.

"Quite a show today." He didn't seem any more happy about it than I was. Of course, I couldn't blame him. What press there were had no doubt been making a damned nuisance of themselves, getting underfoot, and digging around the investigation to see if they could find anything amiss. If anybody had made the slightest mistake it would be trumpeted to the world, and his people would have egg on their faces.

I didn't answer. There wasn't much to say. And I was actually a little bit afraid that if I opened my mouth I'd throw up. I wasn't just nervous, I was terrified. I do great in an emergency, when you react to the situation instantaneously. But this kind of stress was hell for me. I'd had too much time alone to think of worst-case scenarios. What if I was convicted? I'd killed the Thrall in self-defense, but what if—

Stop it, Reilly. Just stop it.

I looked out the window, searching for Tom and my brothers. I didn't see them, but that didn't mean they weren't there. Maybe they were already in the courtroom, waiting. If they weren't, from the looks of things they might not get a seat.

"This isn't all for you, by the way." His voice was a gravelly baritone, and he spoke with just the tiniest hint of a drawl. "There's a full load of cases on the docket this morning. Probably half of the crowd is their families and attorneys."

He was trying to reassure me. It wasn't helping much, but it was nice of him to try.

"Thanks."

"Just the plain truth." He sighed and eased the cruiser over to the curb. A uniformed cop moved aside a yellow barricade long enough for us to drive through, then dropped it back into place. Meanwhile, Sheriff Beall pulled into the spot reserved for prisoner transport at the rear entrance of the building and put the car in park. "Although there're bound to be more than a few of the locals hoping to get a look at a celebrity, and a lot more want to show their support."

"Their support?"

"Your brother wasn't the only person those vampires attacked that night."

I felt my eyebrows rise until I thought they'd slide off my face. It was the first I'd heard of anything like this.

"They did the same thing to Father Raphael as they did to your brother. Only he didn't have a werewolf to find him and dig him out."

I swallowed hard, forcing bile back down. I would not throw up. I wouldn't. But the thought of being held down while a bunch of vampires fed on me, then being buried alive—I swallowed convulsively again. I would *not* throw up.

The sheriff gave a curt nod to the deputy and the two of them climbed from the vehicle. The deputy was a big man. I hadn't realized *how* big until he climbed out of the vehicle and stood, legs slightly apart, hand near the butt of his gun. I was surprised. The press actually backed away a step or two at his order—probably because he so obviously meant it.

Sheriff Beall opened the door for me, and I slid across the plastic seat.

I walked a step behind the sheriff, and a step ahead of the deputy. Reporters yelled questions, cameras flashed. I kept my eyes on the glass doors that led inside the courthouse, staring straight ahead. I caught a glimpse of my reflection as the door swung open. I almost didn't recognize myself as the pale, grim-faced woman in the glass.

Attorneys with briefcases, their clients, and gawkers parted enough to provide a narrow space in the aisle that led to the elevator. I saw my local counsel pull himself away from the group he'd been chatting with to slither like an eel through the crowd to come up next to us.

Jeff Johnston looked completely and totally unremarkable. Average height, average weight. His hair was a shade that was in that fuzzy area between blond and brown, kept neatly at average length. Today he wore a suit that was an unremarkable cut and made of a fabric that could be gray or a silvery green depending on the light.

Appearances, however, were deceiving. Within the first five minutes of meeting Jeff I knew that there was a world-class mind hiding behind the ordinary camouflage. Thank God.

"Sheriff Beall. I'm going to need a moment to talk to my client in private."

The elevator doors whooshed open. The sheriff

held the door for me to precede him. "The district court clerk has a private office. I'm sure she'll let you use it. We'll take Ms. Reilly there."

"Right. I'll see you there."

The doors closed, and I wondered what, exactly, was up. He'd told me in our last meeting not to worry about today's appearance. This was just the preliminary hearing and nothing much was going to happen. They'd read the charges. He'd enter his appearance as my counsel and I'd enter my plea. Bail would be set. But something was definitely up. Because when he'd come up to us I'd felt outward a little with my mind. What I'd found was profound disquiet, confusion, and worry.

The crowd was thicker on the second floor. People were crowding their way into and out of the courtroom. Attorneys, briefcases in hand, had pulled their clients aside to hold urgently whispered conversations.

Sheriff Beall took the lead. I stayed close at his heels with the deputy walking right behind, close enough, in fact, that he actually stepped on my heels a couple of times when I had to stop abruptly. It took a few minutes of concerted effort and polite apologies before we were able to reach the door to the district court clerk's office. Sheriff Beall tapped briskly on the frosted glass window before turning the brass door handle and leading me in.

The office wasn't large, but it was tidy, and a study in contrasts. The old metal secretarial desk and mismatched file cabinets shared space comfortably with a state-of-the-art copier and a top-of-the-line computer system. There was no air conditioning, just a huge old ceiling fan that moved the air just enough to stir the papers that seemed to be stacked on every flat surface.

Jeff had beaten us up here, and was sitting, waiting in one of the slat-backed oak visitor chairs that lined the wall with the windows.

There were two doors: the one we'd come through, and the one to the judge's chambers. Without prompting Sheriff Beall nodded to Jeff and led the deputy back into the hallway to stand guard.

As soon as the door was safely closed, I took the chair next to my attorney. Looking him in the eye, I asked, "What's up?"

"We have a situation. I'm honestly not sure what to make of it." He shook his head. "In a way it's good news."

"What is it?"

"I was just speaking to the prosecutor. They've decided not to pursue the charges at this time."

I felt this huge grin form on my face. "That's *great!*"

"Yes . . . and no."

"Jeff, they're dropping the charges. I'm free to go."

"Kate, they've decided not to pursue the charges *now*. They're going to continue their investigation. If they don't prosecute, and you're not found innocent they can refile at any time. There's no statute of limitations on murder. This could be hanging over you for the rest of your life."

"So, what? You're saying I should *force* them to prosecute? What if I lost?"

He ran his hand through his hair, ruining the effect of the perfect haircut. "I know. You don't want to take that kind of a chance. It would be stupid. But right now you've got your witnesses. Everything is fresh in their minds, the evidence is fresh. You have a lot of public support—Father Raphael was very popular in the community. We could mount an excellent case for self-defense with a good chance of winning. Giving them more time to prepare is only going to be to your disadvantage."

It made sense the way he explained it. But oh God, I didn't want to go through another trial. Just the civil trial over the mess at St. Elizabeth's had been a huge strain on me, physically, emotionally, and financially. I didn't even want to *think* about what a real murder trial would do.

"And really, it's moot. I made some calls as soon as I found out, got the opinion of a professor of mine who's a retired appellate judge. We can't *make* them prosecute. It's their call."

"But you're worried about it."

He ran his hand through his hair again. Apparently it was a nervous gesture. "Yes, I am. This really could bite you in the butt down the road—particularly if you ever get in trouble again."

I looked out the window for a moment, at the clear, intense blue of the morning sky. I wanted out of here. I wanted the charges dropped. "Sufficient unto the day" and all that. I turned to Jeff. Giving him a smile to show my appreciation for his efforts I said, "I understand what you're saying, and believe me I'm grateful. But I want this over with."

"That's just the point. It won't be. Not really. Not ever. Can you live with that?"

"Do I have a choice?"

"Not really."

"Then I guess I'll have to."

We rose at the same time. His cell phone rang. I left him to take the call and do whatever else he needed to before the case was called and went to join my escorts and take my place in the courtroom.

I'd been in courtrooms before. This one wasn't quite as nice as the one in Denver. The paneling was cheaper, the seats old-fashioned wood, but it was set up the same way. At the front of the room was the judge's bench, the court reporter's box, and the witness stand. To the left was a jury box with a dozen wooden chairs that looked as though they'd qualify as antiques and would be wretchedly uncomfortable. Which would, I suppose, keep the jurors from dozing off during the proceedings. Against the right wall, not far from where the court reporter would sit, there was an enclosure that was just a little bit bigger than the jury box. Instead of chairs, it had three old-fashioned church pews. This was the area for the prisoners. Sheriff Beall led me up the center aisle, past the rows of spectator seating. He pushed open the hinged gate that separated the spectator portion of the courtroom from the "business" area and held it open for me. I started toward the prisoner's box, but he stopped me with a light grip on my arm. He nodded toward the defendant's table. "Go sit over there. You're first on the docket."

"Thanks."

I walked over to take my seat, my skin crawling from the sensation of being watched. I wished my attorney was here; wished Tom or my brothers were with me. I turned in my seat, scanning the crowd, but there was no sign of them.

I shouldn't have worried. Seconds later they walked in the back doors with my attorney. Making their way to the front of the courtroom, they took seats directly behind me on the opposite side of the railing, seats that some kind soul had been saving for them.

Jeff took the seat next to me, set his briefcase on the table in front of us, and popped it open. He drew out a three-ring binder, a yellow pad, and a pair of pencils. He puttered around getting things organized to his satisfaction while I squirmed in my seat, wishing to hell this was over with.

I didn't have to wait long. The bailiff closed the door, walked to the front of the courtroom and announced, "All rise. This court is now in session. The Honorable Judge William Woodin presiding."

We rose.

"In the matter of the People of the State of Colorado versus Mary Kathleen Reilly. Is the defendant present?"

Jeff stood and nodded with deference. "Yes, sir."

"And the people?"

"Your honor," The prosecutor stood up. He was a small man, probably not much over five feet and nearly as broad as he was tall. He was almost completely bald, his scalp pink and shining in the overhead lights and the thick glasses he wore magnified a pair of watery blue eyes. His lips seemed to be set in a perpetually thin line of disapproval. "The people would like to defer prosecution at this time and move to dismiss this case *without* prejudice."

Without prejudice is apparently lawyerese for, we want to be able to change our minds later.

The judge looked down his nose at the prosecutor, his expression unhappy. "Would counsel for both sides please approach the bench?"

The lawyers went up to stand right in front of the judge, who switched off his microphone. For nearly five minutes Jeff and the prosecutor whispered intently at each other and made fierce gestures with their hands. Finally the judge whispered something that made the two of them subside. Waving them back to their respective seats, he hit the switch to turn back on the microphone.

"It is fully in the discretion of the district attorney to choose to prosecute, or not prosecute, a case at any time. Thus, I am left with no choice but to dismiss this case without prejudice. The defendant is to be released from custody upon completion of the proper paperwork by the sheriff's department."

There was enough of an uproar in the courtroom that he wound up pounding the gavel a few times and calling for order. Meanwhile, Sheriff Beall and the bailiff had come up to escort me out. For better or worse, this part was over. For the time being I didn't have to worry about lawyers and court. Which just left the Thrall. Then again, that was more than enough.

14

It was a nightmare. A part of me knew it. In real life, real time, my body was asleep in the back of Joe's SUV with my head on Tom's lap. We were driving back from Murphysboro and Bryan was alive. He had scars covering his neck and a haunted look that even the city limit sign in the rearview mirror couldn't erase. But he was alive.

The overwhelming stress of the past few days had exhausted me completely. Let Joe and Bryan drive. I was out.

But the dream felt so incredibly *real*.

I was standing in a cemetery. It was one of the new, modern ones where the landscaping is all perfectly designed and groomed, the roads are paved with actual drains and curbs, and discrete rectangles of marble or granite set on the ground serve as headstones. It was a pleasant, late summer evening. The sun was setting behind the mountains in the west, and I could hear crickets chirping.

A murder of crows perched in a nearby tree. Their bright black eyes stared at me unsettlingly. I shuddered, forcing my attention back to the ground in front of me. The polished granite tombstone read Dylan Shea, and had dates of birth and death, but instead of a grave there was an empty hole in the ground, dug in the shape of a coffin. The earth was rich, black, and moist, the scent of it thick in the still air.

A harsh caw, and the crows took flight. My head jerked to the left and I was suddenly in a laboratory that didn't exist anymore, standing in front of Miles MacDougal.

"Have you followed my advice?"

"What advice? What am I supposed to be doing?"

"You really don't know, do you?" It was Dylan's voice, thick with scorn, coming from behind me. I whirled around to see him standing in the hallway. In some ways he looked as he always had, the same handsome features and dark curls. But the expression on his face—that was different. I'd loved Dylan, but he'd always been weak, diffident, and it showed in his posture. The man facing me now was neither of those things. He stood with supreme confidence, his hand absently stroking the fur of a huge, brindled werewolf that leaned in against his leg. "Not the brightest crayon in the box, are you, Katy-did? Strong as an ox and almost as clever."

I took a step forward, and the wolf didn't like it. It crouched, as if to spring, a rippling growl rolling from its throat to fill the hallway. Its lips pulled back, and I expected to see the same fearsome teeth that Tom, Rob, and the other wolves I've known had. The teeth were there. But there was something else there as well: fangs—vampire fangs.

"I loved you once. We could've been together. But you chose the wrong side; chose him. *You shouldn't have done that, Katydid."*

Dylan's eyes blazed with an eerie light, his features distorted from the intensity of his rage. I could hear the faintest of lisps, glimpse the hint of fangs behind those perfect lips.

I opened my mouth to respond, to say . . . something, anything.

"Kate, wake up."

The dream shattered. I gasped and blinked as I was thrust too suddenly back into reality. I tried to focus on Tom staring down at me. It took a minute.

"You were having a nightmare."

"Yeah." I used the back of my hand to wipe my mouth as I shoved myself upright. Apparently I'd been drooling. How embarrassing.

"Want to talk about it?"

"Maybe." I was blinking, my mind still a little foggy around the edges. I looked out the car window. We were just passing the natural food store on Colorado Boulevard. Just a few more blocks until we turned left into Joe's subdivision. "We're almost there."

"Yeah," Joe answered. "You were out for almost the whole trip."

"I'm not surprised. I haven't slept very well the past couple of days."

Bryan stiffened as if I'd slapped him. It surprised me because I hadn't meant anything by it. It was just the flat truth.

"I'm sorry, okay?" His voice was resentful. "I know it was my fault. I screwed up."

I sighed. I so didn't want to do this. I'm not exactly known for my way with words. I'm not good at dealing with my own angst, let alone other people's. But there you go. Family is family—and mine more than most.

"Bryan, stop it. Just stop." I sounded tired, and I hadn't even come close to keeping the frustration from my voice. "You did what you had to do. I know that. I don't blame you."

He turned in his seat, his blue eyes locking me in a gaze of almost painful intensity over the leather headrest. "But I failed, and it got a good man killed, and put you in jail." His voice shook with anger and shame. "For nothing."

I looked at Tom. He gave me a tiny shrug, which meant he didn't have any more idea what to say than I did. Joe was staring straight out at the road. Great. Why is it girls get all the "fun" jobs? All right, I'm being sexist. But in my family at least, it seemed to be true.

"Not for nothing." I put some heat in my voice, let a tiny hint of my own anger and frustration show through. I hate self-pity and my baby brother was wallowing in it. "Mike sent you for information. You got some. Maybe not as much as he wanted, but you *did* get results. Tom tells me that you learned that the vampires aren't bringing the recovering zombies and coma victims all the way back, that you faxed Mike proof of it."

Bryan started to protest, but I rolled right over him. "It may not seem important to you, but it was to them: important enough that they were ready to kill you and Father Raphael to prevent word getting out."

"But we don't know why." No self-pity there, just good old-fashioned frustration.

"No, we don't. But once people start looking some-one's bound to find out." Tom slid his arm around me, giving me a quick hug. Apparently he thought I was doing okay. Bully for me. "And as for the jail thing, well, it was bound to happen sooner or later."

"What!" Joe was so startled he almost didn't see the car in front of us stop. He hit the brakes vio-lently enough that the tires squealed in protest and we were all jerked back by our seat belts.

"I've killed people, Joe. Yeah, they were people with fangs, but I *killed* them." My eyes met his in the rearview mirror for a brief second before he had to look away. "I didn't go to jail for killing Larry be-cause the queens cleaned up the evidence. It was part of the deal they made to save Monica. Techni-cally I didn't *kill* Monica, she died of natural causes and shock when I fought off being infested. I killed an attacker in an alley on the 16th Street Mall. No, I didn't *know* he would die when I broke off his fangs, but I had a pretty good idea. Again, the Thrall cleaned up the evidence."

The three of them were listening so intently I could barely hear them breathe. Bryan's expression held so many emotions I couldn't even guess what he was thinking. But I was on a roll now, I'd had three days of solitude to think things over, get my head on straight. I'd come to some fairly unpleasant conclusions. I needed to talk it out. These three, my family, were the people I most trusted in the world, so I plowed on. "Amanda—Amanda's where I really started pushing it, and the police took notice. If she'd actually died up in the mountains there would've been hell to pay. As it was, when she came after me in Denver it was pure self-defense, and there were witnesses, including a decorated veteran cop, so they let it slide."

"Then there was Samantha Greeley." Joe flinched at the mention of her name, and I saw his jaw tighten into a hard line at the memory of the torture she'd inflicted on him. "I still don't know how I caught a break on that one. Maybe it's the whole *Die Hard*/she was a terrorist thing that made them decide not to prosecute, but I *should've* seen some jail time for that one."

"You can't tell me you're sorry," Bryan said.

I gave a derisive snort. "Hell, no! Of course not. I did what I had to do, and I'd do it again in a heartbeat. But there are always consequences. Three days' jail time and some public humiliation? After all that I've done? That's cupcakes." I sighed. "We're all alive and more or less intact. I do hate that they killed the priest." My voice caught, and I shuddered at the thought of him being buried alive. I'm a little bit claustrophobic. Just the thought of watching some-one pour dirt over you while you lie there helpless gave me a bad case of the heebie-jeebies. And what they did to Mike—

My eyes closed and I felt the tears well. "Maybe the *courts* will forgive me, but there's still someone else I'll have to answer to eventually."

Tom sensed it, or maybe he smelled the fear on me, because he held me a little tighter, trying to reassure me. I slid my hand up his arm, and his strength gave me the strength to continue. "But that wasn't your fault either. *They* did it, not you. And the information you got for them may give Mike and the church the ammunition they need to prevent even worse things from happening."

"You think so?" Bryan's voice wasn't sullen any more, but it didn't sound as if he believed me.

"I think it gives us a chance. Before, we had nothing."

"I agree." Joe pulled the SUV into the driveway and put it in park. "And I've got to tell you. I'm proud of you." He coughed, and gave Bryan an awkward punch on the shoulder. "Do it again and I'll kill you myself, and I'm still working through a lot of things. But, yeah, mostly I figured out I'm proud of you." He looked at me strongly, and I realized the admission wasn't just meant for Bryan. I was in there too, un-spoken, but real.

It was a very guy way of interacting, but it worked. In fact, I think those few words knocked more of the tension out of all three of us than anything a high-priced therapist could have said. Figures.

The two of them climbed out of the car, going to join Mary who'd stepped into the doorway wearing an apron liberally decorated with what looked like tomato sauce. I started to follow, but Tom held me back with a touch.

"This may be the only privacy we get for the next couple of days."

He was right, of course. I love my family, and it was incredibly kind of Joe and Mary to let us stay with them, but we needed our own place, soon. As in now. The thing is, what money we'd had that could've been used for a down payment on some-thing had been used as a retainer for the attorney. We'd get some of it back. He wouldn't have used most of it. But that didn't put a roof over our heads or get me my cat back.

I snuggled in against his chest and sighed. Some-times my life just sucks. Staying with Joe and Mary was definitely going to put a crimp in the old sex life, because while I *know* we're all adults, he's my *brother,* and as a werewolf Mary would be able to hear, and smell, everything. Ewwww.

"I get paid in a few days. It'll be tight, but between the refund from the lawyer and my paycheck we should be able to get something. How we'll furnish it

I have no idea." Tom shook his head; I felt his chin moving across my scalp. "But we'll manage something." He took my chin in his hand and tilted my face up so that our gazes met. "Unfortunately, I've got a shift starting in the morning, and as soon as I get off that I'll have all sorts of last-minute stuff to do to help the pack prepare for the emergency session of the Conclave. You'll be stuck with the job of finding a place and getting us packed pretty much by your lonesome."

"I can handle it." I leaned up, pressing my lips to his in a gentle kiss.

"It won't be that easy." His expression was so sad, and worried, but there was an underlying anger there too. I hugged him, trying to drive the sorrow from his face. "You remember how bad it was for me before I moved into your building."

Yeah, I remembered. Prejudice sucks and there's plenty of it to go around. People *say* that lycanthropy is a disease, but that doesn't mean they want a werewolf living in their building, or down the street from their kids. Hell, Rob got thrown out of his previous apartment because they said his living there violated the "No Pets" clause. Assholes abound. I had no doubt I would meet more than my share over the next few days—especially since we'd be looking at low-income listings. But I gave him my gentlest smile, and was rewarded with a softening of his expression.

"Don't underestimate the future wife." I poked him in the ribs.

"Fine, right. I give up already." He was grinning, mainly because I'd started tickling him. Of course then he *had* to retaliate. We were wrestling around like a couple of little kids in a matter of minutes. The wrestling was just about to turn adult when there was a firm tap on the glass of the car window.

Shit.

Tom slid his hand out from beneath my top and shifted his weight off me, enough that I could sit up and rearrange my clothing. While I did, he rolled down the window to see what was so important that Mary had left off cooking dinner to come out here.

"What's up?"

Mary held out the cordless extension. "Sorry to interrupt, but Katie has a call. It's Detective Brooks. Something about her missing guns. He doesn't sound happy."

I shot Tom an apologetic look, but he just gave me a resigned smile and tried to shift his trousers so that his erection wasn't quite so obvious.

"Right." I opened the car door and climbed out, taking the receiver from her hand. She turned and walked back into the house, giving me some privacy.

I hoped he wasn't as upset as she made it sound. He understands my situation better than most, so *upset* meant bad things. I met him under "battle conditions" the night Monica Mica infested me. We'd formed a friendship then that has withstood all of the crap the vampires, and life, has thrown at me. It was his mother's house I hid in when Amanda Shea, the press, and Samantha Greeley were after me. He is the one I call when I have to deal with the police—because he's one of the few I *know* will treat me fairly regardless of what kind of political machinations may be going on behind the scene.

At five foot seven he isn't tall, but he still manages to be imposing. His suits are perfectly tailored, and fitted to accommodate the kind of heavily muscled body that only comes from serious weight training. He's handsome, but it's as much because of the keen intellect staring out from his liquid brown eyes as from bone structure and grooming.

"Kate here."

"Hey, Reilly. I just heard the news. Glad things turned out okay for you down there." The rich baritone carried clearly through the receiver. I could actually picture him sitting at his desk, the sleeves of his snow-white dress shirt rolled up to reveal muscular arms—a stack of paperwork in front of him.

"You and me both." I glanced back at the car. Tom hadn't gotten out, which meant our private discussion might not have to be over—if I got done with the call quick enough. "Mary tells me you found one of my guns?" The tone made it a question.

"Two, actually." He sighed. It was a frustrated, weary sound that made me feel bad for him. "But don't expect to be getting them back anytime soon."

"Why not?"

"They're in evidence." He explained. "One turned up at a pawn shop in response to my BOLO—"

"*Bolo?*"

He gave a weary chuckle. "*Be on the lookout.* I took the initiative and faxed your list to the local pawnshops. We got a call back almost immediately. Found your gun and a few other things besides."

"Cool."

"But the investigation's ongoing. So you'll have to wait a bit."

"No problem. At least I'll be getting it back eventually, and it's not on the street wreaking havoc."

Silence on the other end of the line made me wonder if I'd just put my foot in my mouth. His answer made me start chewing.

"The second gun turned up in a liquor store robbery. The clerk died. You probably heard it on the news."

No, I hadn't. Shit. "I'm sorry, John."

He coughed. "Not your fault. You weren't allowed inside the building to get it, and you had the damned thing locked in a safe. Can't expect much more from you. But I do need you to stop by first thing tomorrow and sign all the paperwork. I got it ready when you faxed the list from the bank, but with everything that's happened I need to make it all official."

"Right. What time do you want me down there?"

"Will 8:30 work for you?"

"Fine. Just give me the address."

He did me one better, giving me directions. It would be a long ride on the bus. I'd have to get up obscenely early and there would be at least one transfer involved. But I'd manage. "Right. Got it." I assured him. "See you bright and early tomorrow morning."

"I'll have the coffee ready when you get here."

"You're a good man, Brooks."

He was laughing when we hung up.

I turned, planning to get back in the SUV, but apparently I'd taken too long. Tom was climbing out and any evidence of ardor was gone. Dammit, dammit, dammit.

My disappointment must have shown because he started laughing. It was a low, wicked chuckle, the kind that hints at naughty things done in darkened rooms, and it made my body tighten. His sparkling eyes darkened, the merriment joined by an intensity that comes into a man's face when sex is in the air. My pulse sped, and I felt my skin flush a little in reaction.

"Dinner's ready."

The mood shattered at the sound of my brother's call. I did *not* scream with frustration, much as I wanted to. And oh, how I wanted to.

"What say we go to bed right after dinner?" Tom whispered the suggestion into my left ear as he slid his arm around my waist.

"But—" I started to protest.

"*I* can be quiet. Can you?"

Oh, that was just too much of a dare to resist, even if I'd wanted to.

15

Dinner was homemade tortellini, garlic bread, and salad with tiramisu for dessert. It was absolutely amazing. Mary was a fabulous cook. I ate more than I should have, but I honestly couldn't resist. After dinner everybody else settled down in front of the television to watch a movie on DVD. Instead of joining them, I went upstairs to take a shower and go to bed. I didn't think Tom was going to join me, which just goes to show I underestimate how stubborn, and horny, he can be.

I walked into the bedroom wearing nothing but a bath towel to find him laying naked on top of the covers. He'd set the bedside light to its lowest setting, and the warm orange glow cast deep shadows on the muscled contours of his body, outlining a perfect six-pack, sculpted thighs, and a penis that rose to attention the minute I stepped inside the room.

"Oh my. I take it you haven't changed your mind."

He gave a low, wicked chuckle. "I believe we have a dare going on."

"Oh really." I was blushing. I couldn't help it. Downstairs were both of my brothers and the Acca of his pack, none of whom were exactly hard of hearing. Oh, I could tell it was an action movie they were watching. There was plenty of gunfire and the occasional explosion. But still—

He rolled over on his side and scooted to one side of the bed to make room, then crooked his finger at me in the traditional beckoning motion.

I let the towel fall to the floor, and was rewarded with a look on his face of hunger to the point of need. Never in my life would I have expected a man to react to me like that, but he always did. The sex might be intense, or playful, depending on our mood, but the passion was always there, and love.

I climbed onto the bed beside him, lying on my side so that we were facing each other. I trailed my hand down the length of his body, using just a hint of fingernails against the warm, smooth skin.

He gave a deep, knowing laugh. "Oh no, you don't," he teased. "On your back, woman."

I tilted my head, raising a single eyebrow in an eloquent look, but did what he'd said. He kissed me then, and the kiss gave me the key to his mood: hungry, yes, but playful, which was just about perfect for me tonight. He pulled away from my lips, and I looked up into brown eyes sparkling with mischief and merriment. He raised a finger to his lips and, in his best Elmer Fudd imitation, said "Be vewy quiet. We be huntin' wabbits."

I started giggling. I couldn't help it. But the giggles turned to a gasp of pleasure as he began kissing his way down the front of my body. His hand stroked between my thighs. "Ah. Fur." He shifted position, spreading my thighs and then moving between them. Using his hands he raised my knees and began kissing, and licking, the sensitive skin behind the bend, moving ever so slowly to the inner thighs.

"Is this a wabbit hole?" he teased. But before I could answer he blew a breath of air against the sensitive skin of my moistened opening. I whimpered, my body writhing against the strong hands that pinned my hips to the bed. He teased me with his tongue, flicking it against me, sucking, bringing me to the delicate edge of orgasm, then pulling back, slowing down. I was whimpering, begging him with my words and my body.

"Please, please, *please*."

There was no more joking, no laughter. Only need that stole coherent thought, made me want to scream.

He covered my mouth with his, and I could taste myself in that kiss, a kiss that softened my cries because I couldn't seem to help myself and he knew I wouldn't want the others to hear.

Slow and gentle, he began pushing his way inside me. It felt right, so good, so . . . incredibly . . . good.

The orgasm started with the first thrust. I'd been

hovering on the verge, so the feel of him moving inside me pushed me over the edge. It hit me in waves, building, then ebbing, building again. His speed increased. Each thrust harder, faster, moving against me. I clawed frantically at the bedding, my body struggling against the intensity of sensation at the same time that I craved it. I felt the rhythm change, knew that he was close, so close. I shifted, moving my hips, and that small change did it. I came again in an explosion of pleasure that spasmed my body around him, bringing him over with me. He cried out my name as he collapsed onto the bed, almost too spent to even pull himself free of my body.

I didn't move. I couldn't. The orgasm had left me literally limp and sweaty with pleasure. If I could ever move again I'd need another shower.

16

It was probably because of the nap, but I was wide awake at 2:30 in the morning. Tom needed his sleep. He would be going on shift in the morning. Being exhausted can be actively dangerous for a firefighter, so I slid carefully out from under his arm and pulled on some clothes. As quietly as I could, I padded downstairs.

Mary had left the downstairs hall light on. It was enough light for everyone to be able to find their way around, but dim enough to allow for sleep.

Bryan was sacked out on the couch, mouth open, snoring softly. Rob was curled up on an air mattress on the floor next to the bassinet.

I didn't know when they had arrived, but it didn't matter. They were here now. It made for quite a houseful and I promised myself I'd find somewhere for Tom and me to live before we wore out our welcome.

I didn't see Dusty, but I figured out where she was by following the sounds of soft crooning coming from the direction of the kitchen. Ah, right: middle of the night, baby, feeding. I padded across the carpet in the direction of the noise, hoping that maybe she'd have fixed some coffee. Probably not. I didn't smell any. But hey, it was worth a shot.

I stepped through the swinging doors and found her sitting at the kitchen table. She was wearing a long white nylon nightgown that had an elastic top. One side had been pulled down, and the baby was breast-feeding. From the noises Robby was making you'd have thought he was famished. She looked down at him, her expression so *content* that I felt a stab of intense jealousy.

"Good morning," I whispered, my voice light, pleasant, hiding the darker emotion as best I could.

"Pfft. It's morning, anyway." She looked up and gave me a smile that made me feel guilty as hell. "It's a little too early to be good in my opinion." She pulled him away from her breast, and he wiggled, his face screwing up to cry out in protest, little fists shaking in rage at the unfairness. But she knew what she was doing, because almost as soon as she set him against her shoulder and began patting his back he let out the kind of belch that would do a beer-guzzling frat boy proud.

"That was a *good* one, Robbie." She kissed him on his forehead and moved him back into position. He settled back in, feeding more calmly this time, and she reached over to take a sip from a glass of milk.

She gave me sad eyes. "No coffee for me any more. It makes him hyper."

"Ugh. That sucks." I pulled out the chair directly across from her and took a seat.

"Tell me about it."

"Still, it's worth it." I nodded toward the baby suckling at her breast.

"Absolutely." She smiled down at him contentedly for a moment before looking back up. "Oh, I almost forgot. There's a present for you at the end of the counter." She gestured in the general direction, and I saw a pair of big bags. One bore the logo of a local bookstore. The other had a padded mat sticking out of the top.

"Tom told us that someone stole your meditation mat and the books Henri Tané had given you. Rob and I figured if they were important enough to steal, you needed to get another set pronto." I rose, crossed the kitchen, and began rummaging in the bags. It was all there. The incense, the mat, candles, even the hard-to-find reference books. It had to have cost them a fortune, and they probably shouldn't have done it, but damn I was grateful. Because you couldn't fault the logic. If the vampires didn't want me to have it, then I probably needed it.

"I got myself a set too." She stroked the baby's cheek gently as she spoke. "I figure, I'd better learn how to use my gift right so that I can teach this little guy when the time comes."

It made sense, I supposed, but I wouldn't have expected it. Dusty had always shied away from using her powers before, only stepping up when it was a life-threatening emergency. I'd always figured she'd been scared off by the fact that her stepfather had tried to give her to the vampires because of them. But if she was right and the baby had talent, it would probably . . . no, make that *definitely* be a good idea to train him.

"Thank-you. I really appreciate it."

She shook her head. "*You're* thanking *me*? Excuse me. Who's the one who nearly got herself killed saving my baby? Please. There's nothing Rob and I can *ever* do that will be enough." She gave me a wicked grin. "Incidentally, it shut up your detractors in the pack pretty damned thoroughly too. When Janine gets back she's going to have one hell of a time drumming up support."

"That's good to know. I've been really nervous about the Conclave."

"Yeah. So has Tom and everybody else. Nobody likes that they're sticking their noses in our pack business, but there you go."

The baby was finished eating, and seemed to be fading off to sleep in her arms. She let out a slow, wide-mouthed yawn. "I think I'll put this little guy to bed and see if I can get some more sleep." She adjusted her nightgown to cover herself. Rising to her feet, she carried Robbie in the crook of her arm toward the swinging door. "We've got a rough couple of days ahead of us."

"Night, Dusty."

"Good night."

The room seemed oddly empty after they left, the silence so thick that I could hear Bryan's snores from the other room, and the ticking of the clock hanging above the sink. I hoped Mary wouldn't mind, but I needed coffee. I rummaged in the cabinets until I found what I needed and set a pot to brew. That done, I pulled the books from their bag and moved them over to the kitchen table.

I knew for a fact that there had been a few times these past few days that the queens had successfully blocked my gift, effectively locking me inside my own mind. I needed to find out how they'd done it and, more importantly, how to counteract the effect. I was pretty sure the answer was inside one of these books. Now was as good a time as any to start looking for it.

Three hours and two mugs of coffee later the household was stirring. I could hear a shower running upstairs, which probably meant Tom was getting ready. Bryan was still out of it, but Dusty and the baby were making noises, and I could hear Mary talking to Joe in the other room about running to the store to get breakfast food for the resident horde. She was joking, but there was an edge to it. I couldn't blame her. Company had descended, disrupting their quiet life with no warning, and no end in sight.

"Find anything?" Dusty appeared in the kitchen doorway with Robby on her shoulder. She was jiggling him a little the way mothers do sometimes to keep the baby from crying.

"Actually I did."

She walked over to the table to look at the paragraph I was pointing to. It was in the section on shielding, and it talked about how a shield could be used offensively to trap an opponent inside their own mind. It would cut off the abilities in such a way that the person might not even notice for days, or weeks, by which time it could be made strong enough that it would be nearly impossible to break from the inside. It could only be lifted by the caster, or broken from outside.

"Oooh, nasty." She shifted the baby to a more comfortable position. "You think that's what they've done to you?"

"I don't know. Maybe." I ran my hand through my tangled hair in frustration. "I've been trying to think if I've used my talent lately, and I don't know. I've done a couple of things, but they could just be chalked up to observation. Maybe I heard the vampire moving in the trees rather than sensed him. Maybe yesterday's nightmare was just a dream. Or maybe the fact that I was touching Tom at the time counteracted what they've been doing. I don't *know*."

"Want me to look? It says here I should be able to sense it."

"Unless they did it to you too."

"No harm in trying."

"Yeah, if you *only* look. The book also says that if

you try to break it there's a good chance the power could backlash onto you. Depending on how much energy they've put into it you could be seriously injured."

"Right." She turned to hand the baby to Rob, who'd come into the kitchen to join us. "Look but don't touch. I can do that."

I sat still, watching her reread the paragraphs we needed. I was nervous as hell and trying not to show it. After all, psychic stuff isn't baking cookies. It couldn't possibly be as simple as following a recipe, could it?

I wriggled in my seat, watching impatiently as she closed her eyes and steadied her breathing. I knew better than to distract her, but it was hard to just *sit*. Patience is not, and has never been, my best thing.

I actually saw it when she "hit the wall." Her face reddened, screwing up in frustration, her breathing growing ragged.

"Dusty," I reached out to touch her hand, to tell her to stop before she hurt herself. At the same instant the baby reached for his mother.

It was like being at ground zero of a nuclear blast—only we were the bomb. Our power, which had been dammed and blocked, joined with the backlash, racing outward. My mind's eye saw a queen vampire, her fangs bared to sink into the throat of a former Eden zombie at the same instant as a lesser Thrall thrust a needle into his arm. The power hit her in a burst of white-hot pain; her mind and body snuffed out like a candle in a hurricane. At least three others fell, and their hives with them, and still the power was not done. It raced forward, like flame along a fuse. But this time it didn't reach its goal. The Thrall hive might have changed, but it still was a hive. The caster felt the other deaths, and with that split-second warning managed to pull away from the collective, shield herself and the host she lived in from the blast by throwing a score of lesser vampires in the way of the blast. It killed them in an instant, but left the power with nowhere else to go. So it doubled back, coming straight for the three of us.

I heard myself screaming in terror, felt strong hands grab me, hauling me bodily across the room. I knew it was Tom. Dripping wet, still naked from the shower. He'd sensed what was happening and raced downstairs to help.

Rob held the baby, who was shrieking as hard and as fast as his lungs could draw air while Mary grabbed onto Dusty.

It was the wolves who saved us. Their magic, their power, deflected the worst of the energy, grounded it somehow. It hurt like hell, like fire burning through every nerve ending in a white-hot rush. It had to have taken only a minute, but it felt like an eternity.

"What the fuck was that?" Rob's voice was shaky. At least he could talk. Now that I'd stopped screaming I couldn't have said a word if my life depended on it. I was shaking like a leaf, and the only thing holding me upright was Tom.

Dusty was sobbing incoherently. Mary steered her gently over to Rob and the baby. The three of them huddled together, comforting each other. Almost immediately the infant's screams calmed to whimpers.

Mary turned away from them. She stalked across the kitchen until she was barely an inch away from Tom and me.

"This was your fault." There was a growl underlying the words, and her eyes glowed eerily with her magic. "I want you out of my house. *Now!*"

"It was an accident." Joe stood in the doorway. I knew he'd come as quick as he could, but he'd arrived too late to help. He stood, leaning hard against the swinging door, wearing only a pair of striped boxers. The scars on his legs were hideous, and his knee bent oddly sideways without the brace to support it. He spoke softly, trying to calm Mary down. But there was no calming the rage in her eyes, and power poured off of her in waves. I couldn't imagine how she was holding her beast in check. Hell, I didn't know how any of them were managing. There was so much magic, so much tension in the room I could barely breathe. It was as if the air itself had grown hot and thick.

Tom turned, putting the bulk of his body between me and his Acca. "Do we at least get to get dressed?" His bitterness was palpable, but he stood with his head held high, his jaw thrust forward.

"You have ten minutes." She turned on her heel, and stalked from the room.

"Mary—" Joe turned, as if to follow, but I stopped him.

"Let it go, Joe. It's all right."

"It wasn't your fault." He gave me a look that was equal parts frustration and sadness.

I shook my head. He couldn't know that. He hadn't been here to see. But he believed it, trusted that I would never deliberately put Dusty or Robby in danger. That meant a lot to me, because it wouldn't have always been the case. Just a few months ago he'd have been more than happy to believe the worst of me. It did my heart good to know that had changed. But now was not the time to argue. Mary was simply too angry to be reasonable. She'd been frightened badly. Hell, we all had. And like me, she reacts to fear with good old-fashioned anger. Given a choice of fight or flight, she'd chosen fight. If the circumstances had been reversed I might well have done the same thing.

"We'd better get moving," Tom said. "We don't have a lot of time."

We were out at the curb in nine minutes, what clothes and toiletries we had on hand stuffed into plastic grocery sacks. A cab was on its way. Bryan had slept through the disaster, but not the ensuing commotion. He'd slipped me enough money to cover our needs for a few days and made me promise to call him when I knew where we'd be staying. It was the best he could do. Everybody was walking on pins and needles, trying not to make the wolf pacing upstairs any more unhappy than she already was. Dusty was in tears and kept saying over and over that it was her fault, and how sorry she was.

Tom and I both told her not to worry. "Just take care of the baby. We'll get this all sorted out eventually."

Of course, *eventually* seemed a hell of a long ways away as we stood in the cold waiting for a cab without any clue where we'd be spending the night.

"Would you like to explain just exactly what *did* happen back there?" Tom's voice was colder than the wind blowing back my tangled hair. He was pissed. He'd stood by me in front of everybody else, but now that we were alone he felt free to have an argument. It might not have made sense to anybody else, but I understood and appreciated it. The two of us are a team. We stand united against all comers with no visible cracks in the armor. Once we're by ourselves, however, we hash out our differences. "I've never felt so much power in my life. You could've gotten us all killed."

"Something's been wrong with my psychic abilities. The only times I've gotten anything is when I've been touching you. I asked Dusty to take a look, but to make sure she *didn't* mess with anything. I just wanted to know if the Thrall were blocking me. I specifically told her it was too dangerous to try to break the block."

"So what went wrong?"

"Apparently they were blocking her too. She started to fight it. When I tried to stop her I touched her, and the baby touched her at the same time, and—"

"Boom." He finished the sentence for me.

"Boom." I agreed.

"Shit, I can't afford to go on shift right now." He ran his hands through his hair in frustration. It's a gesture we have in common. My own hair was looking pretty ratty right at the moment from having done the same thing.

"We can't afford for you not to. We need the money."

He closed his eyes. I could almost hear him counting to ten before he answered. "Yeah. We do."

A long, uncomfortable silence stretched between us. I hated it, mostly because I felt guilty. Loving someone is supposed to make both your lives better. Tom improved my life every way I could imagine. But I'd screwed his up all to hell and had pretty much from the first. Worse, it didn't look like it would be straightening out anytime soon.

"I'm sorry." I whispered the words, my throat tight.

"I know. So am I." He set the bags he was holding down on the curb and took me in his arms, gathering me close. I hugged him tight, my head resting against his chest. The rough zipper of his jacket scratched against my cheek, but I didn't move. It was ignorable, just so long as he didn't let me go.

I was so afraid of losing him. Anybody else would've given up on me ages ago. I mean, my life was just too *messy*, violent and ugly. Why would he put up with it? Why would anyone?

My thoughts must have been bleeding over, or maybe he knows me too well, because I heard him say, "I'm not going anywhere, Katie. I'm in it for better or for worse."

"Yeah, well it looks as if worse is likely to be pretty damned bad."

He didn't answer. He just held me. We were still standing that way when the cab arrived a few minutes later.

17

At 8:30 sharp I walked through the glass door of the station house. This particular branch of the Denver Police Department was in a smaller brick building. The front area had a tiny reception area. A desk sergeant sat at an old metal desk behind a thick plate of bulletproof glass that had a slot cut out of it. It reminded me more of a theater entrance than a police station. I gave my name. The man behind the counter called to make sure I was expected. When he got confirmation he buzzed me through.

I stepped into a short hallway with four doors. The one behind me swung closed, and I heard the locking mechanism click on. The three other doors were all open. The first, to my right, led into the desk sergeant's area. The door to my left led to a large, open room that had been divided into cubicles, each with its own prefabbed work station. When I peeked inside the officer at the nearest desk looked up and asked if he could help me. He looked familiar, but I couldn't quite place him.

"I'm looking for John Brooks. I have an 8:30 appointment."

"Right," he smiled. "BROOKS! Company." He gave a bellow that would do a drill sergeant proud. In response a familiar head appeared over the walls of the second to last cubicle.

"Come on back, Reilly. The coffee's getting cold."

"Thanks." Now I remembered, his name was Adams. He'd been one of the officers to respond to the Shamrock Inn.

"No problem," he said, his smile broadening. "It's good to see you still up and around."

"You too." I gave him a cheery wave and hurried down the aisle to where Brooks was waiting. True to his word, he had coffee ready for me—and not just coffee, the good stuff: high octane, from one of the expensive chains that grind their own beans fresh. Not only that, he'd picked up pistachio muffins for us to munch on. I'd never had a pistachio muffin before. They were surprisingly good. Of course, I was also ravenously hungry. After all, I'd been up for six hours and had had a metaphysical crisis already. I definitely needed food.

John had been in the middle of a telephone conversation when I'd shown up. He'd gestured silently toward the cup and muffins. I didn't need to be told twice.

"No. I'm sorry. I've decided not to renew the listing. Yes, I know you've been doing your best. No. I don't agree. I think the price is just fine. My wife and I have discussed it. We've made our decision. Thank-you for your efforts, but no. We've decided to take the house off of the market for the time being."

My ears perked up. The idea hit me so hard that I inhaled sharply, and promptly choked on a half-chewed bite. I was coughing my head off as he set the telephone receiver back in its cradle.

I finally managed to cough up the offending bite, then washed it back down with coffee. When I trusted myself to speak, I said, "I thought you'd already sold your mom's place."

"So did I." He answered sourly. "The deal fell through . . . again."

Aw, damn. "How much are you asking?"

The figure he named wasn't cheap, but it wasn't outrageous either. After all, I'd seen the house. The neighborhood was good. The place was in excellent condition. It was located in a cozy little area on major bus routes with a grocery store within walking distance. Yes, the place was small—two bedrooms and one bath, but it was cozy. It had a fireplace, and a big front porch. Of course, we needed a place now, and who knew how soon I'd wrangle the check out of the insurance people. And I'd have to, because there was no way I'd qualify for a loan right now.

Even B lenders would shudder at the prospect of giving me money.

"Reilly, did you even hear a word I just said?" Brooks grumbled, but he looked amused.

"I'm sorry. It's just . . . I think you may be the answer to my prayers."

"Don't let my wife hear you say that—or Tom either for that matter." He grinned at me over the lip of his coffee cup. He took a long pull. Only after he swallowed did he continue. "Are you going to explain, or are you planning on keeping me in suspense?"

I explained. He just sat there for long moments, looking thoughtful.

"So, would you consider a six-month lease with an option to buy at any time—just in case the insurance company actually decides to pay up?" Like any good negotiator I started with the position that was in my best interest. Ask for the moon. He could always talk me down to something else.

"You wouldn't have a problem after what happened there? The real estate agent says that the 'history of violence' is one of the reasons it hasn't sold."

I flinched. With good reason. It had been my violence. Amanda had tried to kill me in the alley next to the house. Tom and I had wound up killing her instead. Not exactly the best of memories.

I thought about it for a long moment. Yeah, it bugged me. But not *that* much. And really, there weren't likely to be any better prospects.

"I'll be fine," I assured him. Then, with a grin, "Tom will just have to take out the trash."

Brooks laughed. It was a deep, rich sound that caused people all around the room to peek over the top of their cubicle walls to see what we were up to. One or two even smiled in response. "Fine. I'll draw up the paperwork. When do you want to move in? I'll need to move the furniture out. Unless . . ." his expression grew sly, "the two of you would want to pay a little extra to get the place furnished? After all," his voice took on an exaggeratedly wheedling tone, "you lost most of yours when the building collapsed." He gave me innocent eyes. "I'd even cut you a deal."

"*You* just don't want to have to deal with hauling it off or having a garage sale."

"True," he admitted.

"How much would you want for it?"

He named a price that was reasonable, and I was ready to jump on it. Of course, first I had to check with Tom.

"Can I use your phone to call the station? I'm leaning toward saying yes, but I have to check with Tom."

"Go for it." He shoved the instrument in my direction.

I dialed the number for the station from memory. Excitement was welling up inside of me. This was almost too good to be true, the kind of thing that makes me look up and say "thank-you" to the big guy. Because having this happen right now was nothing short of miraculous.

"Bishop here." Tom's voice came on the line.

"What do you think of Brooks's mom's house? We can rent it for six months with an option to buy. He'll even sell us the furnishings." I couldn't keep the excitement from my voice. The more I thought about this the happier it made me.

There was a long, long, silence on the other end of the line.

"Tom? Are you there? What do you think?"

His voice was almost awed. "I'm thinking that I am never again going to underestimate my future wife."

"You're okay with the Amanda thing?" I hoped he was. I *really,* really hoped he was. Because I honestly couldn't imagine us stumbling onto a better deal.

"Eh. She's dead and gone, and I wasn't there for most of it. Are you?"

"Yup."

"Are you sure?" He sounded doubtful.

I paused and thought. "I think so." Yeah, I had a couple of misgivings. But they were small misgivings. "But there's only one way to find out."

"Right."

"So? Whaddaya think?"

"If you're okay with it." I heard the alarm sound in the background. "Baby, I've gotta go. You make the choice. I'll be okay with whatever you decide. I love you."

"Love you too. Be careful." I said the words, but he'd already hung up. I felt the little shiver of fear I always get when I know he's headed out to a fire. He loves his job, and he's good at it. I know that he's as careful as he can be. But it's dangerous as hell. And every time I think about him rushing *into* a burning building it scares the crap out of me. So I try not to think about it. I focus on other things. And right now there was a perfect "other thing" to distract me.

I set the handset back in its cradle and turned to Brooks. "I assume it's okay for me to have my cat?"

Brooks grumbled a little. "Fine. Blank can come with you when you move in." He gave the bags piled at my feet a significant look. "Which I assume is going to be soon?"

"Just as soon as you'll let me."

He sighed. "So I gathered." He shifted his weight and fished in his pants pocket, eventually pulling out a familiar set of keys. "I'd give you a lift, but I'm buried in paperwork this morning." He handed me the keys. I'd been right. It was the same ring I'd used when he'd loaned me the house all those months ago. "Camille and I are going to the theater tonight and tomorrow's her mother's birthday dinner. Is it okay with you if I bring the paperwork by Thursday evening?"

"Perfect," I agreed. "In fact, why don't you bring Camille with you? I'll fix us all dinner."

"Sounds like a plan." He grinned. "She's been dying to meet the two of you."

"I've been curious about her too," I admitted. I'd never met John's wife; I'd only seen her in a vision.

But she'd seemed like one hell of a woman. She'd almost have to be to deal with him.

"Good. Now back to police business." He shoved a stack of papers at me. I glanced through them, noting that old-fashioned, preprinted, triplicate forms were outdated. Now everything was computerized. You could print as many copies as you needed. He'd done just that, and placed little sticky notes on the pages I needed to sign.

I read through the report, signed in triplicate, and slid the papers back across the desk to him. "Is that everything then?"

"That's it."

I gathered up my bags and rose to my feet. It was time to go. I had things to do. Like get my cat, and move into my new home. *Yay!*

"We'll see you Thursday evening. Say seven-ish?"

"That sounds fine." He reached out his hand and I shook it. "Give my best to Tom."

"And mine to Camille. Oh, and pet Brutus for me. How's he doing anyway?" Brutus was Brooks's pride and joy, a huge old Rottweiler. The dog had been seriously injured saving Brooks's life. For a while they'd been afraid they'd have to put him down. After a lot of complicated and expensive surgery he had seemed to be recovering, but it was definitely touch and go for a while.

"All healed up. Oh, he still has a limp, but he's doing fine."

"I'm glad. He's one hell of a dog."

"That he is." Brooks grinned and shook his head. He might have said more, but his phone started ringing. He cast a quick look at it, and shrugged. Duty literally called.

"I'll let you get back to it. See you Thursday night."

I walked out past the row of desks, waving at Adams on my way out the door.

I behaved with dignity all the way out the front door of the building, managing to contain my glee. Once outside, I caved, squealing and doing the happy dance. I wasn't homeless. Not only that, I had a *nice* place, a place I'd be happy to call home, where I could live with Tom and the cat and not have to worry about a prejudiced landlord trying to pull all kinds of bullshit because my boyfriend just happened to be a werewolf. Whoo hoo! Score! I wanted to call someone, to celebrate. But Tom was doing his job. Calling Joe's house right now was a bad idea. If Mike were still in town I'd run by Our Lady of Perpetual Hope, light a candle in the church to say thank-you for deliverance from prison and homelessness, maybe raise a glass with my favorite priest. Of course with him at the Vatican I couldn't do the latter. And the church was *technically* closed. Technically because I still had a key on my ring.

I knew I shouldn't use it.

I really shouldn't.

I could go to any of the thousand-and-one other churches around town and say my thank-you prayers there. But they wouldn't be "Our Lady," the church that had been practically a second home for me since I came back to Denver after my folks died. And really, who would it hurt? Nobody. I didn't even have to go inside.

I kept rationalizing the entire time I walked to the bus stop and waited for the bus to come get me. I continued arguing with myself as it jounced its way down the street, making stops every third block or so. But when the time came, and the bus was coming up on that old familiar stop, I hit the bell to be let off. Maybe it was stupid, but I had to see it one more time. Had to look up at the most beautiful stained glass window I've ever seen anywhere, touch the baptismal font where Brooks had cut Thrall eggs from my arm as I stared up at the hand-painted ceiling, see the altar where I'd been given my first communion. There was just too much of my life tied up in that place. I couldn't *not* go there. Saying thanks for something this big anywhere else would just feel . . . wrong.

It wasn't until I climbed off of the bus that I felt something odd. It was as if someone was watching. The feel of their eyes on me made my skin crawl almost as much as the sense of deep, anticipatory malice. It wasn't the collective as such, but it was Thrall. One, individual Thrall of immense power. Whoever it was, they'd expected me to come to the church—not necessarily now, but sooner or later; and they'd left me a message. The question was, did I have the courage to find out what that message was?

I took a deep breath of exhaust-riddled air and turned, intending to walk in the direction of the church.

A chill wind made the plastic rattle as I gathered up my bags. Stiffening my spine, I looked up and said a quick prayer for strength.

It wasn't there.

The church had been the tallest building for blocks. From where I stood I should have been able to see the old steeple and bell tower over the tree line to the east, even glimpse the top section of the stained glass window.

I swallowed hard around the lump in my throat. They'd torn it down. It was gone. But that wasn't all. I knew it. The mind brushing against mine wasn't finished with me. *Come see. Come see.*

I didn't want to. But I wasn't willing to give that voice the satisfaction of seeing me back down. So, my dread increasing with each step I took down the broken sidewalk, I made my way to the church site.

I'd known intellectually they'd torn it down from the moment I hadn't seen the steeple. I *thought* I'd prepared myself during the seemingly endless walk from the bus stop. I wasn't prepared. Not even close.

What once had been a beautiful red brick edifice was now an open wound in the ground; a pile of rubble taller than my head standing behind a hastily constructed fence of chain link and barbed wire. There should have been a construction crew working, but the scene was completely quiet. I knew then that they'd been ordered to stop. That the scene was meant to stay exactly like this until I came to see it. If I hadn't come, it might well have stayed the same until doomsday.

I stared at the rubble, trying to make sense of the pieces and parts lying on the raw ground. My heart ached when I saw the broken frame of a huge window arch.

They hadn't salvaged the window.

It made no sense. That window had been a gorgeous rendition of the *Pieta,* with Christ's mother cradling his broken body, weeping in her blood-stained robes. It was a work of art and had to have been worth a fortune. What kind of idiot would destroy something like that? My eyes filled with angry tears as I saw that the window wasn't the only casualty. There were huge chunks of broken marble, shattered wood from the hand-carved baptismal font. They hadn't saved *anything.*

Why? I practically screamed the question in my mind.

Look at the sign, Katydid.

I did as the voice in my mind bid, finding the sign on the far corner of the lot. I walked up, circling to the front so I could read.

FUTURE HOME OF NEW DAWN—DENVER

I threw up. My hands curled in the chain link, I leaned forward and heaved onto the ground until there was nothing left but foul-tasting bile and bitter memory.

It made a horrible, sick kind of sense. The Thrall had received one of their first significant defeats here. This was where I'd come when Monica infested me. This was where the hatchlings were killed before I could be taken over. As a result, not only Monica, but the entire Denver hive and most of their herd had died in a single night. Their loathing of this place would demand something, and now they had the power to do it.

True enough. But that's not why I did it.

Not *we. I.* I noticed the phrasing, knew it was significant. The change I'd noted in the hive a few days ago was even more pronounced now. There was only one dominant voice. One queen in charge of everything. I tried not to let that realization swim too far up into my consciousness. I didn't want *him* knowing I knew. Him: Dylan Shea—my former fiancé, the man I'd nearly died for, the man who'd died for me. Or so I had thought. But he wasn't dead . . . and he was my enemy now. The Thrall inside him had turned him, had made him as evil as Monica, or Amanda, or Larry had ever been.

God help us all.

I had to let Dylan think I believed things hadn't changed, that he was just another Thrall in the crowd. Let him believe I would make mistakes based on that belief—that I didn't know the ruthless streak he'd always hidden had given his Thrall the tools it needed to take over the hive.

Then why? I wouldn't have been able to keep either

the rage or pain from my mental voice, so I didn't bother to try.

Because of you.

When I didn't answer his voice in my mind continued, growing in mental volume as his control slipped and anger got the best of him. I stared down at the befouled concrete, my head pounding with my pulse as his words and emotions beat against my consciousness like a club.

I will destroy everything and every one *who matters to you as completely as I destroyed this building. I have stripped you of your home and your belongings; next it will be your friends, your family, your relationship with* him. *I will destroy your life while you watch helplessly. And when it is over, and you have* absolutely nothing, *then I'll take your life.*

It was a movie villain tirade. The thing was, he meant it.

The knowledge that he'd do it, that he'd use others like that just to get to me, filled me with fury. Rage gave me strength. Screw secrecy. I stood tall, stepping away from the mess at my feet. I looked out, clear-eyed. I focused my mind, my will, making sure I put every ounce of intensity I possessed into the response I spoke with both mouth and mind.

"Fuck you, Dylan Shea."

I slammed my shields down as hard as I possibly could, even resorting to the old standby of listening to AC/DC at top volume in my head.

The rat bastard. The more I thought about it, the

angrier I became until I was actually quivering with
suppressed rage. I'd thought, I'd actually *believed*
that Dylan had died a hero's death saving Tom and
Joe.

I shook my head to clear it. It didn't matter how
we got to this place. We were here. And I'd damned
well better be on my toes because the stakes had just
gone up. Hurting me was one thing. I hated it, but
I could live with it. But he was threatening people
who were dearer to me than my own life.

"Strong as an ox and almost as bright." I quoted
the dream in my mind. I almost agreed with it. Because even with this revelation I wasn't any closer
to knowing what his plans were, or how to stop
them—yet.

I started to turn my back on the sign, to just walk
away, when a piece of rubble sticking out from beneath the fence caught my eye. It was a heavy chunk
of plaster about the size of a saucer, broken from
what had once been the hand-painted ceiling of the
church entryway. Generations ago a local artist with
talent had created a ceiling that looked like a cloud-
filled summer sky. But the truly amazing part was
that, hidden in the clouds like figures in a Doolittle
painting were pictures of angels and saints. You'd
had to look closely to see them. I always looked—
even that fateful night when I'd been cuffed to the
baptismal font and Brooks had been performing surgery on my arm I'd sought for those hidden images.
I squatted down and lifted the bottom of the section
of chain link with my right hand as I worked the

piece free with my left. It came loose so suddenly that I fell onto my butt on the hard concrete, still holding my prize.

I stared at it for a long moment, looking at the delicate brush strokes almost hidden beneath the layers of grime. I looked, and found the image of St. Michael, the archangel. Even soiled and broken it was exquisite.

The image painted in the plaster glimmered slightly in the light. I didn't know how the artist managed to make the paint of the clouds pearlescent, but he had. I ran my finger gently over the plaster's surface. My finger came away filthy, but I caught a clearer image of the angel who is considered a leader in battle.

I'd told Tom once that I don't believe in omens, but looking at that chunk of plaster restored me. I felt strength, and peace, fill me. It's the feeling I get sometimes in response to my prayers. Usually, in this very church.

But ultimately a church is just a building, and God is everywhere.

Reaching into my bags I began shifting things around until I had an empty sack. With great care I slid my new prize into the bag and rose to my feet. It was time to go home and ready myself for battle.

18

I was pretty much lost in thought for the entire bus ride. There was plenty of time. I had taken the regular bus rather than an express, and it stopped every block or two to let passengers on and off. I wasn't sorry. I had lots of information to think about, and none of it made sense. It was like a jigsaw with several pieces missing, or as if I were completing a crossword and somewhere I had used the wrong word so that everything was off.

Dylan was a puzzle. The intensity of his hatred for me had been chilling. When in hell had that happened? The last time we'd actually spoken, before he'd "died," he'd made a pass at me and said he wanted me back. Now he was trying to destroy me. I didn't get it, and I felt singularly stupid. He'd said I'd chosen the wrong side, had chosen Tom. I had, and I wasn't sorry. Was it just jealousy? Was it really that simple? I mean, surely when somebody hates you that much you should be able to understand why.

And what about the werewolves? There was a wolf in my vision, and Tom had fought a wolf in the cemetery. But vampires and werewolves *hate* each other. I couldn't imagine them working together. But they seemed to be, at least on a limited basis.

Then there was the kidnapping of Dusty and Rob's baby. Why? Not only why did they take him—but why did they give him back, without any muss or fuss? I'd overheard enough to know that they'd gotten what they wanted. But what was it?

The whole situation was so damned frustrating. Lives were at stake. I needed answers. I just didn't have any.

The bell rang and the bus pulled to the curb and jounced to a halt. Looking down, I realized that I'd been so distracted I'd missed my stop by three blocks. I'd ridden as far as the stop past the neighborhood grocery. *Shit.*

I hurriedly grabbed up my packages and climbed down the rear stairs to step out onto the trashy, leaf-strewn curb. I know Regional Transportation District has crews that go around regularly cleaning the stops. This one was obviously overdue. I might have gathered up some of the detritus myself, but the trash can was overflowing, there would be nowhere to put it. Besides, it was just gross. I mean dirty diapers left lying around? Ewww.

I picked my way past the mess, heading to the grocery. As long as I was in the neighborhood I might as well pick up a few things on the way home. I'd need to eat soon, judging by the rumbling in my gut. The nausea at the construction site was past, and my body had started audibly reminding me that it needed fuel to keep moving.

I was just starting to cross the street when I caught a glimpse of something, some movement out of the corner of my eye. I turned my head to look, but there was nothing there. The hairs on the back of my neck rose. Maybe it was my imagination. *Yeah, right.*

I looked in both directions again and waited for traffic to clear. As soon as there was an opening I hurried across the street. While making my way through the parking lot I used the windows of parked cars as mirrors to check behind me. There was nothing. No one, at least no one I could see.

I tried to look as though I were completely oblivious, "just little ol' me walking to the store to pick up a few things," while in fact I'd lowered my shields and was stretching my psychic senses outward.

There! Got her! But what in the hell? It was Janine. She was trailing me, had been trailing me for days, stalking me really. She hadn't done anything yet; didn't even really have any organized plan to do anything. There was confusion, but underlying that was a black, mindless jealousy. I could hear her thoughts clear as a bell. Running through her mind, over and over like a record stuck in a single groove:

Why her? There's nothing special about her. She's not a wolf, not a surrogate. She's not even particularly pretty. I'm just as strong as she is. Why would he choose her?

She was obsessed, obsessed enough that she'd come back to Denver from Las Vegas against her mother's wishes, and probably against the terms of her bail bond. If I called Brooks he'd probably check for me. They might even be able to pick her up. I'd feel safer with her in jail. I surely would. But that would make her mother my enemy, and Tom's? Could I really afford to do that? Could I afford *not* to?

The automatic doors whooshed open and I stepped into the grocery store. I grabbed a cart from the metal corral just inside the door. Tying a knot in the top of each of the bags I brought in the store, I placed them one by one onto the shelf underneath the basket.

This was the store where Bryan worked, when he wasn't off doing spy missions for Mike. Now that I was moving into the neighborhood it was probably the store where I'd be getting a lot of my groceries. I didn't want to start out my relationship with the owners on the wrong foot, having them think I was shoplifting. Every couple of minutes I would sneak a glance outside. I couldn't see her. But I could *feel* her out there, watching. It creeped me out right proper.

It wasn't a large place, but it wasn't tiny either. There were six or seven aisles that ran most of the length of the building and stocked a bit of everything. Along the far right wall was the produce department. The refrigerator and frozen food sections were on the far left. In between were paper products, pet foods, toiletries, canned goods. But the pride and joy of the owners was the meat section along the back wall. They got their meat directly from one of the large suppliers, and cut it to order in their very own butcher section. There were people who drove all the way across town to this store just to get the freshest and best cuts of meat.

There were only two checkout stands in the front, and usually only one cashier on duty, so you generally wound up waiting in line for a bit. But nobody seemed to mind. It was just a part of doing business in the neighborhood.

I wandered through the aisles, pretending to shop mostly by tossing random things in my basket. I picked up milk and cheese in the dairy department. Bread, I definitely needed bread. Other than that, it didn't really matter.

If Janine had challenged me it would be one thing. We'd fight. I'd lose, mind you. I was unarmed. She was nearly my size and had a werewolf's super strength and speed to her advantage. I'm good, and I practice, but there's only so much training can do to level the playing field.

But she hadn't challenged me. Hadn't really *done* anything. Not *yet* anyway.

Shit, shit, shit.

"Can I help you with something, Ms. Reilly?" A gentle male voice jerked me out of my reverie and into the present. It was the store owner, Shawn Hendren. Tall, in his late forties or early fifties, he was wearing a white cap over his close-cropped white hair. The front of his well-worn blue jeans and black polo shirt were mostly covered by a white butcher's apron liberally decorated with fresh blood from the meat he'd been handling. I looked down to see what was in my hand. Head cheese? Oh, *so* no. I set it back down quickly and actually took a look at what was in the basket. Other than the milk, cheese, and bread, I'd basically grabbed an assortment of things that I wouldn't normally buy if my life depended on it. I mean, *turnips*? Please, I *hate* turnips.

Okay, I was just too distracted. I needed to get my head together and get advice on how to deal with the Janine issue. Of course, the best person to ask wasn't going to be thrilled to hear from me. "Is there any chance I can use your telephone? It's a local call."

"Sure, no problem." He set down the knife he was holding and picked up a black, multiline telephone, setting it onto the glass display counter between us.

I dialed Joe's number. Mary might be furious, but I was reasonably sure she'd want to know Janine was back, and as Acca, or former Acca, she understood werewolf politics enough to be able to give me good advice. Maybe. I hoped.

She answered on the first ring. "Hello?"

"Mary," I started to speak. Before I could utter more than her name she shouted for my brother.

"Joseph, it's your sister." Her voice was only

slightly muffled, as though she'd covered the telephone speaker with her hand. Any hope I might have had that she'd calmed down died an icy death in the chill with which she delivered those words. In fact, I was almost tempted to check for frostbite.

"Katie." Joe picked up the line almost immediately. He sounded harried. I wasn't surprised. I decided to keep the conversation as short as possible. Maybe that would minimize the amount of crap he'd have to deal with. It was at least worth a try.

"Joe, I'm sorry. It was an accident. But just so you know, I've found a place. Tom and I are going to buy Brooks's mom's house."

"Oh, thank God." He let all of his breath out in a rush. Apparently he'd been worried. Maybe even worried enough to argue with his wife. In the background I heard Bryan's voice asking "Where is she? What's happened?"

"She's fine." He repeated what I told him about the house. I heard Bryan's voice saying "Oh, thank God" in an exact echo of Joe, and what sounded like someone moving a kitchen chair to sit down abruptly. You'd almost think my brothers had been worrying about me. Nah.

"He's even selling it to us furnished."

"Give me the address. I'll call Connie for you. She left a message asking where she should bring the cat. Apparently her boyfriend's allergic. And I'll let the insurance guy know too. They're going ahead and issuing a check now that the police have arrested someone regarding the collapse of your building."

"They are?" I didn't squeal. I absolutely did *not* squeal, and certainly not loud enough to deafen my brother on the other end of the line.

"They are. There are photographs and a confession by one of the vampires. Since everybody knows you're the vampire's number one enemy and would never work with them the insurance company is paying up."

I had worked for the vampires once. Under duress. But I wasn't going to tell the insurance company that. Nope, nope, nope. Not me. Nunh unh.

"And," Joe continued, his voice sounding a little bit more pleased, "since good news comes in threes, your luggage has arrived. Airport security delivered it to the house with their profuse apologies."

• "Oh, Lord. I bet Mary just loved that." I hadn't meant to say it out loud. Oops.

"Let's just say that, under the circumstances, I think it's best if I bring all your stuff to the house *now.*"

I took a deep breath. "Actually, I called to speak to Mary."

"Uh, Kate . . . that's not such a great idea."

That was probably the understatement of the millennium. If I'd known anyone else who'd be as well connected and could help as well I'd call them instead. I didn't. "Look, I know she's still pissed. But Janine's in town. She's been following me around. She hasn't done anything yet, but—"

Joe didn't wait for me to finish. He called out to his wife, "Mary, you need to talk to Kate. Pick up the line."

There was a brief argument. I didn't hear the details. Joe apparently had used his hand to cover the speaker and it muffled the sound better than his wife's had. But in the end he won. I knew because she picked up the line.

"What's this about Janine?" Mary asked crisply.

"She's back in town. She's been following me."

"You're sure?"

"Positive." I didn't tell her I brushed the other woman's mind. I wouldn't need to. Mary knows about the psychic stuff. Probably understands it better than anyone else I know at this point.

She started swearing. She actually has a real knack for it. She started out low and slow, sort of under her breath, then let it build in both volume and intensity. I was almost impressed.

"What do you think I should do?"

"How the hell would I know?" she snarled.

"Fine," I snapped. "Never mind. I'll take care of it myself." I started to hand Shawn the receiver, until I heard her shout.

"Wait! Reilly, don't hang up."

I put the receiver back to my ear. "What?"

"I'll call Elaine and get back to you on your cell phone."

I shook my head, then realized she couldn't see it. "Can't. The battery is dead and the charger's in my suitcase."

Her martyred sigh carried clearly over the line. "Fine. Joe and Bryan were going to bring your stuff to you at the house anyway. I'll make the call while they load up the SUV and send word with them how to handle it. In the meantime, for God's sake, don't do anything stupid."

I wanted to object to that, but decided discretion was the better part of valor. She was helping me. It wouldn't do to get her any more irritated than she already was.

"Right. I'll see them at the house. Tell them to be careful. I don't want Joe pushing himself too hard and screwing up his leg again."

"You and me both. Now hang up the damned phone so I can call Elaine."

I set the handset into the receiver. "Thanks, Shawn. Sorry it took so long."

"No problem. Did I hear you right? You're buying the Brooks house?"

I nodded and grinned.

"Congratulations!" He slid off the clear plastic glove he was wearing and reached his hand across the counter to shake. "Welcome to the neighborhood! I was beginning to worry the place would never sell because of all the bad publicity."

"Not the house's fault." I shook his hand. He had a good, firm grip and the smile actually seemed sincere. "It's a nice little place, and it's in great condition. It'll be perfect for Tom and me."

"Just right for a young couple," he agreed. "So, are you stocking up the cupboards? What can I get you?" He gave a sweeping gesture to take in the meat counter. Everything looked, and smelled, wondrously fresh.

"I don't want to pick up too much. I'm on foot and I already have a few packages." I gestured at the bags. "I should probably return some of what I've already picked up."

"No problem. We can deliver. Your place is on my way home. We close at eight tonight, so I can have it to you by eight-fifteen. Unless you need it sooner?"

"No, that would be fine." I gave him a big smile. He was going to deliver. Talk about service! "I'll just take home enough to fix myself some lunch and dinner and you can bring by the rest." I pointed, he weighed and wrapped. When I'd decided I'd had enough, he rang up the amounts on an adding machine and handed me the printout. "Give this to Melinda when you go through checkout." Melinda was his wife and business partner. She was half his age, a petite sandy-haired beauty with a winning smile and a mind like a steel trap. At the moment she was hugely pregnant with their third, or maybe their fourth, daughter. She did checkout duty only when they were short-handed. The rest of the time she handled the books, payroll, ordering, and the general office work.

He gave me a wry look. "If you get a chance, could you tell Bryan that we really need him to get back to work as soon as he can. Stevie quit, and I had to fire Carole for stealing so we're short-handed. I don't want to push, but I'm getting tired of working doubles and Melinda needs to be staying off her feet."

"I'll let him know."

He looked relieved. "Thanks. He really is one of my best workers. We've missed him around here. Even the customers have been commenting on it."

I was glad to hear it. Maybe working in a grocery wasn't the most glamorous job, but it was honest work, and they were being as good to Bryan as they knew how: giving him time off to go into the clinic when he'd only been working there for a couple of months had been nice of them. He'd also been given at least one raise since he started. I didn't know if he wanted to make a career out of it, but for the moment at least it was something he was good at and seemed to enjoy.

I steered the cart through the various aisles, putting back the nonsense I'd chosen earlier and replacing it with real groceries. In my head I was running a mental tally. Sad to say, most of the money Bryan had given me would be gone in this one stop. But what was I supposed to do? We needed to eat. The cat needed a litter box. I wasn't exactly being frivolous here. Besides, I'd be getting the insurance money soon, and Tom was getting paid. It'd work out.

With positive thoughts firmly in place I went through the checkout lane and exchanged virtually every cent I'd borrowed for enough groceries to get Tom and me through the next month. I left all but two bags' worth there for later delivery. With everything I already had to carry even two bags was awkward.

I walked out of the store into a day gone gray. The sky had clouded over, the sun hidden from view.

A chill mist was falling that walked that thin line between rain and sleet. I made sure to watch my step. The sidewalk wasn't iced over yet, but it would be soon. The temperature had dropped like a stone while I'd been doing my shopping, and I could see my breath fog the air. I set off at a brisk clip, in part to stay warm, but also to get to the house as quickly as I could. I felt exposed on foot, knowing that Janine was out here somewhere watching. The bags I'd brought with me from Joe's swung back and forth as I moved, along with new bags containing a pair of frozen pizzas, paper towels, and a six-pack of soda. It wasn't exactly a feast, but I didn't figure my brothers would mind.

It didn't take long to walk the short distance to the house. As I came up the street I found myself grinning. Home. I hadn't even put the key to the door and already it felt like I was coming home.

It looked almost exactly like I remembered it, a small, neat building with green shingles and gleaming white trim. The old metal chairs had been removed from the big front porch, and somebody had put a fancy wreath with russet ribbons and brilliant autumn leaves on the front door. But otherwise it was just the same as when Bryan and I had lived there a few months back. My stride quickened, my arms were getting tired, and I was eager to get out of the chill. I'd dressed in such a hurry this morning that the clothes I had on weren't nearly warm enough. Still, I slowed to a stop when I reached the mouth of the alley.

The third dumpster down was where it had happened. It had been cleaned up, but I could still see some evidence. The fence pickets had been replaced, the new boards were beginning to weather, but still didn't match the old. The dumpster itself still had dents and scars from where Amanda had swung a scrap of lumber at me and missed.

I stared and let down my guard. Did it bother me to be back here? I'd joked about making Tom take out the trash, but would it actually bother me? Could I go down that alley, day or night, and not be bothered by the memory of Amanda trying to kill me?

Fierce barking broke out, and I shuddered. The dog had been barking that night too.

It's just a damned dog, Reilly, I told myself. *Amanda's dead. She can't hurt you. Nothing there is going to hurt you.* It was the absolute truth and I knew it. But that didn't keep my pulse from thundering in my veins; couldn't keep the adrenaline from rushing through my system with each beat of my heart.

I forced myself to take deep breaths. It took a little time, but I managed to calm my raging heartbeat. I would do this. I loved this house. I intended to make it my home. I would *not* be driven away by memories and irrational fear. I would *not.*

When I was as calm and as steady as I was going to get in one attempt I continued on, down the sidewalk and up the steps.

It was a little awkward opening the door, what with juggling the groceries and the key safe attached to the doorknob, but I managed. I stepped over the threshold, and hit the light switch. The overhead light came on, the old-fashioned cut crystal sparkling merrily as it threw a warm glow over a room filled with worn but well-tended furnishings.

The piano was still in the corner, although the lace cover and all the family photos were gone. The big old dark wood instrument had been waxed until it glowed. Someone had filled in the holes in the wall above it with spackle and repainted. If I hadn't lived here before, I might never have known there had once been family pictures hanging there.

The entire room had been given a fresh coat of Navajo White paint. I'm not a big fan of the color, but it's neutral, which is why realtors and landlords use it so often.

I was glad to see they hadn't painted over the bookshelves. The old-fashioned varnish still glowed warmly, the wood stain exactly matching the darker boards in the hardwood floor. I was sorry to see that the cases were empty. Someone had gotten rid of all the old Nancy Drews and classic paperback mysteries that had filled the shelves.

There were logs in the brick fireplace that took up most of the north wall, but I could tell they were for decoration, not for burning. There was no tinder, no kindling, just a tidy stack of three large logs piled in a perfect pyramid.

I closed the door behind me, flipping the latch to lock the dead bolt and started making my way through the house, looking at it with new eyes, from the perspective of an owner rather than a guest.

The kitchen was next. I stepped inside, setting my bags on the counter with a sigh of relief. The big gas stove was old, but I'd taken a good look at it when I'd stayed here before, and it was in perfect condition. Someone, probably Brooks, had recently replaced the piping. The kitchen set was old enough to have become trendy again. The table had chrome legs and a wide band of chrome around the edges, with a gray-flecked Formica top. The chairs had chrome legs, with metal seats and backs painted fire-engine red. They probably weren't the most comfy things in the world, but durable, oh hell yeah. They might well be around for the next ice age. The linoleum was old, but still in good shape, and had been waxed until it positively glowed.

The refrigerator wasn't new either, but it was spotless. When I opened the door I found it echoingly empty, the sole occupant an open box of baking soda.

I put the soft drinks in the freezer in hopes that they would chill before my company arrived, and stripped the frozen pizzas from their packaging and stuck them in the oven to bake. I went to throw the trash in the bin that had been under the sink. It was gone. In fact, there didn't seem to be a trash can anywhere in the kitchen or pantry. Just lots of empty cupboards and shelves.

I wadded up the wrappers and stuck them back into the plastic bag in which I'd carried them, then hooked the bag handles over the back door. I should probably make a list of things I'd need to buy, like a broom, dustpan, mop, and bucket. For the moment, however, I just made a mental list and kept exploring.

Every other room in the house had been as lovingly tended as the living room and kitchen. I loved the workmanship and character to be found in every detail, from the hardwood floors to the built-in, glass-fronted bookshelves that flanked the big brick fireplace. Oh, it wasn't perfect. There was only one bathroom, and it was small, but it had one of those monstrous old claw-foot tubs that is actually deep enough for a person my size to take a real bath and soak my tired muscles.

Right now the place seemed a little barren, mainly because all of the little "personal touches" that had made it a home had been removed—probably at the behest of a real estate agent. I've heard it said that a house with family photos and too much "stuff" won't sell. I don't understand that. To me, it's the little things that make a house a home.

It would take time to add all of those "touches," but there was one thing I wanted to do immediately. With great care I took the plaster chunk from its bag. Using one of the paper towels I'd brought home I gently wiped off the worst of the grime, then walked into the living room to give it a place of honor at the center of the fireplace mantel.

I was glad to see that the master bedroom hadn't been repainted. I suppose it was because they'd have had to steam off the old-fashioned floral wallpaper I loved so much. It would have been a lot of work, and a hired crew would've charged a fortune for it. So the flowers remained, along with the antique furniture and crimson drapes.

Brooks's childhood bedroom was next. The formerly sky-blue walls were now a neutral cream, the blue and white plaid curtains and white chenille bedspread replaced by heavy drapes and a matching comforter in the same shade of midnight blue as the carpeting. The darker color made the room seem smaller to me, almost cramped. Here, too, all evidence of occupancy was gone. There were no athletic trophies on the shelf. It was just a bland, impersonal room.

I wandered from place to place, thinking about where I would put the various possessions Tom and I had that had survived the building collapse to fit them in with the existing pieces, thinking about the changes I'd suggest to Tom when he got off shift.

A heavy knock on the front door startled me enough to make me jump and give one of those odd little "eepy" screams. Okay, maybe I was a *little bit* nervous and creeped, but it wasn't about the house.

I stopped and peeked around the living room curtains to catch a glimpse of who was visiting. A black and white Denver police cruiser was parked in front. A uniformed officer was standing in front of the door, his expression studiously blank.

"I'll be right there," I called out, and hurried over to the door. I swung it open and came face to face with a handsome blue-eyed brunette.

"Can I help you, officer?"

"Ma'am. I just got a call from the neighbors. I

understand that this residence is supposed to be vacant. May I ask what you're doing here?"

"Come on in. I've got to check the pizza in the oven." I could smell it. It wasn't burning yet, but it would if I didn't get the heat turned off.

He followed me into the kitchen. I could see him looking around, his eyes taking in everything from my disheveled appearance to my plastic bag luggage. He thought I was a squatter. I almost didn't blame him.

"The owner is Detective John Brooks. He's renting the place to me furnished with an option to buy. I don't have anything of my own because my building collapsed in the blizzard."

He thought about that for a moment. "Do you know which station he operates out of?" He phrased it pleasantly enough, but I knew he was trying to verify my right to be here. Fair enough. I had nothing to hide.

"It's the one on Colorado and 13th, a couple blocks from the park."

Reaching for his radio, he hit the button and spoke to the dispatcher. "Can you patch me through to a Detective John Brooks at the Colorado station? I need to know if he's rented a house to a . . ." he paused, waiting for me to provide the name.

"Kate Reilly."

He blinked a couple of times rapidly. Apparently the name was familiar even if he hadn't recognized my appearance.

"Kate Reilly," he repeated. He slid the radio back

into its holster. Meanwhile, I began rummaging around in drawers hoping to find something I could use to get the pizza out of the oven. They were empty, of course. Just my luck. Crap.

"I take it you forgot utensils?" He sounded amused.

"Last time I stayed here they were still in the drawer."

Before I could say anything else I heard the slam of car doors and running feet. "Katie! Are you all right?" Bryan burst into the house with Mary at his heels, screen door slamming behind them.

"I'm fine. We're in the kitchen. One of the neighbors just called the cops to make sure I had a right to be here."

"Oh, thank God." Mary stood in the doorway, practically shaking with nerves. She was upset enough that I was surprised. Okay, we're friends, but I really wouldn't have thought she'd care so much. Too, there was no sign of her beast. Then again, she's always had excellent control.

Joe came up behind her. "We thought—" he didn't finish saying what they thought. Probably best, all things considered.

The policeman's radio crackled to life. "Brooks says she's okay."

"I kind of figured that out." He grinned at me when he said it, but he clicked the button on his radio and gave a more "official" response to the dispatcher.

"Well, I'll leave you folks to it." He turned toward the doorway. Joe and Mary immediately moved out of the way. "Have a good evening, and good luck with the pizza."

"Thank-you, officer."

"No problem. I'll tell the neighbor you're the new tenant, ask her to let everyone know you belong."

"Thanks."

I walked with him to the front entrance, watching until he'd reached the edge of the property before closing the door behind him.

"Why would you need luck with a pizza?" Bryan seemed genuinely curious.

"Someone cleaned out the kitchen. There are no utensils, hot pads, plates. Nada." I turned to Joe. "I don't suppose anything survived from my kitchen at the apartment?"

He shook his head.

"Well, doesn't that just suck." I stood there, hands on my hips, staring in frustration at the perfectly cooked meal I couldn't touch.

Bryan laughed. "I'll run over to the store. I need to check in anyway, see if they're willing to give me my job back. Be back in a flash."

He took off, leaving me with only Joe and Mary for company. It could've been awkward, hell, it *should've* been. But apparently Mary was so glad I hadn't killed, been killed, or called the cops on Janine that she was ready to let go of some of her earlier anger. Besides, I think she was legitimately curious about the place where Tom and I would be living. She and Joe were wandering from room to room, commenting to each other about what they saw. They came out to the living room together to give their verdict.

"Nice, very nice," Joe observed. "Is the furnace gas forced air?"

"I think so. I honestly haven't taken the time to go into the basement and look."

"Katie!" He was shocked.

"Joe, don't fuss. We can replace the furnace if we have to. Brooks is giving us one hell of a good price on the place."

"And you're okay about the thing with Amanda?" He didn't sound too sure.

"I'm fine," I told him. Okay, well, maybe *fine* was an exaggeration at the moment. But I'd be fine.

"Hmpfh." He didn't seem to believe me. Then again, I've never been much of a liar.

"Joe," Mary suggested sweetly, "why don't you run out to the car and get the cat. You know how much he hates me."

"You've got Blank with you?" I couldn't keep the delight from my voice. I would've gladly followed Joe out to the car, but Mary kept me back with a hand on my arm. Apparently she'd been getting rid of him so we could have a minute of privacy.

"I didn't tell Joe this, but Elaine had been having one of her people with Janine at all times. Not exactly under guard, but close enough. Annie was on duty the night she escaped. Janine ripped her throat out, stole her husband's car, and disappeared."

My stomach tightened into a knot of worry. "Did Annie make it?"

"She's recovering. It didn't kill her. She may even be okay in a day or two. I understand she has exceptional healing abilities, even for our kind. But the point is, Elaine has sent people out looking for Janine. She's trying to get her back and into a treatment center before the police find out she's jumped bail. So far they haven't had any luck. Now that you've spotted her, they're coming here. The official story is they're coming to help us set up security for the Conclave."

"Okay." I kept looking at her, waiting for the other boot to drop. Because she was holding back something important, some bit of news I wasn't going to like. I could tell by the tense way she held her body and the tone of her voice.

"Elaine is coming with them. She's asked to stay with you."

"No. Oh, hell no. So, so, no."

Mary sighed and closed her eyes. "I'm sorry, Katie. She's insisting. Says it's the only way she can be sure of your safety."

"That's not why she's doing it." I sounded sullen. No surprise there. I felt sullen, and angry. I hadn't even moved into my house yet. Tom was still on shift and already I was supposed to have some werewolf dignitary staying over?

"No, she's doing it to be sure nobody gets killed. Not you, and not Janine."

She stopped talking abruptly. I heard Joe's heavy, unsteady footfalls on the porch steps accompanied by the familiar yowling of a supremely angry pussycat. "Blank," I called to the cat, and was rewarded by the sound of him scratching at the plastic of the cat carrier.

I took the cat carrier into the master bedroom and shut the door behind me. Setting the carrier onto the bed, I opened the cage door.

He came out cautiously, almost twenty pounds of fur so white he practically gleamed.

"Oh, my God, she gave you a bath." I didn't look, but I was betting his claws had been clipped as well. Nothing was going to hide the criss-crossing of old scars that decorated his nose, but other than that he looked every inch the pampered purebred. I was stunned. Well and truly shocked. "And she lived to tell the tale? You didn't tear her apart for her trouble?" I chucked him under his chin and was rewarded with a *look*. He might be purring, but the look in those gleaming green eyes was one of pure disgust and implied accusation. *How dare I!*

"Sorry buddy. I didn't know she'd do that." I stroked him gently in apology, only to have him roll over, grab my hand in his front paws and try to claw my wrist with his left. Lucky for me he'd chosen the left hand, and the foreshortened claws only managed to scrape harmlessly against my cast. "Hey, stop that." I tapped him lightly on the nose with my index finger. It made him sneeze. I laughed, and he glared at me again.

"Yeah, well, can't say as I blame you. It's been rough for me too. And looks like it's going to get worse before it gets better. Just wait until you meet our guest for the next couple of days." I sighed. I didn't want Elaine staying here. I really didn't. And the cat would *hate* it. He's barely gotten to the point where he gets along with Tom. All the other werewolves freak him out completely.

"I'm sorry, bud. I wish I could see a way around it, but I really don't."

That, of course, was the rub.

19

I was asleep, in a comfortable bed, Blank curled up next to me purring. Down the hall I could hear Bryan taking a shower, getting ready for an early shift at the grocery. That was reality. I knew it. But that didn't change what I was seeing, hearing, and *feeling.*

It was morning, about ten o'clock judging from the height of the sun from the horizon. I ran through a deserted park, the snow crisp beneath my pads as my paws touched down. I could feel the grass beneath the thin layer of powder-dry snow, dormant, waiting for spring. My breath misted the air, but I wasn't cold. In fact, it felt good.

In the distance the Canada geese on the lake grew restive, flapping their wings and honking a warning. My mouth watered at the thought of hot blood and raw meat, but I fought down the hunger. There was no time for that. I needed to get back to the apartment and change before going to the convention center.

Even in this small pocket of wilderness I could taste the car exhaust in the air. Denver was known for its "brown cloud" in the winter and today was no exception. Running through the bare trees, I could hear the cars whizzing by on the highway I couldn't see. An eight foot privacy fence had been placed between the park and the highway, but that was on the far side of the lake, by the access road where I'd left the car. It wasn't visible from here.

Stupid human. Her own fault really. The first lesson is always to eliminate anyone who may be a threat. Caesar forgave his enemies, and died with a knife in his back.

There was no warning; just sudden, excruciating pain as a section of my hindquarters literally exploded outward in a mess of blood and bone. I went down in a graceless heap. Only then did the sound of a rifle cut the winter air; a rifle, and howls of challenge. Four—no, six—voices, converging from different directions. I couldn't smell them yet over the scent of meat and blood, but I heard them, and I knew they were coming for me. I wasn't whimpering in pain because I couldn't feel anything below my waist. That was bad. Very bad. Because if I couldn't feel, I couldn't move, wouldn't be able to fight. Already I could feel my strength flowing away with my blood on the snow.

The first of them appeared in silhouette at the crest of the hill. He was a huge, brindled male. He posed there, deliberately letting me catch his scent.

It was the scent of a vampire.

"Katie, wake up!" Bryan was standing by the edge of the bed, shaking me hard. I came to myself with a soft gasp, as if I were relearning how to breathe. It had been so *real*. Too real for a dream. I wasn't that good at telling dreams from visions but sometimes, like now, it was obvious.

I clung to Bryan's arm, trying to wrench myself out of the psychic and firmly into reality. I didn't want to lose the gist of the vision, I knew it was too important to let go of it, but I sure as hell didn't want to get sucked back down for the finale. They say that if you die in your dreams you can die in real life. I *so* didn't want to find out if that particular belief was or wasn't true.

"Are you okay?" He looked down at me with worried eyes. The black polo shirt he wore as part of his work uniform gaped away from his neck just a little, revealing the bandage that covered one of the many healing puncture wounds that still decorated his body. I shuddered, remembering how close he'd come to dying just a few short days ago.

"Katie, answer me. You're really starting to scare me."

"I'll be fine." The whispered words came out hoarse, barely audible. I worked to steady my breathing. Inhale, exhale. Easy. So why was I having such a hard time with it?

"Liar." But he smiled. I'd relaxed my deathgrip on his arm, so he pulled away enough to sit down on the edge of the bed. "Was it a vision?"

"Yeah."

"What about?"

"Blood, death, Caesar."

"Caesar?" His eyebrows rose high enough to disappear beneath the rumpled shock of damp blond hair he hadn't had time to comb out yet.

"It's a long story." My voice sounded normal. In fact, I was getting my act back together. The vision wasn't real. Or at least it wasn't real right now. In the reality of the moment I was me, I was safe, whole, and in desperate need of the bathroom. My brother had less than fifteen minutes to get ready for work. Even if the vision represented today—it had been 10:00 A.M. Denver time. I had a couple of hours. I could pee, get myself some coffee, and let my brother get on with his day before I tried to process the details of what I'd seen and figure out what the hell to do with the information.

"You'd better get moving or you're going to be late," I warned him.

"I can stay if you need me." He was so serious, even solicitous. I didn't mean to peek into his mind, but I caught a stray glimpse anyway. He was worried that staying here, after what happened, was causing me problems.

"Nah. Go. I'll be fine." I shoved him off of the bed with both hands so I could climb from beneath the covers.

"You're sure?"

"Positive." I rose to my feet, grateful that I was decently covered in a baggy old pair of gray sweatpants and matching tee-shirt. Since I've been living with Tom I've spent most nights sleeping in lingerie or the nude. He prefers it. But since Bryan had decided to stay over, I'd gone for modesty. I was glad now. I could run down the hall to the bathroom without flashing him.

"All right. I'll go. But call if you need me." He was talking to me through the closed bathroom door.

"I will."

I don't think he believed me, but he left anyway.

I finished my business and washed my hands. I started a bath running. Considering the size of the tub, it was probably going to take a while to fill. That was fine with me. I wanted to get some coffee started. Bryan, God love him, had given me a housewarming present last night—a coffeemaker. Joe and Mary's contribution had been a set of dishes for eight. Ruby provided pots and pans. It had all been part of the stuff Joe and Bryan had brought over last night. The luggage was in the bedroom. Everything else was in the garage, waiting for me to unpack.

Thinking about it made me smile. I have friends. The kind of friends who come through for you in a pinch. For a long time after Amanda betrayed me with Dylan I hadn't trusted anyone enough to let them close. I mean, when your fiancé cheats with your best friend it kind of makes you doubt your taste in relationships. Oh, Michael had been around, but he'd been around forever. Peg had broken through, but other than that, I really hadn't let myself go. But over the past couple of years things had changed. I'd started socializing again. Loving Tom had given me the courage to let others into my life as well, people like Brooks, Mary, Dusty and Rob, even Ruby.

And despite Dylan's threats, I didn't think they were going anywhere. For one thing most of them are just too damned stubborn. They've seen me through "battle conditions" before. They wouldn't abandon me. As to whether he could kill them— well, most all of them are pretty damned tough, particularly when they're on their guard. I'd warn them all, of course. But I doubted they'd back down, or change much of how they handled their lives.

I wandered into the kitchen and retrieved the coffee can from the pantry. It was only when I'd opened the bin to the coffeemaker that I realized why Bryan hadn't started a pot brewing. No filters. Crap.

It was still dark outside, dammit. I needed caffeine, and I wanted it steaming hot in my very own kitchen. There had to be something I could use. *Think, Reilly. Think.*

I glanced around. My eyes lit up at the sight of salvation. Paper towels. Perfect. Well, not perfect, but good enough, by God. I might get a few grounds in my cup, but I'm tough. I can handle it.

Just the aroma of the ground coffee made me feel more alert. Pavlovian probably, but who cares? I sure didn't. I set up the machine to make a full six cups, hit the button, and went back to the bedroom to pick out clothes for the day.

I started rifling through the dressier clothes from the suitcase, mainly because I expected to be meeting with the insurance adjuster and running other important errands. Theoretically it should not make a damned bit of difference how you're dressed under these kinds of circumstances, but the fact is that you are judged by your appearance every time you step out the door. Women are judged more harshly than men, too, or at least differently. I needed to look businesslike, competent, but nonthreatening enough that nobody would be defensive right out of the box. That meant no leather, which was really okay since my most recent purchases were still in the evidence locker at the police station in Beaver Falls. The brown suit Joe had bought me was still dirty and wrinkled, so that was out. I hated the idea of wearing my good coral suit, but it was still clean and reasonably unwrinkled. I hadn't wound up using it on the Vegas trip. Of course it didn't offer much opportunity for weapons concealment—once I got weapons—which I *really* needed to do. Sooner rather than later.

So coral it was, with a cream colored silk blouse and, ugh, hose and the matching heels. Here's hoping I didn't have to do any running, or even much walking.

I carried the clothes into the bathroom with me and hung them up by hooking the hanger necks over the handle of the linen cabinet. If I was lucky the steam would get rid of the last of the wrinkles. If not, too bad. I didn't have an iron yet.

The tub was just about ready, and the temperature was perfect, hot enough to relax me but not so toasty as to leave me parboiled. I had my coffee. There was only one more thing I needed before I could strip and sink gratefully into my bath. The cell phone. Because I knew that just as soon as I was naked, wet, and relaxed the damned thing would ring. Not psychic premonition. Just experience. Lots and lots of past experience.

True to form, I had just started shampooing when it rang. I ducked underwater long enough to rinse out the worst of the bubbles before grabbing the phone from off of the toilet lid. "Good morning, gorgeous," I sang. It was Tom. Had to be. Only he would have the courage to call me this early in the morning.

"Good morning yourself. How was your first night in the house?"

"It would've been better with you here," I answered forthrightly. "But Blank and I managed. Bryan stayed over. He had an early shift at work."

"Sounds like you didn't miss me at all."

"Oh, I missed you." I made my voice a sexy purr. "As soon as you get back home I'll prove it."

"Promises, promises," he teased.

"Are you alone? Would you like a little phone sex?" I made the offer. I'm a little shy, and still somewhat awkward at it, but I discovered that playing along sometimes keeps things very, very hot between the two of us. I guess it's all that anticipation. I might blush purple and squirm with embarrassment at some of the things he says, but it gets under my skin. And I just can't stop thinking about it. Apparently neither can he, because the times that we've talked dirty he's come back from his shift rarin' to go.

"No to the first, which means no to the second."

"Aw, damn." I was actually disappointed.

He laughed, and it was as thick and rich as chocolate. "I love you, Katie."

"I love you too."

"So, is there any news?" he asked.

I had to think for a minute. An awful lot had happened in a really short period of time. I wasn't even sure where to begin. I did know one thing for a fact. I was *not* going to tell him about Janine stalking me, Dylan or the threats he'd made, or even the vision of the werewolf I'd had this morning. Those bits of bad news were all going to wait until he was off duty. His job regularly puts him in life-and-death situations. I *so* didn't want him going into one of them distracted. The disasters could wait. Good news, however, was fair game. I could share it all in good conscience and did. I started with the insurance check, then moved on to the luggage being returned, our stuff being moved for us by my brothers, and Joe's second interview.

"What aren't you telling me?"

Damn, he's a suspicious man.

"Katie—" his voice carried a very real warning. Tom has a thing about my keeping secrets from him.

He thinks I shut him out of the dangerous parts of my life. I don't, not anymore. I learned my lesson after I almost lost him. But timing is everything and now was so not the time to tell him some of this stuff.

"All right, there are some things that aren't great news too, but they can wait until you're off shift."

"I don't like that."

"Let's just say you'd better come home prepared for company."

"Why?"

"Elaine Johnston is going to be staying with us, at least until the end of the Conclave." It was actually the least of the bad news, but I was crossing my fingers that it would be enough to sidetrack him from asking more questions.

"Oh, fucking goodie."

I let out a harsh bark of laughter. I couldn't help it. He'd summed up my feelings on the matter to absolute perfection. "That's kind of how I felt."

"This has something to do with Janine, doesn't it?"

Damn. There are times when I really wish he wasn't as bright as he is good looking. This was definitely one of them. Thinking on my feet, I managed to answer his question with one of my own. Oddly enough, I even wanted the answer. It might even be important.

"Tom, did Janine follow you out here from Vegas before or after all the publicity with Samantha?" Tom had been around for my original confrontation with Monica Mica, in fact it was when we'd first started dating. But while there'd been plenty of publicity at the time, none of it had mentioned him. He'd managed to stay under the radar quite a lot longer than I had.

"Before. It's one of the reasons the pack was pushing me to dump you. She was agitating even then."

"But how did she find you? I mean, you knew she was unstable. I assume you didn't just leave a forwarding address."

There was a long, intense silence. When he answered it was very quietly. "No. I didn't. And no one I know would've told her."

"Would someone in the Denver pack—" He interrupted me before I could finish the sentence.

"Not a chance. They all knew it had ended badly, and she has a reputation for being . . . difficult. Nobody wanted that kind of a diplomatic mess."

"So how'd she find out?"

"That's a damned good question. I've chewed on that for a long time."

I knew he'd be thinking about it for the next two days, too. It was the kind of puzzle that would worry at your mind when there was nothing else to occupy you. But I knew he'd be able to set it aside to do his duty.

"Is that everything?" Persistent little devil. Dammit.

"No, it isn't," I snapped irritably. He was pushing. He knows how much I hate that and he was doing it anyway.

"Well?"

"Tell you what. I'll show you mine if you show

me yours." I didn't mean for it to sound as bitchy as it came out.

His voice dropped almost an octave, and took on a dangerous edge. "What's that supposed to mean?"

"It means that you've been keeping things from me too. 'For my own good' no doubt."

I heard him inhale sharply. I'd hit a nerve. But he kept his cool enough to act innocent. "I don't know what you're talking about."

Bullshit. My mind brushed his, and I saw clearly a lot of the things he'd hidden. Some of them were incredibly important, and it pissed me off. I couldn't help myself. I just started spouting words, not even sure where they were going until they reached air.

"Really? Are you saying you just *forgot* to tell me that the werewolf you fought at the cemetery wasn't a rogue working with the vampires—that it smelled, and tasted, *like* a vampire, and that a good third of the bites on my brother and the priest who died didn't come from human mouths, and that they showed signs of having had blood sucked through them anyway?"

Silence stretched for long moments on the other end of the line. I knew he was still there. I could hear his harsh breathing. I let it drag on for a bit, mainly because I really was angry now. Maybe I could have found out more from my dreams if I'd known what to look for.

He sighed, but didn't answer.

"Fine." I tried not to sound bitter and failed. "We can talk about it when you get off shift. Along with everything else. But know this, if I have to tell you everything the reverse is true too."

"I suppose." His enthusiasm was underwhelming. In fact, he sounded just a teeny bit bitter, which meant it was probably time to change the subject. Because ultimately I didn't want to cause a real fight. "Before I forget. Thursday night we're having dinner with Brooks and his wife to sign the lease. I was thinking maybe we'd fix steaks. There's a brick barbeque pit in the back yard."

"Sounds great." It sounded flat and cold, even though I knew he meant it. But he wasn't quite ready to let go of the previous conversation. He sighed again, and this time the sound was more sad than martyred. "Look, I'm sorry I didn't tell you about that stuff. I should've. I've gotta go now, but we really will talk when I get off shift. I love you, Katie."

"I love you too. I'll keep the bed warm for you." If he could bend, so could I. I'm proud, but I'm not stupid. I love him. I want the relationship to work. That means sometimes one, or both, of us is going to have to swallow our pride a little and compromise.

"Do that." I could sense his gratitude. It was warm and gentle as a blanket against my psychic senses. It made me a lot more hopeful about the conversation we'd be having in a couple of days.

I finished getting ready and was on my way out the door by 8:30. Before I left I took my cell phone off of the charger and called Mary. I knew she'd taken the whole week off to get ready for the Conclave. I was hoping she hadn't already left for the convention center because I didn't have her cell number programmed into my phone yet.

"What do you need now, Katie?" She sounded tired and stressed. I knew she'd be glad when the meetings were over and life could get back to normal. I was pretty sure everyone who'd had to deal with her the past few weeks felt the same way. But even I have enough sense not to say something like that out loud.

"I'm headed out to take care of a bunch of errands and I wanted to know if you have a time for Elaine's flight? I want to make sure I'm home by the time she gets here."

"Hang on. Let me look it up." I heard her rummaging around for a minute in the background. "It arrives at 7:00 P.M., on United. She's taking a cab, so we won't have to meet her at the airport."

"Oh good. That should give me plenty of time."

"What all are you planning on doing?"

I gave her a quick rundown of my list. She laughed. "Your day sounds almost as bad as mine. I bet you won't manage even half that."

"Probably not," I admitted. "And while I'm out, is there anything you need me to help with?" *Say no. Please say no.*

"Not today. Go run your errands. But if I don't make some real progress I may be asking you for help tomorrow."

"In that case I won't schedule anything."

"Thanks."

I hung up and slid the phone into my jacket

pocket before heading out the door. I was looking good, feeling sharp as I hurried down the street to the bus stop. Mary's words had motivated me. The best way to get me to do something is to tell me I can't, that it's impossible. Not that I'm contrary or anything.

I plopped myself onto the wooden bus bench and pulled out my phone. I might as well make calls and schedule as many appointments as I could manage while I waited. Yeah, strangers might overhear. I could live with that.

My first call was to my insurance agent. He transferred me to the adjuster handling my claim. Ralph Hendrix was not a happy man. Part of it was personal. His daughter was currently enrolled in a vampire halfway house. Too, I was costing his company money. A lot of money. He hated it and would've taken it out on me if he hadn't suspected (correctly) that I'd report him to his superiors if he behaved as anything less than a professional. I wished I'd had a chance to talk to him when Tom was with me. He was enough of a chauvinist to at least hide his emotions when a man was present. But Tom had to work. So I was going to handle it alone. And professional self-preservation wasn't quite enough to keep the hostile tone from his voice when he explained that they were considering the building a total loss. They'd already cut the check for the bank and sent it to them, so the loan was paid off. I could pick up my checks for the contents and the remainder on the building itself. But had I chosen someone to do the cleanup and demolition? Or, if I wasn't planning to rebuild, he'd been contacted by a couple of different developers who were interested in the property and would include clearing the lot as part of the package. Had I considered that option?

I hadn't, but I told him I would.

Did I want to sell, or rebuild? Land in lower downtown is at a premium. I would get a great price. I could pay off all the debt I'd incurred and probably still have more than enough to buy the house and replace my vehicle. It would give me a fresh start. I'm not a builder. I'm more a handyman. Give me the basics and I can do maintenance and improvements, but building something from scratch? I'd have to hire that out. I've heard more than a few horror stories about that sort of thing over the years. And then there's all the bureaucratic red tape that I'd have to wade through. Could I even *afford* it? And more than one developer had already expressed an interest in buying. That was a good sign. But did I really want to give it up?

There was only one way to be sure. I needed to actually see the ruins for myself. I'd managed to avoid it yesterday, but it was time. And if seeing Our Lady of Perpetual Hope Church in ruins had been hard I knew that facing this would be downright hellish. I'd poured so much of myself into the renovations. It had taken years of literal blood, sweat, and tears.

Damn Dylan anyway.

I climbed onto the bus that would take me downtown along with a couple of commuters dressed for a day at the office. Taking an empty seat near the back, I thought about everything that had happened to me recently. How much of it had been manufactured by the Thrall? The attack at the airport was obvious; and we had proof about the building collapse and the church. Bryan's injuries had definitely been Thrall-induced, although frankly, that could've been the result of his spying more than an attack on me. Someone had let Janine know where Tom was. It would have been a perfect way to unbalance my relationship. In fact, it had almost succeeded. Had that been a "gift" from Dylan as well? How long had he been planning his revenge? When did his heart turn from love to hate? There was no way of knowing. But I wouldn't have put any of this past him, thinking back.

The blocks rolled by. The bus was getting more and more crowded. Pairs of people were sharing nearly every seat, but nobody made any move to sit next to me. I suppose I probably looked forbidding. I was certainly getting more and more angry. As we drove past the stop that would have led me to Our Lady Church I found myself grinding my teeth, my fists clenched in impotent fury. It took a real effort to relax my jaw muscles, to fight down my rage. He wanted me angry—too angry to think, so that I would react, play right into whatever plans it was he'd made. I would *not* give him that satisfaction. I was better than that. I had to be. But oh, God it was hard.

A few more blocks and we were nearly to the Market Street Station, easy walking distance from the old place. The lurching of my stomach had nothing to do with the abrupt stop the bus made. I trooped off after the other passengers, but where most of them headed across the street to catch the mall shuttle toward the highrises uptown, I walked in the opposite direction, my heels clicking harshly against the dark stone squares that formed the station pavement.

Already it was a warm enough morning that I didn't mourn the lack of a coat. My suit jacket was enough, so long as I moved at a brisk pace. My breath didn't even fog the morning air. Hard to believe that just a few short days ago the city had been locked in the throes of a freak fall blizzard.

I passed a couple of restaurants, a high-end liquor store, and the building that warehoused all of the books for one of the city's big independent bookstores. If I went two more blocks straight ahead I'd come to Bernardo's. But not yet. That was where I'd head *after,* assuming I wanted either breakfast, liquid restoration, or both. I turned right, and caught my first glimpse of the disaster—yellow warning tape that flapped in the breeze, making a sharp slapping sound. It had been wrapped around parking meters and attached to temporary construction fencing that reminded me forcibly of yesterday.

I paused, steeling myself, then continued forward.

It was both better, and worse, than I'd expected.

Oh, the building was a total loss. No doubt about that. But the sight of it didn't hurt me the way I'd expected. Maybe it was because I'd had all this time to prepare; maybe I was just numb. But it didn't devastate me the way the loss of the church had. It was just a wrecked building: something to be torn down and replaced in the never-ending cycle of life and death in the city. Don't get me wrong, I was sorry and sad. But I'd seen glimpses of it on television; and had been warned by Tom and Joe's reaction to my coming here and the condition of those few of my things they'd managed to salvage.

I heard a vehicle slow down near the curb behind me. There was a soft whirr as the window rolled down.

"Hello, Buffy."

I knew that voice, knew who I'd see when I turned to look behind me. Part of me brightened at the voice, and part of me wanted to turn and punch him in the nose.

Lewis Carlton is a former NBA all-star. In his prime he played power forward and no one in the game had been better. Three championship rings decorate those oversized hands. He stood seven foot two inches in his bare feet, every bit of it solid muscle. He sported tattoos, piercings, and, now that he'd retired, a perfectly lovely set of fangs. He was the queen of the Pueblo hive, thanks to my intervention. From the minute we'd met I'd found him fascinating, pretty much the same way birds find snakes fascinating. The former Denver queen had brought him into Denver for the sole purpose of intimidating me. It had worked. But in the process we'd formed an odd bond. He still scares me, and I don't trust him, but I can't help but like him.

He pulled his Hummer to the curb and unfastened the seat belt. He was moving slowly, but I really didn't notice it at first. I was too busy wondering how he'd tracked me down. I was so curious, in fact, I asked. After all, the worst he'd do is refuse to tell me.

"How'd you find me?"

He shrugged one shoulder and tipped his head. "Wasn't hard. Our people have been tapping your brother's phone for months. I made a couple of calls to my peeps, the ones who don't know I'm on the big guy's shit list. They read me the conversation you had with the wolf bitch this morning." He climbed out of the vehicle, slamming the door closed behind him.

"They're *what*?"

"Oh for God's sake, Buffy, grow up," he snapped. "If you keep expecting your enemies to behave themselves and play fair you'll wind up getting killed."

I stared at him for a long silent moment, too shocked to speak. Normally Carlton is the epitome of style. Today, he just looked bad. His burnished black skin had gray undertones and he slouched in a way that spoke of injury and pain. He wore his usual dark shades, so I couldn't see his eyes, but the black nylon warm-up pants and a matching tank clung to his body in spots and the dark color didn't quite hide darker stains. That's when I noticed he was swaying on his feet. If he dropped, he might bring down the rest of the building.

"What in the hell happened to you?" I hurried over to his side. Sliding my arm around his waist I walked him over to the steps of the building next to mine and helped him lower himself carefully into a sitting position.

I sat next to him, not quite propping him up, but available if he needed it.

He was moving badly enough that I had to wonder just how hurt he was, and whether I should be taking him to the emergency room or calling an ambulance.

He gave me a watered down version of his usual smile. "Tactful as always."

"Should I dial 9-1-1?"

He shook his head. "Don't bother. I've only got a few minutes before they shut me down. I'll be dead before an ambulance could get here."

The words were all the more shocking because he said them so matter-of-factly. I didn't doubt him. I couldn't. I've seen the collective cut down individual members who defied it. But killing Carlton would wipe out his whole hive. Why would they do that? What had he done?

"Why—" I started to ask, but he waved me to silence. "Things have changed, Buffy, but you've probably figured that out by now. The Thrall isn't a collective any more, at least not the way it used to be.

It's the difference between socialism and a dictatorship. He's killed all of us who were strong enough to
stand up to him. Every one of us who argued against
his plan is dead or dying. He's replaced all of us with
his puppets." Giving a grunt of pain he twisted his
body, reaching to pull a large brown envelope from
the small of his back. "Use this. Find a way to stop
him."

As I reached out to take the envelope my hand
brushed his. I felt the attack he'd been fighting hit like
a crushing pressure against my mind. It hurt. Oh *God,*
how it hurt. I threw everything I had, every ounce of
strength and training I'd developed in my years fighting against them, into my shielding. It was too much
power for me to simply block the attack. This was so
far beyond what Monica had been capable of that it
was breathtaking.

I wasn't strong enough to fight it straight on. Instead, I created a dome of power that would take the
energy and redirect it downward, channeling it into
the earth until it grounded itself in the soil beneath
our feet. I pulled power from the wolves, from the
Thrall themselves, to channel into the former NBA
queen. Light and heat surrounded me and then
pain . . . flashes timed to my heartbeat that I let bleed
into the ground. I felt Dylan's rage as he fought to
destroy the one I protected. He poured more power
into the link, tried to reestablish what he'd given up
freely.

It felt similar to when I'd channeled power into
Bryan's brain to reopen scarred tissue. But this time,

I was closing *down* tissue. I could feel Carlton's symbiont react, felt the desperation it used against me to control the big man. As I let the power slide over and past us, I felt Dylan's hive react with alarm. But it was too late. They'd severed their ties with him too much in an attempt to protect themselves from his death. And in doing so, they'd allowed me to save the *man,* at the expense of the beast.

If I hadn't been sitting, I would've fallen. As if from a distance I heard Carlton collapse, his face smacking the concrete with an audible snap that told me he'd broken at least one of his fangs.

I'd done all I could. But if he didn't get help in the next few minutes he was going to die. His daughter would lose the father who had loved her enough to become a Thrall to save her from a coma. I wondered if she even knew.

It was hard to focus my mind and my eyes were watering so hard that everything was a washed-out blur. But I fumbled in my bag until I found my cell phone. I dialed for help and prayed, prayed for a man who should have been my enemy and just wasn't.

20

I had a migraine. I hate the damned things, but they seem to be the price I pay for psychic trauma. I sat in a darkened room off of the emergency room of the new St. Elizabeth's Hospital, waiting for Dr. Watkins, the neurologist who'd worked with me before, to prescribe one of his magic potions to take the pain away. He'd promised to stop by for a second before he scrubbed up for Carlton's surgery.

It hadn't been the closest emergency room, not by a long shot. But St. Elizabeth's had the best research and treatment facilities in the country for working with the vampires.

The new St. E's had moved into what had been scheduled to be the VA facilities out by the Anschutz Medical Campus, before Congress had forced a change of plan. It was on the grounds of what had formerly been Fitzsimons Army Medical Center. It had been easier and less costly to convert the VA buildings than to tear down and rebuild what Samantha had destroyed. Down time had been minimal. Almost none of the staff had been lost. But the new location wasn't downtown, it was in one of the eastern suburbs. I'd wound up taking a wild ambulance ride all the way across town to get here.

Carlton wasn't dead. His Thrall was. He was injured and unconscious, but there was hope. His doctors were saying things like "unprecedented" and "a first." I think there was actually a line of people competing for the privilege of watching the surgery. They were going to try to go through his nose and remove the symbiont from his brain. If they managed it, they might be able to save his life. They didn't have much hope, but it was his only chance.

The cops, the EMTs, and the doctors were all confused. At first they'd assumed I was the one who'd beaten him. I am, after all, reputed to be the scourge of vampire kind. That I hadn't, that I was in fact working to save him, just baffled the hell out of everybody, me included.

"Ms. Reilly." Dr. Watkins stepped into the room, turning the dimmer switch just enough to give him illumination to work by, but still keeping it dim enough that it wasn't excruciating. He was wearing green surgical-style scrubs at the moment and I wasn't sure if it was from a previous patient or if he was getting ready for Carlton. He was not only a neurologist, but a skilled surgeon as well. I might not like the hospital

administrator, but Simms had called in the best when
I collapsed after healing his daughter.

"I thought we agreed you weren't going to be doing this any more." He looked down his nose at me.
At six foot one I'm tall enough that not too many
people can do that. But Dr. Watkins was a big man,
tall and angular. His build was gangly enough that
I'd originally expected him to be awkward, but he
wasn't. And those huge hands had an almost miraculously delicate touch. He pulled a stool up in front
of me and sat down. Using his penlight he checked
my pupils, then had me track his pen, moving just
my eyes.

"It wasn't a healing," I told him. "We were under
psychic attack. I was just trying to keep us alive."

He made a disbelieving noise. "Do I have to remind you that the last time actually killed you? We
had to revive you, and it wasn't easy."

No, he didn't have to remind me. I didn't remember
dying, but I remembered hearing about it, from the
doctors, from Tom, from Joe. It probably shouldn't
have freaked me out. After all, I've had more than
a few close calls. But truthfully, the mere thought
scared me into cooperation better than anything else
would've done.

"Although I have to admit," he said the words
grudgingly, "you do seem to be in much better shape
this time. I don't even think we'll need to admit you.
I'll have the nurse give you your shot. We'll give it a
half hour to take effect. If you're doing better, you

can take a cab home. But I want you to *rest*. No physical activity for at least twenty-four hours. And if the pain comes back, or you start having any of the side effects, I want you to come back to the emergency room stat."

"Did the nurse send for Miles?" I'd asked her to, but that didn't mean she'd had the chance to do it. This was, after all, the emergency room. There were plenty of other things that could've taken precedence.

"Dr. MacDougal is outside."

"Oh good." I was relieved. I'd tried to take a peek at the papers inside the envelope Carlton had given me. I could tell they were research notes. I could tell it was medically related. Other than that, I didn't have a clue. As an internationally known Thrall researcher, I figured Miles MacDougal was the perfect person to have look at the file. It made me nervous dragging him into this. I mean, the vamps had already killed to protect their secrets. But lives were at stake and I didn't know who else to ask.

"I asked him to wait outside until we were finished." The doctor scooted the stool over to the counter and set down both my file and the pen. He seemed to be gathering his thoughts as he slid the penlight back into the pocket of his lab coat. When he turned back to me his expression was serious. "I don't know what you've gotten yourself into this time, Ms. Reilly. I don't know, and I don't *want* to know. But you are not indestructible. Don't delude yourself into thinking otherwise." He rose to his feet in a smooth movement.

"Before you get any more deeply involved than you already are, I want you to ask yourself: is it really worth dying for? Because that's exactly what you'll be risking."

On that cheery note he walked out the door. I heard him say, "Go on in, Miles. Maybe you can talk some sense into her."

Miles isn't a big man. Standing five foot six or so, he's slender, with thinning dark hair and a luxuriant moustache that dominates his face. I hadn't seen him in person for a while and I was shocked at the change. He looked like he'd been dragged face down through hell. His body was emaciated, his eyes sunken and haunted. Normally a fastidious man, his clothes were stained and rumpled, as though he'd actually been wearing them when he'd eaten and gotten what minimal sleep he'd managed. Even the moustache that had been his pride and joy was unkempt.

"Um . . . *Miles*?" I tried to hide how shocked I was, and failed miserably. It earned me a weak version of the wry smile I'd grown so accustomed to over the years.

"Hello, Kate. I'd ask how you're doing, but it's obvious you're not in much better shape than I am."

"I haven't seen you since . . . that night. What have you been doing to yourself?" He didn't need to answer. I knew the moment he flinched when I said *that night*. He blamed himself for having supported Samantha Greeley's research project—for helping her to start the chain of events that eventually led to her thrall infestation, madness, and death. He firmly believed that if he hadn't helped her none of it would have happened. She would be alive and well. Joe would be whole. I wasn't so sure. She'd been a very determined woman. His influence might have helped, but I didn't doubt she'd have managed it without him. Besides, hindsight is always 20/20. I sighed. "I keep telling you, it wasn't your fault. You did what you had to do."

He shrugged. "We'll have to agree to disagree on that." He moved over to the stool the doctor had vacated. "The nurse who called said it was urgent; that you had some papers you wanted me to look at?" The tone of his voice made it a question.

I hesitated. The information was important, but I hated using him. Besides, did I really have the right to put him at risk?

"So, you don't you trust me either." The weary sadness in his voice suggested there were other people who had done more than hesitate to trust him in his current state. I wasn't sure I blamed him, but I didn't doubt the knowledge made him worse. His work was probably all that was keeping him afloat right now.

"It's not a trust issue, Miles. The Thrall have tried to kill people to keep this information secret. People like Lewis Carlton. People like me. I don't like putting you in that sort of danger."

His eyebrows rose until they would have disappeared beneath his hairline if he'd had one. He pursed his lips, and a hint of the old fire lit his eyes. "Dangerous indeed. Let me take a look."

I handed him the envelope and he pulled the sheets from inside, spreading them across the counter. He started reading, muttering under his breath as he did.

"My, my," he whispered. "Isn't *that* interesting. I never would've considered that possibility, although why one would want to—"

A light tap on the door interrupted his monologue and the duty nurse appeared with my shot.

"I'm sorry. I didn't mean to interrupt. But Dr. Watkins—" She gave Miles an uncertain look. He gathered the papers up rapidly, sticking them into the envelope before she had the chance to get so much as a glimpse.

"Go ahead. Give her the injection." He turned to me. "Kate, I need to look at these more closely, make a couple of calls. I should know more by the end of the day. I'll get in touch with you." He was on his feet now, hurrying toward the door. I didn't mean to eavesdrop, but his thoughts were right on the surface. He'd never seen anything like this. It was amazing. He couldn't contain his eagerness to get back to the lab where he could check his reference books and call trusted colleagues.

"Miles, we need to be discreet." I warned him as the nurse rubbed a spot on my arm with the little alcohol pad and popped the tip off of the needle.

He stopped in his tracks. "Of course. I understand. But I need to make one call at least, to confirm that what I'm seeing is actually possible. I've known Chuck since college. I'd trust him with my life."

I hissed in pain as the nurse jabbed the needle home and carefully didn't say that he might be doing just that.

21

I'm not a big fan of hypocrisy, Tom." I didn't
snarl. I was too tired. The medicine hadn't started
to work yet and the pain was kicking my ass. Besides, it had been a rough morning.

He'd burst into the room just as the nurse was
leaving. I could tell he was worried, but he was also
angry—the kind of angry you get when someone
has scared you, but you know it's going to be all
right. He'd spoken with quiet intensity about how he
shouldn't have to hear that I was in the hospital from
one of the EMTs, that I should've called him.

"First, I haven't had a chance. You'll note there
isn't a phone in the room, and I seem to have lost
my cell phone. Second, it's not that bad. It's just a
migraine. I'm just supposed to go home and lay
down."

"*Just* a migraine . . . like the one that almost killed you not so long ago. And for *him*."

"This was shielding, not healing or opening his mind. And you say *him* like Carlton hasn't saved your butt more than once."

"You swore you wouldn't take these kinds of risks. But here you are." His voice carried more than anger. I remembered suddenly he'd overheard something Carlton said to me when we both thought he was unconscious after being roughed up by Mary. Carlton told me if he hadn't turned Thrall, he would have given *Fido* a run for his money with me. That didn't mean I was interested, but I also hadn't slapped him or laughed at him. I don't think Tom's ever quite gotten past Carlton's interest and continued attempts to help me, even against his own kind. It's something that Tom hadn't done yet.

Thus far I'd been trying to be reasonable. I hadn't meant to scare him, or make him jealous. I know how it feels to worry like that. But he was pushing his luck because I was rapidly running out of patience. It was the same old fight every time. *You don't include me. You don't tell me things. You have male friends who fight for you.* Well, it was bullshit. I might not get on the phone the minute something happened, but I did tell him. I'd never given him a hint of being interested in another man. And unlike *some* people who just never seemed to get around to sharing bad news at all, I did eventually tell him everything. "I'm not fond of hypocrisy, Tom," I repeated, my voice dripping venom.

His head snapped back as if I'd slapped him. "What's *that* supposed to mean?" He was managing to keep his voice in check, but his eyes were flashing and a dark flush was rising up his neck. He was clenching and unclenching his fists, as if he really didn't quite trust himself. I felt his magic start to rise, and waited while he struggled to stifle it.

"It means that I'm tired of it being all right for you to risk your life every day to save total strangers, but I'm supposed to stay safe; that I'm supposed to be *fine* with you doing things like asking my own brother to design you a special parachute so you can jump out of a perfectly good airplane *into the middle of a freaking wildfire,* but I'm supposed to 'be careful' and 'not take chances.' I'm supposed to wait for you to help, instead of using those who are closer and who offer. Fuck that. You're a hero. You always have been. I know that. I've known it from day one. You run toward the things that scare the crap out of the rest of us. You can't help it. It's part of who you are, and if I'm going to be with you I have to live with that. I can't ask you not to be you. So I swallow the fear, put on my game face, and yell '*Go, Tom*' like some frigging cheerleader." I spat the words out at him. It made my head pound, hard enough for my stomach to roil in protest, but I didn't care.

I'd been crying a lot lately. I'd figured it was the stress of everything, the botched wedding, all the crap that Dylan had pulled. But those hadn't been the only reasons. This had been back there all the time, like a

festering wound. Because while I was trying so
damned hard to support him, not to ask him too many
details about pack life, or ask him to change—he'd
been doing the opposite, and it *hurt*. But the tears
were gone for the moment, replaced by the long, slow
burn of real anger.

Tom stared at me for long moments, his jaw
dropped so low that it nearly touched his chest. Most
fights escalate when both people are angry. It doesn't
seem to work that way with us, thank God. My anger
seems to stop his cold. "I've always wanted to be a
smokejumper." It was a whisper.

"I know."

"I don't want to give it up." I could barely hear
him.

"Did I ask you to? Did I ever *once* ask you to give
up *anything*?" My head was throbbing in time to my
pulse. I was whispering, not only because of the
pain, but also because if I didn't I was liable to
scream. Staring into his face, he looked so lost, so
confused, and I knew that until this minute it honestly had never occurred to him that I could be just
as afraid for him as he was for me, every single
freaking day. I let out a ragged breath. "It's who you
are, and I love you. I don't want you to change. So
I have to live with it. There are probably support
groups, but if there aren't, damn it, I'll start one.
Whatever it takes. Because I love you, and I don't
want to lose you: not to the fires, and not to my fear.
But aren't I entitled to the same luxury? Shouldn't I
get to be who *I* am?"

He sat down abruptly, on the stool the doctors had abandoned. It was almost as if his knees wouldn't hold him upright. "I'm sorry." He leaned forward to take my hands in his. "I didn't know. I should've. I've heard other guys talk about it—seen their marriages fall apart because of it. But it honestly never occurred to me—" He shook his head. "I . . . I need to think about this. You're right, but I need to think. Can you stand that?" He brought my hands up to his lips and kissed my knuckles.

I nodded. It was all I could ask for, just like letting Joe deal with his issues. "Do you need to go back to the station?"

"Nah. Bob's covering the rest of my shift."

"Good. After my nap, when the migraine's gone I want you to do something with me."

He raised one eyebrow in inquiry. "Not that I mind, but are you sure you'll be up to it?"

"Not that!" I rolled my eyes in mock exasperation. "I've read in the books that sometimes, if the psychic is strong enough, they can bring another person along with them in the vision."

His hands spasmed around mine, and he gave me a skeptical look. "Katie—" Just my name, but I could tell he thought it was a really bad idea, that he wanted to argue with me.

I cut him off before he could say more. "Tom, too much is happening and all of it is important. I need someone to help me put together the pieces of the puzzle. Dusty could do it, but after what happened the other day, I can't bear the thought of risking—" I let the sentence trail off.

"And Mary would kill you both for trying it. If it didn't kill you to begin with anyway."

I gave a small nod. A *very* small nod because that's all I could do as the tension . . . and the control . . . left my muscles.

He stared at me for a long silent moment before giving a grim nod. "I don't like it," he admitted. "But I understand why you have to do it. And I'll come along for the ride. But it won't be until after the headache's completely gone. I want you to be at full strength."

"Agreed. Now go see if you can find out what's happening with Carlton, and call us a cab. I want to go home as soon as I wake up."

"Sounds like a plan to me."

He left quietly, pulling the door closed behind him. I climbed back up onto the examining table and closed my eyes. I was so tired. Not just physically weary, but mentally and emotionally exhausted. I was beginning to understand on a visceral level what the doctors had been trying to tell me. I didn't have much more in me. If I didn't rest, soon, my body would *make* me rest. But could it have picked a worse time? I mean, the Conclave was only a couple of days away; the Thrall were pulling something major; and I had a jealous and possibly psychotic werewolf stalking me. But the thoughts faded as my consciousness succumbed to the drugs. I slept.

I woke in my own bed, spooned against Tom, still dressed, but without my shoes, tucked under the comforter. The smell of Chinese take-out drifted to me faintly through the closed door. Turning my head I could see the green glow of the clock on the night-stand. It was 3:00 A.M. *Damn, what was in that shot?* I'd slept through the whole day and most of the night. Whoa. Still, I had to admit I felt better than I had for a while. The absence of pain is a wonderful thing, and so totally underrated.

I wiggled out from under Tom's arm. Using the light seeping through the crack under the door to guide me, I tiptoed around Tom's discarded clothes and our shoes to the door and headed down the hall to the bathroom.

He'd left the hall light on. It made sense since we had company. In fact, I could hear Elaine's snores coming from behind the closed door to the second bedroom. I felt a little guilty. I should've been up to meet her, should've fixed a nice dinner. If she de-cided to take insult there would probably be hell to pay. Werewolves are big on their own brand of eti-quette. Call me silly, but I doubted I'd get a pass for having injured myself in the process of rescuing a rogue Thrall.

My bare feet were nearly silent as I padded over the hardwood floor. I used the facilities quickly, washed up, and checked my reflection in the bath-room mirror.

I looked rumpled. The suit would have to go to the cleaners to remove the creases that had set themselves deep into the fabric. But otherwise the rest had done wonders for me. I hadn't realized how many lines of pain and strain had been marking my features until now that they were gone. My skin was still a little pale, but my features weren't drawn, my skin sagging and jowly. There were still dark circles like smudges of soot under my eyes, but the bags had definitely gotten smaller. They were more the size for a weekend getaway than a year-long tour of Europe. Whatever had been in that syringe was good stuff. I was impressed. I hoped I'd never have to use it again, but it was good to know stuff like that was out there.

I ran a quick comb through the mass of tangles on my head that passed for hair and then pulled it back into a ponytail. I'd braid it after I had a chance to shower and shampoo. Right now I just wanted it out of the way while I rummaged around in the kitchen for something to eat.

I was famished. Not surprising considering the number of meals I'd missed. When I'd finished cleaning up as much as I was going to for the moment I left the bathroom for the kitchen. I switched on the overhead light, expecting to find things pretty much the way I'd left them this morning. Instead, the place practically sparkled. It looked like something out of a cleanser commercial. I half expected some bald guy in white to step out of the pantry and tell me how to disinfect while I mopped.

I shook my head. Either the shot hadn't completely worn off after all or my blood sugar was bottoming out, because I was getting a little loopy.

I stepped over to the refrigerator. Opening the door I shoved aside the little white take-out boxes. Chinese leftovers was definitely not what I wanted this morning. I wanted a "real" breakfast: bacon, eggs, some biscuits. Homemade would be good, but the ones in the tube were quicker, and I remembered buying some on my grocery run—was it only yesterday? But most of all, I wanted coffee. Nectar of the gods and fuel of champions, the day couldn't officially get off the ground without at least one cup.

I went about my cooking as quietly as I could. Still, I wasn't quiet enough, or else Tom missed having me in the bed with him, because it wasn't too long before I heard his soft footfalls coming down the hall.

"I smell bacon," he whispered, "and coffee, and *biscuits*." He came up behind me, sliding his arm around my waist to pull me close against him. Nuzzling my neck he whispered, "Have I mentioned before how much I adore the fact you can cook?" He nibbled my ear as he said it, the coarse stubble of his beard rubbing against the sensitive skin of my neck and jawline.

"Once or twice." I leaned into him, enjoying the warmth of his body while my hands kept busy turning the bacon and then flipping the eggs. He was wearing pajama bottoms, but his chest was bare, and I could feel the solid bulk of his muscles against my back. "But it's not like this is difficult."

"Not for you anyway." He could see the food was almost done, so he stepped away from me and began gathering plates and silverware from the various cabinets.

"Thank-you for buying coffee filters."

"Yeah, well, I noticed we were out when I cleaned the kitchen." His grin was a flash of bright teeth and dimples. "And I was so not going to deal with you in the morning without your coffee."

"I'm not that bad," I protested.

"Of course not, sweetie." He said it with a chuckle that made it clear he was lying through his teeth, and set up the place settings, giving me the biggest mug in the house.

I heard scratching, but couldn't pinpoint where the sound was coming from. "Blank? Where are you, boy?"

A piteous mewing came from the general direction of the pantry. "Oh, crap. How'd he get stuck in there?"

"I dunno." Tom walked over and opened the door. The cat wound his way around his feet, purring like a motorboat. He was begging for breakfast. We both knew it. But I also knew that Tom would give in and feed him, in part because he was so tickled that the cat liked him. Growing up he'd never been able to have pets. Most small animals could sense the predator in him and were too terrified to let him come anywhere close. Maybe it's because Blank lived with Dylan and Amanda before he was given back to me. They'd no doubt smelled of Thrall. A werewolf might be the lesser of two evils to a cat. Tom reached down to run his hand over the thick white fur. "I think I'll feed him some breakfast too."

I hid my grin by stepping behind the refrigerator door and pulling out the butter and a carton of orange juice. While I was pouring a glass for each of us Tom was opening one of those tiny cans of expensive gourmet stuff for the furball. I knew for a fact that *I* hadn't bought it. It's too damned pricey. Which meant that Tom had done it. But no, he doesn't spoil Blank. Of course not.

Just a nice, domestic morning. I loved it. Maybe even more because I knew that in an hour or so everything was liable to go to hell.

Tom set the saucer of food onto the linoleum a few inches in front of the cat. Blank dived into the food as if he'd been starved for days when there was a nearly full bowl of hard food barely six feet away.

I set both glasses of orange juice onto the table and put the carton back in the fridge. That done, we settled into our places and tucked wordlessly into our breakfast.

Tom waited until I was mostly finished before starting the conversation. "So, how much do you remember of yesterday afternoon?"

"The last thing I remember, you'd gone off to call a cab and I climbed back up on the examination table to close my eyes for a minute."

"That's it?"

"Yup." I grabbed another biscuit and buttered it. Yes, I was making a pig of myself. I didn't care. I was *hungry,* dammit. "So, what did I miss?"

Tom sighed and started ticking items off on his fingers. "Let's see. When we got home Janine had vandalized the house: tomatoes, eggs, some spray paint. It was a mess. One of the neighbors came up while I was hosing down the mess, told me that he'd called the cops, but they'd gotten here too late to catch her at it. But he'd taken pictures with his cell phone. It was her. And he gave copies to the cops, so they're looking for her."

"Oh, crap." That sucked. It wasn't that I wanted Janine on the loose. I didn't. But being at ground zero with Elaine when her daughter got arrested again wasn't likely to be a load of giggles either.

"Elaine showed up while Joe, Bryan, and I were painting over the graffiti. She started following the trail, but she didn't have any more luck than I did. The scent trail dead-ended at a park about eight blocks from here."

As if cut off with a switch, my hunger disappeared. In fact, the food I'd already eaten began sitting a little uneasily. "Was it the one near the highway with a lake?"

Tom stared at me, the biscuit he'd been eating hovering forgotten halfway to his mouth. "Katie, what's wrong?"

I thought of the vision I'd had. I'd been a werewolf, probably Janine, running away from a park.

"Katie?" There was an urgency to his voice. "Come back to me. Tell me what's wrong."

I took a deep, shuddering breath and very deliberately worked to ground myself psychically. Almost

immediately I felt more calm, more capable of dealing with reality.

"I had a vision yesterday morning." I said it calmly.

He set the biscuit down, shoved the plate away
from him. "Tell me."

I did, as succinctly as I could. Unfortunately, a lot
had happened in the interim. Some of the details of
the vision were definitely fuzzy. Still, there was no
mistaking that it was the same park, and I clearly remembered her disdain for "the human."

Tom rose to his feet in a sharp movement that
scraped the chair across the floor, making it teeter
and nearly fall. He strode restlessly around the
kitchen, swearing under his breath. I could feel the
heat of his magic rise in an overwhelming tide. It
washed over him, and I knew that this time he
wouldn't be able to keep it at bay.

Blank hissed, his back arching, every hair standing on end before he bolted through the door and out
of the kitchen.

Transfixed, I watched in horrified fascination as
Tom's body began to shimmer. His bones shattered
and popped, moving visibly beneath his muscles
and skin, which had begun to flow with thick, coarse
fur. It took what seemed an eternity, but was actually
only a few minutes, for the entire process to take
place; for the man I loved to be replaced by a huge
beast of fur and fang the size of a small pony.

He took up most of the space between the table
and the door. I couldn't have escaped that way if
I'd wanted to. But I didn't want, or need, to escape.

Unlike most werewolves Tom was always Tom, whatever his form. He might not be able to talk to me in his wolf shape, but he was still in his right mind.

Of course that didn't keep me from swallowing hard and staring. I mean, I know intellectually that he's in there. But staring at the reality from a few inches away made me a little . . . nervous. *Grandmama, what big teeth you have, indeed!*

Tom, are you okay? I thought the words directly into his mind.

I'm fine. Angry, a little frustrated that I don't have better control than this, but other than that I'm just peachy.

His irritation actually comforted me. If he was coherent enough to be capable of sarcasm we were in good shape.

"Do you still want to try what we talked about yesterday? I might be able to go back to not only that vision but the other ones, too, maybe get a few more details."

There was more than one? He didn't say "and you didn't tell me," but I could feel the thought brush by before he was able to stifle it.

"We were going to talk about it when you got off shift, remember. It's not like I've had a chance to tell you before now." I pointed my finger at his nose and was rewarded with a half-hearted wag of his tail.

Are you sure you want to do it with company in the house?

Not really. But Elaine had been anxious to come here before anything bad had happened. I didn't for a minute believe she'd wander off and leave me alone now that we had proof Janine was going off the deep end. Right now, when she was still deeply asleep, might be our only chance for any privacy at all.

I hadn't answered in words, but Tom must have caught the gist of my thoughts because he answered. *The meditation gear Dusty bought you is in the hall closet. Let's do this while we can.*

I let Tom lead. I wouldn't have been able to fit past him anyhow. The kitchen was a mess, half the food would be wasted. It didn't matter. I wasn't hungry anymore anyway. I could clean it later. Who knows, maybe I'd even have a girl/girl bonding session with Elaine doing the dishes. I doubted it, but stranger things have happened.

It took a few minutes to set everything up. I had to move one of the chairs and the coffee table to the side of the room to make enough space for the both of us, but I managed it without making too much noise. I could tell because the snoring hadn't diminished. If anything, it had increased in volume. Whether that meant she was sleeping more or less deeply I didn't have a clue.

I spread the mat on the floor. The blue nylon cover looked bright and cheerful against the hardwood. I set pillar candles at each of the front two corners. I was glad Dusty had chosen white, according to the books it symbolized protection, and I wanted all that I could get.

The incense burner was brass. Shaped like Aladdin's lamp, it had been intricately cut with a lace-like pattern of holes. I flipped open the hinge lid, dropping in two small cones of sandalwood incense. I used one of those trigger-style lighters to make sure it was burning steadily before flipping the lid closed. I knelt on the mat a little to the left of center and signaled for Tom to join me. When he was lying down comfortably, I lit the candles and settled next to him, sitting cross-legged, my left hand resting palm up on my knee, my right buried deep in the fur of his ruff.

I expected to have time to relax, to focus my mind. I didn't. The vision came in a rush of sensation so real I would have sworn I was standing there, rather than sitting quietly in my living room.

It was Bernardo's Pool Hall. I recognized it immediately. The large, mostly open room was filled with pool tables, each with enough room to move comfortably around. Fluorescent lights hung above the individual tables, creating a spotlight effect. There were probably forty or fifty individual pools of light above tables with green felt. The rest of the room, however, was dimly lit.

There weren't many patrons at this time of day. Most everybody had left shortly after last call. But there was a big money game being played at the center table. A few of the regulars sat at nearby tables, or had turned their bar stools around to watch as they sipped cups of steaming coffee.

Leo, the night barman and someone I like to call

friend, was washing dishes, his shaved head gleaming in neon colors from the beer light hanging from chains above his head.

It felt as though there should be stale cigarette smoke swirling in air moved in lazy circles by the overhead fans. There wasn't. The city had passed a complete smoking ban not too long ago. I considered it excessive, but knew just as many people who were relieved to be able to go out without having to deal with other people's nicotine habit.

I glanced around, looking for someone with a watch. In the perpetual gloom of the pool hall it wasn't easy to tell what time it was. Hours could pass, even most of a day, without the patrons realizing it. It was good for business since the tables were rented by the hour. It had to be sometime between 2:00 and 7:00 when first call rolled around and liquor could be served, but other than that I didn't have a clue.

I turned at the sound of familiar voices coming through the front doors.

Bryan was at the front of the group. His reddish-blond hair gleamed like burnished gold. He was laughing, his walk a little unsteady. I could see the bandage at his neck. So this was probably the present or the very near future.

I sighed inwardly. He was drunk. Coming in behind him were a pair of girls I knew by sight if not necessarily by name. I felt my body tense in anger. They'd been part of the crowd he'd hung out with back when he'd done drugs. Maybe they'd even been the ones to dump him on the street when he got the bad Eden. Maybe not. Bryan swore he didn't remember. I'd never know. But his being with them meant he was running with that crowd again, and that thought filled me with such fury that I almost lost control of the vision. I felt Tom move beneath my hand as the picture wavered, felt him giving me his strength, his calm. I took a minute to control my breathing, to still my emotions, letting my anger drain into the ground. The vision steadied, becoming clear once more.

"You're sure Toby said he'd meet us here?" Bryan seemed a little worried. "He's been avoiding me the past couple of weeks."

The shorter girl was a pretty brunette wearing a cropped red top that showed a flat, tanned abdomen in the middle of winter. A piercing winked at her navel, and her denim skirt barely qualified as decent. She'd dressed for sex rather than the weather. She took Bryan by the arm, leaning into his body so that he could get a good look at her cleavage if he wanted. He did. "That's what he said." She dragged a blood red nail across the skin of his chest where the neck of his black dress shirt was unbuttoned. "But I think it's time the two of you made up. Besides, we don't want Laurie to be lonely, do we? And I don't share." She stood on her tippy toes to kiss him. It was one hell of a kiss. She was practically eating him alive, face down. His body reacted predictably and she pulled away with a laugh. "Later, tiger." She dragged her hand down the front of his body, deliberately stopping just above the bulge in *his trousers. He groaned, and she laughed again, a wicked, possessive sound that just irritated the hell out of me.*

She led him by the hand up to the counter. He registered for a table, giving his ID to Leo, who was giving him a studiously blank expression.

I recognized that look. That was his blank bouncer face. He knew this girl, knew she was trouble. Terrific.

Bryan missed the hint. No surprise. He wasn't thinking with the big head at the moment. The brunette led him by the hand toward a table in the far corner of the hall, as far away from everyone as she could get. Laurie followed the two of them, carrying the rack of billiard balls. She watched Bryan as he moved, her eyes glittering with malice. I realized then that the real threat to my brother wasn't the brunette.

They were playing eight-ball when Toby arrived at the front counter. I saw him walk in the door and stop, letting his eyes adjust. It had gotten light outside, he had to take off the dark sunglasses he'd been wearing. The money game was over. Leo was busy cleaning up the place and was away from the counter, so that Toby had to wait. He turned, his eyes scanning the room. When he saw Bryan his expression changed to one of horror and panic. I could see the pulse throbbing in his throat.

He moved, taking a quick step backward, but he wasn't quite fast enough. Laurie saw him. Their eyes locked. I watched as sweat beaded on his skin, his body taken with a fine trembling. God help him, he was trying to fight, but his own body wasn't his any more. She was controlling him, moving him like a sock puppet. I knew how that felt. Monica Mica had taken over my arm, making it move of its own volition, in an effort to get me to claw out my own eyes when I'd offended her.

He made her work for it. Each step forward was an individual battle. You could see the effort, and the rage, on her face. Bryan had been lining up a shot when he saw it.

"What the fu—?" He set his cue down and turned to stare, first at Laurie and then across the room to where Toby stood.

"Toby, buddy, what's wrong?"

"I . . . won't . . . do . . . thisss." The last word had a hissing lisp. I shuddered, thinking I knew what that meant. Bryan either knew or guessed.

"You didn't. You're not—" he stared, his expression horrified.

"You will do what I tell you. Kill him, or die." Laurie's face shifted, the illusion and mind tricks falling away as more and more energy was being used against Toby. She became taller, the soft female curves hardening and flattening into a body I knew all too well. So did Bryan.

Dylan.

"No!" Toby threw back his head, shouting the word at the ceiling, his voice changing. I watched the bones begin moving beneath his skin, heard the familiar popping and breaking as his body began to *shift. The word changed, becoming a long, mournful howl that somehow perfectly captured both his rage and despair.*

The ring of a telephone snapped me back into the present so abruptly it was almost painful.

Tom was lying on the floor panting. He was hurt? How in the hell had that happened? I blinked in the kind of confusion that comes from returning too suddenly to the here and now. It was like being woken from a particularly vivid dream, in those first few instants when you can't quite tell which is reality.

"Tom, are you all right?" I said it with both mouth and mind.

"Just tired. I tried to help him fight. But I wasn't there, wasn't touching him. So it drained me more than I thought it would."

I shifted positions until I was kneeling and blew out the candles. "If you can change back I can help you back to the bedroom."

He gave a small whimper, but I felt his magic rise. It took longer than usual, but his body reversed the earlier changes until he lay human and naked beside me.

It took effort, but we managed to get him onto his feet. He was practically dead weight dragging me down as I hauled him bodily down the hallway. We made it to the edge of the bed before the last of his energy gave out and he collapsed, falling sideways on top of the covers. The mattress squeaked in protest, but the bed held.

Too tired to move, he lay passive as I tugged the

covers out from under him and rearranged his body into a more normal position. I tucked the pillow under his head, running my fingers through his soft brown curls. "I love you, Tom Bishop." I whispered the words to him and was rewarded with an inarticulate grunt that was supposed to be a response. "I can't believe you actually tried to send your power through a vision that might not even be in the here and now. And you say *I'm* impulsive." He gave another grunt that might, or might not, have been "stupid." Shaking my head, I bent down and kissed him tenderly on the mouth. "Yeah, well, I'm proud of you. It was generous and brave, even if it was really, seriously dumb. Now get some rest."

He was snoring softly seconds later when I left the room. The sound was oddly comforting. He was a werewolf. I knew that given enough time he could heal almost any injury. But it seriously scared me to see him like this. Nor was he the only one I was frightened for at the moment. I'd told him that the vision might not be in real time; and it might not. But it had *felt* real; real enough that I wanted to talk to my baby brother.

The last time I'd seen my cell phone it was on the kitchen counter, plugged in to recharge. Evidently Tom had gotten it from the hospital staff. I was glad. I would hate to lose it. The screen showed a missed call. I hit the button and it displayed Mary's cell phone number. I'd call her in a minute. Before I did, I wanted to check on Bryan.

I dialed the number of his cell phone without

luck. Either he'd turned it off or had chosen not to answer. I left a voice-mail asking him to call me as soon as he could and then hung up. I thought I still remembered the number for Bernardo's from back when I was more of a regular. I dialed, hoping I had it right. A familiar voice answered on the third ring. Not Leo, but Stevie. "Bernardo's Pool Hall. Can I help you?"

"Steve, it's Kate . . . Kate Reilly. Is Leo on shift?"

"Nope. It's his night off." *Not tonight then. Which means Tom exhausted himself for nothing. But, there's still time.*

"Is my brother Bryan there?"

"Nope. Haven't seen him for a couple weeks. Shame too. I can usually take him for a couple of bucks when he's had a few beers."

I didn't answer that. It was none of my business if Bryan wanted to throw away his money. As long as his bills were paid and he wasn't mooching off family to get by, it was his life.

"Well, if he comes in, have him give me a call."

"Sure. Is that it?"

"Yeah."

"Should I tell Leo you called?"

I thought about it for a minute as I grabbed the mug of cold coffee from the table and dumped its contents into the sink. "Nah. I'll check back later. Thanks, though."

"No problema."

He hung up without saying good-bye, but I was okay with that. Steve has his issues, but he's dependable enough in his own way. He'd give Bryan the message, but he'd expect me to buy him a beer and a shot the next time I was in, as payment. Seemed a fair price to pay.

I hit the series of numbers that would ring back the last person who called me and tucked the phone between my shoulder and ear. It was uncomfortable, but it left my hands free to run dishwater in the sink and start cleaning up the breakfast mess. I was sliding the biscuits into a zipper-top plastic bag when she picked up the line.

"Good morning, Kate."

"Morning. What're you doing up and about so bright and early?" I glanced up at the clock. It wasn't even 5:00 yet.

"I could ask you the same thing," she sighed. Just those few short words, and I could tell she was not only tired, but weary. There's a difference, at least to my mind. Tired is a physical state that comes from overwork or lack of sleep. Weariness is usually the result of stress and frustration. Tired I get by itself sometimes. Weariness almost never travels alone.

"So?"

"I'm at the hospital. Ruby had the baby. She's a girl. Eight pounds three ounces with thick brown hair and a set of lungs you wouldn't believe."

I was grinning as I threw the bag of biscuits in the refrigerator.

"Are they okay?"

"Mostly. It was a hard delivery. Ruby will need to stay in the hospital for a day or two, and the baby's a little jaundiced, so they're going to put her under the bilirubin lights."

"That's not serious, is it?"

"Nah, not really. Lots of kids are jaundiced at birth. For a werewolf delivery it actually went pretty well. They're both going to be fine."

I grabbed Tom's plate and began scraping the uneaten portion of his food into the trash. "Then what's wrong?"

"Nothing really. I'm just tired. But before I get caught up in the day I wanted to give you a call, see if you and Tom would stop by the hospital during visiting hours. Ruby wants to talk to the two of you."

That seemed a little odd to me, but the kid had been lonely since Jake died, and we had started getting more friendly in Las Vegas. "Okay. No problem. It's going to be a couple of hours before we can manage it, though. Which hospital is she at?"

"St. E's." Mary gave me the room number.

"Cool. I'll bring flowers."

"That'd be nice. She'll like that."

There was an odd inflection in Mary's voice. I couldn't quite pinpoint what the problem was. She'd said Ruby was fine, that the baby was fine. So why wasn't she happy? The pack had been desperate for babies. Both surrogates had now delivered; a boy and a girl. She should be practically delirious. She obviously wasn't.

Mary, can you hear me? I sent a thread of thought in her direction. She might or might not be psychic. I'd found out after Jake's death that most of the wolves are connected to each other through the pack. It's a bond and it's psychic, but it's not as direct or concrete as what I have and the hive mentality the Thrall used. They might not know when a fellow pack member was in trouble, but they felt the absence if one died, and sometimes strong emotions could bleed over from one to the other. I'd never seen it, but I've been told that watching a tight-knit pack hunt or fight as a unit was impressive as hell.

"What are you doing, Kate?" She sounded suspicious.

"Oh, just cleaning up from breakfast," is what I said out loud. Mind to mind I said something entirely different. *We need to talk. There are things I need to tell you that we can't discuss on the phone. Can you come to the house? It's important.*

"Breakfast sounds pretty damned good about now. I haven't eaten since lunch yesterday." *Fine, Reilly. But it better be important. I've got dignitaries arriving all day, security measures to take care of, and last-minute crap to deal with at the convention center. I do not need anything more on my plate.*

I kept my voice light and cheerful, despite the worry in my mind. "Well, drive on over then and I'll feed you some fresh biscuits."

That's fine, Mary, but don't talk about anything important over the phone.

I'd never heard a growl in my mind before. But there it was as she replied psychically. *Why not?*

Your home phone's been bugged. They may have done your cell phone too.

"WHAT!?" She shouted it out loud. I flinched, and the phone popped out from between shoulder and ear to clatter against the edge of the sink. I had to bat at it with my hands to keep it from falling into the soapy water.

"What in the hell are you talking about?" I could hear her clearly, even though the phone had fallen to the floor. She was snarling, and there was a guttural quality to her voice that I didn't like hearing at all. She'd been a long time without sleep or food. Her control over her beast might not be at its best. But hopefully, if her phone was being tapped, those listening would just think I'd suggested doing something kinky with biscuits that outraged her, rather than getting suspicious.

I picked up the cell phone and spoke lightly, my voice utterly bland, but tinged with a bit of faked embarrassment. "Gosh, I didn't mean it like *that*, Mary. I just think we need to have a little chat about some things a friend of ours told me yesterday. I would've called you sooner, but I wound up with a migraine."

Mary! Stop. You need to separate what you think from what you say. I know it's a shock to find out, but I think we can use it to our advantage. That's one of the things I want to talk about. Just don't let on that you know about the tap until after we've had a chance to talk, okay?

I heard her let out a slow breath and when she

replied, she chuckled lightly. It definitely sounded forced, but that was better than angry. "Actually, Joe wanted to bring by a present for you anyway. Think you could whip us both up some breakfast if we stop by?"

Her thoughts brushing mine were horrified and filled with fear. I didn't blame her. *Saints preserve us, Kate. I've made all of our plans for the conference from the house. All our security measures,* everything *was discussed on that phone. This is a disaster.*

I was afraid of that. *Trust me. Please. At least long enough to hear me out.* "Sure, come on over. I'll put the coffee on."

"We'll be there just as soon as I can haul Joseph out of bed. And yes, coffee sounds wonderful."

"Bye then."

She paused and her voice sounded distracted as she replied. "Bye."

I hung up the phone, setting it on the counter as far away from the sink as I could get it. Even if Joe drove like a lunatic I probably had a half hour before they could get here; say twenty minutes to be on the safe side.

With no time to lose, I moved like a madwoman through the kitchen, throwing out what couldn't be kept, putting the dirty dishes in the sink to soak and putting another pot of coffee on to brew. I finished with ten minutes on the clock, barely enough time to shower and throw on clean clothes.

I dashed through the house, my bare feet slapping against the hardwood. Tom was still out of it, but I could tell from the squeaking of the bedsprings that Elaine was moving about restlessly. If she got up we'd have to include her. I'd like to prevent that if at all possible. I didn't want to give her an excuse for criticizing Mary and the pack, blaming me, or both.

I couldn't make her sleep, but I did tiptoe around as quietly as I could, barely daring to breathe as I passed by her door on my way back to the bathroom carrying the clothes I'd be changing into.

I didn't dawdle under the spray, didn't take advantage of the hand-held shower massage. There was simply no time. I needed to be clean. I'd spent a long, hard day and night in the same clothes. I stank. So I scrubbed myself down, rinsed myself off, and climbed out so fast that the mirror hadn't even misted over. Grabbing the knob, I pulled open the linen cabinet and found nothing. Not even a freaking cobweb. *Shit! There were towels here yesterday. Bryan took a shower, I took a bath. I hung the towels back up to dry. Where are they?*

I checked the hamper. No luck. They were simply gone. Maybe Tom had thrown them in the wash—or the guys had used them for something when they were cleaning up the graffiti. It didn't really matter. I didn't have time to worry about it. I'd have to figure out what to do by the time Elaine took a shower, but right now I needed to get dressed. So I took the tee-shirt I'd been going to wear and used it to dry off and wrap my wet hair. That left me wearing sweat pants and a sports bra, but hey, I was decent, and in the living room waiting by the door when I heard Joe's SUV pull up.

It was cold enough that my breath misted the air as I stepped onto the porch and pulled the door closed behind me. The wooden floor of the porch was cold and rough beneath my bare feet as I paced over to the steps to greet my company.

"Are you drying your hair with a tee-shirt?" Mary stood next to the open door of the vehicle. Her voice sounded incredulous. I opened my mouth to explain, but Joe beat me to it.

"Oh crap, the towels! Kate, I'm sorry." His expression was a mixture of horror and guilt. "I didn't even think. And you with company."

Mary and I turned to him simultaneously with curious expressions.

He stood, leaning his arms on the roof of the car. He was trying for a relaxed pose, but I could tell that he was actually supporting a lot of his weight with his upper body; something in his posture showed the strain his face concealed. "Bryan and I came over yesterday to help Tom clean up and paint over the graffiti. I'm still kind of clumsy, and I accidentally knocked over one of the paint buckets on the kitchen floor. The only thing I could think to use to clean it all up in a hurry was the towels. It didn't even occur to me that they were probably the only ones you have right now."

"It's all right, Joe, really." He was mortified, and obviously feeling guilty. How could I be angry? He'd come over at a moment's notice to help get the place cleaned up before Elaine arrived despite the fact that his legs *aren't* steady, and moving is not only still hard, it *hurts*.

He shook his head. "Your guest is going to be getting up in a little bit. She's going to want a shower. You *need* towels." He turned from me to Mary. "I'm going to run down to the SuperCenter. It's open all night. You can fill me in on what I miss when I get back."

"Let me get my wallet," I called out as he climbed back into the SUV. He heard, but he waved the suggestion away irritably and slammed the door.

"Let him take care of it." Mary shut the door and stepped away from the car. "It'll make him feel better."

"But—" I started to protest, but she shut me up with a very pointed look.

"Let him take care of it," she repeated firmly.

"Right. Well, okay then. Come on in where it's warm. I've got the coffee on."

I opened the door and stepped gratefully back into the warmth of the house, shuddering a little from the change in temperature. I draped the damp tee-shirt over the back of one of the chairs, promising myself I'd take it downstairs and throw it in the dryer before Elaine got up.

"You shouldn't have gone out with wet hair. You're liable to catch your death," Mary scolded. She kept her voice soft so as not to wake anyone who was still sleeping and stepped carefully around the meditation gear that was still spread out on the living room floor.

"You sound like my mother. She always used to say that." I walked back to the kitchen with her at my heels. She took a seat at the table while I went to the cabinet and got us fresh coffee cups.

"So did mine." She grinned. "I think it's in the manual." I filled the mug and handed it to her. She took a long drink, closing her eyes as she did to inhale the aroma. "Oh, I needed this. I really did." She gave a long sigh. "But back to business. Explain to me about this little 'bomb' you dropped on me at the hospital. What in the hell is going on?"

"Let me check on Tom first. I haven't told him any of this yet, and he may want to get up to hear it. In the meantime, there are fresh biscuits in the fridge, and jam if you want it. I'll be making breakfast again later, but you look like you could use a quick pick-me-up."

In fact, she looked like something the cat dragged in—after having played with it for quite a while.

"I could at that," she admitted. She groaned, and started to rise, but I waved her back into her seat.

"Never mind. I'll get it. You just rest." I went to the fridge and retrieved not only the muffins but the rest of the leftovers as well. A few seconds in the microwave and the bacon would be good as new. The eggs, not so much. They tend to get rubbery. But it would only take a minute to scramble up some more. I'd do it while we were talking.

I slid the bacon slices between a pair of paper towels and stuck them in the microwave. With the push of a button they were on the way to warming up.

"I'll be right back."

I moved silently through the house, listening as hard as I could. Everything sounded peaceful behind Elaine's door. Tom, on the other hand, was "sawing logs." I opened the bedroom door to find him curled up next to the cat. Blank gave me what I would've sworn was an embarrassed look before jumping off the far side of the bed.

"Yeah, you're just terrified of him. I can tell," I chuckled. I love that cat.

"Hmnn?" Tom rolled over onto his back. He looked up at me through slitted eyes, his mind obviously still sleep fogged. But he wasn't as pale as he had been, which was good. And I knew he'd be angry if I didn't at least *ask.*

"Mary's here. I'm going to tell her about everything I know or have guessed about what's going on. Do you—"

"I'll be right there." He rolled out of bed in a smooth movement and snagged a tee-shirt from the pile of dirty clothes on the floor. He wasn't quite back to normal, but nearly enough to be moving quickly. I fought down a twinge of envy. Oh, how I wish I could heal like the lycanthropes. But I'm human. I just don't.

"Don't start without me," he said as he ducked out the door and headed down the hall to use the bathroom.

"I won't." I said it softly, but I knew he'd hear.

When we joined Mary in the kitchen she was making significant inroads into the leftovers. Tom got himself a fresh cup of coffee and took up a position leaning against the counter. I sat down on the chair nearest to where he was standing, but angled so that I could watch him. I wanted to see how he would take some of this. I knew he wouldn't be happy. But I wasn't sure exactly how he'd react. I could only hope he wouldn't get pissed at me and think I was hiding things. I hadn't been. I had barely had time to even think over the past few days, let alone talk things out. I just hoped he'd understand that.

"So." Mary gave me a long hard stare. "Spill it."

I hesitated. I wasn't sure where to start. "Um, okay then." I took a deep breath. "Dylan Shea is alive. According to Carlton he's taken over the collective so that it's more like a dictatorship." I looked from one to the other. Neither said anything. Was that good or bad? "Anyway," I continued. "I think there are two separate things going on here. Dylan's personal agenda with me; and the Thrall plan for the werewolves, but they kind of overlap. Some of this I know, some of it I'm guessing."

"Just start already," Mary snapped.

"All right. Okay. The Thrall started 'curing' zombies and coma victims, set up the halfway houses, got a lot of good press. Everybody thinks they're wonderful."

"Not everybody," Tom growled.

"Not the wolves," Mary agreed.

"Right. But the average populace thinks it's great and look at all the good they're doing."

"Yeah," Mary said bitterly. "Tell us something we

don't know." She had pushed away from the table now, and was leaning back into her chair with her arms folded across her chest.

"But then Mike and some of the others started noticing that there's something not quite right about some of the people being brought back. It's like they're not quite back all the way." I looked at Tom for confirmation.

"That's right. Mike sent Bryan in undercover. He found proof that a fair number of the former Eden zombies in particular are being brought back enough to function, but they're still . . . malleable. Bryan told me he couldn't be sure, but it was like they were almost dependent on the hive, without any real will of their own. It creeped him out." I didn't blame him. It bothered me too.

I continued. "In the case of people like the prince's son, that could give the vampires a *lot* of power. I mean, he's the heir to the throne in one of the most oil-rich countries in the Middle East. I think that was how it started out. Control a few key people. Sort of the same idea that Monica Mica had a few years back."

Mary nodded.

"Now not many people can hold out against a Thrall anyway. There weren't ever a lot of Not Prey, and most of us got killed. So we're kind of a nonissue. But the wolves are a problem. The wolves are immune to the psychic stuff. They hate the Thrall, and they're strong enough individually and as a group to keep the vampires from becoming too powerful and they can see through all the illusions and bullshit. If you're head of the Thrall, and you want to get rid of any resistance, any chance of somebody interfering with your big plan, whatever it is, what would be the first thing you'd do?"

"Eliminate the wolves." Mary said it and Tom nodded his agreement.

"But how? When it comes right down to it, the wolves really do have an advantage when it comes to fighting. Teeth, claws, healing ability, working together as a pack. It's a tough package to beat."

"Glad you noticed." Elaine had appeared in the kitchen doorway. I hadn't heard her coming. Neither had Tom. But Mary didn't act surprised at all. She'd either heard or scented the other woman. I would've bet on it.

She walked into the room wearing an oversized pink tee-shirt adorned with the dancing hippopotami from Fantasia, her hair tousled from sleep, and she still looked dangerous. Every eye in the room was on her as she pulled out one of the two vacant chairs and took a seat, helping herself to one of the biscuits and then spreading it with jam.

"He wanted to create a fighting force equivalent to the wolves, but one that he could control, preferably using the Thrall psychic abilities. His own private little army."

"Wolves are born, not made," Elaine said between bites.

"Are you absolutely sure?"

"Oh, do go on." She smiled and it was poisonously sweet. "I *love* a good fairy tale. Tell me how Little Red Riding Hood plans to slay the big bad wolves."

Mary sat very, very still. I could see her eyes darkening, but that was the only sign that she was getting angry. Tom, on the other hand, flushed. He stood up and was moving toward her, until I scooted my chair back in his way.

"You forget yourself, Thomas." There was a rumbling growl to her voice, and I could feel the power of her magic crawling up my arms. I didn't say anything, just stared at her for a long, slow heartbeat. Not in challenge, precisely, but not backing down either. Her eyes stayed locked with mine, even after she'd begun talking again. "Monica Mica was an aberration. The fact that the Thrall are a collective mind means that they have the knowledge of the consequences of every action taken by any individual host. It makes them very conservative in their dealings. They've scored big with their "helpfulness," and they'll use every chance they can to play on the humans' fear and make us look like rabid animals, but even if it were possible, they would never risk a direct, open attack. They wouldn't dare."

I could feel Tom stiffen, hear him inhale to start to speak. I didn't want him to. First, she wouldn't believe anything we said. She was just that sure of herself. It was pure hubris, but there would be no getting past it. But more than that, I didn't trust her. My psychic sense was picking up something, but the fact that she was a powerful werewolf was interfering with me getting anything specific. I could probably have talked to her mind-to-mind like I had with Mary, if she'd wanted. But if she wanted to shield me out she damned well could.

Don't argue. It's what she wants, and you can't win.

I knew he heard me. I could see a reaction flicker through those warm brown eyes. There was no hiding the fact he'd been about to say something, but he could change what it was.

"Maybe you're right." His smile was bright, shiny, but without any depth or feeling. "But where are our manners? No one's gotten you any coffee. How do you take it?"

"Black, thank-you." Her words were fine, but her eyes had narrowed with suspicion. She looked from Tom, who was moving around me to get her coffee, and back to me. I hid behind my cup, taking a long drink, so that all she could see was my eyes, and I kept them wide and, hopefully, innocent.

"Would you like some bacon and eggs?"

"No. Thank-you. I'm not usually one for breakfast." Her smile was a baring of sharp teeth. "But I smelled the biscuits and just couldn't resist."

"I'm a big biscuit fan myself," Mary admitted. She was making small talk. Even without sharing thoughts the three of us all seemed to be in agreement. Anything we needed to talk about would be discussed when she wasn't in earshot. Unfortunately, she had no intention of letting me out of her sight.

Wasn't that just ducky.

22

"Is it bad that I find myself hoping Janine tries to kill me soon?" I wasn't asking anyone in particular.

Joe had arrived back at the house just as Elaine announced her intention to take a shower. He'd come bearing towels, sheets, dishcloths and matching dishtowels, hot pads, scissors, even a complete set of gourmet chef and kitchen knives in a butcher block stand. There were other goodies, too, but while the towels were the most urgently needed, it was the knives that made my little heart go pitty pat. I love edged weapons, and these were beautiful, functional, and honed to an edge you could shave with.

So now Joe, Mary, Tom, and I were sitting around the kitchen trying to talk softly enough that Elaine wouldn't hear. And while we wanted to talk about the serious stuff, none of us felt really comfortable doing it with her awake in the house.

I'd asked the question because it had occurred to me that I was supposed to spend the entire day running errands, sitting around *bus stops* with that woman. She'd been up less than a half hour and already I was ready to commit violence. I normally like sarcastic, caustic people. But Elaine—Elaine was just a bitch.

"I'll be there with you," Tom reassured me.

"No, you won't." Mary's voice made it an order. She stopped the argument he was about to make by raising her hand. "You make it worse. Just seeing the two of you together is bringing out the worst in Elaine. It'd be a diplomatic incident waiting to happen."

"But—" he started to protest, but she waved him to silence.

"I don't know why. Maybe it's because of Janine, maybe it's something else, but we can't afford to piss her off as a pack, and you, especially, can't afford it. So, after we take care of our business at the hospital Joe's going to drop you and me off at the convention center and then he'll spend the rest of the day acting as chauffeur and mediator so that they don't kill each other."

I raised my eyebrows at that. Joe, a mediator? Um, she *was* married to the man. Surely she knew just how bad of an idea that was.

The thought must've shown on my face because

Mary smiled. "It's not perfect, but she's much less likely to try pushing you around if there are two of you."

"If you say so." I sounded doubtful. I couldn't help it. I mean, yeah, Joe and I were seeming to get along better the past few days, but we have years of tension between us. The problems might not come from dealing with Elaine.

"Look, let's just do this one thing at a time," Mary suggested. "We'll go to the hospital. Joe will drop off his resignation and clean out his office while we visit with Ruby. Then we'll go to the convention center. If we're lucky, my mother will be there. She's in charge of the Surrogate Council and enough of a political bigwig that we can count on her keeping Elaine busy for a bit. The Conclave officially starts tomorrow. I need to know what's going on, and I think that's the only chance we'll have of getting in a private talk. We can worry about the rest of the day later. Okay?"

I couldn't help but agree with the logic. She did need to know. It would've been nice if Elaine was open-minded enough to be supportive. She wasn't. Having her in the loop would just screw things up. So we would work around her and hope like hell it didn't bite us in the ass.

"All right," I agreed. "But there's something I want to tell everybody right now while I've got the chance." I took a deep breath. "All of you need to be very, very careful. Dylan is unhinged. He specifically threatened all of you."

"Threatened *how*?" Joe asked.

I thought about what Dylan had said by the church, tried to think of a way to tell them that didn't sound silly and melodramatic. It was hard. Because while the words were overblown, the hatred behind them had been very real and very terrifying.

"Katie—" Tom's voice had a warning note that I didn't like. "What exactly did he say?"

I closed my eyes, and forced myself to remember it exactly, trying to get not only the words but the tone. When I was sure I had it right, I open my eyes and spoke. "I was at the church. They've torn it down. They didn't salvage anything. It was deliberate. He meant it as a message for me. And when I saw it, he spoke to me, mind to mind: *I will destroy everything and every* one *who matters to you as completely as I destroyed this building. I have stripped you of your home and your belongings; next it will be your friends, your family, your relationship with* him. *I will destroy your life while you watch helplessly. And when it is over, and you have* absolutely nothing, *then I'll take your life.*"

"Fuck." Joe said it, and swallowed hard. Mary simply sat, grim and pale on the kitchen chair. But it was Tom's reaction that I was most worried about. Because this was a threat to me, and while he respects my strengths, he's also very, very protective of me.

He stood very still, every muscle in his body tense, jaw clenched tight enough that I would've sworn I heard his teeth grind. When he spoke, it was in a slow, controlled voice, every syllable perfectly enunciated. "You didn't tell me this until now?"

"Tom, I haven't had the chance. I was going to show you when we did the meditation. I wanted you to see it for yourself, it and the visions I've been having. I wouldn't hide something like this from you. I wouldn't. It's too damned scary. Because he meant it. He really, truly did."

Tom turned his head toward me slowly, and something about that movement wasn't entirely human. His eyes held a golden cast. I could feel his magic like a weight pressing against me, crushing the air from my lungs. I couldn't talk. I didn't know what to say. I was telling him the absolute truth. Life had been hellish the past few days. There had been no time to think, plan, or talk about anything. Of course, that probably had been part of the plan, keep the blows coming hard enough and fast enough that I was always reacting instead of taking the offense.

"So it's personal then." Joe meant the words to break the tension, but they rolled over us, unheeded. Our gazes were locked, and I, without any psychic effort on my part, could feel Tom trying to test me, trying to see if I was lying to cover the fact that I had done the one thing he hates most. I couldn't make him believe me; couldn't force him to trust me. Either he did, or he didn't. But God help me, I *wasn't* lying.

"It's always been personal." Tom's voice was lower than normal, and there was a rumbling growl to the words, as if a very large, dangerous dog had suddenly learned speech. "He wanted her back; thought if he died a hero, he could come back later and she'd go running to him."

"Not going to happen." I stated it as the fact it was. I would never leave Tom for Dylan. Never. What I felt for Tom was so far beyond what I'd ever had with my former fiancé that there was no comparison.

Tom unbent enough to smile just a little. "I do know that."

"Just making sure."

"Dylan knows it too, obviously," Mary observed drily. "Which is why he went off the deep end." She shook her head, and tried for humor. "You two and your exes."

The lighthearted words were more than a little forced, but this time Tom was ready to heed the intention behind them. I watched as he slowly, deliberately unclenched his tense muscles, forcing his body to relax first, then his mind. It was a good thing, too, because distantly I heard the shower shut off.

"Right," Joe's voice was a little higher pitched than usual, as if he'd been really afraid of what might happen. I certainly had been. "So, one thing at a time. We start with the hospital."

IT WAS EIGHT-THIRTY by the time Joe pulled into the parking lot behind the emergency room at St. Elizabeth's. It had taken a while for everyone to get ready. I'd changed into a pair of black jeans, black polo shirt, and a brand-new black leather jacket that

Joe had bought me. It wasn't as heavy as an actual biker jacket, but it was better than mere cloth, and I wanted to show him that I appreciated everything he was doing for me. Whether it was Mary, the therapy, or both, I didn't know, but these past few days I'd been seeing a side of Joe that had all but vanished since our parents' death.

Tom was wearing an almost identical outfit, but in blue and brown. Both the shirt and jeans were new enough to still be crisp with sizing and a deep, vibrant color that always seems to fade out after the first few washings. His brown leather bomber-style jacket was back, or replaced, and the color looked perfect with his dark curls and brown eyes. I probably should have noticed what everyone else was wearing; but honestly, I couldn't seem to take my eyes off of Tom.

I was nervous, twitchy and high-strung. I couldn't seem to help it. Tom is usually so calm and reasonable, the perfect foil for my temper. I've gotten used to holding hands, having him slide his arm around my waist—small, reassuring touches. Not today. He was still too angry. Oh, he had it under control, and I didn't *think* his rage was directed at me, but he'd pulled himself in on himself. It was affecting everyone. Casual conversation had all but ceased, making for a long, uncomfortable car ride.

We crossed the parking lot in a group, with Joe in the lead. He was carrying an empty box in one hand. Mary walked beside him. They weren't touching, but somehow you just knew they were a couple.

Body language, probably. I couldn't define it, but it was there. And despite everything I found myself smiling. Joe had found a woman who was right for him, who made him happy. She was strong in all the right ways, capable of standing up to him when need be, and standing behind him when he needed that. I was so glad.

I turned to look at the man who did all that for me and saw him watching me. His expression had softened, probably in reaction to what he was seeing on my face. He reached out, and I slid comfortably into the crook of his arm, sliding my arm around his waist, reveling in the warmth of him and the scents of leather and clean skin. When Elaine scowled at us we both chose an attitude of lofty indifference, although I did have to fight down the wild urge to just flip her off and be done with it.

The glass doors slid open as we came up the walk, but before they did I caught a glimpse of our reflection in the glass. We looked dangerous, coming in as a group. We might mean no harm, but that didn't change the appearance of it. The effect was impressive, right up until Tom whispered a movie quote in my ear: "We bad, we bad." He probably would've started strutting like Richard Pryor if I hadn't given him a warning squeeze.

Nobody else I knew would've gotten the joke, but Tom and I love Gene Wilder movies. We'd spent a Saturday evening at home munching popcorn and watching a double-feature of *Stir Crazy* and *Blazing Saddles* on DVD just a couple of weeks ago.

Mary gave us a *look* over her shoulder, but not a glare. "All right, you two. Behave yourselves."

"Yes'm . . . ma'am." I had been about to say "yes, mother," but sarcasm probably wasn't appropriate in front of company. With Janine out of the picture, Mary was the Acca of Tom's pack. Family or not, we were supposed to show her respect in public. We'd just stepped inside when the first nurse caught sight of Joe. She stepped around the desk holding a clipboard to front of her Looney Toons scrubs.

She cried out in mock alarm, "No, Joe . . . not a box. Dammit! You are *not* leaving us."

At her words staff members started poking their heads out from behind desks, office doors, and various cotton curtains. Several voices called out my brother's name. More than a few groaned when they saw what he was carrying.

A slender black woman with graying hair came up. I recognized her, but couldn't place the name. "It's official then, you're quitting?"

"Yeah. I got the job at DG—thanks in part to your recommendation. Thanks."

"Every word was true. We're really going to miss you around here. Makes me wish I would've lied."

Joe laughed. "I'm glad you didn't."

He was in his element. These were his people, his friends. I knew he'd miss them terribly. But the job at DG was going to be a great move for him. And there he wouldn't have to deal with a lot of the political bullshit he had here. Oh, there'd probably be *other* political bullshit. There almost always is. But at least it would be different, and it probably wouldn't involve the vampires.

Mary spoke up. "Darling, we need to get moving. Meet you back here in forty-five minutes?"

"Sounds good." He smiled at her. "It shouldn't take any longer than that."

We followed Mary down a wide, well-lit hallway with pale gray walls and sparkling linoleum to stop in front of a set of elevator doors. "Elaine," Mary's voice was sweet, light, sugar with just the hint of something uglier underneath. "You'd mentioned you wanted to buy our surrogate a baby gift to make up for what Janine did. If you're still interested, the gift shop is just down that hall to the left about twenty yards."

"Are you trying to get rid of me?" If she was joking, it fell flat. Then again, I got the impression she didn't joke much. At least not with the likes of us. Maybe around everybody else she was a barrel of laughs. I'd probably never be in a position to find out.

"Actually, yes. I am." Mary answered her forthrightly. "We have some private pack business I want to take care of. I'm sure you understand." Saccharine this time, accompanied by a mile-wide smile that would have done a used car salesman or televangelist proud.

"Fine. I'll meet you upstairs in fifteen minutes." She sounded huffy, but at least she left.

"Thank-you so much," Mary called out as Elaine stalked out of sight. Only when we were safely inside the elevator with the doors closed did she say "God, how I hate that woman."

"I think the feeling's mutual, boss," Tom said. "Watch your back."

The bell rang as the elevator eased to a stop. "I always do," she answered as she passed through the doors that whooshed open.

We followed her down another wide hallway. We were obviously on the floor with the nursery, as the hall had wallpaper with flowers and colorful cartoon figures of baby ducks and geese. We slowed a little walking past the wall of glass windows looking in on rows of newborns in identical white bassinets. It occurred to me that I didn't know Ruby's last name, so I couldn't pick out which of the tiny infants behind the glass was hers.

Mary led us to the last room on the left. It was semiprivate, which meant Ruby only had one roommate. The roommate had taken the bed next to the door, and was filling it to overflowing. She was huge, easily 350 pounds. She lay there blithely breast-feeding the biggest infant I'd ever seen in my life, in full view of the open door and anyone who happened to walk by.

I don't think of myself as being a prude, but I'm kind of old school. If you're going to breast-feed in public, fine, but be a little discreet; use a baby blanket or something to cover yourself so the whole world doesn't have to watch. Apparently Ruby's roommate didn't agree.

I hurried past her bed toward the young woman propped up in the next bed, holding a tiny red-faced bundle wearing a pink hat.

"You had the baby." I hurried over to her bedside to get a better look. "Is she okay? Are *you* okay?" I asked the second question because she'd been crying, hard. And like many blondes, me included, she didn't do it well. Her nose was chapped, her eyes bloodshot and swollen.

"She's fine. She's beautiful." Ruby's voice was choked with tears. She held the baby out for me to hold and I took her in my arms. She was so tiny and light that it didn't even hurt the arm in the cast to do it.

"What's her name?" Tom asked the question gently. He'd come up behind me and was reaching around me to stroke the baby's cheek with a single finger. His breath was warm against my neck as he leaned in close. He was obviously just as enchanted by the infant as I was.

"I figured I'd let her parents name her."

I looked at Ruby in shock. I couldn't have heard her correctly. She'd been crazy about Jake. The pack had saved her from the street. Surely they weren't making her—I turned to Mary.

"Don't look at me. It's not my idea. We're more than happy to help her keep and raise the baby." She held up her hands in a warding gesture, as if she sensed that I was ready to fight for Ruby's right to keep the child.

"Nobody can force you to give up your child, Ruby." Tom spoke gently to her. "We won't let them."

"It's not Janine, or the pack." Ruby's voice was tight with the tears she was fighting, but she held her head high. "It's my decision. I want my baby to have two parents who can protect her and who will take care of her, no matter what. I want her to have a real home with people who will raise her to be the kind of person I can be proud of."

"But—" I started to interrupt, but she talked over the top of me, her voice gaining strength with each word she uttered.

"My mother threw out my stepfather. They're getting a divorce. She says if I give up the baby I can come home. I want to go home, Kate. I've missed her so much—missed so much of my life living out on the streets. I want to finish high school, go to a prom . . . maybe get a real job that I earned instead of something that someone gave me because they felt sorry for me." She looked long and hard at the baby, then stroked a gentle finger across the tiny forehead. "But it's not fair to this baby that her mother's still a kid. But I have to be sure, really *sure* that she'll be all right; that she's going to be okay."

I thought I knew what was coming, but I didn't know what to say. My God, was she really going to—

She swallowed hard and then the tears began to flow again. "Dusty's different—she thinks like an adult. Robbie would be fine even if something happened to Rob. If Jake were alive we could raise the baby together. But he's not. And I can't do it without him. I'm just not that strong . . . physically or emotionally." She took a deep, shuddering breath. Her eyes met mine. In that gaze was a burning intensity that demanded complete and total honesty. "Mary tells me you can't have children, but that you want them. Is that true?"

I turned my head so I could see Tom's expression. He was standing so very still, as if he barely dared breathe. He wanted this, wanted it so badly he didn't even dare hope; wanted it almost as badly as I did.

"Yes." My voice came out as a croak; my throat was too tight with emotion for me to be able to speak normally.

"Tom's strong enough to handle her when she gets older and you won't put up with any shit either. I'd like you both to have her, to adopt her." She paused, suddenly unsure of herself. "If you *want* her, that is."

"Ruby." Tom's voice was hushed, almost awed. "I don't know what to say."

Her tears were falling again, and her voice was thick and wet with them. "I'll sign whatever papers they say I have to so she's yours forever. Just promise me you'll send me word once in a while. Let me know she's okay."

"We can do better than that." Tom turned to the bed and took her hand. "If you're really *sure* this is what you want, we can make it an open adoption. You can come see her, spend time with her. She can even know you're her biological mom." He looked at me when he said it, making sure I agreed. I did, completely. If Ruby wanted to be a part of the baby's life, I wanted her to have that chance. I truly

believed it would be the best thing for her and for
the baby.

"I'd like that." She gave us a watery smile and
reached out to gently touch the child. *Our* child.
My God. I had a baby.

But oh Lord—Dylan, the vampires. Did we dare?
I looked at Tom. I wanted this, wanted her. But I
wouldn't, couldn't risk—

Mary saw the look I exchanged with Tom, knew
what it meant without my saying a word.

"We have a couple of days. The baby has to stay
here in the hospital, we'll keep someone on guard at
all times. By the time she's ready to come home the
Conclave, and the crisis, will be over."

Are you sure? What if . . .

*Reilly, if Shea so much as thinks about doing any-
thing to hurt that child I will hunt him down and kill
him myself. You and Tom want the baby. Ruby needs
you to raise her. I'm not letting some asshole vampire screw this up.*

"What are you going to name her?" Ruby asked
as she took the tiny hand in hers, letting the infant
grab her finger.

Tom coughed, and I could tell he was fighting to
hold his emotions in check. Even Mary wasn't un-
moved. So I said what I was thinking, and hoped
Tom wouldn't object. "What do you think of the
name Jacqueline Ruby Bishop?"

"I think that would be perfect," Tom whispered.
"Absolutely perfect."

"I'll have them put it on the birth certificate," Ruby said.

"Jacqueline Ruby, yes," Mary agreed. "But not Bishop. Not until after the Conclave."

Ruby stared at her, aghast. "You're not going to let those assholes break them up, are you?"

"No. Of course not," Mary assured her. "If Tom's listed as the father on the birth certificate, then Kate's automatically a surrogate when they marry. Nobody will break them up. But there are some things going on that make it safer for Jacqueline if nobody knows about the adoption until she can come home from the hospital. So we'll keep this just between us."

"Okay," Ruby agreed.

I heard footsteps coming up the hall outside the door. Without even thinking about it, I sent my mind outward to check. Joe was on his way, and Elaine and Brooks were with him. Time to hand the baby back to Ruby and change the subject. But I didn't want to. Little Jacquie was sleeping sweetly in the crook of my arm.

But I knew that, once we got through the next few days, I'd have the rest of my life with this child. Ruby wouldn't. Even with an open adoption, today and tomorrow were all she really had. I could understand that she wanted to hold Jacquie while she could. Cram all of the love she could manage into that brief bit of time.

There are people who think it is terrible for someone to give up their baby for adoption. I could only marvel at her courage. Even knowing it was in the child's best interest, I'm not sure I would have had the strength.

I turned and bent over the bed, handing my daughter back to her birth mother.

23

"Hey, Reilly." Brooks stepped into a room that was becoming increasingly crowded. The mother in the other bed had pulled the curtains closed around her bed in a huff. I wasn't sure what had annoyed her, and honestly didn't much care. She'd get over it, or she wouldn't. It wasn't like she and Ruby were going to be best friends.

"Come out in the hall a minute," Brooks suggested. "We need to talk."

"Okay."

I started to step away from the bed and stopped. On impulse, I leaned down and gave Ruby a hug. "Thank-you. Thank-you more than you'll ever know." I whispered the words to her as I leaned over to kiss Jacquie on the forehead.

Ruby didn't answer. I'm not sure she was capable

of speech. That was okay. There was nothing more to say anyway. So I stepped away from the bed and walked out the door after Brooks, with Tom at my heels.

Tom closed the door firmly behind us and gestured toward the sitting area at the far end of the hall. Either nobody was in labor right now, or the fathers were all in delivery rooms, so we had the place to ourselves. Seemed like as good a place as any for a private chat. It might even be far enough away from the room that the wolves wouldn't be able to overhear. It wasn't a particularly big room, about twelve by twelve, painted a simple, soothing dove gray. The chairs were made of chrome and heavy, dark gray plastic in rows of four all welded together into one unmovable piece. There were four rows total, with the inside pair of rows joined back-to-back, facing out toward the other two. They looked a lot like the seats in airport concourses, and were probably just as uncomfortable. But they were practical, cheap, and easy to clean, a staple of public buildings everywhere.

Brooks sat in the far row, gesturing for Tom and me to take seats across from him. He looked grim, determined, and a little bit intimidating. The suit he wore today was solid black. He'd paired it with a pale gray shirt that was almost the exact color of the walls of the room we were sitting in and a tie that had charcoal, black, and silver stripes.

It took me a minute to realize why he was probably angry at me. I winced. One of us should've called and told him about the vandalism. We were only renting after all and I certainly would want to have known if one of my tenants had their place broken into. But it honestly hadn't occurred to me. "Look, John, I'm sorry. We should've called. But Tom and my brothers got the mess cleaned up. You can't even tell—" I would've finished, but he waved me to silence.

"I'm not here about the house, Reilly. I already heard about it from Mrs. Loren next door." He kept his voice low. "I'm here on police business."

My heart sank, my throat going suddenly dry. He was a homicide detective. Judging from his voice, police business meant somebody was dead, possibly somebody I knew. My first worry was Bryan. I still hadn't heard from him. Without thinking I sent out a tendril of psychic power. He was alive, busy unloading paper products at the store.

My next thought was Miles. I said the name out loud, knowing for a certainty as I did that my friend was dead. As I thought about it, I even knew how.

He'd been at the computer, typing. His seat was an antique wooden office chair, wheeled, but with a high, carved back. He'd tied a cushion onto the seat so that he could sit on it longer without his rear going numb. It was a match for the huge old wooden desk that he used. The file with the notes I'd given him was lying open on the desk next to the keyboard. The doorbell buzzed, but he ignored it in favor of finishing what he was doing. This was important. Whoever was at the door could wait, or not.

He wasn't expecting anyone, so it didn't matter to him.

He hit "send" and closed out the e-mail program. Whoever was outside was persistent. They were leaning against the doorbell now, so that it was an angry, constant buzz in the background.

"Fine, fine. I'm coming!" he called out. Shoving back the desk chair he rose. For a moment he considered closing out the word processing program and shutting off the computer, but decided against it. He'd take care of whoever was outside first.

He walked down a paneled hallway, turning right into a living room that was well, if sparsely, furnished. Looking out the peephole he saw a petite woman in a familiar blue and red uniform and hat. She was standing at the door, holding the red vinyl zipper pack used to hold pizza boxes and keep their contents warm.

He undid the chain and dead bolt and opened the door. "I'm sorry. But I didn't order—" He didn't finish the sentence. He couldn't. A force slammed into his mind, overwhelming his free will in a single, powerful wave.

The Thrall moved his body like a puppet, making him step back from the door so that she could come inside. Sweat beaded on his forehead. I could feel him struggling, trying to fight. Every move he made was stiff, slow, as she forced him to walk down the hall in front of her.

"Sit down." She gestured to the chair by the desk. "Put your hands on the armrests and don't move."

He did as he was bid. He couldn't not. Every muscle quivered with the effort he was making to fight. She, on the other hand, was calm, smiling; she wasn't even straining herself.

Setting the vinyl box on the desktop she unzipped it and began pulling things from inside. First, latex gloves. She pulled them on with the practiced ease of someone who uses them regularly. Next, the box that had given the case its shape. Flipping open the lid she removed a length of plain white nylon rope, the kind you can buy almost anywhere. One end had been tied into a hangman's noose.

Sweat poured from his reddened face, every sinew in his neck showing as he strained to make his body obey his will. With casual ease she climbed up onto the desktop to wrap the loose end of the rope around the ceiling fan, securing it with a quickly and competently tied knot before jumping lightly down to the floor.

"Time to join your true love, doc." She turned to him, giving a bright smile that showed a flash of fangs. "Upsy daisy."

He didn't move. Her smile vanished instantly, replaced with a vicious and angry expression. "I said, get up." She gestured with her hand and he jerked to his feet like a badly controlled puppet. He stood there quivering as she wheeled the chair beneath the noose.

"Now up on the chair."

Miles didn't move. It was costing him to fight her. His eyes were bulging, and I could see flecks of foam at the corner of his mouth, but by God he wasn't going to go easily, not if he could help it. It made me proud, and sad. Because I knew how the story ended, knew he'd lost.

Tom's arm went around my waist, pulling me close. At his touch I was back in my body, back in the present. I felt tears well in my eyes. I'd killed him. Oh, the vampire had done the dirty work, but I was the one who'd come to him with the information from Carlton, *knowing* they were ready to kill to keep it quiet.

Brooks noticed my distraction. Any other cop would've pounced on the fact that I'd known it was Miles, thinking I might be involved. But John also knew my history, my abilities. He wouldn't just jump to the conclusion I was involved merely because I'd known the victim.

"It was made to look like a suicide. Like he'd hanged himself in his home office. Considering he's been depressed for months, it wasn't a bad plan."

It wasn't a suicide. I knew it. Hell, Brooks knew it. I could tell by the way he was holding himself. There was contained power in his bearing, like a fighter poised to enter the ring, a cat waiting for the right moment to pounce.

"The CSI folks found some inconsistencies." He gave me a long look. "They also found a couple of e-mails he'd sent a few minutes earlier. One of them was to you."

I couldn't talk. Tears were choking off my voice. Miles was dead. My friend was dead and it was my fault. It was all I could do not to sob violently against Tom's chest. I wanted to. I wanted to break down under the weight of the pain and guilt. There should be anger too. But there wasn't. I didn't feel any rage. Not yet. The shock of loss was too fresh. But when the rage came, I'd use it to drive me, to help me do what needed to be done. Because there were other lives at stake; lives that could be saved with the information in that e-mail. I held myself as still as I could, trying hard to breathe, panting for air because my nose was too stuffed up from suppressed tears to let oxygen through.

"I've read the e-mail, Reilly. So have the techs. What in the *fuck* is going on?" His voice was practically quivering with anger, and I could see a flush rising beneath his dark skin. Brooks controls his emotions well, but almost no one can hide emotions that intense completely.

"She hasn't seen it yet." Tom spoke for me. "Dr. Watkins gave her migraine medicine yesterday that knocked her out. She was home until we came here, and we haven't replaced her home computer."

"So she was home with you all last night?"

"Home with me and a houseguest," Tom assured him. "And there were others who came and went during the course of the evening."

Brooks nodded, as if he'd already known the answer. He might have. Who knew what witnesses he'd interviewed before he got to me. But it didn't matter. Only two things mattered right now. Miles's death, and that it not be for nothing. I wouldn't let his life be wasted.

I felt the heat of anger beginning to build and I welcomed it. Felt the strength of it flowing through me, shoving aside the tears and grief. I put my hand on Tom's chest, pushing gently so that he'd let me loose. When he did, I turned to face Brooks.

"I need to see that e-mail." My words still sounded wet, but there was no weakness in them.

Brooks gave me a long look. I saw a flicker of . . . something, recognition, satisfaction, maybe both, pass through his eyes. He reached a hand into the inside pocket of his suit jacket to pull out a folded slip of paper. He handed it across to me, watching me carefully as I unfolded it and read.

Kate, I was right in my suspicions. These are case notes. It's rather complex, but the simplest summary I can give you is that it is a retrovirus designed to introduce the DNA of a psychically gifted werewolf into a human simultaneously with Thrall infestation. The result is a werewolf host that can be psychically linked to the hive.

The notes also indicate that the hosts chosen for this have been very carefully selected, using Eden zombies who were not brought completely back to free will.

In short, the Thrall plan to create an army of werewolves over which they will have complete psychic control.

The e-mail went on, but I couldn't read it. My

hand was shaking so hard the paper was rattling. Shit. *Shit, shit, SHIT!* It was horrible. But it exactly matched what I'd seen in my visions. Toby, a former Eden zombie, as both a vampire and werewolf; the werewolves that smelled of vampire and attacked the lone wolf in the park, even the wolf that Tom fought in the churchyard. It explained everything.

"Breathe, Katie. Breathe." Tom was pushing against my back, forcing my head between my knees. Apparently he thought I was going to pass out. He might be right, based on how light-headed I felt.

I put my head down, taking deep breaths. Slowly, deliberately, I used everything Henri Tané and his books had taught me to build shields around my thoughts. But this time I did it differently. I needed more than a single shield, which could be broken with enough power; this one was more like the layers of an onion. Each individual layer just a little different from the last. It would take a lot of energy, a lot of *work* to break through those layers. And this was a good thing. Because I was going to be coming up with a plan to stop the Thrall in their tracks, and I wanted the element of surprise.

"The e-mails refer to notes you gave him, but we didn't find anything like that." He gave me a long look. "That was one of the inconsistencies. There was a suicide note typed on the computer. It had a typo. His secretary tells me he was fanatical about those sorts of things." He sighed. "But what makes me not believe it was suicide are the e-mails. I didn't know Dr. MacDougal well, but I'd met him, and I can't believe he'd check himself out when there was something this dangerous he could help with. Not after what happened with Samantha Greeley. He blamed himself for that. This would be his chance to make up for it."

He was right.

"It wasn't a suicide." I spoke softly. "The vampires killed him."

"For what was in the notes." Brooks nodded at the e-mail.

"Probably." I folded the e-mail and handed it back to him. It was evidence. I could print my own copy later. Print it and keep it to remember him by.

"Do you know what's going on? Why the vampires would be building their own army of vampire–werewolf cross-breeds?"

"Why does anyone ever build an army?" I sounded almost as angry and bitter as I felt. Damn Dylan. Miles MacDougal had been a good man, and a good friend. Yes, I've killed, but it's been in self-defense, and defense of others. With Dylan in control the Thrall were killing people to further some abstract plan, and sometimes just because they could.

Brooks slid the e-mail back into his inner pocket. "There are really only two reasons. To defend themselves, or to attack somebody else."

Tom nodded. "And we all know who the Thrall would attack first, who their enemies are."

Brooks gave Tom a hard look. "You're thinking this has something to do with the Conclave that's starting tomorrow at the convention center. I know Mary Connolly had to get a city permit to hold it there. The city clerk insisted there be officers in uniform present." It wasn't a question, but I answered as though it had been.

"Don't you?" I asked him. "It's the perfect opportunity."

Tom continued where I left off. He was leaning forward, his expression serious and intense. "They could wipe out the heads of virtually all the established packs, along with their top enforcers; because nobody comes to these things without a security force of their own. We've never had to worry about that before. Security was mostly to protect the various leaders from each other. Werewolves are stronger, better fighters than vampires. But with these new "troops" they can take out the leaders. Manage that and wolves everywhere will be disheartened and disorganized. It wouldn't take much to hunt them down. Especially when you consider that, without the werewolves to interfere, the vampires won't have much of anybody capable of blocking their mental control."

I spoke softly. "If they do it right, they can make it look like it was an internal fight between werewolves. Make the werewolves look like animals with no self-control so that the humans hunt down the rest for them, either kill them or stick them in 'containment camps.' "

Brooks gave me a long look. "So take out the

werewolves, and they can do what you like with the humans?" Brooks's voice was cold. "Is that what you think?"

"I think that's what *Dylan* thinks," I answered.

"Dylan. As in Dylan Shea?" Brooks gave me a shocked look. "I thought he was dead."

"We wish," Tom said bitterly.

Didn't we just.

24

I had always liked Mary Connolly's mother. I've only met her a few times, but she is almost a match for Mary herself. She's a little shorter, has a little more gray in her hair, but she's feisty, opinionated, and takes absolutely no shit off anybody, ever. When we arrived at the convention center she strode up, gave her daughter and my brother each a perfunctory hug, and immediately set her hooks in Elaine Johnston and dragged her off for a private chat.

"I swear," I said as I gratefully watched their backs retreating down the carpeted hallway and into one of the private meeting rooms, "If I wasn't already engaged, I'd seriously think about marrying your mother for this."

"Wrong gender," Rob pointed out as he walked

up. He was wearing jeans and a plain white tee-shirt that was stretched tighter across the chest than it would've been a few months ago. I'd realized dimly that he'd put on some weight. I hadn't realized just how buff he'd become.

Ahem. Tom gave a none-too-discreet cough that let me know I'd stared a little too long. Oops. I turned to see if he was jealous. He wasn't. He knows I don't think of Rob that way—don't think of anyone but him that way. But I couldn't help but notice. Rob had always been scrawny and kind of starved looking. Now he just wasn't. Lucky Dusty.

"Yeah, but she got rid of *Elaine*," I joked. Well, half-joked. Getting rid of Elaine was a really big deal to me. Maybe it shouldn't have been. But that "Little Red Riding Hood" crack had annoyed the hell out of me.

"She's that bad?" Rob asked.

We were saved from answering by the ringing of Joe's cell phone. Normally I get annoyed when people take calls in the middle of a conversation, but this time, not so much. Because any honest answer would not have been diplomatic and I was under the impression that everybody else pretty much felt the same way.

"Hi John. Long time no hear from," he joked. It had been all of maybe a half hour since we'd left him at the hospital. As I watched, the humor in Joe's expression was replaced with a kind of thoughtful determination. "I suppose. I had been going to help Mary with the setup—" Another pause as he listened.

"You did? He had. Wow. Yeah, I can see where it would be."

Okay, hearing half of the conversation was driving me crazy. But none of us wanted to leave him out of the important plans we needed to make. Joe can be aggravating, but he's got a brilliant mind. His input in the planning stage could make the difference between success and failure. So we waited with varying degrees of impatience until he finished his phone call and stuffed his cell phone back into the pocket of his jacket.

"That was Brooks," Joe explained. "He's called in some personal favors and gotten some cops to pull security duty here tomorrow. *Not* in uniform."

I opened my mouth to speak, but Joe talked right over me. "He specifically chose people who scored as head-blind on the police tests, because they're less likely to be affected by the vampire mind tricks."

I started again, but he rolled relentlessly on. "*And* he contacted the widow of that old friend of mine. She still has the molds from when we were going to mass-produce the neck braces. He wanted to know if I thought I could make a dozen of them by tomorrow."

"Can you?" Tom was the one who asked.

"I don't know," Joe admitted. "But, if it's all right with you," he looked at Mary, "I want to try. It could make all the difference to those cops if things go wrong."

"I think you should do it," Mary smiled. "We can get by here without you. Rob and the others have gotten a lot more done than I'd expected. I still need to go over the schedule with the caterers about the banquet, but that's nothing you need to be here for."

"You're sure?" I could see he was both relieved and worried. His body wasn't up to a lot of physical labor yet, so he wouldn't be as useful here as he'd like to be. But building the shields, that was something only he knew how to do, something he was good at.

"Go. We'll get someone else to drive Kate and Elaine around."

"Oh!" His face lit up, and the first glint of mischief sparkled in his eyes. "About *that*." He looked at me, and I could tell he was holding back laughter. "I know you're going to be heartbroken not to have your buddy by your side, but Brooks told me that Janine got picked up by DPD last night when they were patrolling your neighborhood. She's got outstanding warrants for failure to appear. *Sooooo*—" he let the word drag out, but he didn't need to finish the thought. No Janine. No need for Elaine as a bodyguard. *WHOO FRIGGING HOOO!*

I didn't recite "Free at Last" or do the happy dance. It wouldn't have been politic. Appropriate, perhaps, but not politic.

Mary fought to suppress a grin at the expression on my face. "Would you like me to go break the bad news to Elaine for you? Maybe while you ride with my husband back to the house so you can borrow the car?"

"What about making plans?"

"Reilly, I know this will be hard for you to believe, but I actually do understand the basics of what's going on. I've got a good grasp of tactics too. Think about why I might have *allowed* Janine to take the pack on the drive. I can handle this without you. Go. We can talk later."

She stood on tiptoe to give Joe a quick kiss, then turned and headed in the direction of the room her mother had gone into. Tom did her one better. No quick good-bye kiss for me. He pulled me into his arms, giving me a long, slow kiss that weakened my knees and left me breathless and aching with hunger. I hadn't expected it, but I managed to give as good as I got. So good, in fact, that there were more than a few catcalls, wolf whistles, and "get a room" comments thrown at us from the various folks helping with the setup. It made me blush to the roots of my hair, but I wasn't sorry. Not one little bit.

We left as fast as Joe could walk. He was babbling excitedly, the words tumbling over themselves in a torrent. If the police had the shields they could help guard the entrances. Not only would it help with whatever Dylan was trying to pull, it would be another level of protection. Uniformed officers could keep the humans who'd be attending the self-improvement seminar and trade show upstairs tomorrow afternoon completely separate from the wolves.

I shuddered at the thought. It honestly hadn't occurred to me that the convention center management would have scheduled another event to run simultaneously with the Conclave. Yeah, technically there was plenty of space. And yeah, the werewolves *aren't* monsters. But geez. I wouldn't have done it. Then again, it's a business. They're in it to make money. Letting the entire exhibition floor and the Wells Fargo Theatre go empty when they could be rented out would waste a ton of money. And while the Conclave could probably afford to rent the whole place, it would be awfully pricey when all they needed was the meeting floor.

I didn't like it. It made logical sense, but the thought of all those unprotected humans so close to what I was afraid would be a war zone made my blood run cold.

Plans within plans, within werewolf plans, within Thrall plans. *My, what sharp teeth you have. All the better to eat you with, my dear.* Why would Mary have let Janine take the pack? What could she do now that she couldn't as the leader? Why would Carlton risk death just so he could drop by to wish me well after the building collapsed? Why steal the paperwork only to have Dylan take them back? What could Carlton do dead—had that part of the plan occurred—that he couldn't as leader?

It was no use. I'm only an adequate chess player, and this would take Deep Blue to solve. But Bryan called while we were on our way to Joe's. He was on his break and wanted to know why I'd called. Telling him what was going on took most of the drive time. Listening to him swear got me into the driveway and as far as Joe's garage door.

"What do you want me to do?"

I thought about it for a minute. I *wanted* him to stay home, hide under the bed, and be safe. Of course he wouldn't, and I couldn't very well ask it of him. He was a man, and was as vested in this fight as I was. They'd tried to kill him. He had a right to be involved. I hated it. But it was his right.

"Joe," I looked at my older brother. One look told me he felt exactly the same way. More, that he felt the same way about not just Bryan, but *me*. Wow. "Do you think you'll need any help with the neck braces?"

"Actually," he gave me a look that told me he knew exactly what I was doing. "I might." He lifted the garage door handle, and it slid smoothly open. Now that my stuff had been moved out I could see that he had set up a workbench to tinker with his inventions. A long, wide table, it had a rule built into the top to measure with, and there were shelves and hooks in the wall above it for the various tools he might need. An overhead fluorescent fixture gave him plenty of light to see by. It was a neatly organized, well-planned work space that suited him to a T.

He walked over to a cabinet in the wall and pulled it open. He obviously didn't like what he saw because he reached for the phone.

"Bryan, it's Joe. I'll need your help with some stuff here. Get here as fast as you can, but on the way I want you to stop by an art supply shop and the hardware store. Have you got a pen and paper? It's going to be a long list."

I raised my hand, asking to interrupt. Joe told Bryan to hold on, covered the speaker with his hand, and gave me a quizzical look.

"Make sure you keep him here overnight, Joe. Dylan's set a trap for him, using a friend of his from high school. If he's here they can't get to him."

Joe's expression hardened to granite. "Got it."

He uncovered the speaker and I heard him say, "Bryan, I need you here as quick as you can manage. Oh, and this is going to take all night. You'll need to cancel any plans you had made."

I gave Joe a nod of thanks, then took his keys and left. I wasn't too worried about leaving my phone. I could always pick it up later. For the moment at least, my brothers were safe—as safe as I could make them. Tom was with the wolves. He'd be fine. Knowing that, I could move on to taking care of my own mundane business with a clear conscience.

The first thing I wanted to do was stop by the church. I wanted to set up a mass for Miles. More than that, I needed someone to talk to, someone who wasn't involved in the thick of things. So I drove out to the suburbs to visit Father Atkins at St. Patrick's.

St. Pat's is a beautiful church. An octagonal building of gleaming white stone, it sits on the crest of a hill so that you can see it for quite a distance in any direction. The day was sunny enough that the stone edifice seemed almost blinding in stark contrast to the jewel tones of the stained glass windows. I parked at the base of the hill and walked up the long set of steps that led, not to the church itself, but to the rectory and parish offices. The door was locked, but when I rang the bell I heard movement. In a matter of minutes Father Atkins came to the door.

"Katie. It's been a few weeks. Are you here about changes to the wedding plans?"

"No. We're still on as scheduled for next week."

Tom and I had been going to have two weddings. The first one, in Vegas, to get the legalities out of the way the minute we could. The idea had been, once we were legally married, the pack would back off. Unfortunately, we still hadn't managed to pull that off. But without threat of the destruction of the church itself, I refused to reschedule the big church wedding I'd waited for my whole life. I didn't know *how* we'd work everything out by next week, but by God we would. I was *not* postponing this again.

I smiled and stepped through the door the priest held open for me. Father Atkins is short for a man, probably about five foot five, and nearly as round as he is tall. He's got a mop of dark curls liberally laced with gray, a beak of a nose, and eyebrows that look like caterpillars ready to crawl off his face. We'd had a rocky start to our relationship. He disapproves of violence in general and in the specific. I understand that. But my life is violent. I don't want it that way, don't go looking for trouble. But I'm also not willing to martyr myself for no good purpose. He'd unbent a little when he'd seen some of the violence firsthand—a shooter had tried to gun me down in front of this very church. I'd been saved by pure luck, and the fact that he'd dragged me back under cover by my ankles.

"You're in trouble again." His expression was grim, his voice disapproving.

There was no point in denying it. "Can we count this as a confession visit? I need the confidentiality."

He nodded and then let out a sigh that would have had me cringing in my youth. "Go into my office and sit down." I heard him lock the dead bolt as I walked past the secretary's desk and through the doorway that led to the book-lined study where he usually worked. A modern computer workstation took up most of the space, but there were a couple of well-worn wingbacked chairs for visitors, and a row of four-drawer file cabinets of different colors and vintages lining the far wall. Hanging above them was a crucifix. It was a modern, abstract sculpture primarily of black iron, the body a stick figure. The thorn crown, however, was polished silver, with razor sharp prongs that would draw real blood if you handled it carelessly.

I took my seat in the guest chair closest to the door and waited for him to join me. It took a few moments, but when he did he brought a fresh pot of coffee and a matching pair of large, ceramic mugs.

"I figured this might take a while." He spoke with a dry humor that I'd begun to appreciate the longer I knew him. "Your confessions are always . . . interesting."

I supposed that was one way of looking at it. Sort of like that old curse about living in *interesting times*.

He poured coffee for each of us, setting a mug on a coaster in front of my seat before settling comfortably in behind the desk. "So, talk to me."

I talked. He winced, visibly, when I told him about Bryan, and about Miles. His eyes widened as I related that Dylan lived, but was fully evil.

I steeled myself and waited for the judgment I just knew would come when he heard that I planned to be in on whatever happened tomorrow.

He sighed. "It's a hard life you live, Mary Kathleen."

"Yes. It is."

"I've come to know you fairly well over these past several months. You and Tom both. I've listened to your confession some few times, and I've learned a thing or two about you."

I winced, sure I was in for it now.

"And I know now that you do not enjoy this. You loathe the violence; hate the attention. Given your choice you would much rather stay at home with your husband and your cat, eating pasties and minding your own business."

"Amen!"

"But that's not an option, is it?"

"No. It isn't. Father, Dylan is in charge of the hive now. He's outright told me he plans to kill everyone I love and destroy everything I care about. No matter if they've harmed him directly. *Then* he intends to murder me. Do you really expect me to sit by and let him?"

"No. Nor do I consider it a sin for you to protect yourself and those you love."

I blinked. Okay, this was new. When it had been Amanda—

He gave me an impatient look, as though I was being particularly dense. Maybe I was. "You will remember, the last time you were being threatened you *didn't* simply act to protect those in danger. You were actively seeking out Amanda Shea in a pre-emptive manner."

Oh. I hadn't really thought of it that way.

"There is a difference, you know."

I supposed there was. But it was a pretty fine line. I started to speak, but he shushed me.

"Kate, I know you well enough now to know that while you may have threatened vengeance for what they did to Bryan in the heat of anger, it isn't really your style. If you can, you'll avoid killing. But I also know that there's a very good chance that you won't be able to sidestep it this time. The head of the Thrall has effectively declared war on you and yours."

I took a deep breath and let it out slowly. I'm not stupid. I can accept reality. "Yes. And there's a very good chance I won't survive. The creatures he's created have all the strengths of both the vampires and werewolves. I'm tough, Father, but I'm only human."

"You sound afraid."

"I am." I could admit it here, to him. Outside these walls I'd put on my armored shell, be Kate Reilly "Not Prey" extraordinaire. But here and now I would admit, to myself and my priest, that I was scared. Not so much that I might die. I've faced death enough times now that I'm not as scared of it as I probably should be. But I could lose Tom, one or both of my brothers, Mary or any of my other friends. In fact, if the vampires used their "shock troops" to attack the Conclave tomorrow it would be nothing short of miraculous if I *didn't* lose someone I loved. Most of us were pretty damned tough. But the odds weren't in my favor. I'd come to love one heck of a lot of people, and Dylan had specifically chosen them as targets. "I'm afraid for myself. But more than that, I'm afraid for everyone else. I'm glad Joe's building neck guards for the cops. It could really make a difference. But ultimately, if Dylan does this, people are going to die. Probably a lot of people. And if I take out Dylan the entire Thrall hive will collapse. *All* of the hosts, most of the herds will die with him. When Monica died, nearly a hundred and fifty people died with her. Dylan could take down thousands . . . maybe tens of thousands. I honestly don't know how many Thrall exist. I don't want that on my conscience. But I don't think he's going to give me a choice."

"I pray that you're wrong about that."

"So do I. But if I'm not?"

He touched the cross around my throat with reverence and smiled sadly. "I'll pray for you, and for those fighting with you."

"Please do. Because I'm afraid we're going to need it."

We talked a little longer, but there wasn't much more to say. I arranged for a mass in Miles's honor, talked to Father about the guilt I bore in his death. He offered words of comfort, of absolution. I tried to take them, but it was too soon. The loss was still too fresh.

I left the church shortly thereafter. I'd hoped to find peace there, but I was just as unsettled and restless leaving as I'd been when I first walked through the door.

If I couldn't escape my guilt, I'd just have to work through it or live with it. In the meantime, life hadn't come to a stop. There were all sorts of ordinary things that needed to be taken care of.

I started with the insurance claim, stopping by the office to pick up the checks. I was lucky. The claims adjuster was out. All I had to do was sign a few forms and the secretary handed me a pair of checks. She also gave me a brown envelope with the offer from the developer.

I hadn't checked with Tom yet, but I, personally, was leaning toward selling the property. I'd look at the offer the claims adjuster had taken, but I'd check with some of my own contacts as well. There was a good chance he'd received a legitimate offer. But there are always people looking for a "bargain" by taking advantage of folks who are desperate. Whether or not it is unscrupulous depends on your point of view. They do get the folks they buy from out of a bind in a hurry, but usually at a huge discount. I wasn't that desperate. I could be a little more choosy.

I used the drive-through of the Wheat Ridge branch of my bank to deposit most of the checks. I kept out enough cash to pay back Bryan, and also to buy some of the things I was going to need, not the least of which was new leathers.

The bank branch was at 44th and Wadsworth, just a few minutes away from the biker shop where I'd ordered my boots and had bought my leathers. I needed another set for tomorrow, and the damned things weren't cheap. At the rate I was going through them I might well be the biker shop's best customer. Maybe they'd give me a discount for buying in bulk.

Probably not.

I had more errands, lots more. But I just couldn't bring myself to do them. Depression sucked at me like quicksand. I needed to do something to break myself out of it; needed to remind myself what I was fighting for.

On impulse I took the 38th Avenue entrance onto the freeway, driving east toward St. Elizabeth's. I wanted to see Ruby. More than that, I wanted to see Jacqueline . . . hold her . . . remind myself that she was real. I had a daughter. I had a fiancé. There were good things, good people in this world. Things and people worth fighting for—worth dying for if need be. I didn't want to. God knows I had a lot to live for. But Ruby had chosen Tom and me because we'd protect her baby, "no matter what." Protect her from exactly the sort of threat Dylan was posing.

It didn't take long to reach the hospital. I parked in the parking garage and made my way through the front doors. There, to the right, was the gift shop, and I stopped in to buy Ruby some flowers. A stuffed wolf caught my eye, and I bought that too.

I carried both with me into the elevator and pressed the button for the floor with the nursery. The bell had rung and the doors were just beginning to close when a manicured male hand slid between the doors, activating the sensor to make them reopen.

The minute I saw who it was I wished I'd been just a little quicker.

Dr. Edgar Simms was an attractive man, well groomed, well spoken, and a world class ass. I'd had dealings with him in the past. I'd done it because it was necessary. But after he suspended Joe, I had little to say to the man. He'd never even thanked me for restoring his daughter to her mind. He'd insisted I'd done it in order to save Bryan, but I'd never heard word one from him afterward.

Today he looked harried and more tired than I'd ever seen him. Oh, he was still handsome. There was no doubt of that. His hair was still perfectly coiffed, his designer suit tailored to fit a tall, slender frame. But there were lines at the corners of those piercing blue eyes that hadn't been there the last time I'd seen him, and the self-confidence that had bordered on outright arrogance seemed to be missing.

"Good evening, Ms. Reilly," he greeted me and turned to face the elevator doors. Reaching in front of me he pressed the button for the fourth floor. The doors rolled smoothly closed, giving the two of us complete privacy for the span of a few moments.

"I take it you're visiting a patient. Would it by any chance be Lewis Carlton?"

"No. Actually, one of my acquaintances had a baby. I thought I'd check in and see how they were doing."

"Ah."

The elevator started moving. I was glad. The silence was getting a little bit strained. I mean, at one point he'd been allied with the vampires. As far as I knew he still actively supported them. He'd certainly been quick to throw my brother under the bus when Joe had spoken out against them.

But I, the bane of all vampire kind, had saved his daughter.

Miss Manners and Emily Post just don't cover this sort of thing.

"So, how is Carlton doing? Or can't you tell me?"

He reached across me in an abrupt snakelike movement, hitting the emergency stop button. Alarms began to sound almost immediately, and a light came on above the telephone handset attached to the wall just below the button panel.

"What in the hell—"

"Ms. Reilly. We don't have much time. I was friends with Doug Richards. Carlton is an acquaintance of mine. I know a bit about the Thrall, or thought I did. But I've spoken to Carlton since he regained consciousness. If what he's told me is true, I owe your brother more than an apology. And you are in very real danger."

I stared at him in shock, completely at a loss as to what to say. I don't think I would've been more surprised if he'd sprouted horns and a tail—maybe less.

"There is no more collective. Only one mind is running the hive now. And it is someone who bears you a personal grudge: your ex-fiancé, Dylan Shea."

The emergency telephone rang before I could respond, and Doug picked up the receiver. In a job of acting that should have won him an award nomination he cheerfully answered the voice on the other end of the line. "No, we're absolutely fine. It was just an accident. I tripped and fell against the controls. Oh, good. Just pull out the button? All right then. I'll do that. Thank-you."

He hung up the emergency phone, then reached over and pulled out the red button. The alarms silenced immediately, and the elevator began to rise once more.

He spoke quickly, but with startling intensity. "I owe you my daughter's life, and quite possibly my wife's sanity. So I'm warning you that something very dangerous is going on. Take a few minutes to talk to Lewis. And be very, very careful."

The elevator stopped, the doors opened smoothly. He'd stepped out and was gone before I could thank him or even come up with a coherent response.

25

I wandered through the kitchen, opening and closing drawers, looking for the scissors and my knives. I hadn't slept well at all last night. I knew I needed to get some rest. I just couldn't manage it. I'd spent the entire night tossing and turning, sending my thoughts out every few minutes to check on the people I loved. I didn't interrupt them, they were all too busy. I probably could've gone to either the convention center or Joe's house, but I knew I'd only be in the way. So I'd stayed home, fretted, and tried to sleep.

I finally gave up and climbed from my bed just as the sun cleared the horizon. I fixed myself a good healthy breakfast, and forced myself to try and eat it before showering and brushing my teeth.

I wandered around the house in a white silk robe

that was supposed to go over a negligee, gathering together everything I needed to arm up. First, I set my neck brace, turtleneck, and brand-new biker leathers onto the bed. The boots I'd special ordered had arrived. I'd picked them up with the leathers. I retrieved the box from the closet, setting it onto the floor by the bed. I hoped they'd be comfortable. They'd seemed to fit well enough when I'd tried them on, but you always have to be careful. Sometimes shoes feel good from the start, other times you have to break them in a bit. I was hoping for the former, because I was probably going to be spending a lot of time on my feet today. Enough time that it was tempting to just go ahead and wear running shoes. But there were things to consider besides comfort. It would take a lot more work to hamstring me through steel-reinforced boots. And the high tops would allow me to carry the present I'd bought myself.

Last night, when I'd bought the replacement leathers, I'd picked up a pair of boot knives and sheaths at the biker shop. They were good quality, with wickedly serrated edges. I'd tried them on with the sheaths stuck in the new boots. The fit had been perfect.

Still, I wanted more. Call me crazy, but I wanted as much weaponry on me as I could carry. So I was looking for just the right blade to tuck in my cast. I knew the perfect one, too. It was one of the set of knives Joe had bought me at the same time he'd gotten the towels. Unfortunately, I couldn't remember where I'd put them. Damn it anyway! They were in a stand. I should have just left them on the counter. I thought I *had*.

I glanced up at the kitchen clock. It showed 9:15. I needed to get moving. Dusty was going to be picking me up at 10:00. The opening addresses weren't scheduled to start until 11:30, but we'd promised Mary and Brooks we'd get there early and use our psychic gifts to check the place out.

As a last resort I checked the pantry. There they were, center shelf, right at eye level. I sorted through them, picking a blade I'd be able to slide beneath my cast.

I was nervous; fidgety. I tried to meditate. But while I'd been getting better with practice, I was just too tightly wound to get into the right state this morning.

Maybe I should call Carlton. But what could he remember that I didn't already know? Dylan is fiercely paranoid. Always was. And he always had to be in control. It was one of the things that nearly broke us up when we'd been together. But like a fool, I'd given in . . . let him run the show. That had been a big mistake and I didn't plan to repeat it.

It might have helped if Tom had been home. Logically, I knew how important it was that he help patrol the building to make sure nobody snuck anything in. Just like it was important that Joe and Bryan make the neck and chest guards for the police officers Brooks was bringing to the party. But that didn't make me miss him any less. Was that a weakness? Maybe, but I didn't think so. Over the past two years I'd learned that our strengths complemented each other. There are things I can do that Tom can't; and others that he does better than I do. As a team we can do more, better, than either of us could individually.

I heard a car pull into the driveway and heavy footsteps coming up onto the front porch. I glanced at the clock again. If it was Dusty she was running early. But it didn't sound like her. I sent a thought outward, just as the doorbell rang.

It was Elaine. I could tell that much. Unfortunately, I couldn't sense her thoughts. Then again, I never really could. She shielded better than anyone I'd ever known, including Henri.

Well, hell. Wasn't this just what I didn't need. I set the knives on the kitchen counter and went to open the front door.

"Good morning, Kate."

"Elaine." I glanced toward the car, looking for her driver. I didn't see anyone, but the trunk lid was open, so I couldn't get a good look inside the vehicle. Apparently the driver was going to stay outside. That meant Elaine and I got to talk alone. Oh goody.

I shifted my gaze to the woman on the front porch. She looked tired, standing in front of me wearing the same dark jeans and simple white blouse she'd had on when she left here with us yesterday morning, and while she'd obviously freshened her makeup and combed her hair, there were dark circles under her eyes. It didn't look as if she'd been crying. Then again, maybe she had, but her werewolf healing had gotten rid of the evidence—the kind of chapped nose and lips I get.

"I came by to get my things." She gave me a smile that didn't reach her eyes. It was a politician's smile meant more for the sake of politeness than anything else. "Since the police have Janine in custody, there's really no point in my staying here. I think we'll all be more comfortable if I check into a hotel near the convention center."

Since I couldn't honestly deny that, I didn't try. Instead, I held open the door for her to come in.

"Janine's failure to appear for the federal charges in Las Vegas will make things go badly for her. That she attacked the police officer who tried to take her into custody here will make it worse."

"I'm sorry." The words were automatic, but I meant them. Unfortunately, she didn't believe me.

She glared at me and I felt the power of her magic pressing against me like a living thing. "Don't lie to me, Ms. Reilly."

"Fine. I'm *not* sorry she's in custody. I think she's unstable, dangerous, and needs serious help. I *am* sorry that it came to this." It was the absolute truth. Janine was a wolf, but that wasn't why I disliked her. It was her human side that had *issues*. A good psychiatrist might have been able to help her before things got this far out of hand. As it was, she was probably going to prison. Most likely, she'd be there for years. For a wolf, being caged like that would be a form of torture, a type of hell. I knew it was necessary, but that didn't make me happy about it.

Elaine gave me a long, hostile look from half-lidded eyes glowing golden with power. "You can't actually mean that."

I threw up my hands and turned my back on her. It was pointless trying to talk to her. There are people who hold their belief in their own rightness so tight to their chests that there is no room for anything else, no room for new ideas, other opinions, nothing. Elaine was one of those people. I was too strung out this morning to deal with her diplomatically. More, I didn't *want* to.

"Whatever. I'll let you pack. I need to start getting ready." I walked down the hall to my bedroom and began viciously ripping the price tags off of my new clothes. After tossing the tags into the waste bin, I started rummaging in my drawers for a pair of thick socks and some clean underwear that would allow for comfortable movement. Sexy is well and good when I'm trying to impress Tom, but today I needed something I'd be able to fight in.

I was interrupted by Elaine's voice, sounding tense and strained, calling me from down the hall. "I'm finished packing, but I could use some help carrying my bags to the car. *If* you don't mind." That last just dripped sarcasm.

Not if it will get her out the door quicker, I thought. What I said was, "Sure. No problem."

I tossed my sweat socks onto the bed and shoved the dresser drawer closed before walking out into the living room.

She had three bags. Two large suitcases and a

cosmetic bag. All of them high end, high quality. All together I couldn't imagine they weighed enough to cause her trouble. She could have carried them out by herself if she wanted. But she was being petty. She was the bigwig. I was the peon. I was *supposed* to carry her bags, kiss her heinie, and act happy to do both.

I am *so* not good at politics. But I *am* fond of my sister-in-law, and I love Tom, and this bitch could make either or both of their lives hellish if she really put her mind to it. So I forced my face into a semblance of a smile by reminding myself that she was, at least, leaving and grabbed the cosmetic bag and larger suitcase. Kicking open the screen door, I walked down the steps to where a mid-sized sedan had been backed into the driveway. The trunk was standing wide open. I set the cosmetic bag in first, leaving both hands free to wrangle with the big suitcase.

I was bent over double when I heard a high-pitched buzz, felt a blur of movement behind me. I tried to turn, but it was too late.

I felt the prongs jab into me through the thin fabric of the robe, and at the same instant a shock of electricity jolted through my body. Pain, intense enough to steal my breath and make me sweat. She kept the prongs pushed against me, the charge surging into me for seconds that seemed to last an eternity. My whole body spasmed, my legs giving out beneath me. I couldn't seem to breathe, couldn't think. She caught me easily and tossed me bodily into the trunk of the car and slammed the lid closed.

I'm claustrophobic. In those first few moments, had I been able to think, I'd have been terrified. Instead, I lay on the thinly carpeted surface, my muscles still quivering and spasming, unable to think clearly or do much of anything.

Time passed; how much time I don't know. I vaguely felt the car moving beneath me, heard the sounds of traffic. Not much later, we pulled to a stop.

The trunk opened. I could see Elaine standing outlined against a background of tall grass. In the distance there was a playground set and the sound of geese.

I should move. I knew that. But neither my mind nor my body was capable of it. I could only watch, distant and detached, as she reached into the trunk and removed her makeup case. Setting it onto the ground, she hit the latches and flipped open the lid. I heard it, but I couldn't see. Couldn't stir so much as a muscle. When she came back in view she was wearing latex medical gloves and had a syringe in her hand. She grabbed the arm without the cast and turned it sharply to expose the bend of my elbow, where the veins are near the surface and easy to find. Pinning my unresisting flesh between her arm and body, she used her free hand to jab the needle home and hit the plunger.

The world went dark.

KATIE! KATIE! WHERE are you? A frantic female voice cut through the fog muddying my mind, prodding me. Dusty. It was Dusty. I knew it, but vaguely. Everything was muddled. I couldn't seem to think.

What's happened to you?

I knew I should be frantic, should try to shake off the effects of the drug, but it was just too hard. I let myself drift downward, back toward oblivion.

TOM! THEY'VE DONE IT TO KATIE TOO. YOU HAVE TO HELP ME.

I felt a second, familiar presence join the woman, felt his absolute terror when he realized what condition I was in.

Katie, baby, you have to fight this. You have to let us help you. He used his thoughts as a hook, trying to pull my mind free of the drug and shock-induced lethargy. Every time I started to slip away I felt him dig in further, shoving more of his consciousness into me, forcing me to stay.

Dusty, can you see where she is, what happened to her? I heard Tom's voice as clearly as if he were here with me, we were that connected.

I felt Dusty's consciousness brush against mine lightly. A moment later, another touch. This time deeper. It was . . . odd . . . as though my mind was a door that she could walk through, my memories and consciousness rooms for her to visit. I'd done it before, but from the other end. Experiencing it as the person being probed was both weirdly intimate and profoundly disturbing. Each memory she touched, each thought she brushed against brought me closer to consciousness, closer to being myself.

She was healing me.

When I was coherent enough to realize that, and to realize the incredible danger she'd put herself in, I started to break the connection.

No! Don't! I'm okay. WE'RE okay. Dusty's voice was clear in my mind.

How?

I'm linked to the pack, and some of the other Accas, the ones who believed. They're helping me to do this without getting hurt. Now, what happened? Where are you?

I don't know. I didn't tell her what happened, I showed her, and through her Tom, and all of the wolves linked to her. I showed them everything, including that small glimpse of tall grass, a playground set, and the distant sound of geese.

The Accas were horrified, furious at Elaine's betrayal. But it was Tom who gave me hope. Because now that I was conscious, I was aware of being confined in a small dark space. My pulse began racing, thundering loudly in my ears. I closed my eyes, trying to keep my breathing even, keep the panic at bay.

I know where you are, Katie. Hang on, baby. We're calling the cops now and I'm on my way.

Inhale, count to ten, exhale. I made myself concentrate on every breath. If I didn't I would hyperventilate. I hated the fact that my fear had that much power over me. It wasn't sane, it wasn't logical. But that's the definition of a phobia in a nutshell. Unfortunately, breathing deeply gave me a good, long whiff of what I smelled like. It wasn't pretty. Panic-laced sweat and urine. I wasn't sure when I'd wet myself. Maybe the electric charge had done it. Or perhaps I'd been close to death when Dusty "found" me. The body usually lets go of everything in that last moment—which is why so many people die on the toilet. As an old friend once observed, there's a reason "the king" died on "the throne."

Stupid, thinking of that. But thinking of anything was better than letting the fear have its way.

I could hear sirens in the distance, growing louder as they came near.

Kate, are you still there? There was a hint of fear in Dusty's mental voice. *Are you all right? The police are on the way with an ambulance.*

I'm okay. Stop by the house and get my clothes. I'll need to change. I didn't elaborate. It was too embarrassing. Either she knew from my thoughts, or just guessed, because she agreed. *I'll try. Tom's pretty frantic. After what happened with Mary he wants to see for himself that you're all right.*

My heart sank. I swallowed hard, afraid to ask, but unable not to. *What happened to Mary?* The sirens were almost here. I could distinctly hear both the ambulance and police sirens, closing in fast. I rolled over as much as I could, fighting to position myself so that I could kick against the trunk. I wanted them to hear me, wanted them to get me *out*. I might not be able to get enough leverage to do any damage to the trunk, but I could make noise, and as soon as I heard the crunch of vehicles stopping on gravel I did just that. Kicking, screaming, and pounding against the closed trunk lid with my fists.

She'd been everywhere around here, working her ass off. Then she just vanished. Everybody figured she was running an errand, maybe went to the restroom. But she was gone too long. So I looked for her the way you always talk about doing. She'd been given an overdose of paralytic and shoved into a closet. She was almost dead. Her heart kept stopping. I tried to do what I did with you, but—

I shuddered. Oh God, Mary. She wasn't dead. I'd be able to feel it if she was. But it was bad. I knew that without even trying to reach out to her, or to Joe.

They took her to DG. She's not dead . . . but it doesn't look good. When we found her like that, Tom tried to call you on the phone. When you didn't answer, he panicked and had me look for you too.

I heard car doors slam, and male voices. "Shit, would you look at all those crows."

At the sound of them talking I pounded and kicked with renewed vigor, screaming for help at the top of my lungs. I heard them pause, and swear. Seconds later I heard running footsteps approach the trunk of the car.

"Hang on, lady. We'll get you out."

I stopped kicking, stopped pounding. They were here. They knew I was here. They'd get me out. It was going to be okay.

"What's your name?"

"Kate Reilly."

The cops are here. Tell Tom I'm all right, and I love him. And get me some clean clothes.

Right.

"Ms. Reilly, are you hurt?"

"I'm all right. She drugged me, but I'm okay now. Just get me out of this damned trunk!" My voice cracked as I shouted that last bit and I forced myself to take more deep breaths. Not long now. Easy. Easy. It was going to be all right. *Oh, God. Mary.* Breathe. Inhale, count to five, exhale.

I heard the scrape of metal against metal, saw the rubber of the trunk lip shoved back as the edge of a crowbar was shoved beneath the trunk lid near the lock. With a grunt, and the screaming protest of metal, the lock gave. The trunk popped open and I was blinded by beautiful, glorious sunlight.

26

They put me in an ambulance and took me to the emergency room at Denver General. I didn't argue. If I said I didn't need medical assistance I'd have been stuck answering questions at the crime scene for hours. The crows hadn't been hanging around for nothing. Elaine's body had drawn them.

It was murder. Oh, I wasn't a suspect. I didn't have the fangs to have pulled it off. And, thank God, Tom and the rest of the wolves I cared about had been getting ready for the Conclave with a few dozen well-respected witnesses and several cops to vouch for them. Just as good, Joe had been at the hospital working on Mary. Every one of the "good guys" had an alibi. If I hadn't been terrified for my sister-in-law it would actually have been refreshing. As it was, the police seemed to find it a disconcerting change of pace.

Dusty and Tom were waiting at the door when my ambulance pulled up. She was carrying a big plastic bag that, presumably, held my clothes and definitely the new neck brace. I could see the dark green acrylic peeking out over the top edge of the sack.

Tom ran up as soon as the ambulance doors opened, standing aside only enough that they could get the gurney out and wheel me to the door.

"She's fine, Tom," one of the EMTs assured him. "This is just a precaution."

I smiled. I should have known the ambulance crew would know him. The community of rescue workers is a small one. They take care of their own.

"Are you? Are you really?" He grabbed my hand, walking next to the gurney as they wheeled me through the automatic doors.

I nodded. "Really." *I would've refused the ambulance, but then they would've kept me at the scene asking questions. You and the wolves need me at the convention center. I know it.*

I felt his relief flood across my mind, even though he was still worried.

A female voice interrupted. *Are you sure? Nothing's happened. It's been dead dull except for the thing with Mary—and I'm thinking that was Elaine.* Dusty had joined the mental conversation without being invited and it looked like without even trying. Not that I minded. It just surprised me. I keep forgetting just how powerful her psychic abilities are. She's probably as good, or better, than I am, and she's never actually been bitten by the Thrall.

The EMTs wheeled me into one of the little curtained areas. I climbed off of the gurney by myself and moved up onto the examining table. With a friendly wave, the ambulance workers made their way out to the desk, where they spent a few minutes filling out forms and updating the on-call doctors and nurses with additional information that they hadn't transmitted over the radio.

I snuck out of the room, unseen by everyone except Tom. I needed to see Carlton . . . find out what was so important that Simms would risk Dylan's wrath to contact me. And hey, if I smelled bad, he wouldn't mention it. Nice thing about athletes—there's an unspoken code about ignoring bad smells in the locker room.

Tom followed at a discreet distance, curious about my plans, but not wanting to make a scene that would get me noticed.

The room was dark, the blinds and curtains closed. The only sound was the soft hum of equipment and beeping of the EKG. "Carlton? Are you awake?"

His voice was faint, rasping—so different from his normal deep baritone that I wouldn't have recognized it if he didn't respond with my name. "Hey, Buffy. How's Fido?"

"I'm here. How you doin', big guy?" Tom's voice was likewise quiet. He seemed subdued now that he could actually see Carlton's condition. I stepped over to the bed and touched his hand. He seemed shrunken somehow, no longer seven feet tall, but closer to a normal size. But that smile, while slow, was pure Carlton. Cocky, confident, and at peace.

"Better now. Simms found you, huh?"

I nodded and he squeezed the hand I put on the bed next to him. "Sorry about the doc, Buff. I didn't realize you'd go to him. Should have. I knew you were tight." He coughed, and then fought to catch his breath. I had no idea what it had taken to remove the Thrall from his body. But he had stitches running up both sides of his face, and his eyes were puffy and black, like they'd had to remove his entire nose to get inside.

"Yeah, I know," he chuckled, noticing that I was staring. "Frankenstein facial. But it's gone. Really gone. Can't hear the buzzing in my head and that bastard Shea isn't kicking my ass anymore. Thanks for that, Reilly."

"You're welcome. I wish I could stay, but I don't have much time. What do you have for me?"

Another cough, this one weaker. We needed to leave him to rest, but I had to know. He gripped my bad arm, and he was still strong enough with just human strength that I couldn't pull away without ripping out the stitches. "Not much you probably don't already know by now. But you need to know . . . they fear you. The queens. There's something about you that's different. Different like Shea. You can do things you don't know about yet. Even I don't know what that might be, but Monica wanted you because you could have remade the entire Thrall

species in your image and we would have ruled the
world. Dylan thinks he's got a handle on you, but
he's an idiot—self-centered and weak in his ego-
tism. You need to pull out all the stops for this one,
Buffy. He's got something big planned. Something
that he didn't tell anyone about. I know it involves
the wolf project, and I think he's planning to do
something at the Conclave." He released my hand
and I could see how much of a toll holding me still
had taken on him. He collapsed back onto the pillow, the tattoos on his head that normally blended
with his dark skin now standing out in sharp relief
against the paleness.

Tom reached forward and held out a fist, looking
at Carlton intently. After a long moment, the big
man curled his fingers and they bumped fists. How
very guy-like. So why did that simple, macho thing
make my eyes tear up?

Moments later, we'd snuck back into the ER and I
grabbed the bag from Dusty's hand as I made a run
for the bathroom. I wanted out of my wet, stinking
robe and underwear. *Now.* If the doctors didn't like it
they could kiss my lily white ass. I wouldn't put on
the neck guard. I mean, that would just be rude when
I knew for a fact they'd need to listen to my heartbeat,
etc. But the clothes definitely had to go.

Tom rolled his eyes as I dashed past, but was wise
enough to keep his mouth shut. The nurse, however,
gave a squawk of protest that I blithely ignored in favor of pulling the bathroom door firmly closed and
flipping the lock.

Having been designed for handicapped access, the bathroom was actually fairly large. Painted white, it had handicapped handles next to the toilet and a motion-sensor flush, a pass-through cabinet for urine samples. The sink was lower than normal too.

I dropped the robe into the trash, quickly followed the underwear. I pulled the plastic bag from the container, tied it closed, and set it on the floor. If the police decided they wanted it for evidence, they could have it. Otherwise, the whole outfit was bound for the trash heap.

Pulling paper towels from the rack, I wet a handful at the sink, hit the button for the soap dispenser, and used my improvised washcloth to give myself a sponge bath. It took a few repetitions before I felt clean enough to be willing to pull on the fresh clothes. Quite a few repetitions. I didn't care. I wanted to be *clean*.

"Kate, are you all right?" Tom's concern was obvious.

"I just wanted to wash up. I'm almost done."

"If you say so." He was being exceptionally gentle, understanding. Then again, he was the only person I'd ever confided my phobia to. I'd never trusted anybody else enough to let them know my weakness. It's the kind of thing that can be used against you too easily.

I pulled the neck brace out of the bag and set it aside. As I'd expected, Dusty had brought me the clothes I'd laid out to wear. I was glad. I was practically ecstatic when I saw she'd packed the knives as well. *Attagirl, Dusty.*

I slipped into the clothes as quickly as I could, which wasn't really all that quick. There's a certain knack to pulling on leather trousers, particularly *stiff* leather trousers. I'd picked a black pair that was a little bit big, I needed to be able to move, but that didn't make dressing a quick and easy process. The boots were another issue. They were black, steel-reinforced, and came almost to my knees. I had to lace them all the way up. But they were long enough and could be laced tight enough to let me slide a knife between leather and sock and not have it wobble around and cut me.

I came out of the bathroom carrying the neck brace and looking dangerous enough that the doctor standing next to Tom stepped back a pace when she saw me, her eyes widening in surprise.

"Ms. Reilly. Um . . . I'm Doctor Jones." She recovered herself quickly, putting on her game face and gesturing to the examining table. "Please take a seat. I want to get your vitals."

I climbed up and sat, the leather of the pants making a weird little squeaking noise as it rubbed against the imitation leather of the examining table. Dr. Jones listened to my heartbeat, took my pulse, then shoved back my sleeve to get a better shot at taking my blood pressure. When she did, she saw the bruising from the shot Elaine had given me. It was ugly and dark against the pale skin of my inner elbow.

"I take it this is how your attacker subdued you?"

"After she'd hit me with a Taser."

She winced. Tom's expression darkened. If Elaine hadn't already been dead, I'd have worried about what he'd do to her. There was that much rage in his eyes.

"Do you know what she gave you?" She slid the gray and black cuff over my arm, fastened the Velcro, and began pumping it tight.

"No. Haven't got a clue. But it doesn't matter."

She rased her eyebrows at that, but didn't say anything. She was too busy listening for the change in heartbeat that would signal the bottom number of my blood pressure. When she heard it she let the air out of the cuff with a soft whoosh and stripped it from my arm.

"I think perhaps we should take a blood sample just in case." It wasn't a suggestion. She intended to do it, whether I liked it or not.

I didn't. I didn't have time for this. The trick was finding a way to convince her. "Dr. Jones, have you heard anything about the psychic healing I did for my brother and another Eden zombie?"

"Of course. Who hasn't? Amazing stuff." She paused, her hand on the curtain.

"Well, another person did a psychic healing on me," I explained. "Whatever Elaine gave me, it's long gone now." I hoped she'd believe me. It was probably a coin toss. But I didn't want to waste any more time. I felt *something* building. A sense of urgency filled me that I couldn't quite explain. We needed to leave, now. I needed to be at the convention center. There wasn't any time to waste. I glanced up at the clock. It was 11:30. All of the delegates would have filed into the main ballroom for the introductory speeches and the catered luncheon.

All of them. Gathered together in one room. Expecting strangers to move among them to bring food and drinks.

SHIT!

"Ms. Reilly!" The doctor grabbed for me as I jumped down from the table and grabbed the neck brace.

"We've got to get to the convention center. NOW!" I shouted it to Dusty and Tom as I dived under the curtain and ran for the exit.

Tom and Dusty didn't argue. They ran beside me as I tore out of the ER, past the startled doctors and nurses, the patients and families waiting in the reception area, the startled shouts of protest from doctors and nurses following in our wake.

Dusty's Mustang was parked in the short-term emergency lot. She hit the alarm button as we ran, it beeped, the lights flashing to let us know it was safe to climb in. I felt a wave of heat, knew that Tom was changing form. Good. He'd need his claws and fangs. We jumped into the car. Dusty in the driver's seat. Tom in the rear. I climbed in front. I didn't strap in. I needed my neck brace on. That meant stripping down to my bra while we were moving, but it didn't matter. I'd have flashed the entire third infantry to get that brace on my neck before we got to the convention center.

"Can you feel it?" My voice was muffled by the turtle neck I was pulling off.

"Oh God. Yes." Dusty whispered the words, and stomped her foot hard on the gas pedal. We pulled out of the parking lot with a squeal of tires, leaving trails of rubber on the pavement. When she took the first corner I was slammed sideways into the door frame. I grunted in pain and irritation, but managed to reposition myself so that I could fasten the latch that held the brace closed. I felt the familiar constriction, and my heart began to race, a touch of the claustrophobia rearing its ugly head. I squashed it like a roach. I couldn't afford the fear. Not now. Later, if I survived, I could have a full-blown nervous breakdown, heebie-jeebies, and posttraumatic stress disorder. But not *now.*

We raced down Speer, Dusty swerving around every vehicle unfortunate enough to be in our way. I was thrown back and forth like a rag doll, and I swore like a sailor. It didn't matter. We were almost there. I was armed, armored, and dressed in my leathers when the Mustang took the last turn, blasting over the curb to come to a skidding stop inches from the glass doors of the building entrance. Just inside, a man lay sprawled and dead, his throat a mess of bloody meat, the carpet beneath him stained with blood.

I leapt from the car with Tom at my heels. In the

distance I heard sirens, *LOTS* of sirens. The cops were converging on the scene.

Oddly though, standing just outside the center itself was almost quiet, the eye at the center of a hurricane. If I hadn't seen the body at my feet, I would never have known anything was wrong. There were no crowds fleeing, no screaming people outside. Nothing.

He has the humans enthralled, upstairs. They don't know anything's wrong. I hadn't noticed what Dusty did, but it made sense. He had wanted this to be laid at the wolves' door. He wouldn't want human witnesses to Thrall presence. Just like Dylan to plan it so carefully.

All these thoughts passed through my mind in the instant it took me to dash from the car to the door. I didn't pause going in. There was no helping the man at my feet. He was dead. I burst through, my boots squishing on the blood-soaked carpet, running full out toward the sounds of screaming, growls, and chaos.

The battle had started.

27

*S*ome of the fight had spilled out of the ballroom and into the hallway. A pair of wolves the size of small horses circled each other, snarling, their lips drawn back to reveal fangs as long as my fingers. One, a huge, brindled male, bore the exact markings of the wolf in my vision. But he wasn't alone. *All* of the vampires' wolves were marked identically.

There was a knife in my right hand. I didn't remember drawing it. But as I came through the door I was glad to have it, because almost instantly one of the vampires moved to attack.

I ducked, and her strike missed. She turned, and would have come at me again, but Tom was there. He leaped onto her, teeth and claws tearing at her flesh with deadly efficiency.

I turned, thinking I'd help him, but he didn't need it. My eyes moved past him, to the scene in the ballroom. For a single instant I froze, taking it all in.

Our werewolves were losing. Individually, they could take down the vampires. They could even take down individuals among the vampires' wolves. But while the werewolves were terrific fighters, there was no unity. No organization. The vampiric wolves were a unit, working together seamlessly as if driven by a single mind.

Because they were.

One mind. *Dylan's* mind. If I could find him, take him down, every one of those identical brindled wolves would have no leader, no coordination and will of their own.

I turned, searching with eyes and mind. He was here. I knew he was here. Where *was* he?

Dusty grabbed my arm. Screaming my name, she yanked me backward hard enough to make me stumble. But it worked. The brindled wolf missed in his strike. He crouched low, growling, and I saw four others move into a coordinated position behind him. They were going to flank us if they could, and they were fast enough to do it.

Tom crouched low, guarding our backs, his growl a low rumble that sent tremors along my spine. I might not have heard it over the battle noise, but I felt it, knew that he was there with me.

We need to find Dylan. He's the key to this. If we can take him down, the vampires will fall.

Uncle Dylan? Her voice in my mind was surprised.

It occurred to me that she hadn't been present for any of the conversations. She honestly didn't know. But now wasn't the time to discuss it.

He's alive and he's gone nuts from the Thrall infestation. He's the one in charge.

It was enough for her. She'd known Dylan her whole life. I had no doubt she knew what he was capable of.

The wolves were moving forward, cautiously. Their huge copper-and-black bodies moved with a fluid efficiency that was disturbingly beautiful, almost dancelike in its coordination. I braced myself, waiting for the attack, and heard the crack of a gun. The lead wolf fell in mid-leap, a tranq dart sticking from his neck. I looked for the source, and saw three of Brooks's men on the dais: Adams and one other were standing guard behind a barricade of overturned tables. The third, acting as sniper, was methodically taking down as many vampires and attacking wolves as he could.

The three remaining wolves leaped. Tom collided with the largest in midair, teeth and claws tearing as each tore into the other, looking for an advantage.

Dusty screamed, a cry of both rage and pain. I wanted to look, but I couldn't. The third wolf was on me. His paws hit me solidly in the chest, and I fell to the ground with him riding me, the wind knocked from my lungs in a rush. He could have had me then, would have, but the brace saved me. His fangs and claws scraped uselessly against the fiberglass carapace. He threw his head back, howling in frustration.

I didn't think, I acted. Using my cast as a guard, I thrust upward with the knife in my right hand, the razor sharp blade slicing through the thick ruff of fur and skin protecting his neck, ripping through the major arteries, sending scalding hot blood in a pulsing spray that soaked me. The wolf tried to scream, tried to fight. But it was too late. I clubbed him with my cast, bringing up my knees so that I could thrust him off of my body. He fell, dying. In my heart, I knew I'd just killed a person. But it was also an abomination. In its place, I would want to have died. Rationalization, true, but it was honest.

I rose, wiping the blood from my eyes with the back of my sleeve. Dusty was still fighting her foe a few feet from me. Tom was alive, I could see him circling his enemy. But beyond him, in a corner, surrounded by a ring of wolves standing guard, was Dylan.

I could see him clearly. He, alone, was not under attack. He stood wearing jeans and a navy blue dress shirt, completely unmarked, handsome as ever. Looking at him chilled me because I could see that he felt *nothing*. All this pain, all this death, none of it mattered to him so long as he got what he wanted. All he wanted was to see me in pain.

I turned back to Dusty. I couldn't leave her under attack. I needed to take the fight to Dylan, but I'd see her safe first. The wolf attacking her didn't see me. Didn't know. Nor had Dylan noticed me. Not yet. I started forward, intending to use my knife, but a shot rang out. The wolf fell victim to the marksman. I heard Dylan's shout of rage over the chaos. Turning, I saw him gesture. Half a dozen of the wolves of his personal guard flowed forward as a unit toward the sniper and his two guards.

Shoot the man in charge. Shoot Dylan. I tried to force my thoughts into the mind of the sniper, but it was useless. I should have known it would be. Brooks had chosen these men for the simple reason that they were completely head-blind. He wouldn't hear me. He *couldn't.*

There were still a dozen of the brindled wolves surrounding Dylan. I needed something to draw them off. A distraction.

And then it occurred to me.

He could control his wolves, lead them as a unit. Could I lead ours? Was I strong enough psychically? Would the werewolves accept my lead? Is that what Carlton had meant . . . why the queens had feared me?

I grabbed Dusty's hand as I grabbed her power. Using our combined gifts I called to the Accas who had been part of my healing, whose power had been linked to me and mine. I used no words, they were wolves now in full blood lust. Words meant nothing. But I offered them a target, offered them coordinated attack, leadership, *pack.*

I knew it was working when the first howl belled through the room, a furious challenge. Furred shapes began converging around me, their voices raised in a defiant chorus that joined to become a single song . . . of unity . . . of strength.

The brindled wolves hesitated, because Dylan hesitated. He sensed what I was doing, sensed *me*.

I watched as he turned, slowly, his eyes blazing with hatred as he sought me, now standing in a circle of wolves that matched his.

I will kill you. His words were a hiss in my mind. I saw him draw a blade, probably six inches long, from a sheath at his waistband. He took a step forward, and the vampiric wolves surged forward in a wave.

You can try.

With a thought, all of Dylan's wolves returned to him, abandoning their various fights to join the charge against me and mine.

But the werewolves joined me; along with the cops, and the human surrogates, even the few waiters and staff members who'd survived the first onslaught. Brooks came, fighting beside a pair of wolves I recognized as Rob and a half-healed Annie from Las Vegas, Bryan, my brother, his shirt in tatters that revealed the green fiberglass of his neck guard, a broken chair leg in one hand, knife in the other. The vampires and their wolves charged, and we met that charge head on, and this time *we* weren't the ones losing.

The battle surged, and it was chaos. There were enemies everywhere. So many enemies, but there was only one Dylan. He could only look one place at a time, while I gave my wolves the freedom to think for themselves—connected them just enough to know, but not to control. I fought with every ounce of strength and skill I'd earned through years of training, practice, and experience, forcing myself to ignore the cries of pain, the sight of friends and allies falling to our foes. I fought, ignoring the pain and exhaustion of my body, carving my way toward Dylan inch by bloody inch, determined that it would be me who finally took him down.

And then I was there. He turned, pulling his bloody knife from the corpse of one of the surrogates, his eyes blazing with a burning hatred.

I grabbed his arm with both hands.

He expected an attack, expected me to shove as much psychic power as I could gather into him, as I had when I'd killed Samantha Greeley. But he was expecting that. He was ready for that. Instead I *pulled*. Pulled energy from him as hard and fast as I could, shoving it into my allies to give them strength. It shocked him. He stumbled, staggered for just a moment: gave me an opening. It wouldn't last. It couldn't. Yes, he'd taken over the collective, brutalized them, made it a dictatorship. But if he died, they'd die and they wanted to live.

I felt their will to survive and for a split second I hesitated. How many of them were like Toby, forced to do something they hated because they weren't strong enough to fight him off? I hesitated.

Tom didn't.

He leaped, snarling, the full weight of his body slamming into Dylan's chest. I heard a masculine scream, Dylan's scream, cut off abruptly in the wake of a wet tearing sound and the crunch of crushed bone.

The vampires fell first, felled in their tracks, hands grabbing their heads as they collapsed to the floor screaming and frothing at the mouth.

The vampiric wolves followed, each muzzle raised to give an almost unearthly keening that ended with their collapse and death.

I swayed on my feet in the middle of a charnel house. The carpet beneath my feet was so soaked with blood you couldn't even see the black-and-gray pattern any more; so soaked it squished when you stepped on it. There were mangled bodies everywhere, ripped apart to show parts of the body not meant to be seen by human eyes There were so many bodies, not all of them our enemies.

I swayed on my feet, and would've fallen. But Tom's strong arms caught me before I could hit the floor. I felt the room spinning and darkness was eating at my vision. But I heard his voice, clear and strong . . . even though it was just a whisper. "Before you pass out, I need to say something. I'll make you a deal. I'll try not to freak out if you ever have to do your superhero thing again, just like you try to support my firefighting. And we'll both go to counseling or find a support group or whatever. Because I'm not going to risk losing you. Not ever. Not to any vampires we didn't get, not to my crazy ex-girlfriends or your crazy ex-boyfriends, and not to *my* fear."

"It's a deal." I fought to smile, but all I could manage was a soft sigh before the lights went out.

It was over.

28

The first two days I slept the sleep of the completely exhausted. The doctors hadn't been wrong. I'd pushed myself too hard, and I paid the price for it. But it was worth it. The Thrall were gone. All of them. I try not to think about it, but it's impossible not to. I hesitated to kill Dylan, not because of some lingering affection for him. Any feelings I had for him were long dead. But not *every* Thrall host had been evil. Carlton was spared because of his surgery Otherwise he'd have died with them. Just like Toby. Taking down Dylan killed thousands of hosts around the world.

It feels—odd not to have to shield out the hum of the hive. The silence in my head is almost frightening. I suppose I'll get used to it. But right now I'm a little unsteady. Tom understands. He's been incredibly gentle with me, putting up with my mood swings and the nightmares, where I relive being shut in the car trunk.

From what Carlton tells me, Elaine wasn't working with the vampires. She underestimated them. She considered Mary a threat to her power base and decided to get Mary and me out of the way so that *she* would be the one who saved the day—permanently cementing her position at the top of the wolf hierarchy. Her mistake cost her her life.

The doctors got to Mary in time to counteract the worst of the drug overdose. She actually is recovering better than I am. Still, we're both expected to be just fine by my wedding day.

Yes, *wedding day.* The wolves have officially given their blessing to the marriage of one Mary Kathleen Reilly to Thomas Bishop and the adoption of Jacqueline Ruby Bishop. I am considered a surrogate with all of the powers and privileges thereof, including participation in pack decisions. Mary was the one to deliver the news. She seemed a little uneasy about it. It was almost as if she's afraid I might cause trouble. Me? Trouble? Not if I can help it. I've had more than enough trouble for one lifetime already.

29

I stood in my slip, balancing Jacqueline on my hip as I watched Peg zip Mary into her dress.

It was really happening. No more delays. No more *crises*.

I was getting married.

Holy crap.

Outside that door, friends and family were filing into the church. I could hear them through the paper-thin walls. Carlton arrived, along with his daughter. There was no mistaking his voice as he introduced her to *Fido*. For the first time, I heard Tom laugh when the word was spoken.

I heard a knock on the door and knew it was Ruby and Mrs. Connolly.

"Come on in," I called as I stepped out of the line of sight of the door. They came, bringing with them the baby carrier. It was their job to look after Jacqueline during the ceremony. That they were here meant that it was almost time.

I gave the baby one last kiss before passing her off to her birth mother and then, on impulse, gave the girl a hug.

Ruby looked good. Wistful, but happy. My mind brushed hers. I wanted to know if she was doing okay. It was a relief to find out that she really was. Moving home had been the right choice for her. She believed that. Yes, she missed Jacqueline, but she knew that Tom and I would love her, give her a good home. And knowing that, and that she could visit whenever she wanted, made it okay.

She hugged me back fiercely. "Congratulations, Katie. I'm so happy for you. For all three of you."

"Thanks."

"Okay," Mrs. Connolly announced. "Everybody out. The bride has only got a few more minutes to get ready and you're all in the way. SHOO!" She scooted everyone out the door, then closed it firmly behind them.

"Let me help you into the dress," she offered. I didn't argue. I was terrified I'd rip it. It looked so fragile, the beaded ivory silk seeming as delicate as a spiderweb to a woman more used to leather and denim.

I slipped it on, letting her pull the long zipper up my back. It fit like a glove. No surprise. She'd tailored it perfectly to my body. This dress was her wedding gift to me. It wasn't my mother's dress.

That was long gone, and wouldn't have fit anyway. But she'd used a copy of my parents' wedding picture to re-create it, just for me.

Taking the hairbrush, she pulled the two front sections of my hair back, pushing the combs of the veil back to hold it in place. Only then did she step away, letting me turn in front of the mirror and look.

Um . . . I was *beautiful*. Really and truly, for the first time ever. The dress, the veil, everything looked like a magazine ad. It might not be my mother's wedding dress, but it was the image of what she'd worn the day she'd walked down the aisle as Da's bride.

Joe's reflection joined mine in the mirror. I hadn't heard him come in, or Mrs. Connolly leave. He looked handsome in his rented tux, a broad smile on his face and a touch of brogue in his voice. "You look lovely, Katie lass. Almost perfect."

I arched a perfectly waxed eyebrow at that. "Only almost?"

His reflection grinned at me, his eyes sparkling. "There's something missing." Reaching into the pocket of his jacket he pulled out a blue velvet jewelry box, faded a little with age, the metal clasp just a little tarnished.

"Those aren't—" I gasped.

He sighed. "No, not Mom's pearls." I wasn't surprised, but tried not to be disappointed that he hadn't managed to pry them from Aunt Anne. She wouldn't have parted with them, or any of mother's other things willingly. She'd felt *entitled*. After all, she'd been saddled with us kids for years after they died. I brushed back the bitter thought. No, this was a day for joy. I would not let it be dimmed by ancient history best forgotten.

"Tom's grandmother insisted. Something about *"something old."* They're one of their wedding gifts to you. I had them restrung. Some of the knots were iffy." He opened the box, gently drawing the glimmering orbs from their resting place. Stepping forward, he put them on me, fastening the clasp.

Stepping back a pace, he checked my reflection. *"Now* you look perfect. Are you ready?"

I nodded. My throat was suddenly tight, making it hard to talk. Despite all the trouble and fights we'd had over the years I love my big brother. He could drive me crazy one minute, then he'd go and do something like this.

"Then let's go. Tom's waiting." He held out his arm and I took it, letting him lead me out of the dressing room and into the lobby of St. Patrick's Church. Mary, Dusty, and Peg stood waiting patiently just outside the chapel doors. Each wore a bridesmaid's gown in a slightly different color: Peg's a pale pink that suited her fair coloring; Dusty, a dusty rose; and Mary, my matron of honor, a rich burgundy. At a signal from the usher the organist began to play, and Peg began a stately pace up the center aisle. When she reached the halfway point it was Dusty's turn. Lastly, Mary. Only when the three of them had reached the front of the church did Joe bring me up to the doors. The wedding march began to play, the guests rising to their feet and turning to watch.

I glanced around, finding familiar faces. Some I'd expected to see. Others were a shock. Pete was in the audience. So were Leon and Leo. And on the groom's side, in the front row, were Mr. and Mrs. Thomas.

"How?" It was a shocked whisper.

"They took the train." Joe whispered the answer out of the corner of his mouth as we started up the aisle.

My eyes went to the front of the church, seeking, and finding, Tom. He was devastatingly handsome in a cream colored tux that suited his dark coloring. But more than that, his face beamed with such pure *joy* that it made my heart sing to see it. He winked, and I had to work not to laugh. It would be so undignified. Eyes sparkling, he nodded toward the space in front of the altar.

As I turned to look, Father Atkins stepped aside to reveal Michael in his wheelchair, wearing his best wedding robes, the Bible laying across his lap. His expression was nervous at first, as if he were afraid that I might be unhappy with the change.

I gave him a smile. Silly, silly man. I might not love Michael the same way I had when we were teenagers, but I will always love him. He has and always will have a place in my heart as one of my dearest friends. I treasured the knowledge that he was willing to come all the way from Rome to officiate at my wedding to Tom.

"Are you okay?" Joe whispered.

"I couldn't be happier."

It was the truth. Every life has a few perfect moments. This was one of mine. Today I would become Mary Kathleen Reilly Bishop. The threat of the Thrall was no more, the wolves were more united than ever in their history—and had blessed our union.

I was about to start a new life with a man I adored, a baby we would raise as our own, surrounded by friends and family. What more could I ask?

What more could anyone ask?

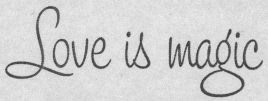

Love is magic

Upcoming Paranormal Romances
FROM TOR

Fallen

Claire Delacroix

978-0-7653-5949-0 • 0-7653-5949-9

OCTOBER 2008

Red

Jordan Summers

978-0-7653-5914-8 • 0-7653-5914-6

NOVEMBER 2008

Cursed

Jamie Leigh Hansen

978-0-7653-5721-2 • 0-7653-5721-6

DECEMBER 2008

Magic's Design

Cat Adams

978-0-7653-5963-6 • 0-7653-5963-4

JANUARY 2009

www.tor-forge.com

TOR
ROMANCE

Believe that love is magic

Please join us at the website below
for more information about this
author and other great romance
selections, and to sign up for our
monthly newsletter!

www.tor-forge.com